www.imagecomics.com

INJECTION, VOLUME ONE. First printing. October 2015. ISBN 978-1-63215-479-8. Published by Image Comics, Inc. Office of publication: 2001 Center Street, Sixth Floor, Berkeley, CA 94704. Copyright © 2015 Warren Ellis & Declan Shalvey. Originally published in single magazine form as INJECTION #1-5. All rights reserved. INJECTION, its logos, and all character likenesses herein are trademarks of Warren Ellis & Declan Shalvey unless expressly indicated. Image Comics® and its logos are registered trademarks and copyrights of Image Comics, Inc. All rights reserved. No part of this publication may be reproduced or transmitted, in any form or by any means (except for short excerpts for review purposes) without the express written permission of Warren Ellis & Declan Shalvey or Image Comics, Inc. All names, characters, events, and locales in this publication are entirely fictional. Any resemblance to actual persons (living or dead) or events or places, without satiric intent, is coincidental. Printed in the USA. For information regarding the CPSIA on this printed material call: 203-595-3636 and provide reference # RICH-647600. FOR INTERNATIONAL RIGHTS, CONTACT: foreignlicensing@imagecomics.com

INJECTION™

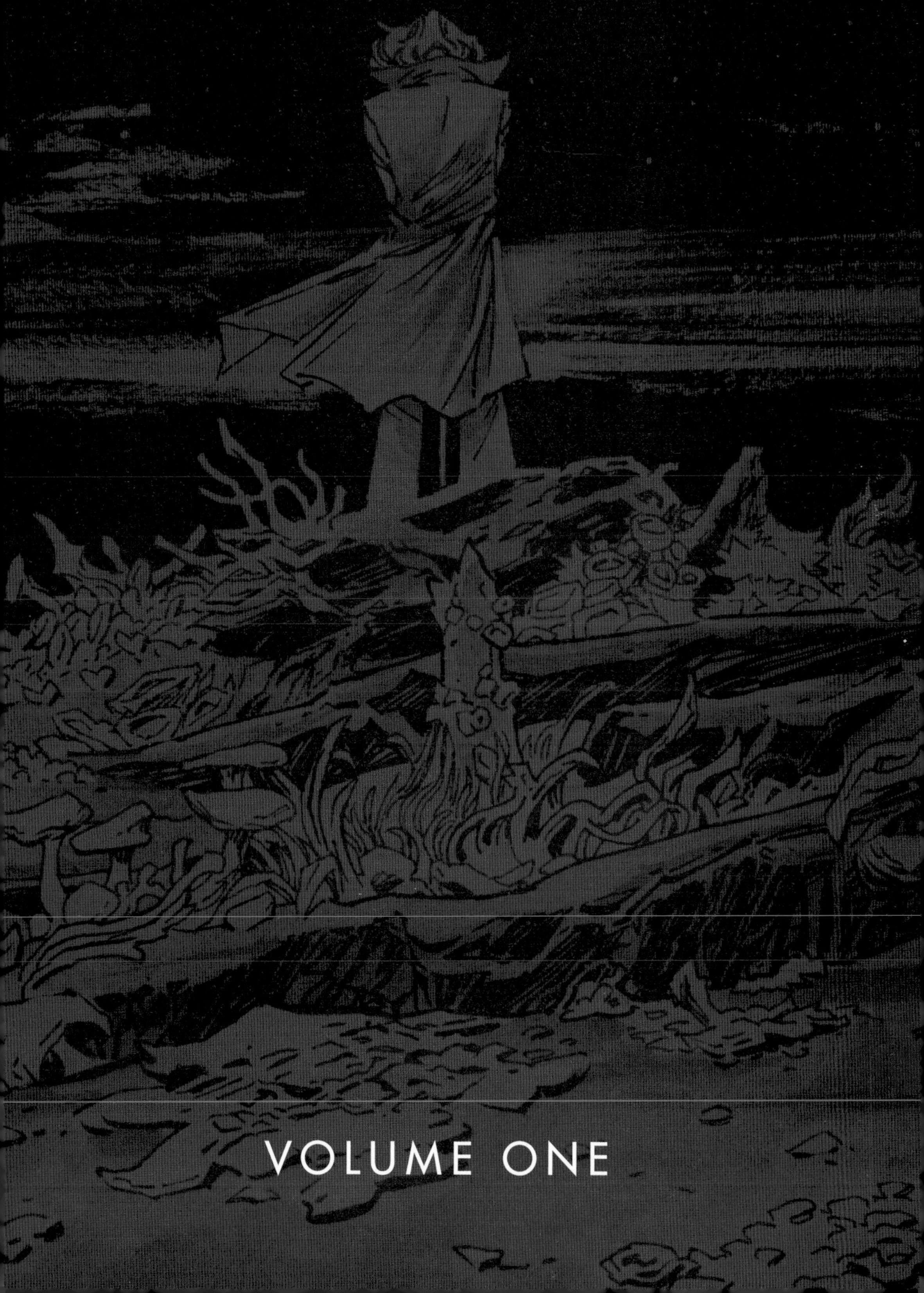

VOLUME ONE

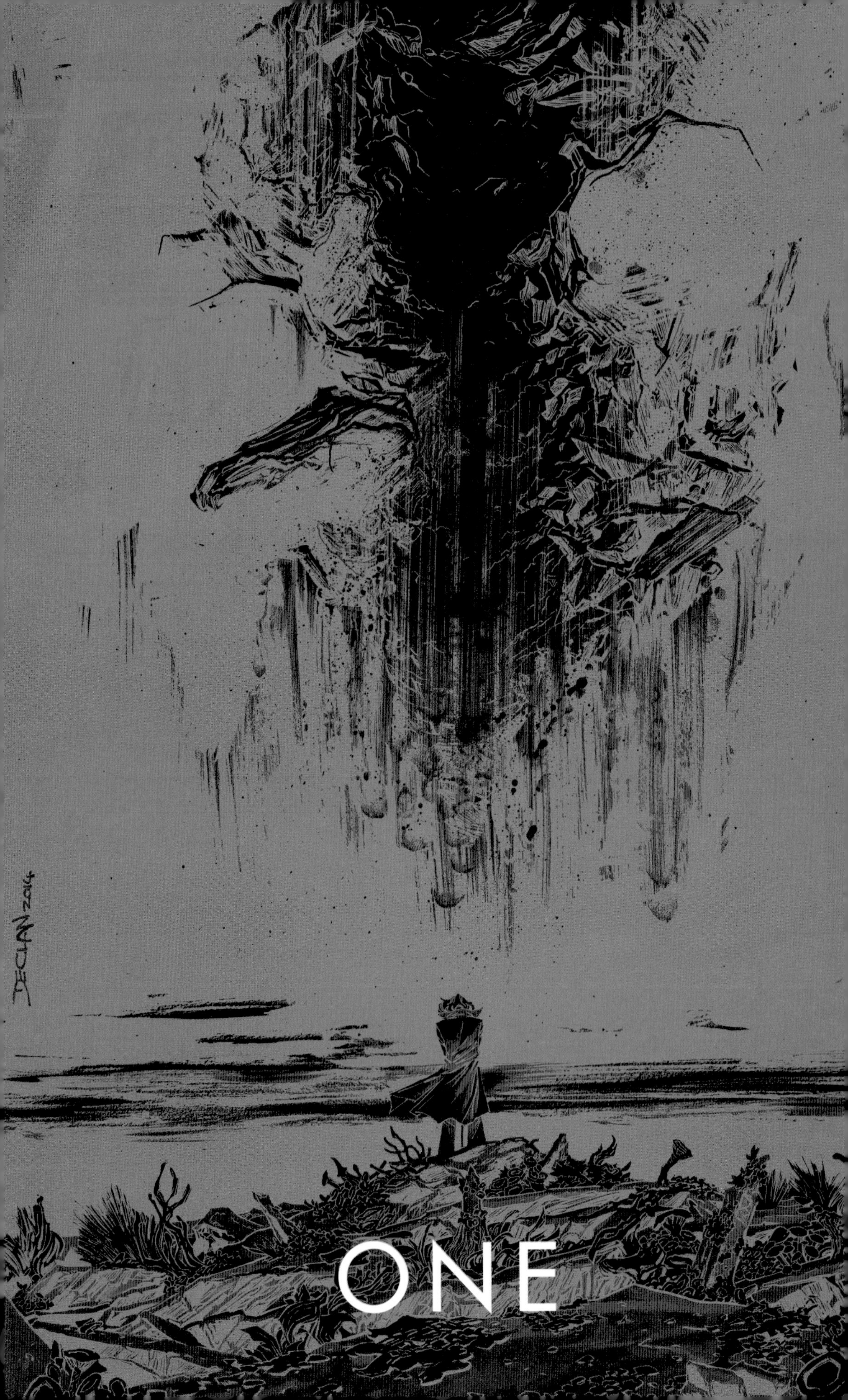
DECLAN 2014
ONE

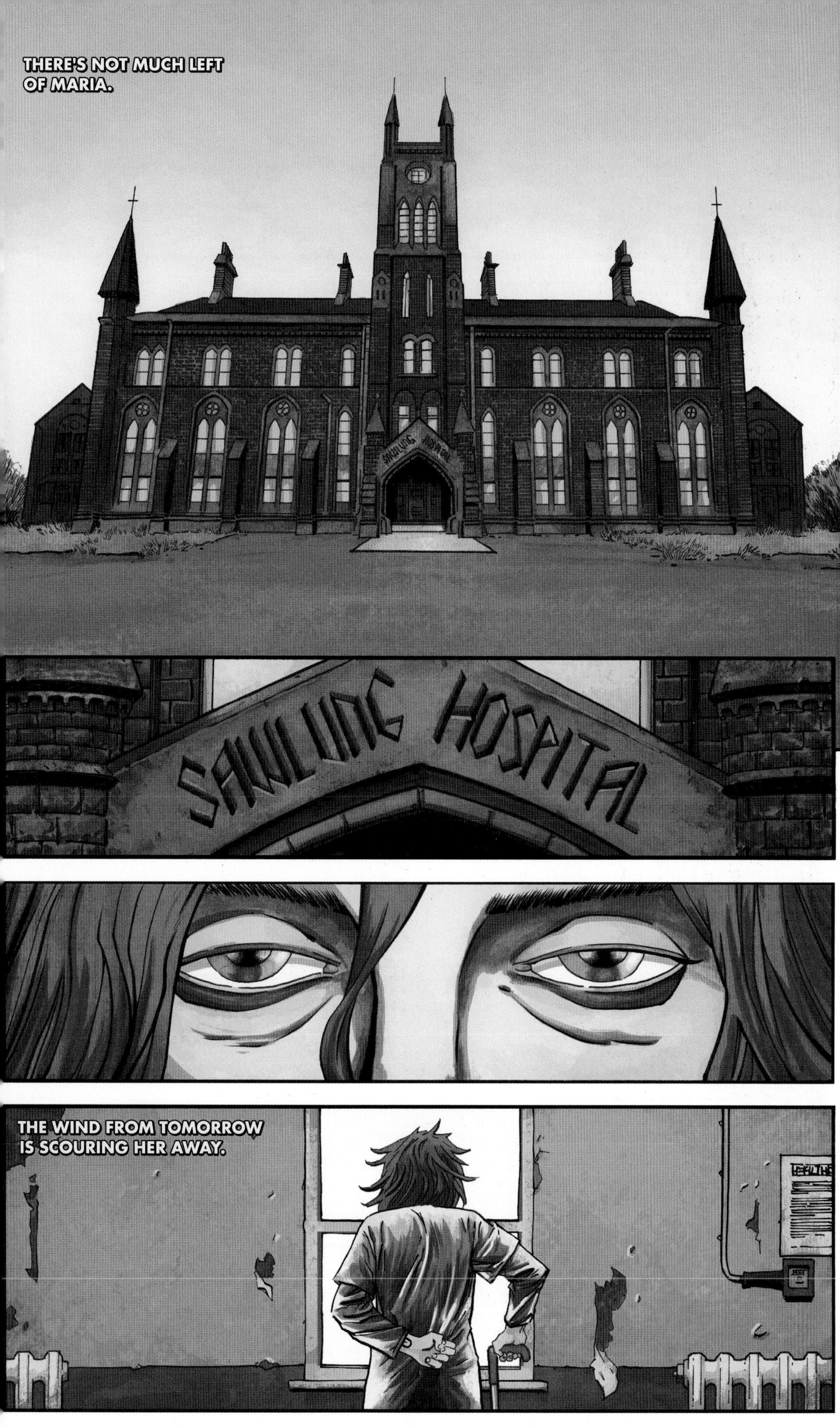
THERE'S NOT MUCH LEFT OF MARIA.
THE WIND FROM TOMORROW IS SCOURING HER AWAY.

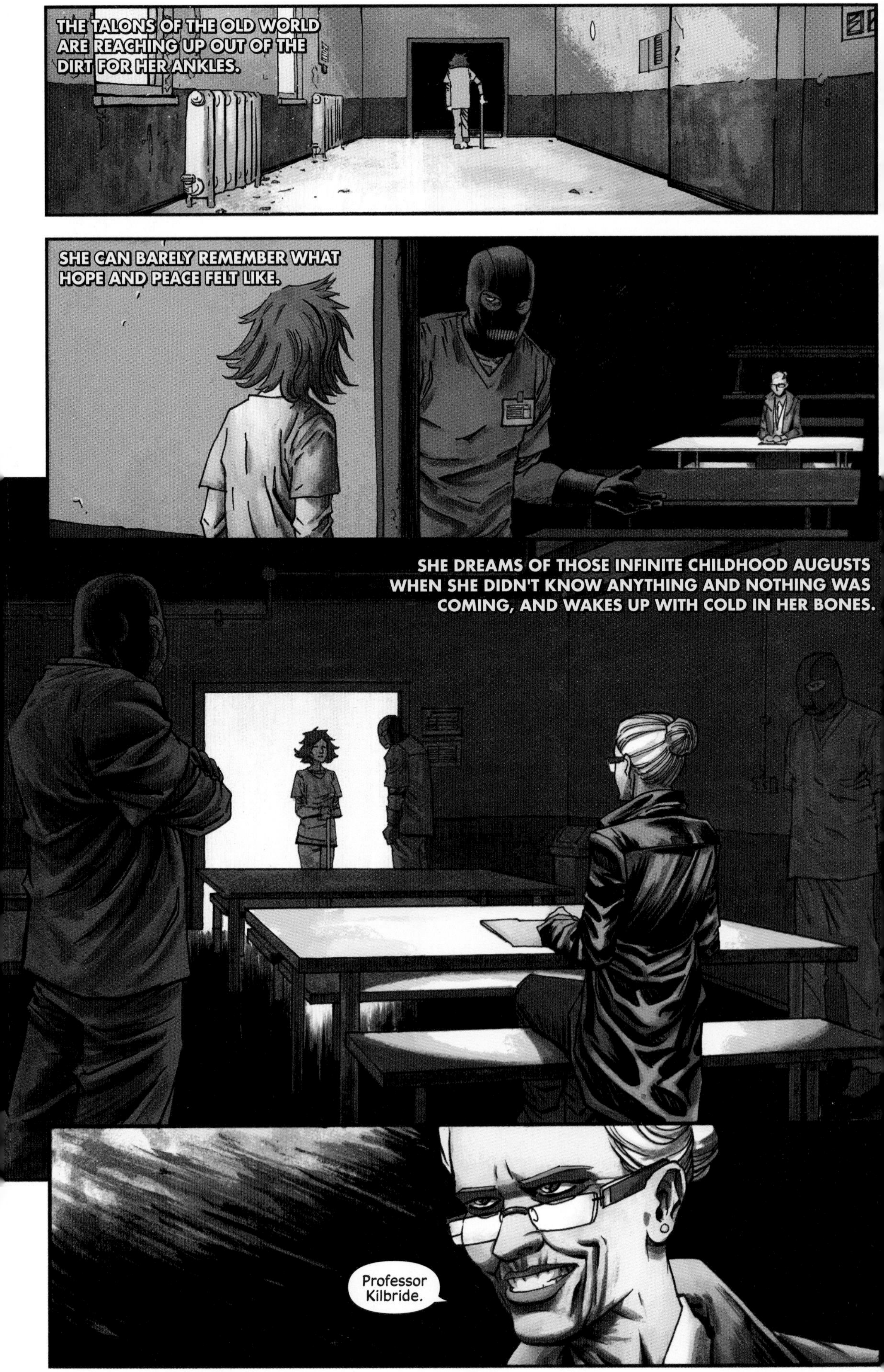
THE TALONS OF THE OLD WORLD ARE REACHING UP OUT OF THE DIRT FOR HER ANKLES.
SHE CAN BARELY REMEMBER WHAT HOPE AND PEACE FELT LIKE.
SHE DREAMS OF THOSE INFINITE CHILDHOOD AUGUSTS WHEN SHE DIDN'T KNOW ANYTHING AND NOTHING WAS COMING, AND WAKES UP WITH COLD IN HER BONES.
Professor Kilbride.

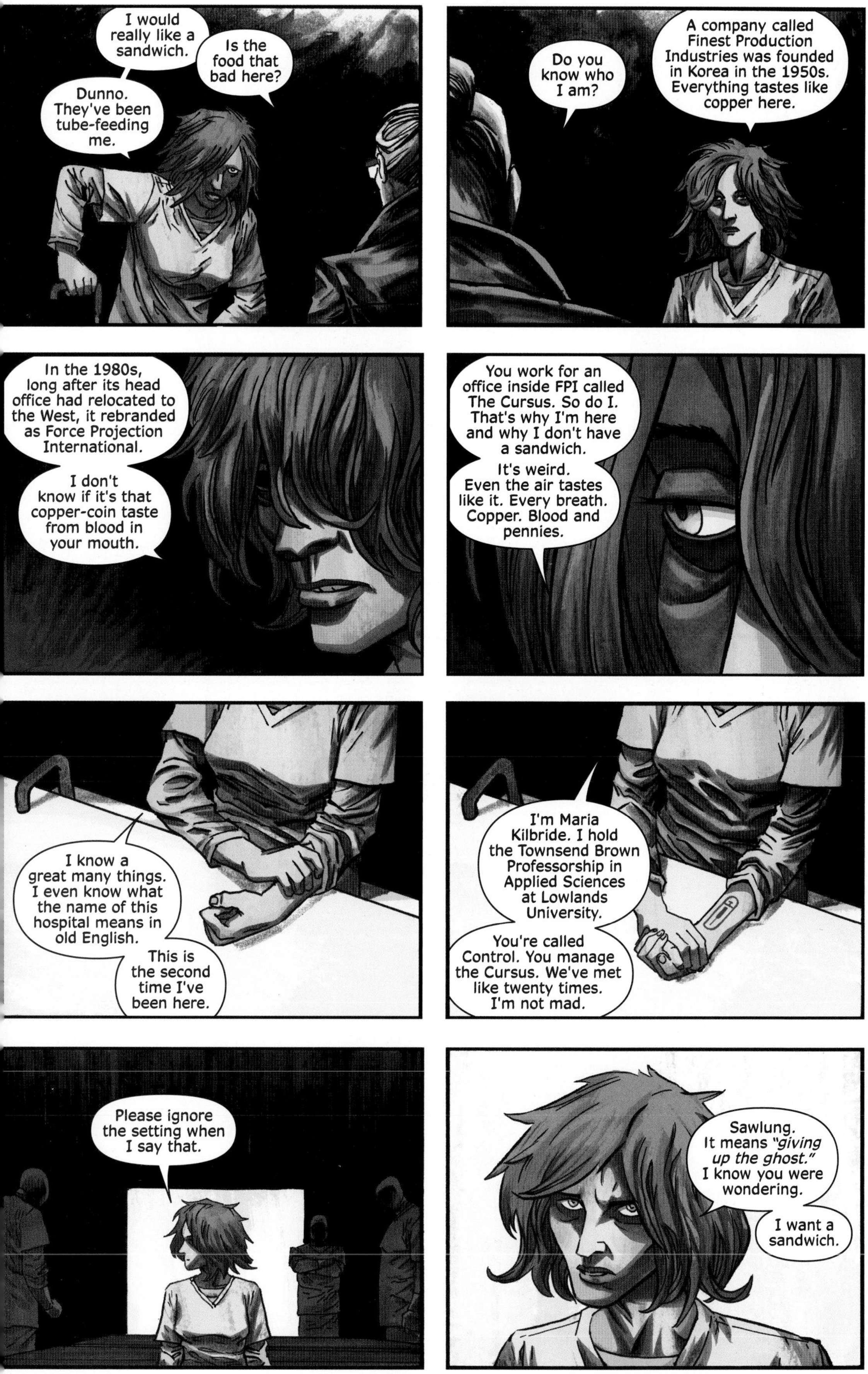
I would really like a sandwich.
Is the food that bad here?
Dunno. They've been tube-feeding me.
Do you know who I am?
A company called Finest Production Industries was founded in Korea in the 1950s. Everything tastes like copper here.
In the 1980s, long after its head office had relocated to the West, it rebranded as Force Projection International.
I don't know if it's that copper-coin taste from blood in your mouth.
You work for an office inside FPI called The Cursus. So do I. That's why I'm here and why I don't have a sandwich.
It's weird. Even the air tastes like it. Every breath. Copper. Blood and pennies.
I know a great many things. I even know what the name of this hospital means in old English.
This is the second time I've been here.
I'm Maria Kilbride. I hold the Townsend Brown Professorship in Applied Sciences at Lowlands University.
You're called Control. You manage the Cursus. We've met like twenty times. I'm not mad.
Please ignore the setting when I say that.
Sawlung. It means *"giving up the ghost."* I know you were wondering.
I want a sandwich.

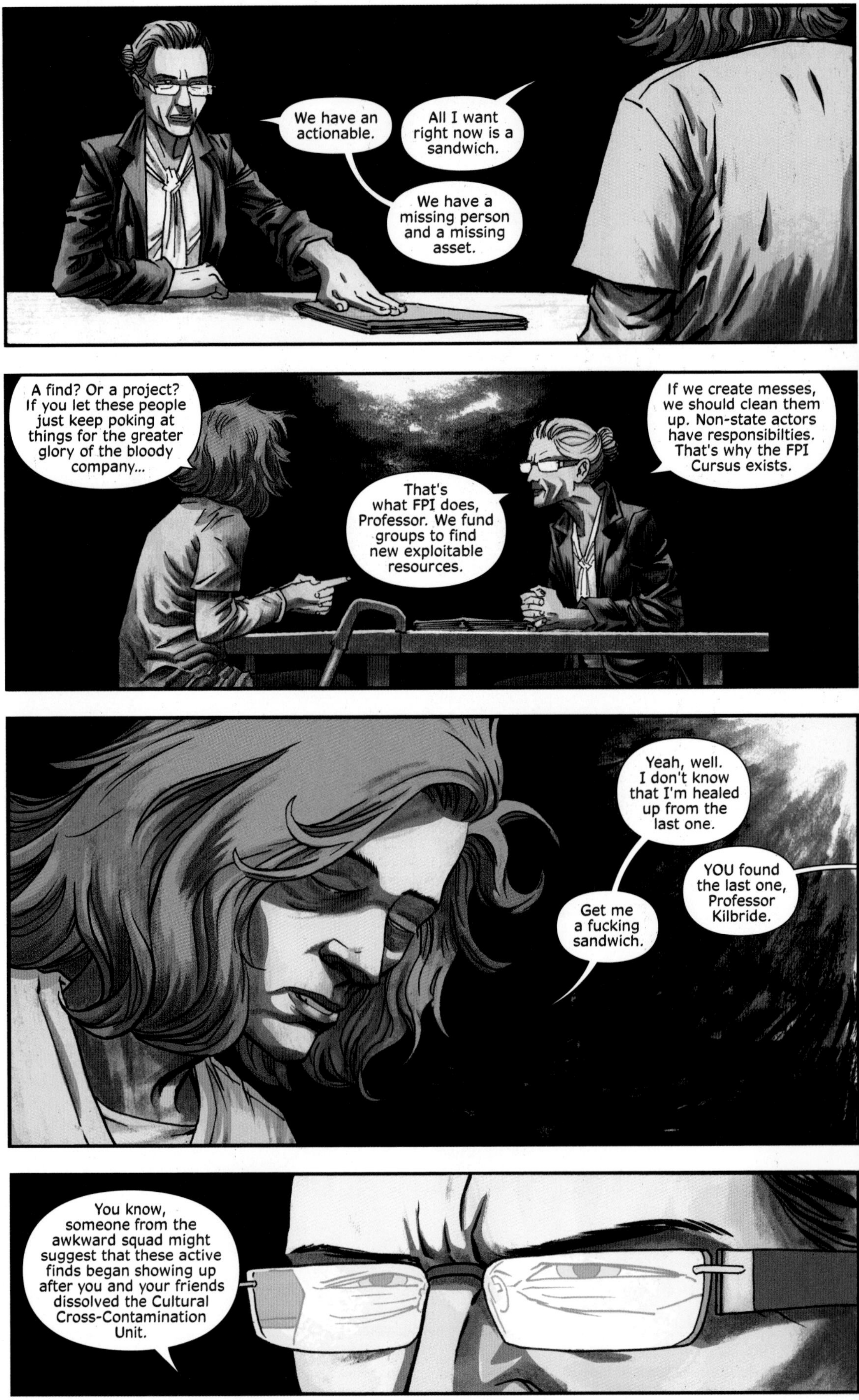
We have an actionable.
All I want right now is a sandwich.
We have a missing person and a missing asset.
A find? Or a project? If you let these people just keep poking at things for the greater glory of the bloody company...
That's what FPI does, Professor. We fund groups to find new exploitable resources.
If we create messes, we should clean them up. Non-state actors have responsibilties. That's why the FPI Cursus exists.
Yeah, well. I don't know that I'm healed up from the last one.
YOU found the last one, Professor Kilbride.
Get me a fucking sandwich.
You know, someone from the awkward squad might suggest that these active finds began showing up after you and your friends dissolved the Cultural Cross-Contamination Unit.

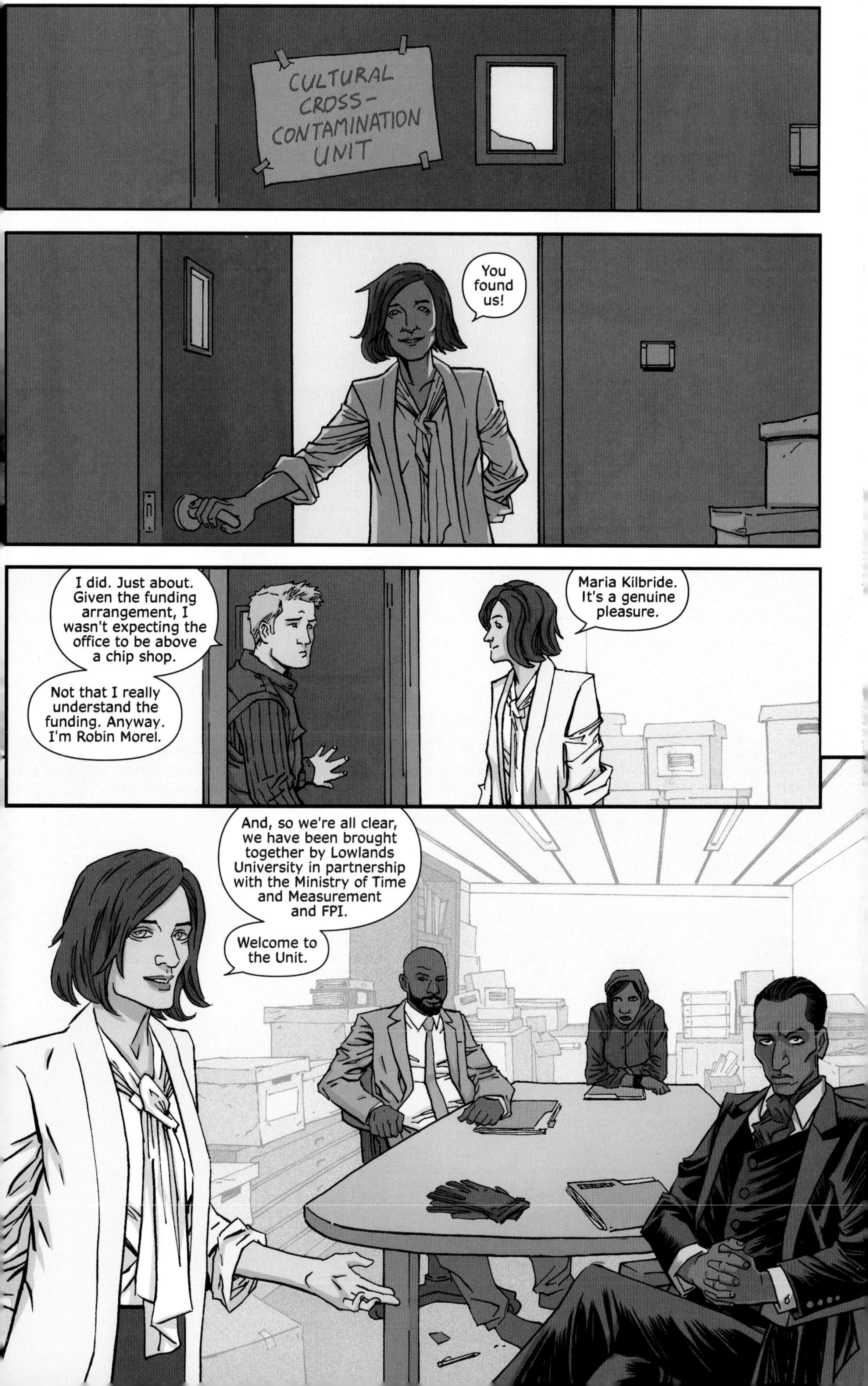
CULTURAL CROSS-CONTAMINATION UNIT
You found us!
I did. Just about. Given the funding arrangement, I wasn't expecting the office to be above a chip shop.
Not that I really understand the funding. Anyway. I'm Robin Morel.
Maria Kilbride. It's a genuine pleasure.
And, so we're all clear, we have been brought together by Lowlands University in partnership with the Ministry of Time and Measurement and FPI.
Welcome to the Unit.

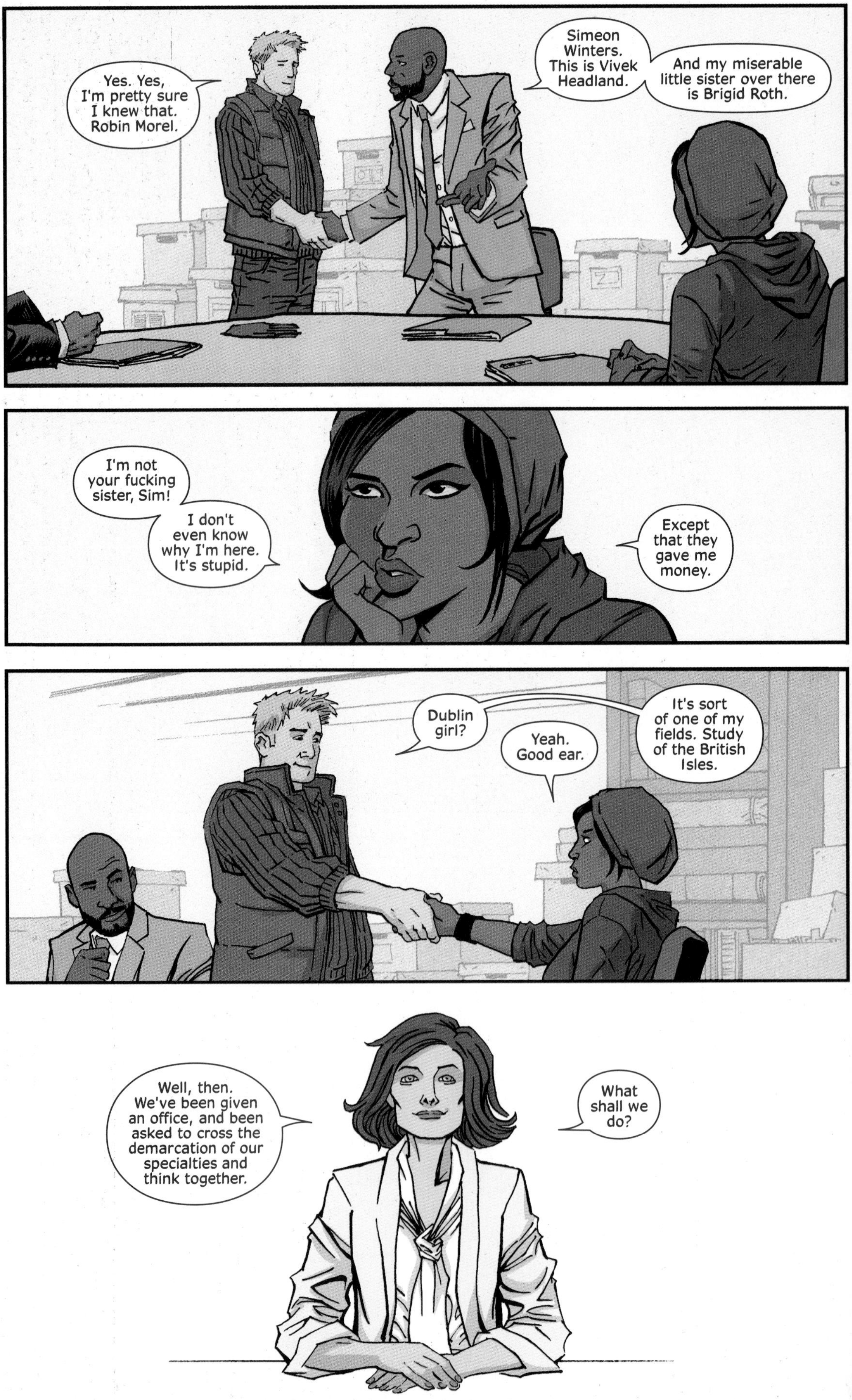
Yes. Yes, I'm pretty sure I knew that. Robin Morel.
Simeon Winters. This is Vivek Headland.
And my miserable little sister over there is Brigid Roth.
I'm not your fucking sister, Sim!
I don't even know why I'm here. It's stupid.
Except that they gave me money.
Dublin girl?
Yeah. Good ear.
It's sort of one of my fields. Study of the British Isles.
Well, then. We've been given an office, and been asked to cross the demarcation of our specialties and think together.
What shall we do?

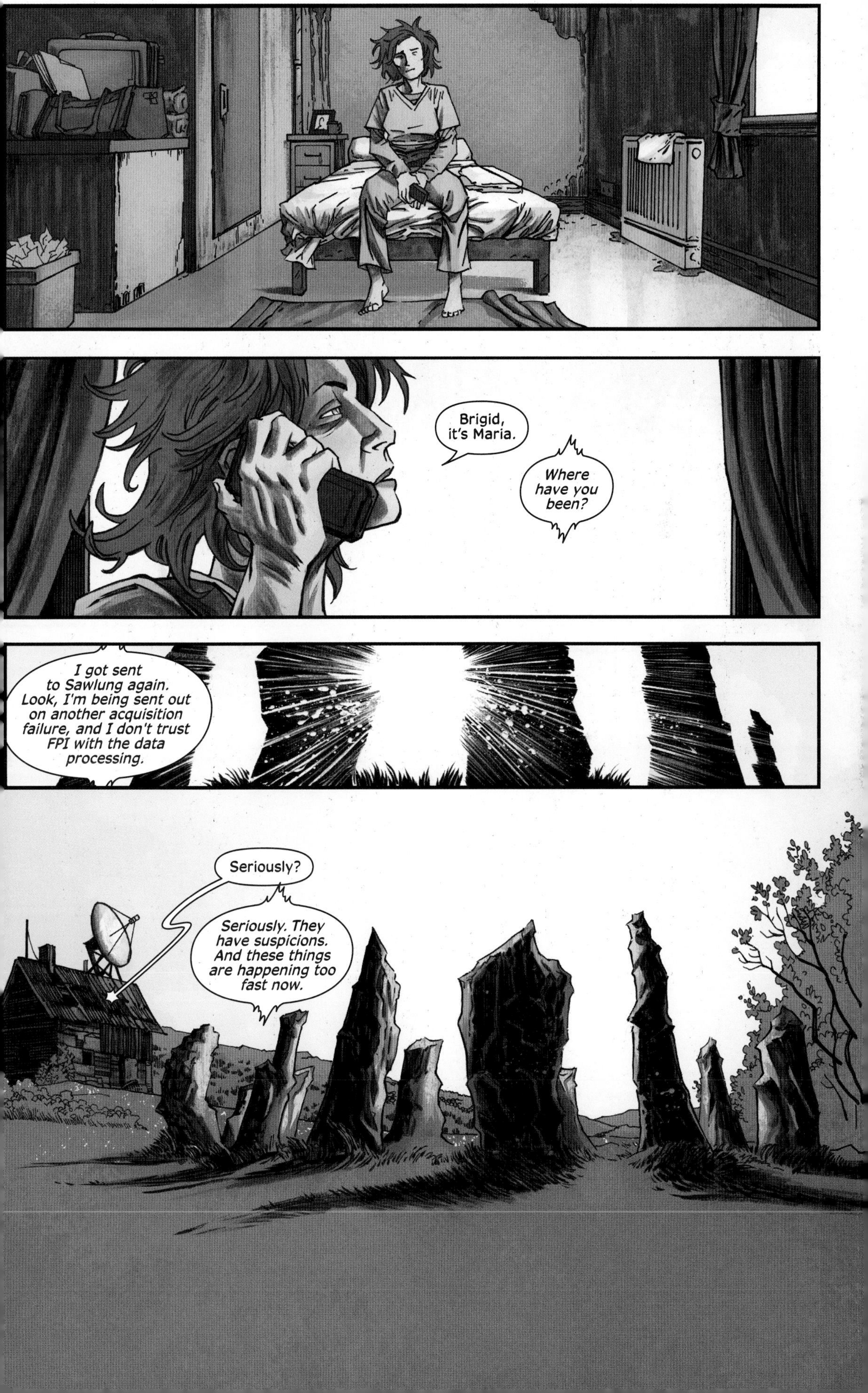
Brigid, it's Maria.
Where have you been?
I got sent to Sawlung again. Look, I'm being sent out on another acquisition failure, and I don't trust FPI with the data processing.
Seriously?
Seriously. They have suspicions. And these things are happening too fast now.

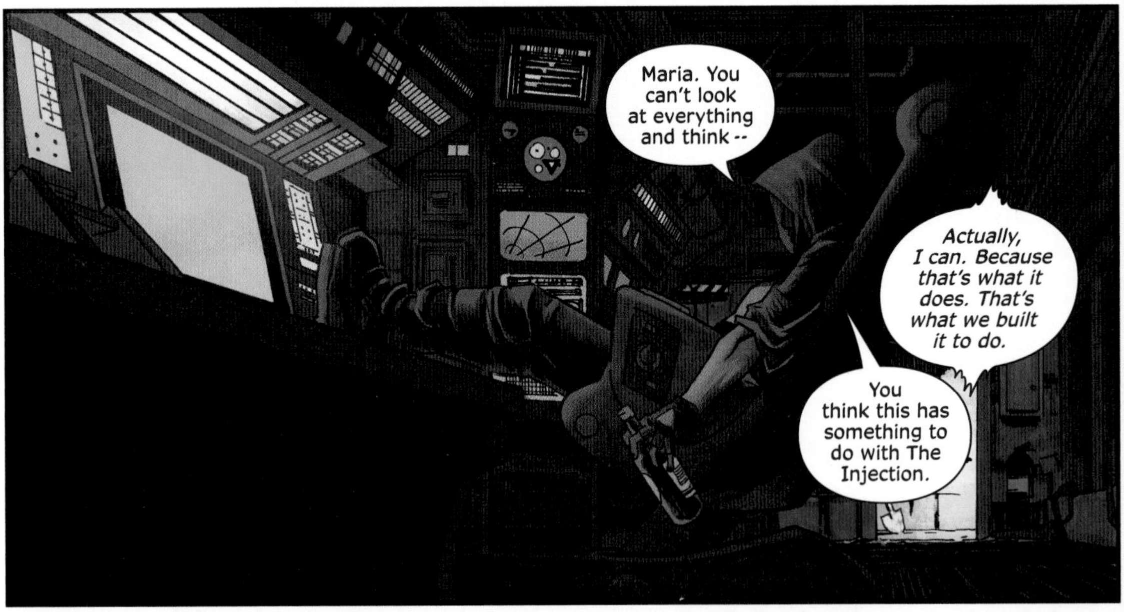
Maria. You can't look at everything and think --
Actually, I can. Because that's what it does. That's what we built it to do.
You think this has something to do with The Injection.

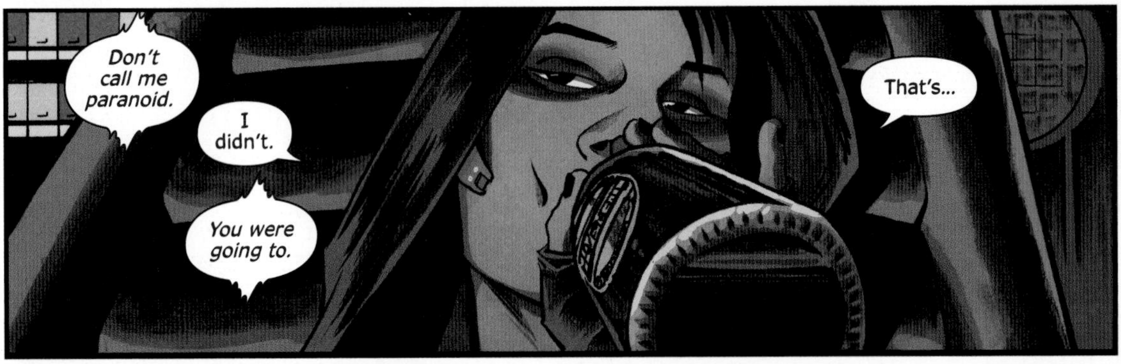
Don't call me paranoid.
I didn't.
You were going to.
That's...

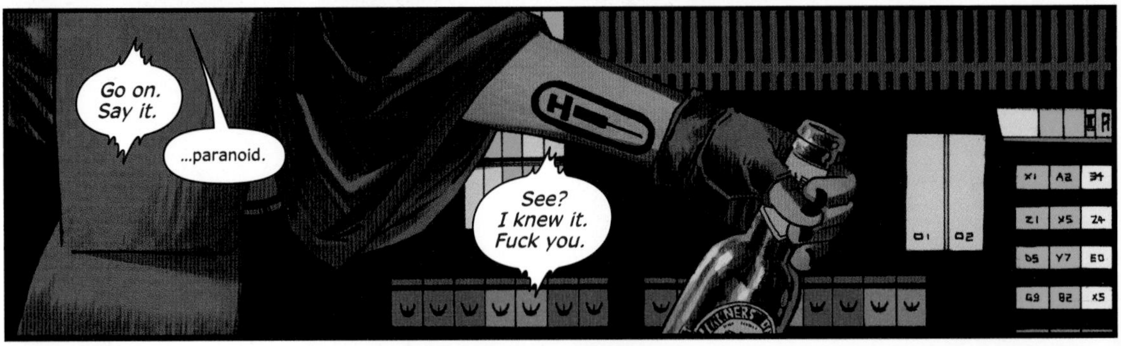
Go on. Say it.
...paranoid.
See? I knew it. Fuck you.

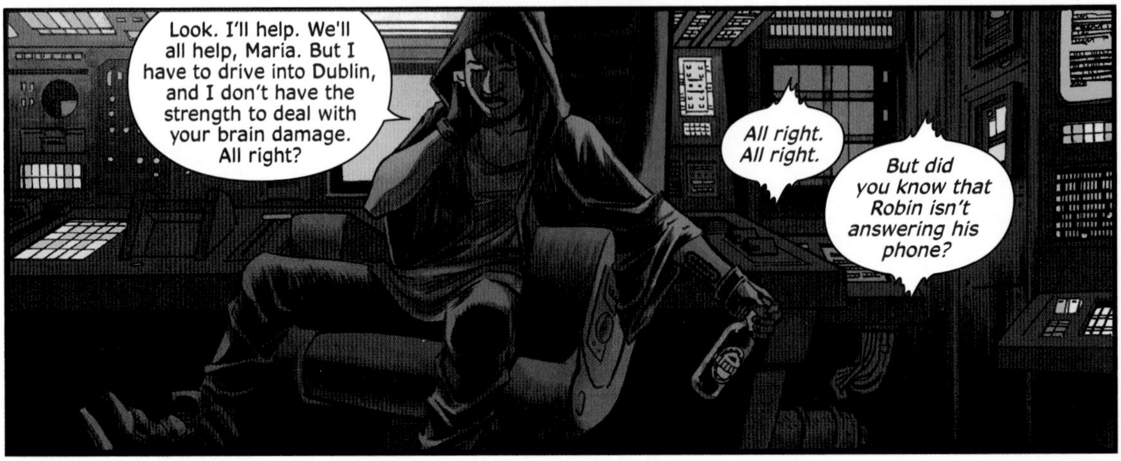
Look. I'll help. We'll all help, Maria. But I have to drive into Dublin, and I don't have the strength to deal with your brain damage. All right?
All right. All right.
But did you know that Robin isn't answering his phone?

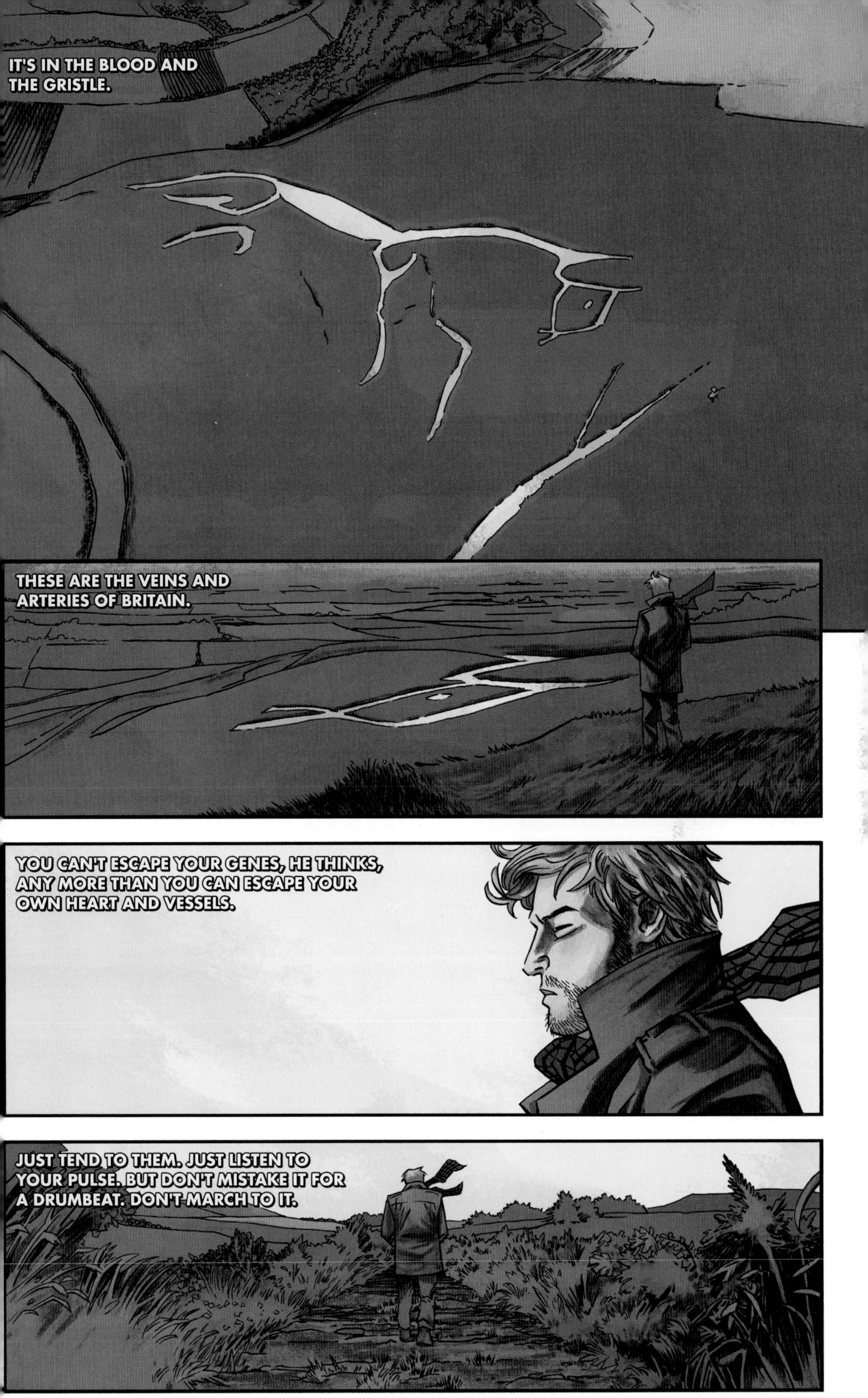
IT'S IN THE BLOOD AND THE GRISTLE.
THESE ARE THE VEINS AND ARTERIES OF BRITAIN.
YOU CAN'T ESCAPE YOUR GENES, HE THINKS, ANY MORE THAN YOU CAN ESCAPE YOUR OWN HEART AND VESSELS.
JUST TEND TO THEM. JUST LISTEN TO YOUR PULSE. BUT DON'T MISTAKE IT FOR A DRUMBEAT. DON'T MARCH TO IT.

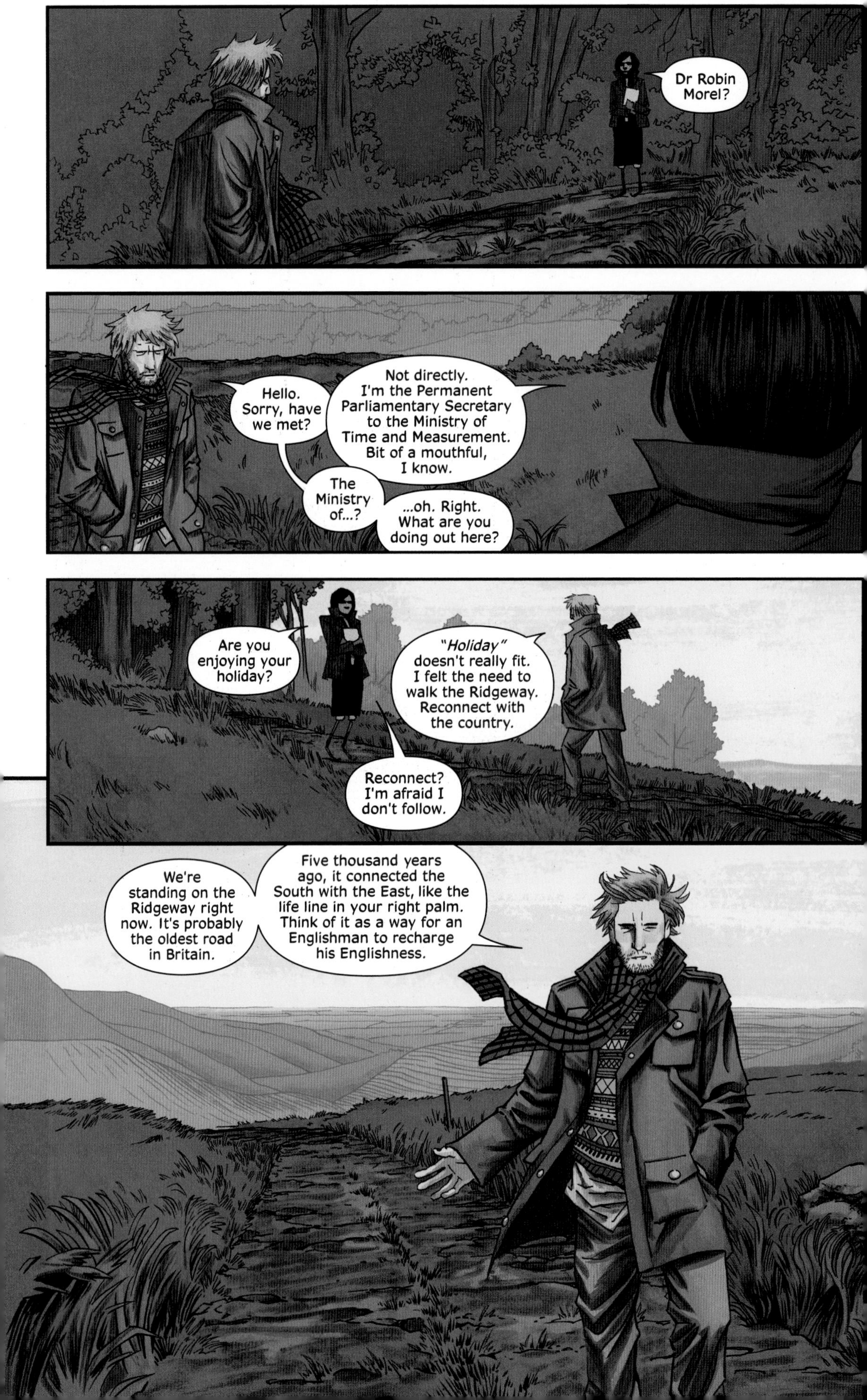
Dr Robin Morel?
Hello. Sorry, have we met?
Not directly. I'm the Permanent Parliamentary Secretary to the Ministry of Time and Measurement. Bit of a mouthful, I know.
The Ministry of...?
...oh. Right. What are you doing out here?
Are you enjoying your holiday?
"Holiday" doesn't really fit. I felt the need to walk the Ridgeway. Reconnect with the country.
Reconnect? I'm afraid I don't follow.
We're standing on the Ridgeway right now. It's probably the oldest road in Britain.
Five thousand years ago, it connected the South with the East, like the life line in your right palm. Think of it as a way for an Englishman to recharge his Englishness.

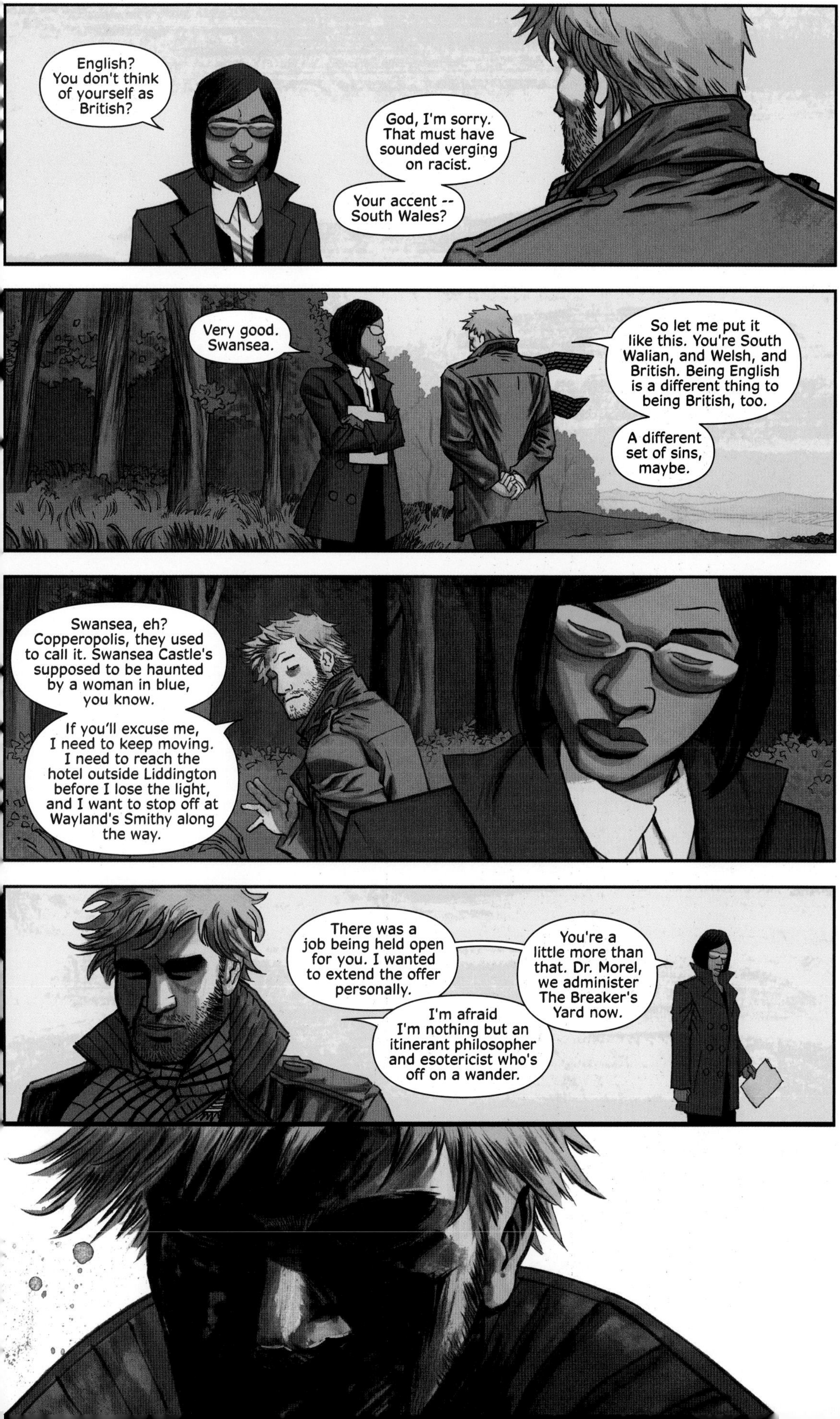
English? You don't think of yourself as British?
God, I'm sorry. That must have sounded verging on racist.
Your accent -- South Wales?
Very good. Swansea.
So let me put it like this. You're South Walian, and Welsh, and British. Being English is a different thing to being British, too.
A different set of sins, maybe.
Swansea, eh? Copperopolis, they used to call it. Swansea Castle's supposed to be haunted by a woman in blue, you know.
If you'll excuse me, I need to keep moving. I need to reach the hotel outside Liddington before I lose the light, and I want to stop off at Wayland's Smithy along the way.
You're a little more than that. Dr. Morel, we administer The Breaker's Yard now.
There was a job being held open for you. I wanted to extend the offer personally.
I'm afraid I'm nothing but an itinerant philosopher and esotericist who's off on a wander.

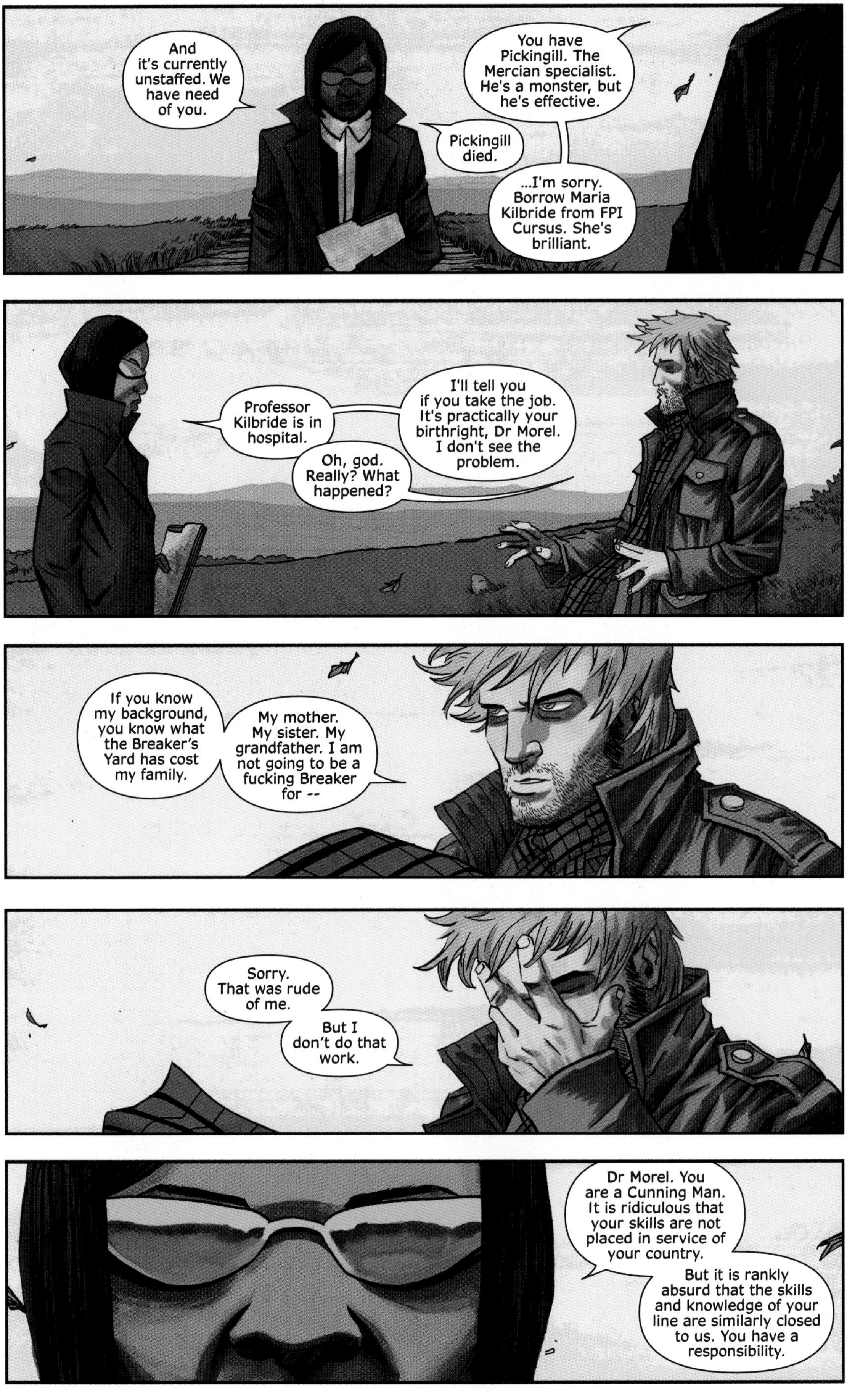
And it's currently unstaffed. We have need of you.
You have Pickingill. The Mercian specialist. He's a monster, but he's effective.
Pickingill died.
...I'm sorry. Borrow Maria Kilbride from FPI Cursus. She's brilliant.
Professor Kilbride is in hospital.
Oh, god. Really? What happened?
I'll tell you if you take the job. It's practically your birthright, Dr Morel. I don't see the problem.
If you know my background, you know what the Breaker's Yard has cost my family.
My mother. My sister. My grandfather. I am not going to be a fucking Breaker for --
Sorry. That was rude of me.
But I don't do that work.
Dr Morel. You are a Cunning Man. It is ridiculous that your skills are not placed in service of your country.
But it is rankly absurd that the skills and knowledge of your line are similarly closed to us. You have a responsibility.

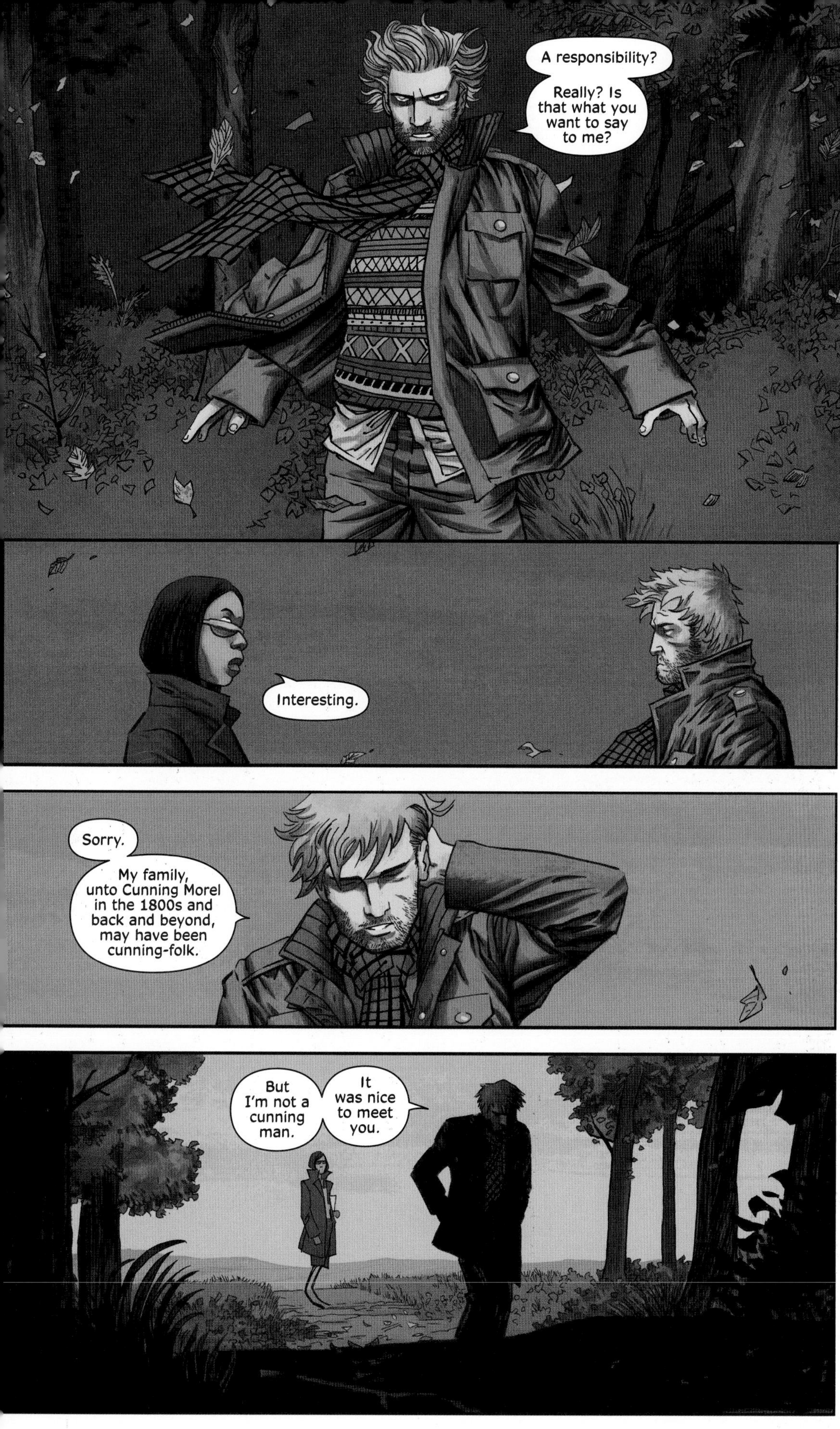
A responsibility?
Really? Is that what you want to say to me?
Interesting.
Sorry.
My family, unto Cunning Morel in the 1800s and back and beyond, may have been cunning-folk.
But I'm not a cunning man.
It was nice to meet you.

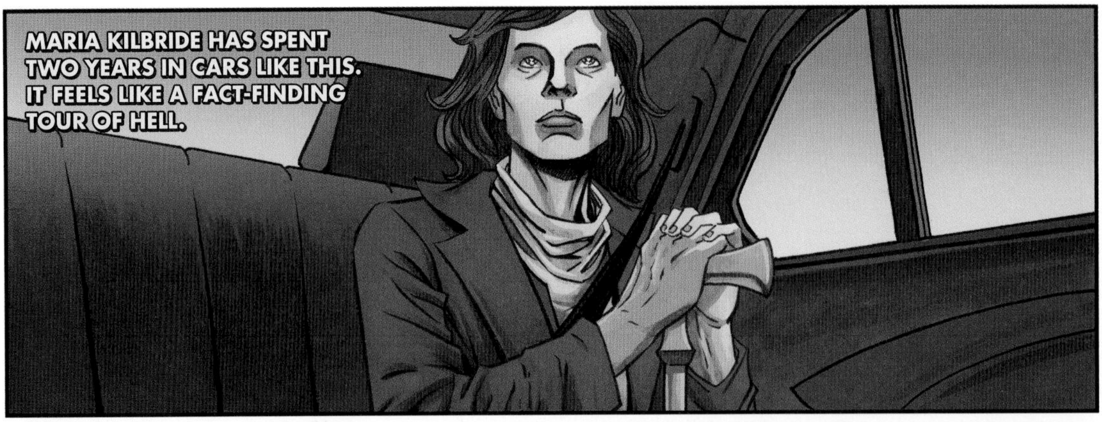
MARIA KILBRIDE HAS SPENT TWO YEARS IN CARS LIKE THIS. IT FEELS LIKE A FACT-FINDING TOUR OF HELL.

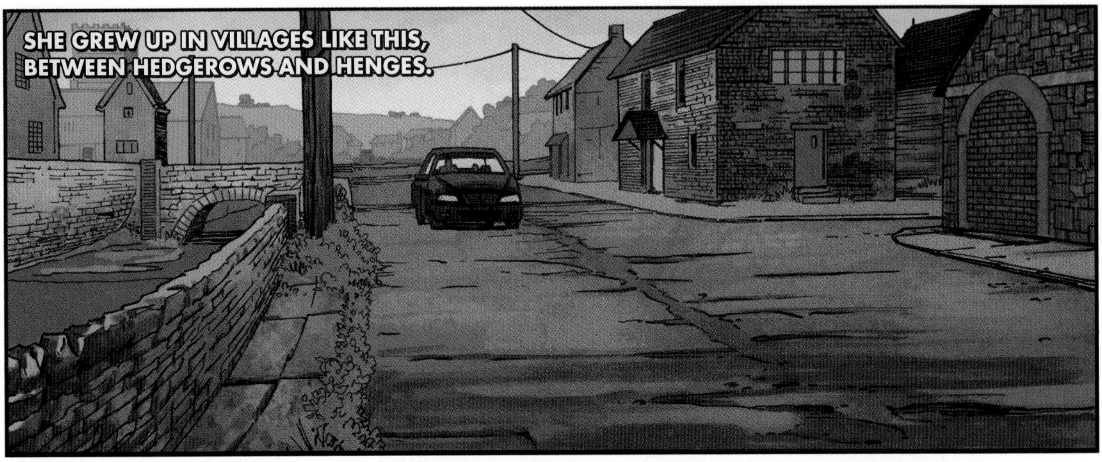
SHE GREW UP IN VILLAGES LIKE THIS, BETWEEN HEDGEROWS AND HENGES.

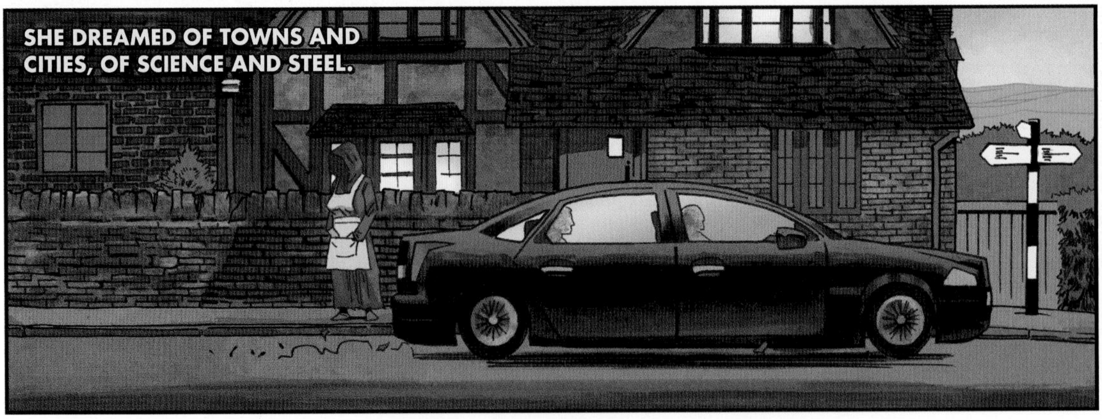
SHE DREAMED OF TOWNS AND CITIES, OF SCIENCE AND STEEL.

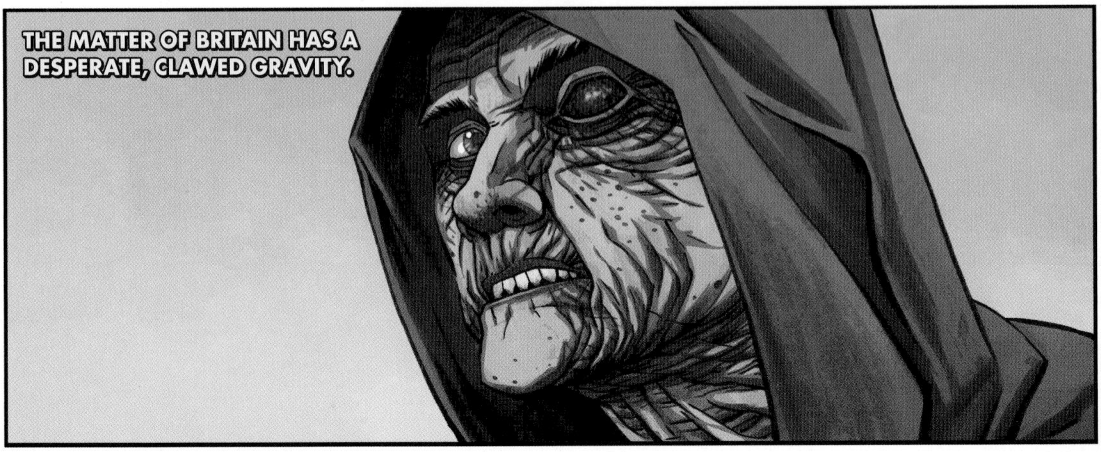
THE MATTER OF BRITAIN HAS A DESPERATE, CLAWED GRAVITY.

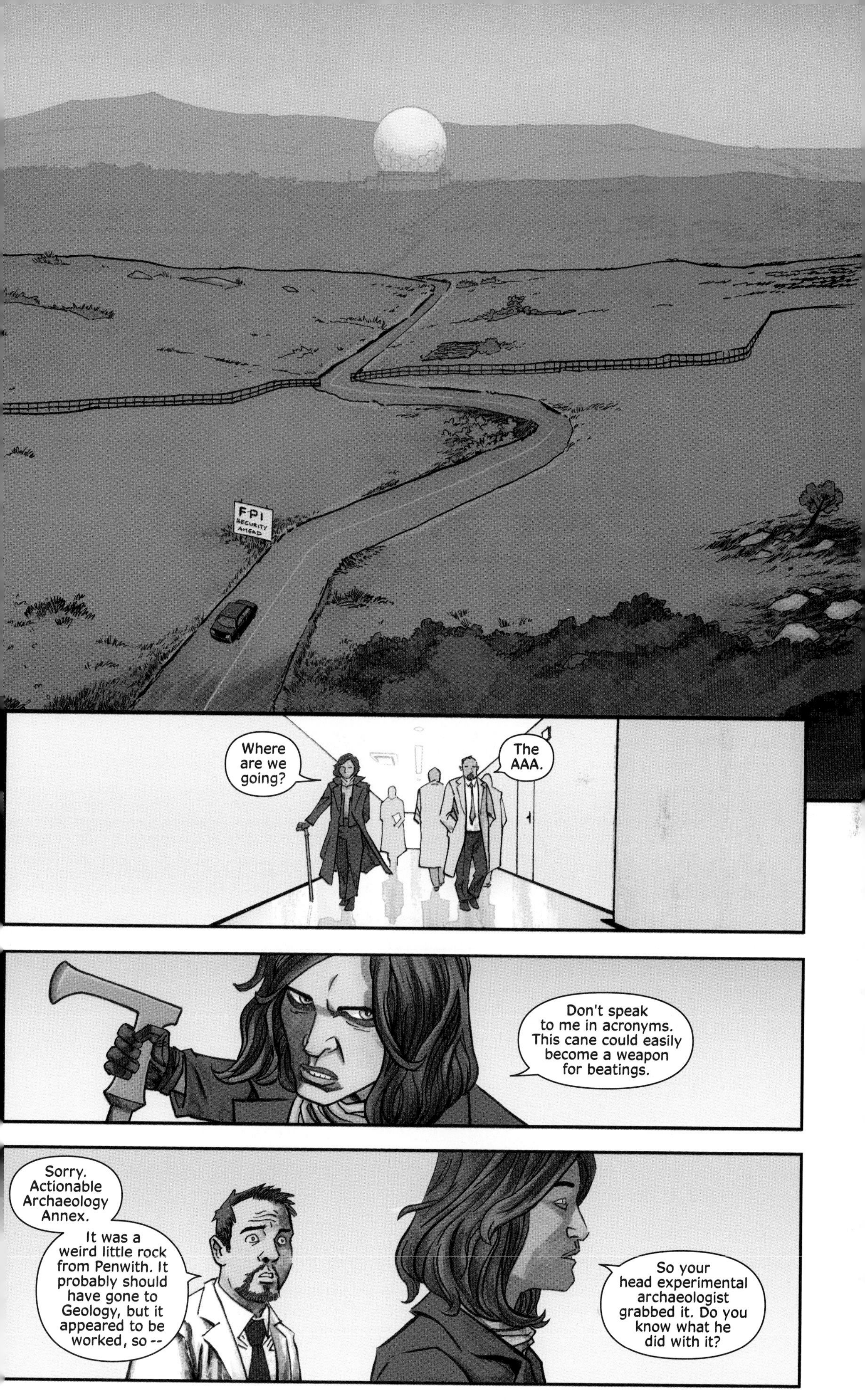
FPI SECURITY AHEAD
Where are we going?
The AAA.
Don't speak to me in acronyms. This cane could easily become a weapon for beatings.
Sorry. Actionable Archaeology Annex.
It was a weird little rock from Penwith. It probably should have gone to Geology, but it appeared to be worked, so --
So your head experimental archaeologist grabbed it. Do you know what he did with it?

Records indicate he may have tested it with sound? We can't go beyond this point.

We have three people missing. The archaeologist. Two security personnel. This is all we know.

All right. Tell your head of security to unseal Workplace Safety Advisory Seven and establish an incursion perimeter as per Protocol F.

And I suppose you'd better open this door.

Let the dog see the rabbit and all that.

Could someone make me a sandwich while I do that?

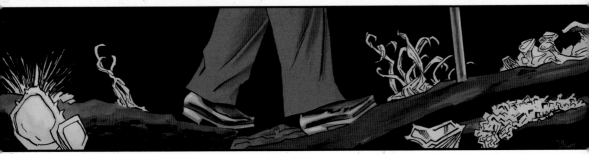

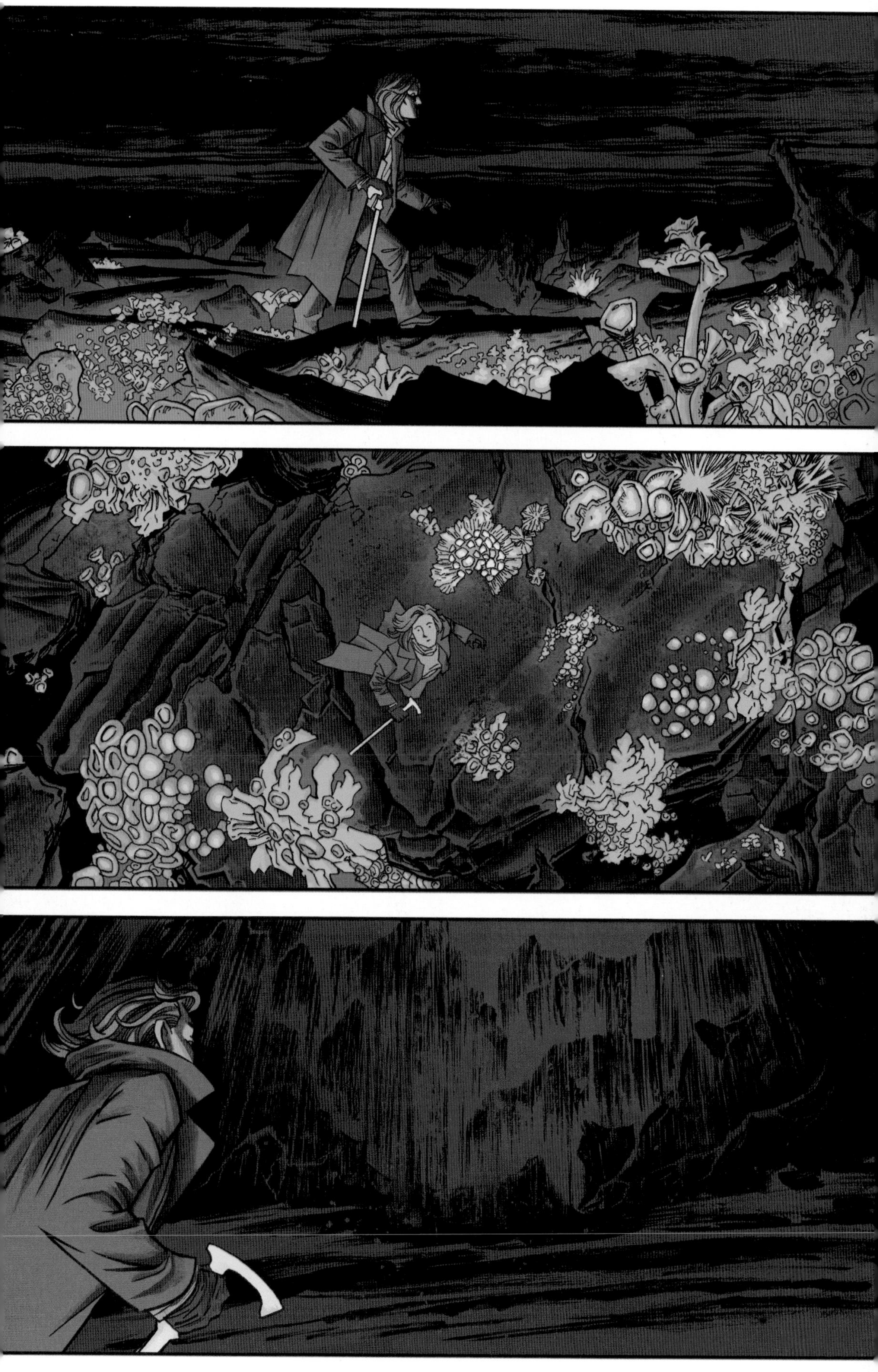

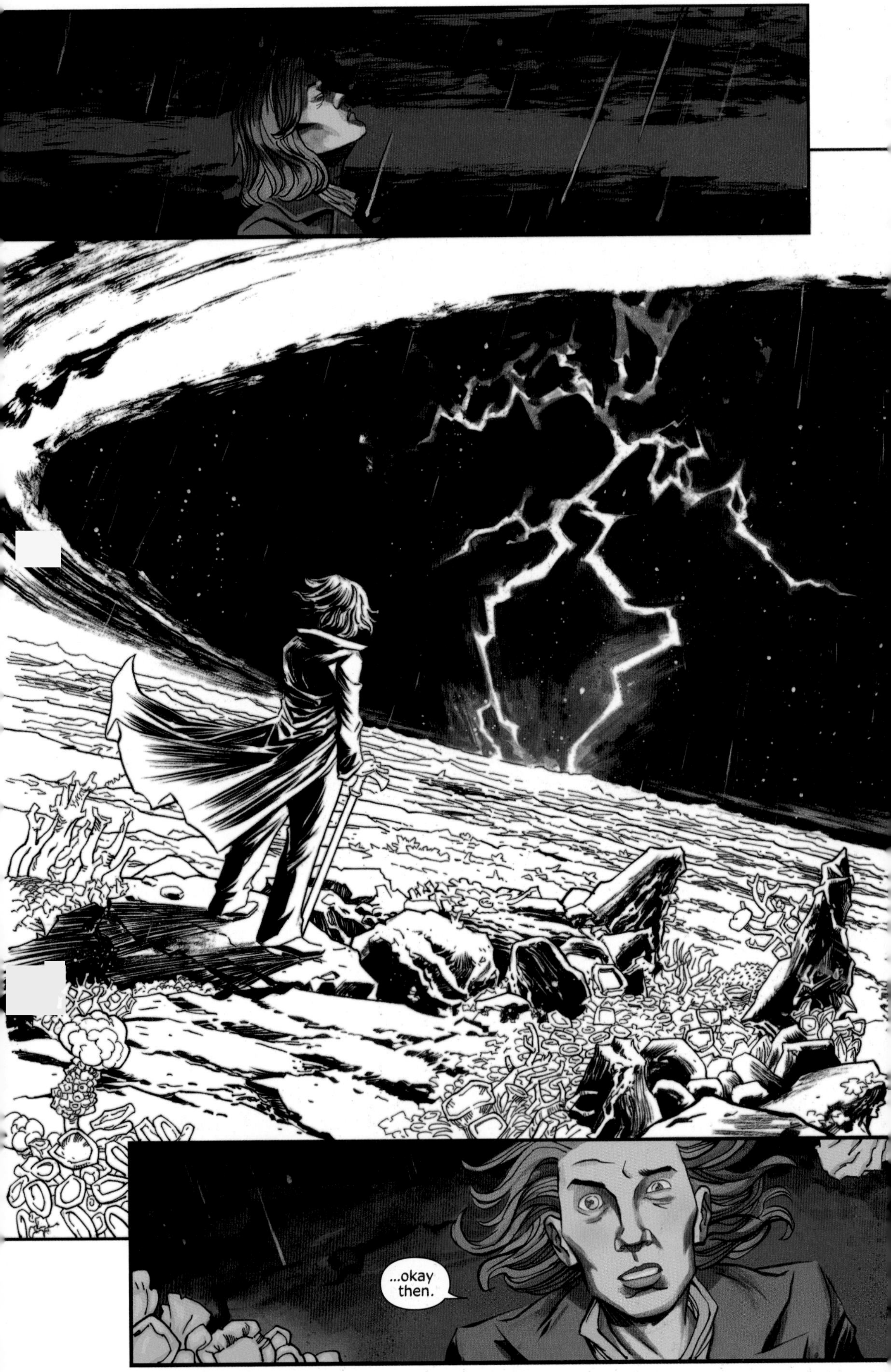
...okay then.

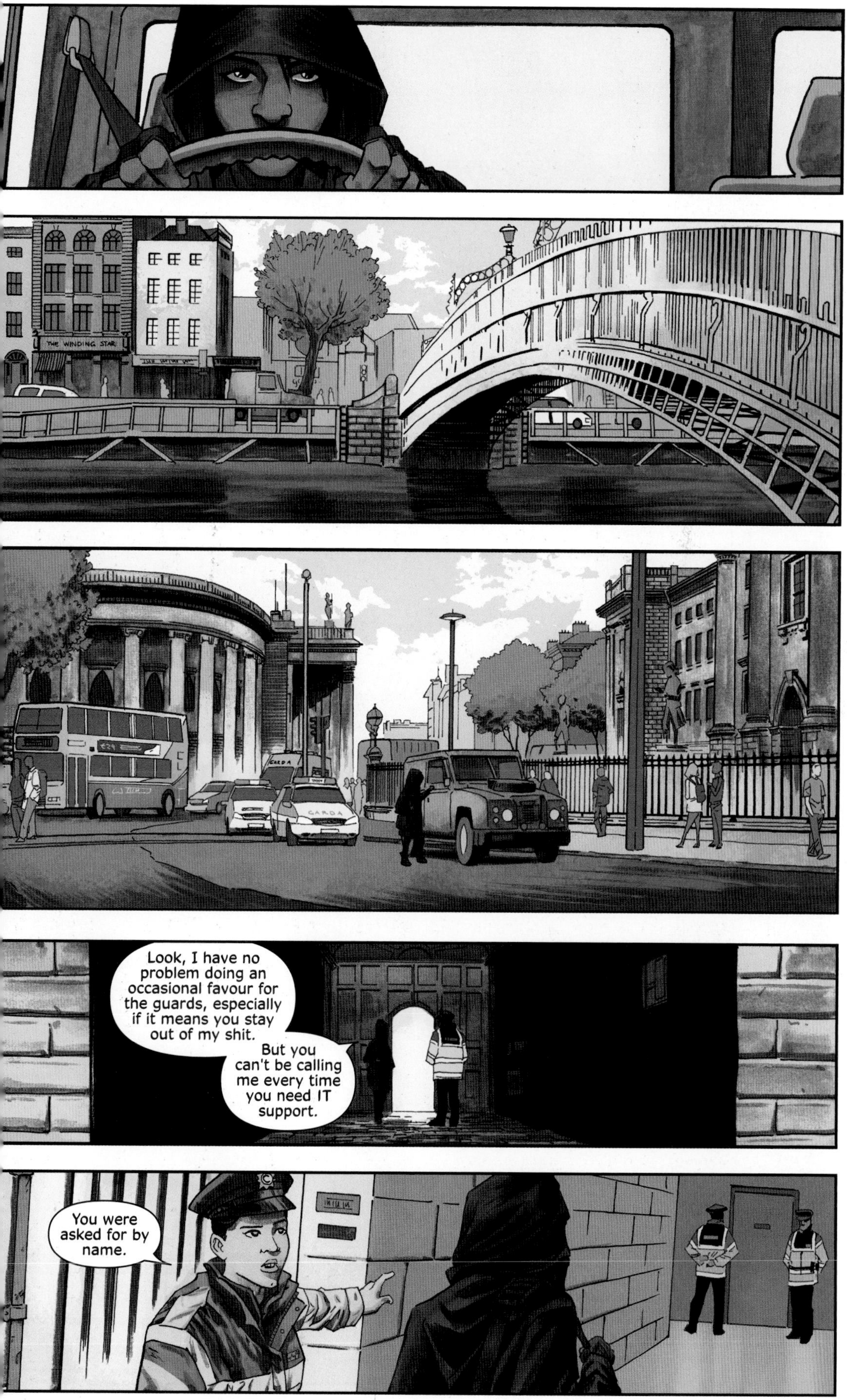
THE WINDING STAR
GARDA
Look, I have no problem doing an occasional favour for the guards, especially if it means you stay out of my shit.
But you can't be calling me every time you need IT support.
You were asked for by name.

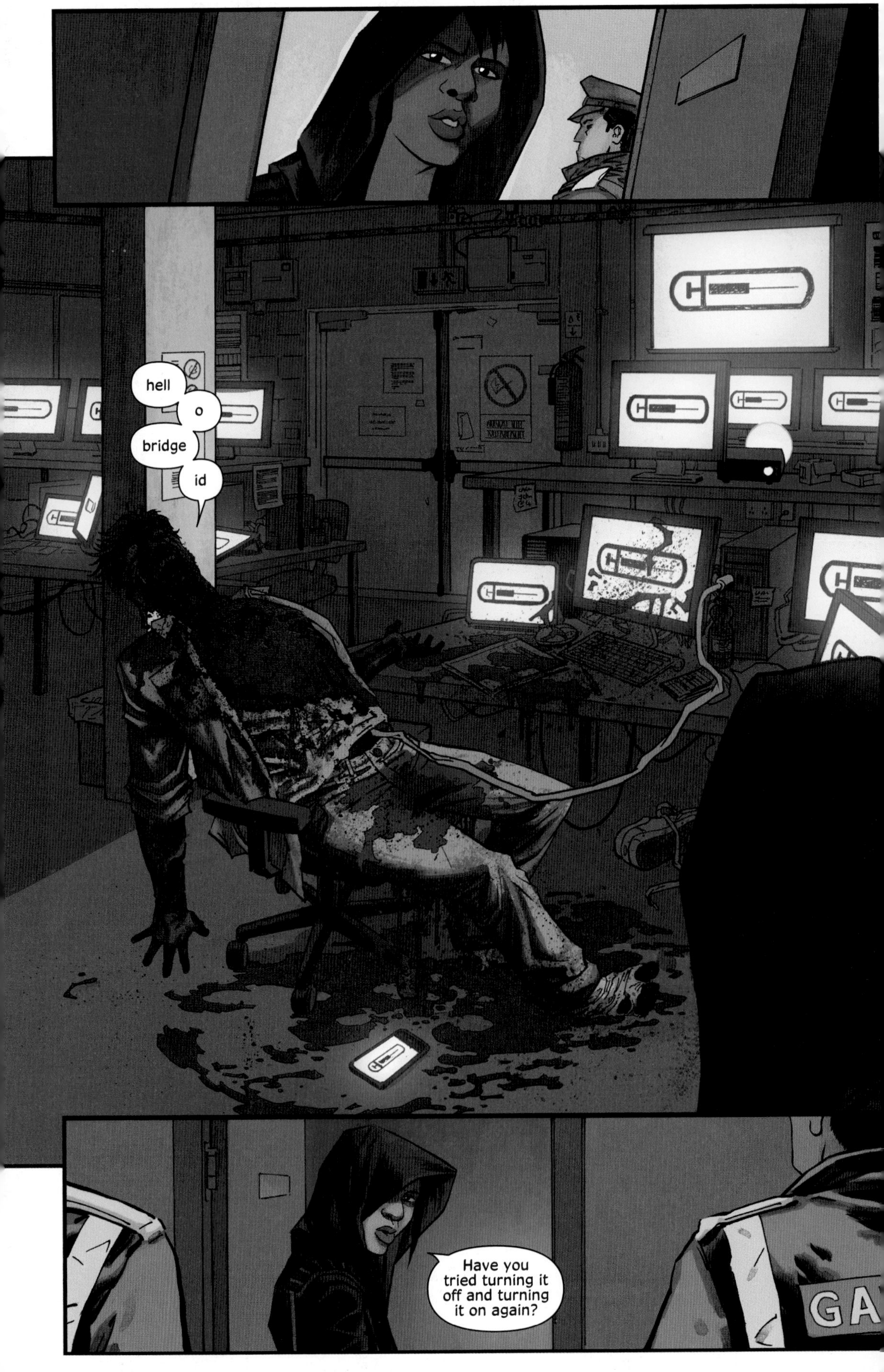
hell
o
bridge
id
Have you tried turning it off and turning it on again?
GA

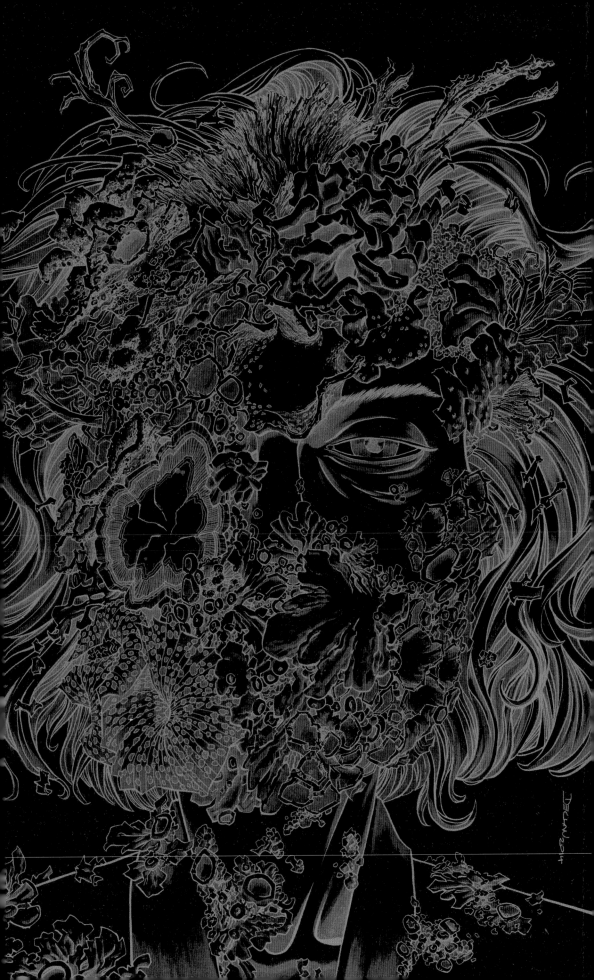

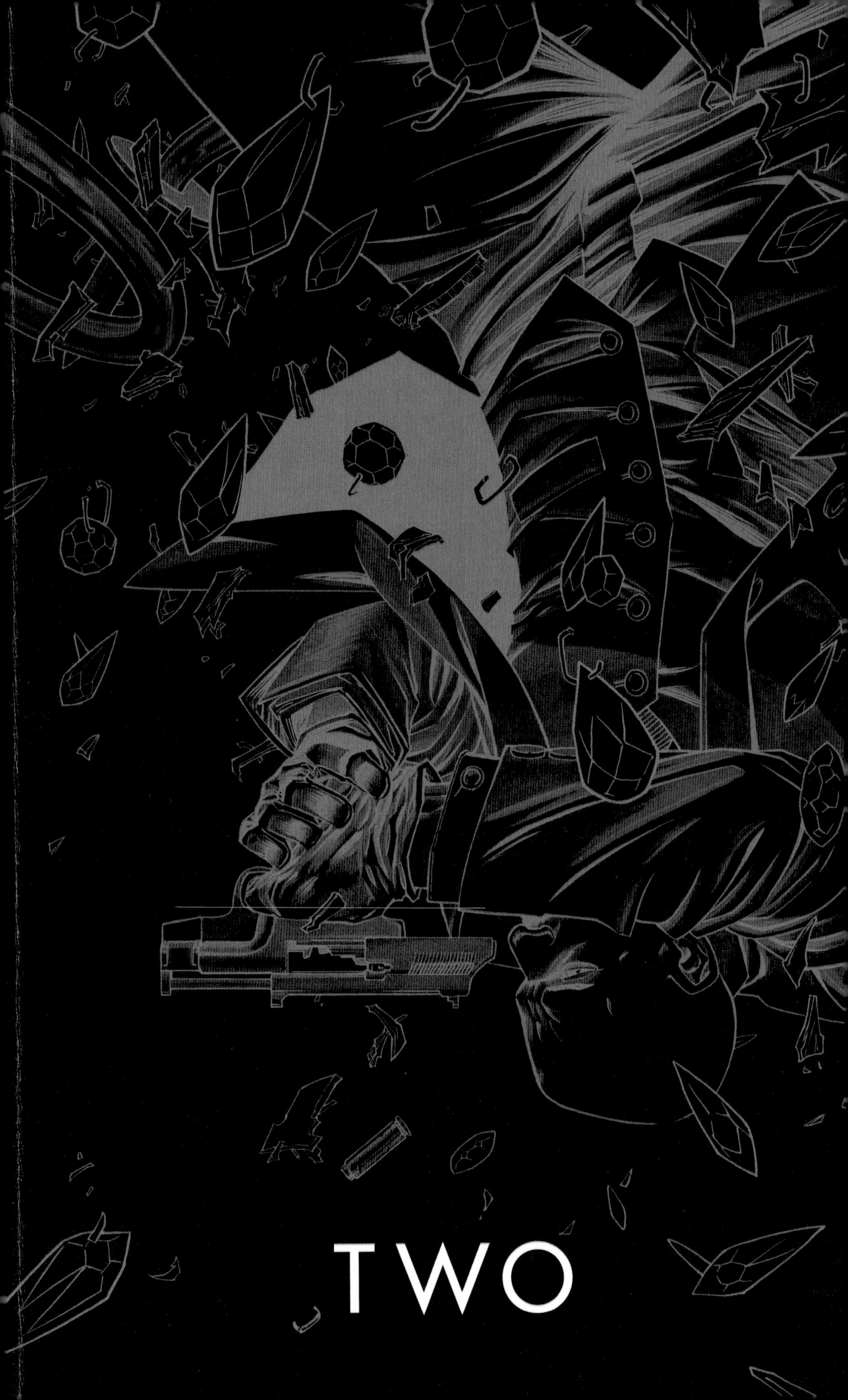

TWO

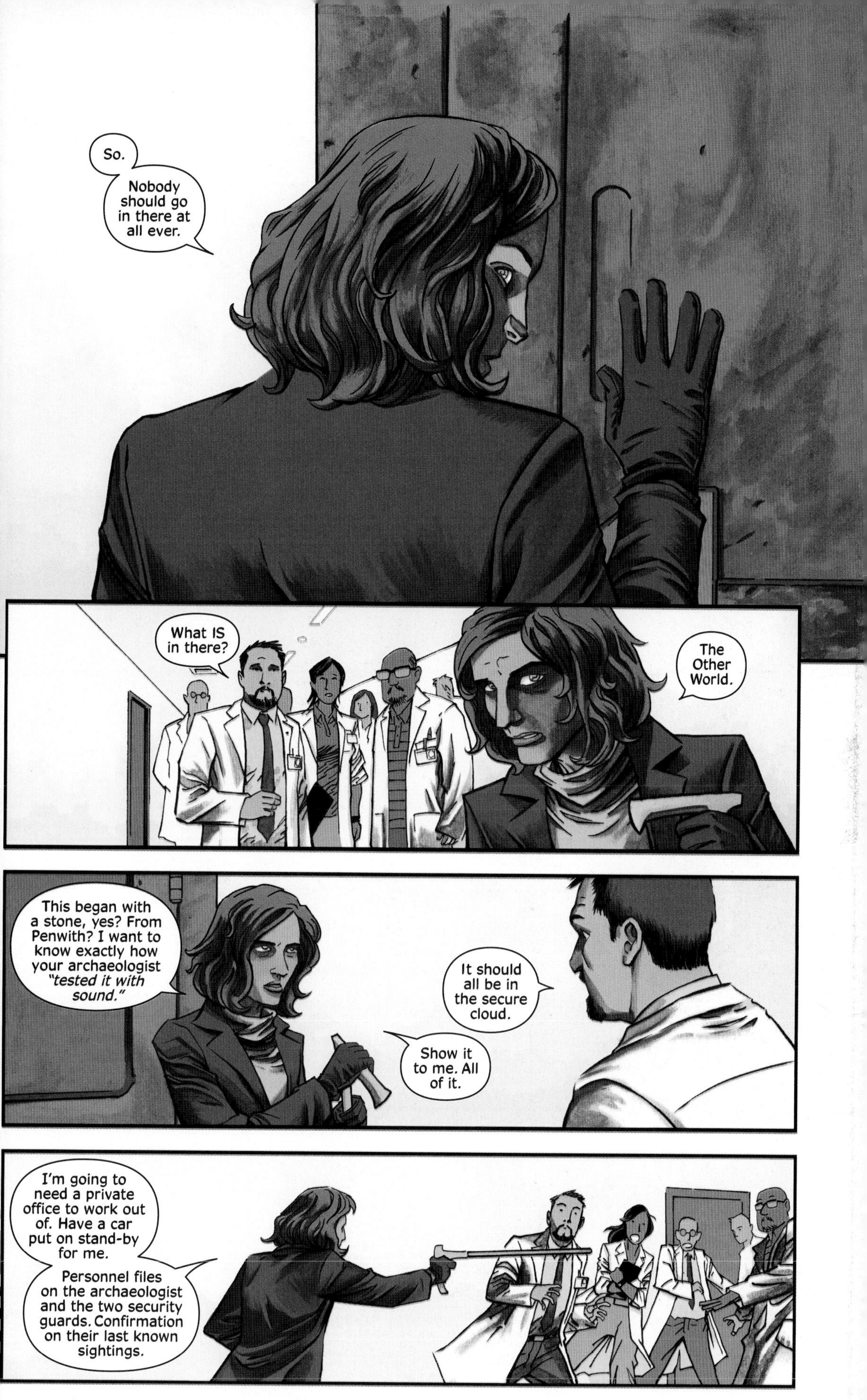
So.
Nobody should go in there at all ever.
What IS in there?
The Other World.
This began with a stone, yes? From Penwith? I want to know exactly how your archaeologist *"tested it with sound."*
It should all be in the secure cloud.
Show it to me. All of it.
I'm going to need a private office to work out of. Have a car put on stand-by for me.
Personnel files on the archaeologist and the two security guards. Confirmation on their last known sightings.

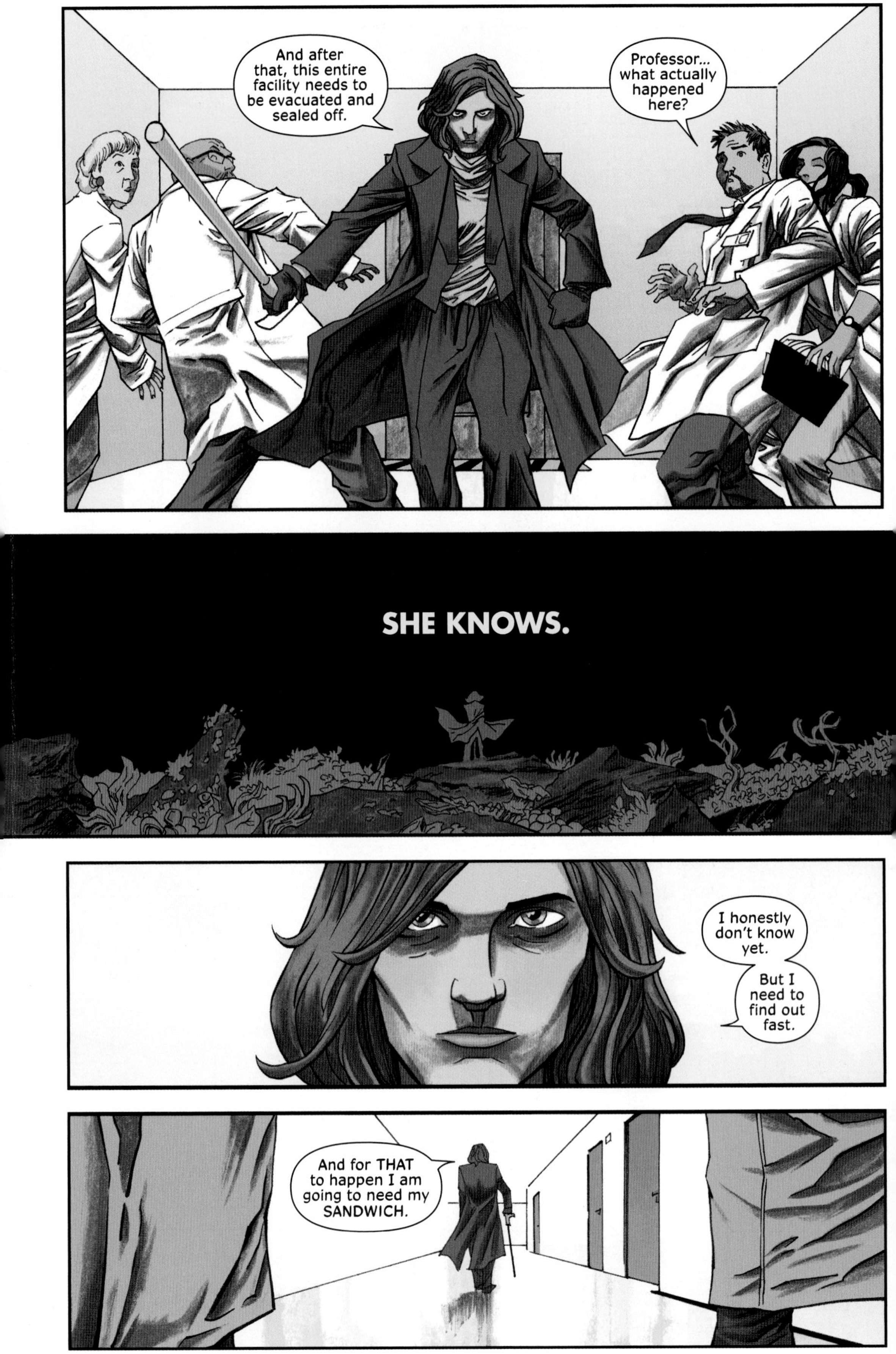
And after that, this entire facility needs to be evacuated and sealed off.
Professor... what actually happened here?
SHE KNOWS.
I honestly don't know yet.
But I need to find out fast.
And for THAT to happen I am going to need my SANDWICH.

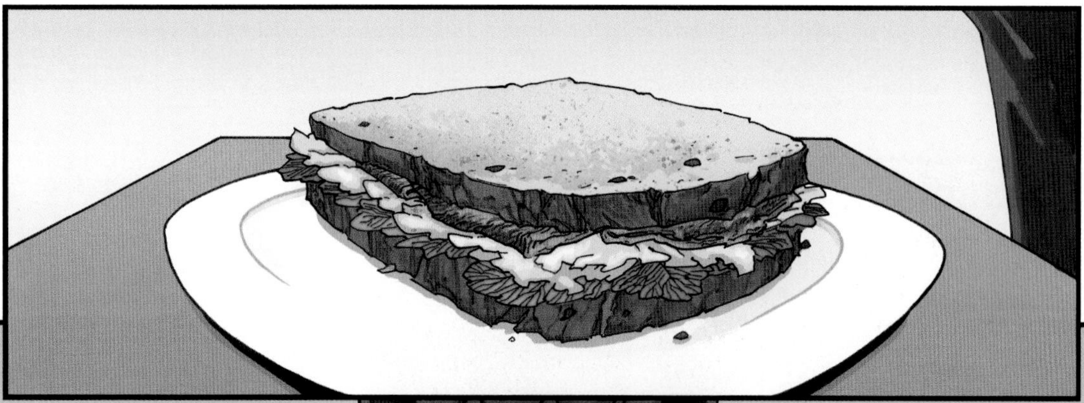

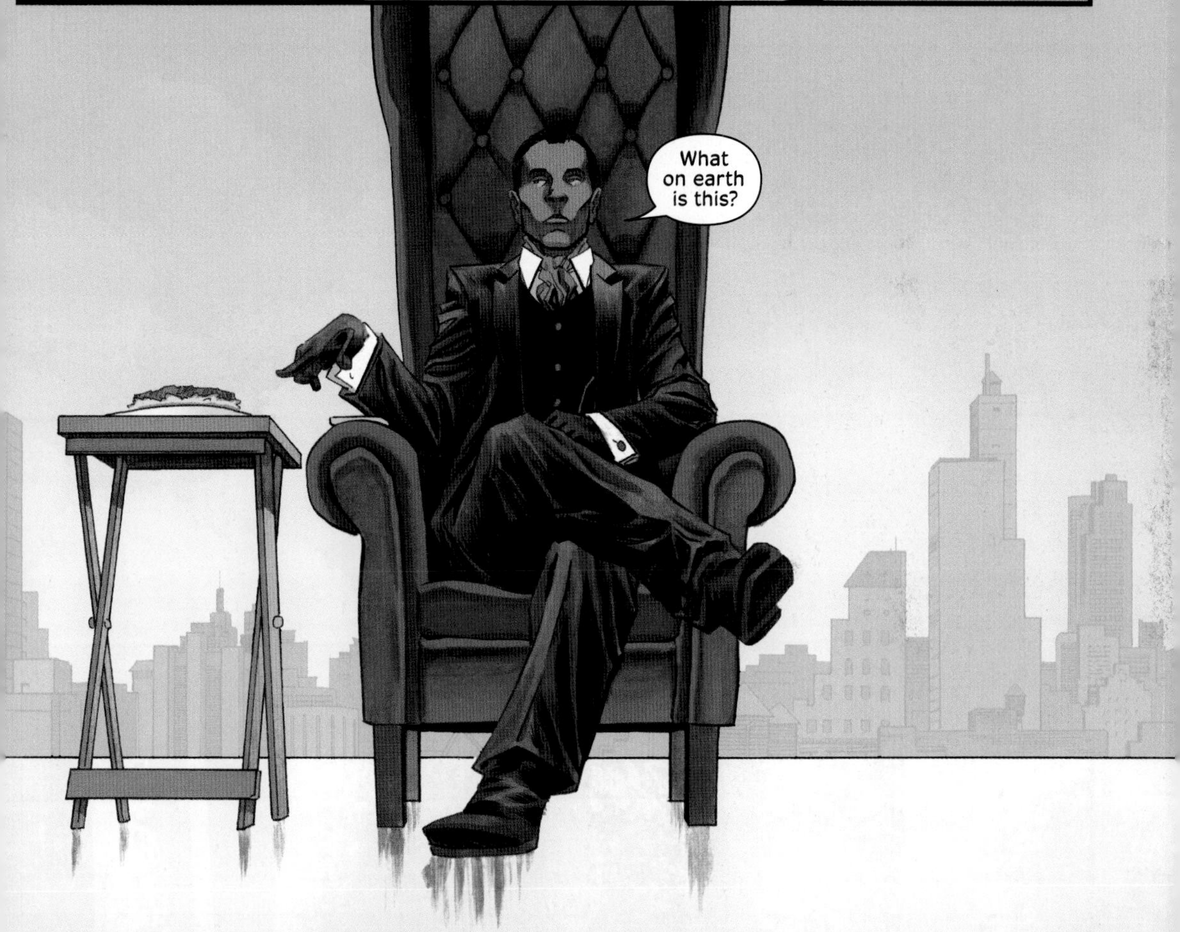
What on earth is this?

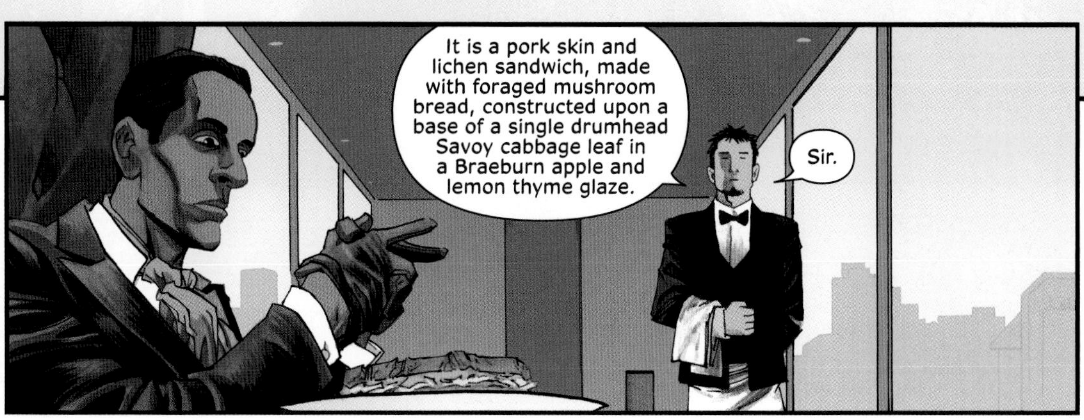
Sir.
It is a pork skin and lichen sandwich, made with foraged mushroom bread, constructed upon a base of a single drumhead Savoy cabbage leaf in a Braeburn apple and lemon thyme glaze.

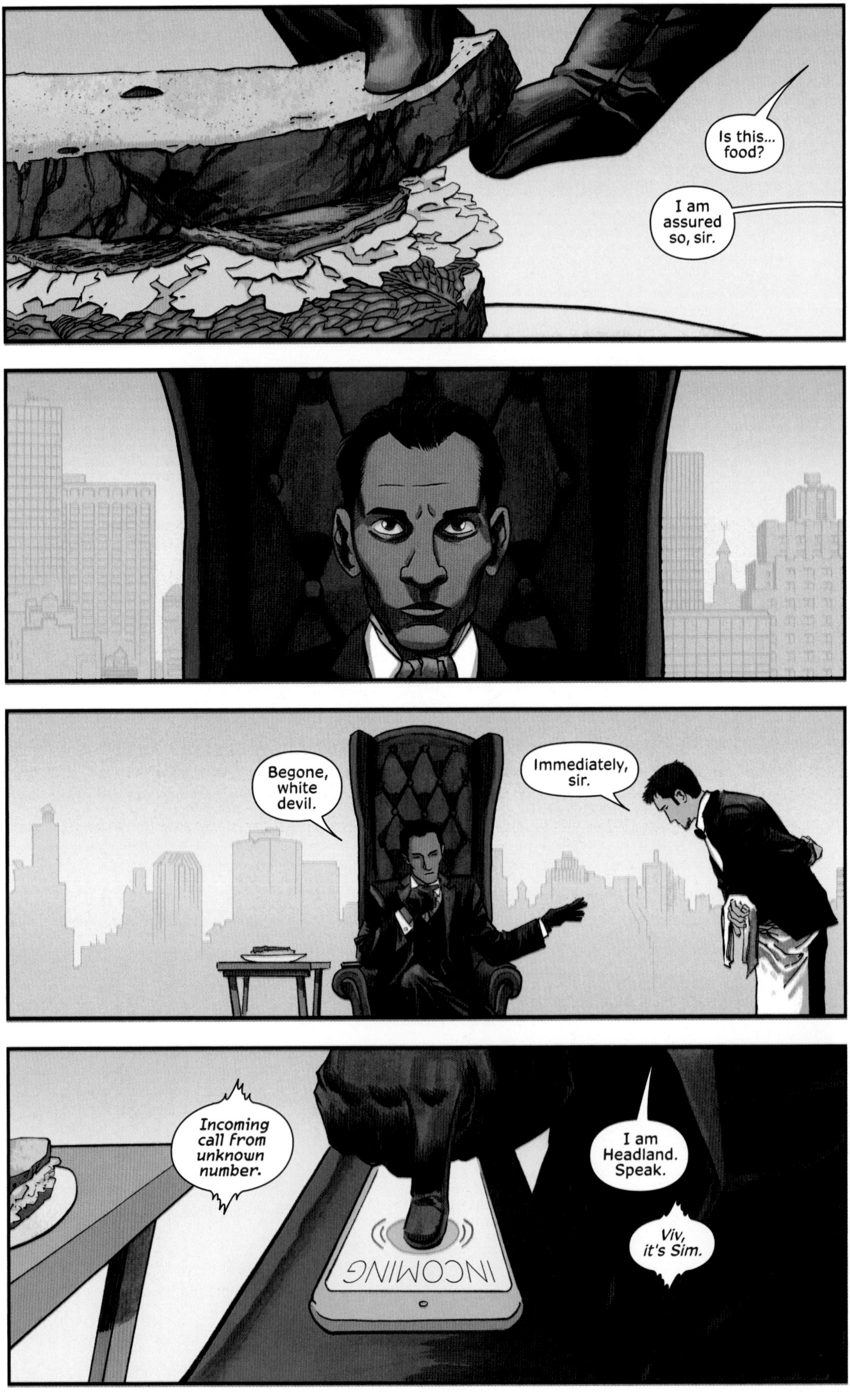
Is this... food?
I am assured so, sir.
Begone, white devil.
Immediately, sir.
Incoming call from unknown number.
INCOMING
I am Headland. Speak.
Viv, it's Sim.

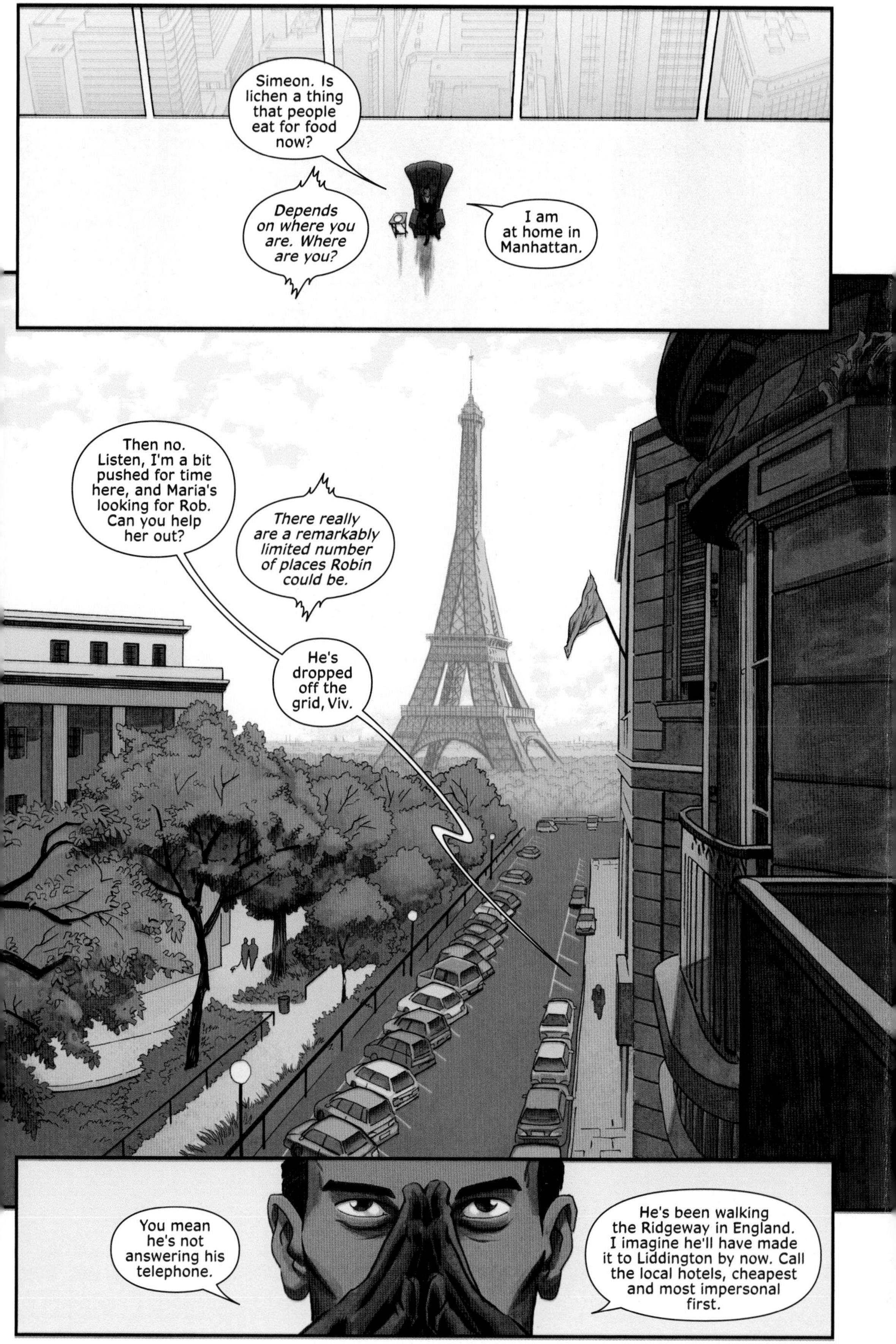
Simeon. Is lichen a thing that people eat for food now?
Depends on where you are. Where are you?
I am at home in Manhattan.
Then no. Listen, I'm a bit pushed for time here, and Maria's looking for Rob. Can you help her out?
There really are a remarkably limited number of places Robin could be.
He's dropped off the grid, Viv.
You mean he's not answering his telephone.
He's been walking the Ridgeway in England. I imagine he'll have made it to Liddington by now. Call the local hotels, cheapest and most impersonal first.

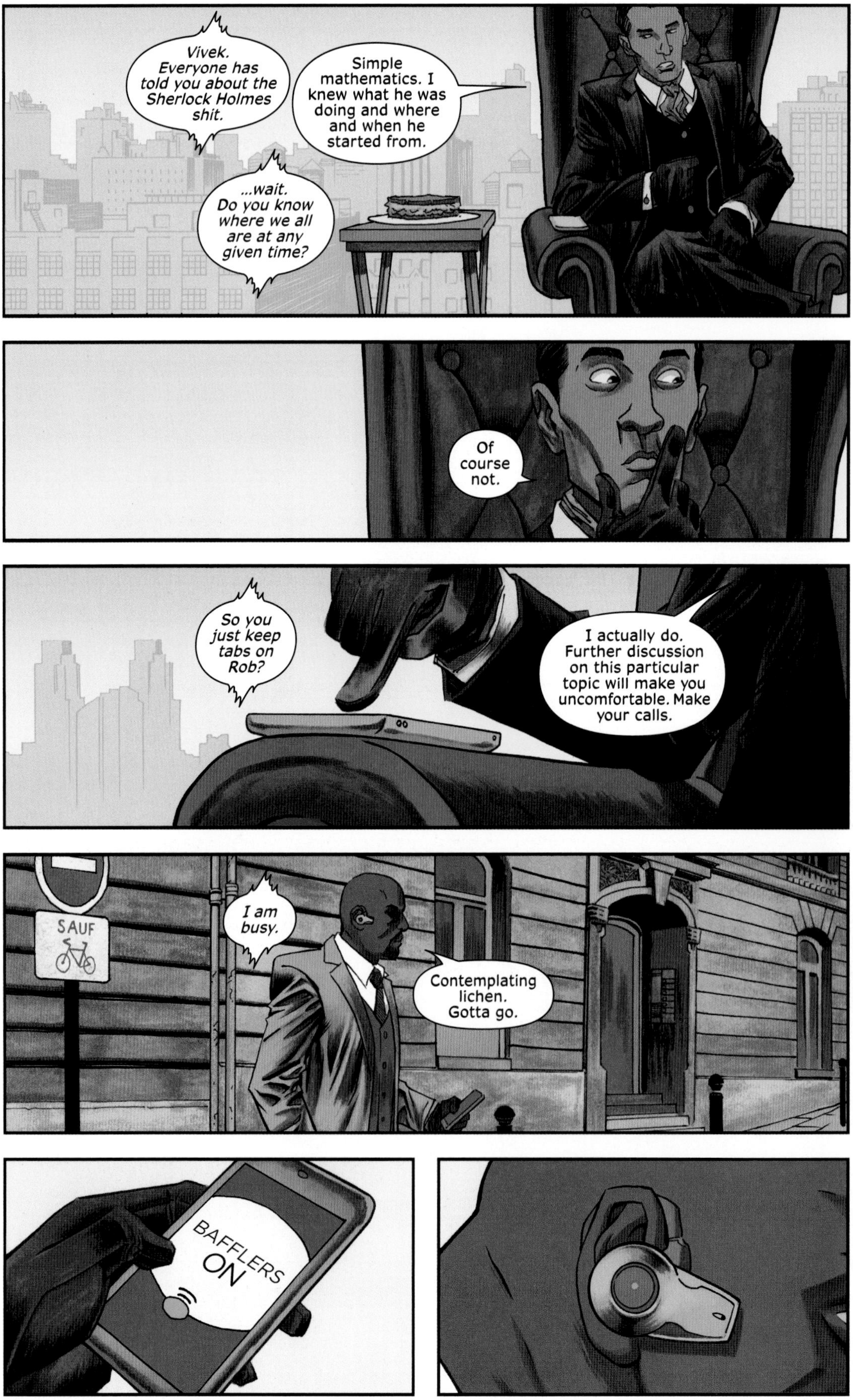
Vivek. Everyone has told you about the Sherlock Holmes shit.
Simple mathematics. I knew what he was doing and where and when he started from.
...wait. Do you know where we all are at any given time?
Of course not.
So you just keep tabs on Rob?
I actually do. Further discussion on this particular topic will make you uncomfortable. Make your calls.
SAUF
I am busy.
Contemplating lichen. Gotta go.
BAFFLERS ON

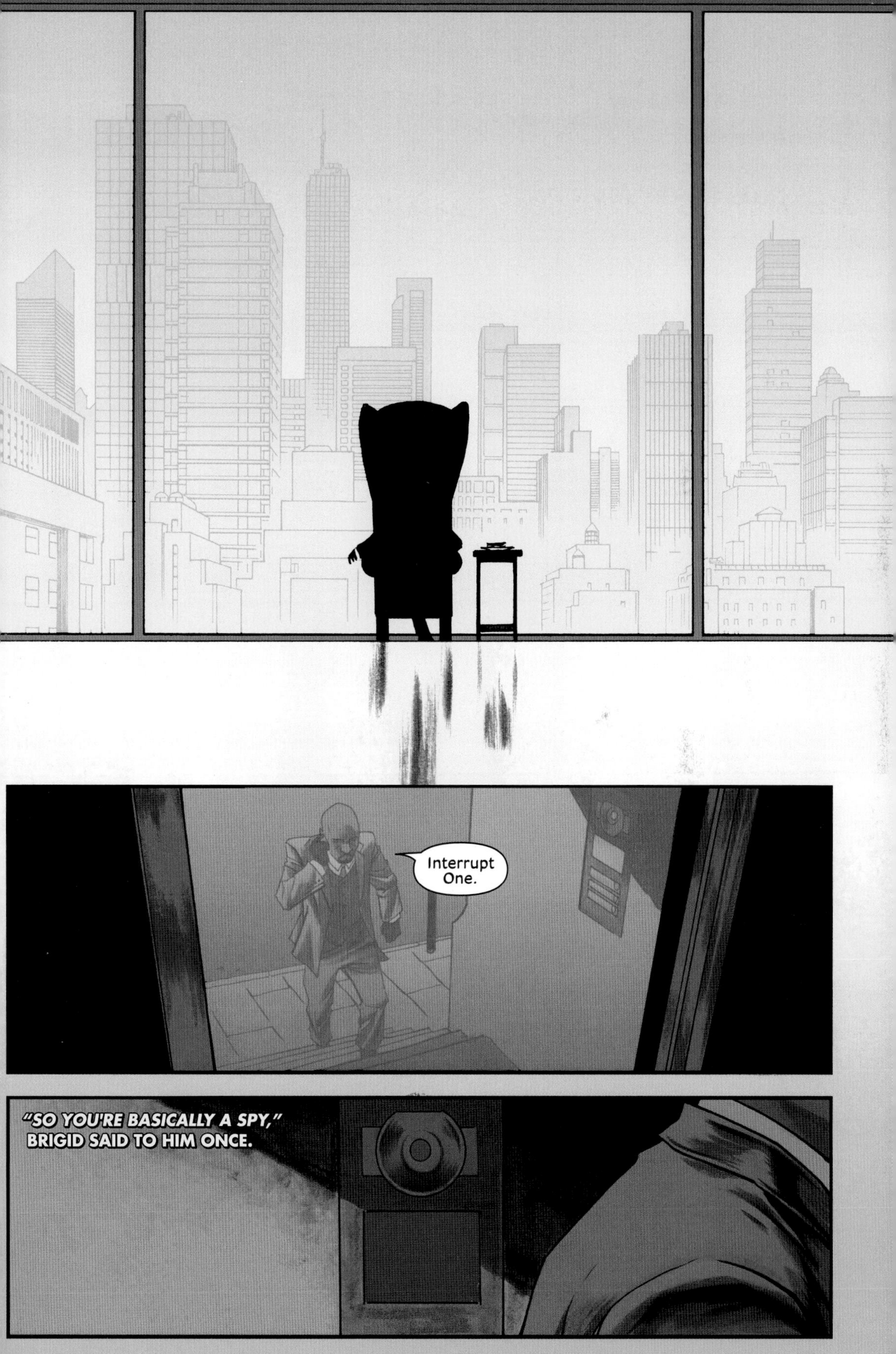
Interrupt One.
"SO YOU'RE BASICALLY A SPY," BRIGID SAID TO HIM ONCE.

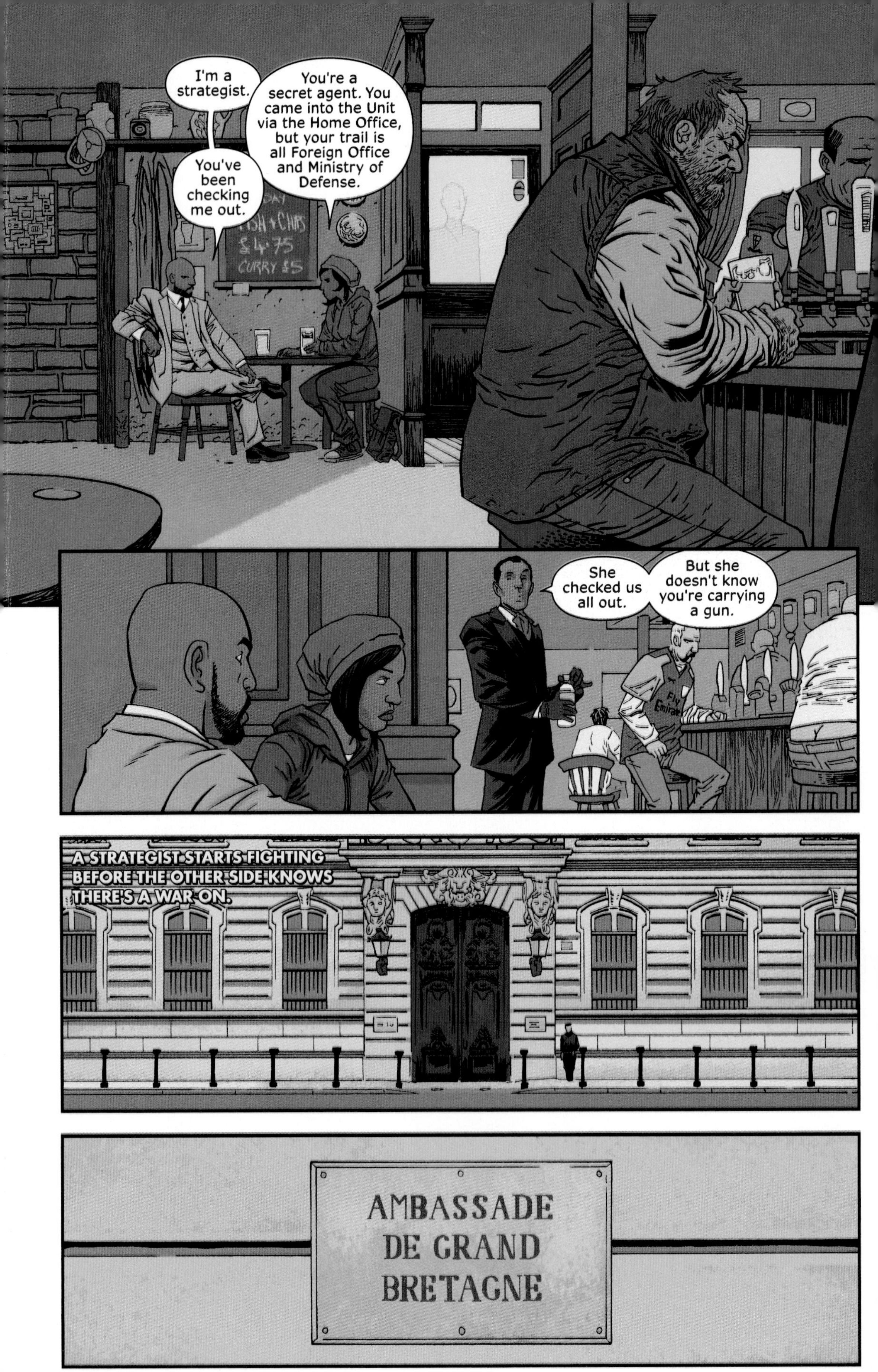
I'm a strategist.
You're a secret agent. You came into the Unit via the Home Office, but your trail is all Foreign Office and Ministry of Defense.
You've been checking me out.
CURRY £5
She checked us all out.
But she doesn't know you're carrying a gun.
A STRATEGIST STARTS FIGHTING BEFORE THE OTHER SIDE KNOWS THERE'S A WAR ON.
AMBASSADE DE GRAND BRETAGNE

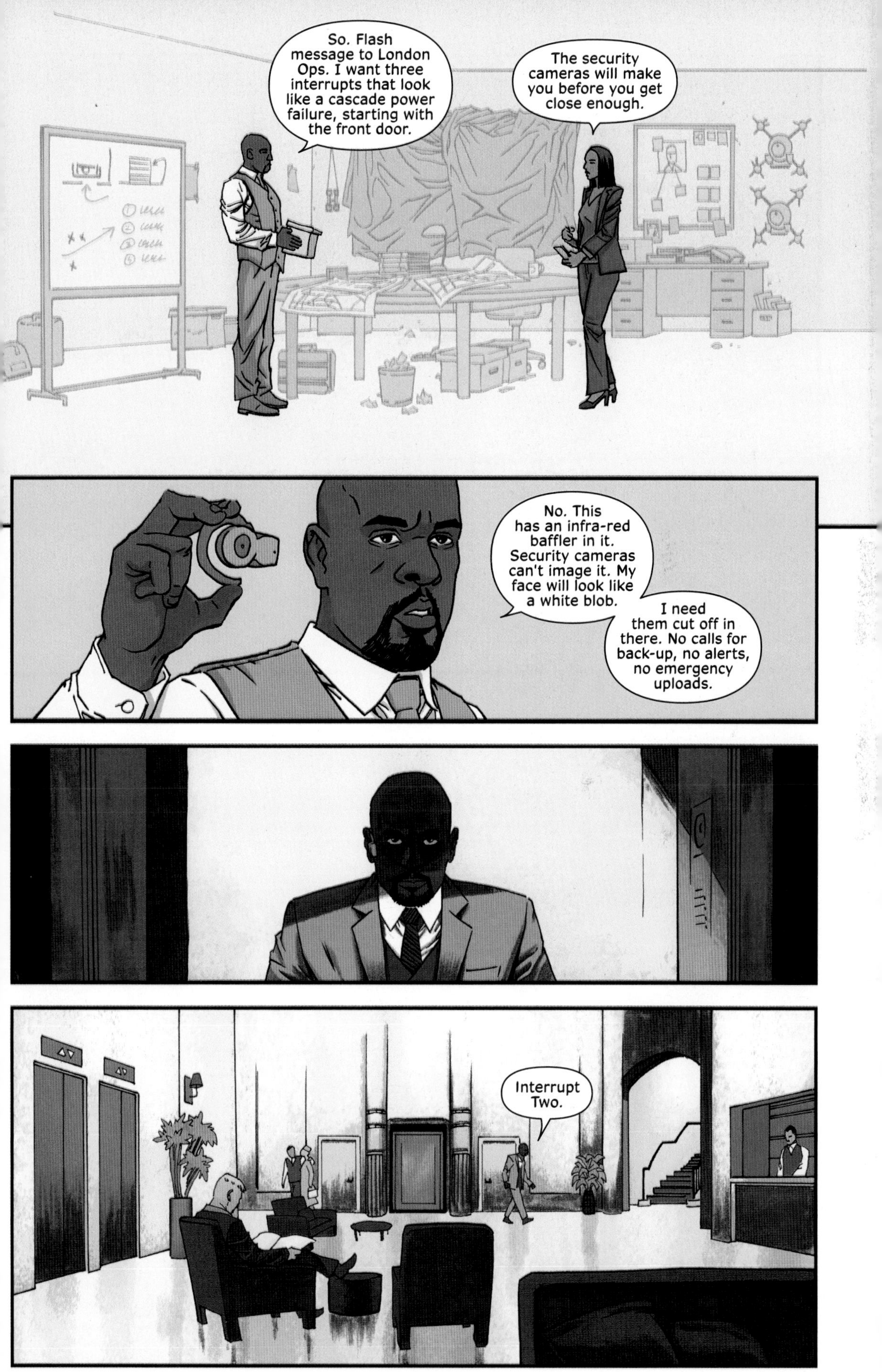
So. Flash message to London Ops. I want three interrupts that look like a cascade power failure, starting with the front door.
The security cameras will make you before you get close enough.
No. This has an infra-red baffler in it. Security cameras can't image it. My face will look like a white blob.
I need them cut off in there. No calls for back-up, no alerts, no emergency uploads.
Interrupt Two.

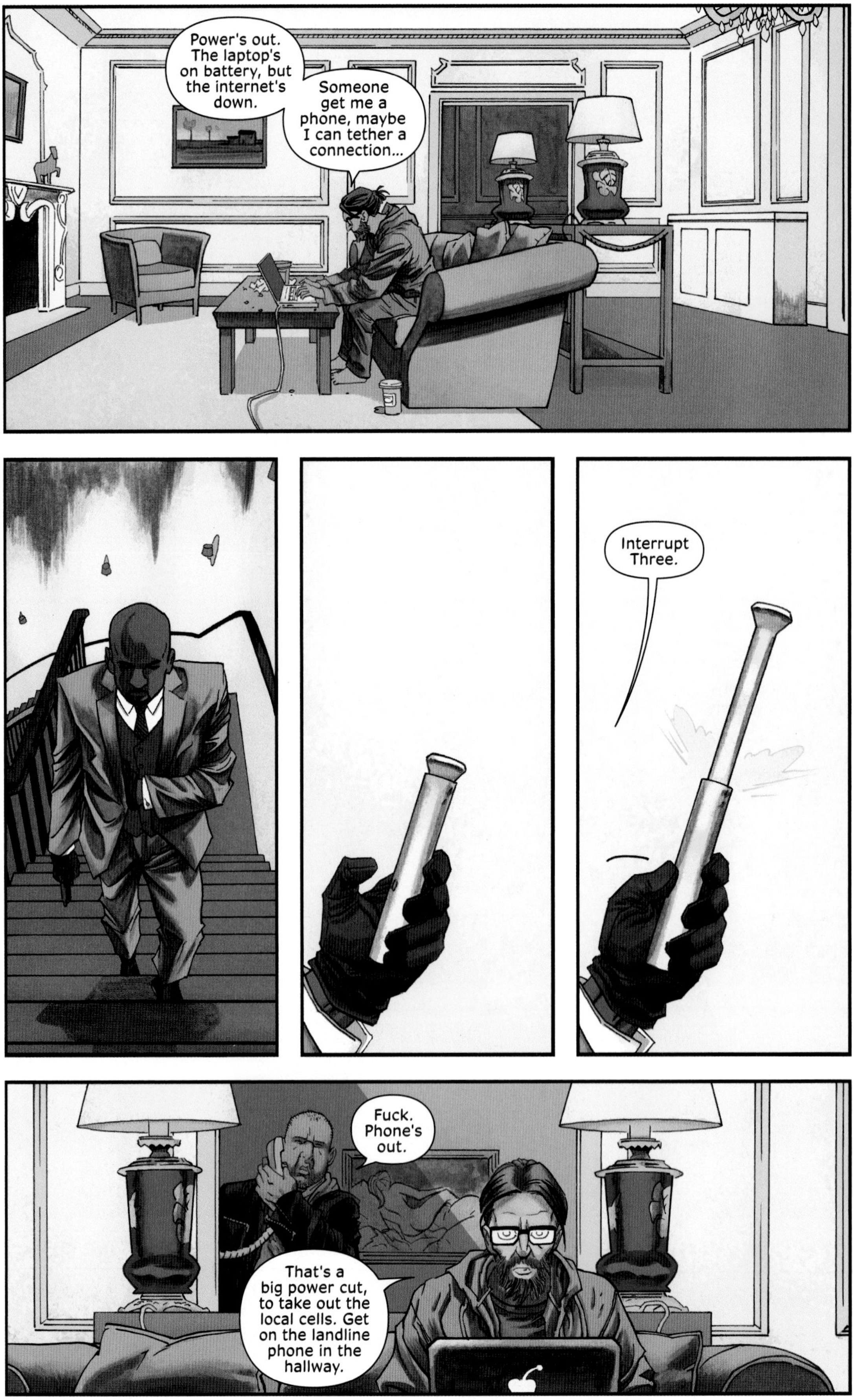
Power's out. The laptop's on battery, but the internet's down.
Someone get me a phone, maybe I can tether a connection...
Interrupt Three.
Fuck. Phone's out.
That's a big power cut, to take out the local cells. Get on the landline phone in the hallway.

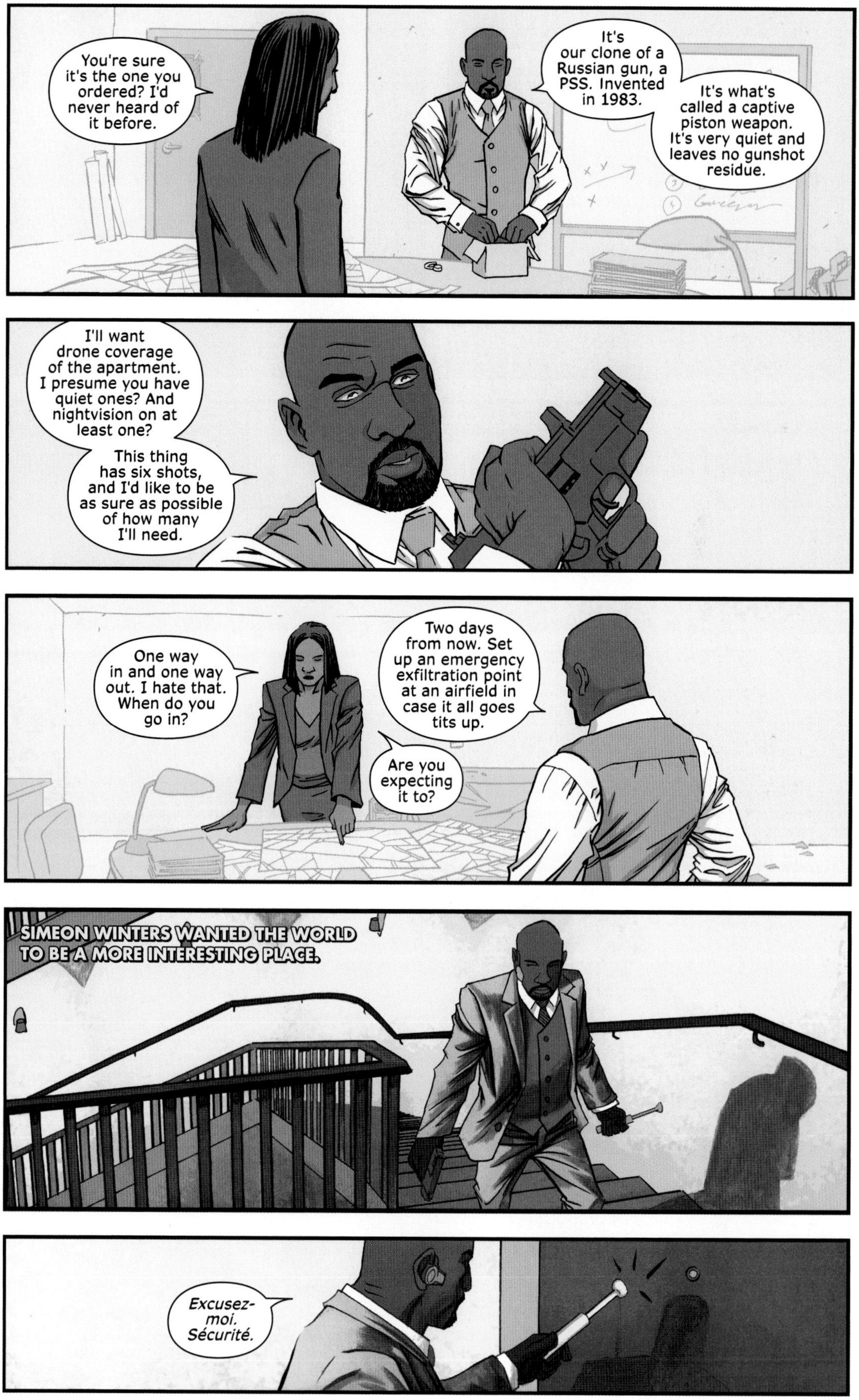
You're sure it's the one you ordered? I'd never heard of it before.
It's our clone of a Russian gun, a PSS. Invented in 1983.
It's what's called a captive piston weapon. It's very quiet and leaves no gunshot residue.
I'll want drone coverage of the apartment. I presume you have quiet ones? And nightvision on at least one?
This thing has six shots, and I'd like to be as sure as possible of how many I'll need.
One way in and one way out. I hate that. When do you go in?
Two days from now. Set up an emergency exfiltration point at an airfield in case it all goes tits up.
Are you expecting it to?
SIMEON WINTERS WANTED THE WORLD TO BE A MORE INTERESTING PLACE.
Excusez-moi. Sécurité.

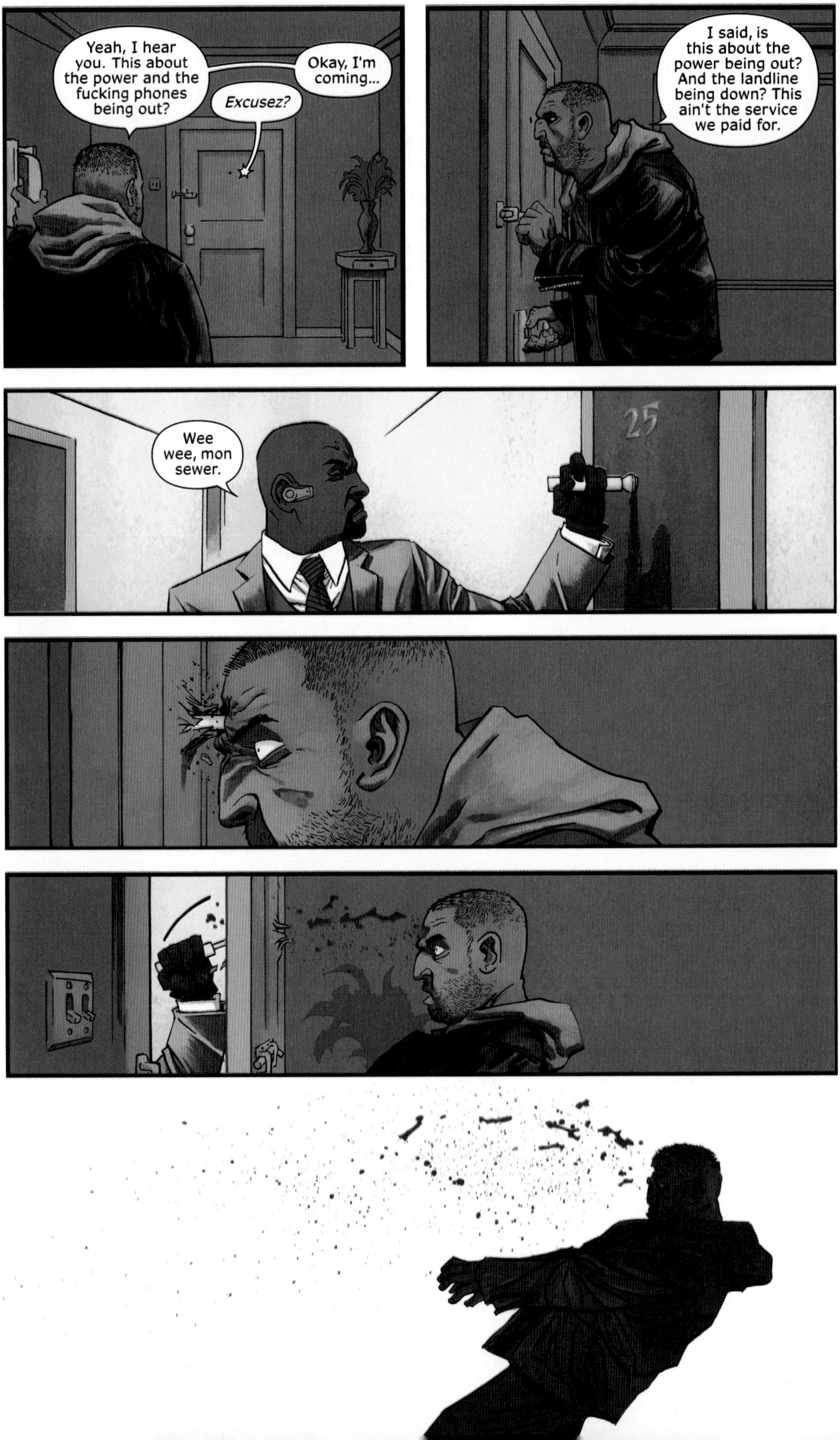
Yeah, I hear you. This about the power and the fucking phones being out?
Okay, I'm coming...
Excusez?
I said, is this about the power being out? And the landline being down? This ain't the service we paid for.
Wee wee, mon sewer.
25

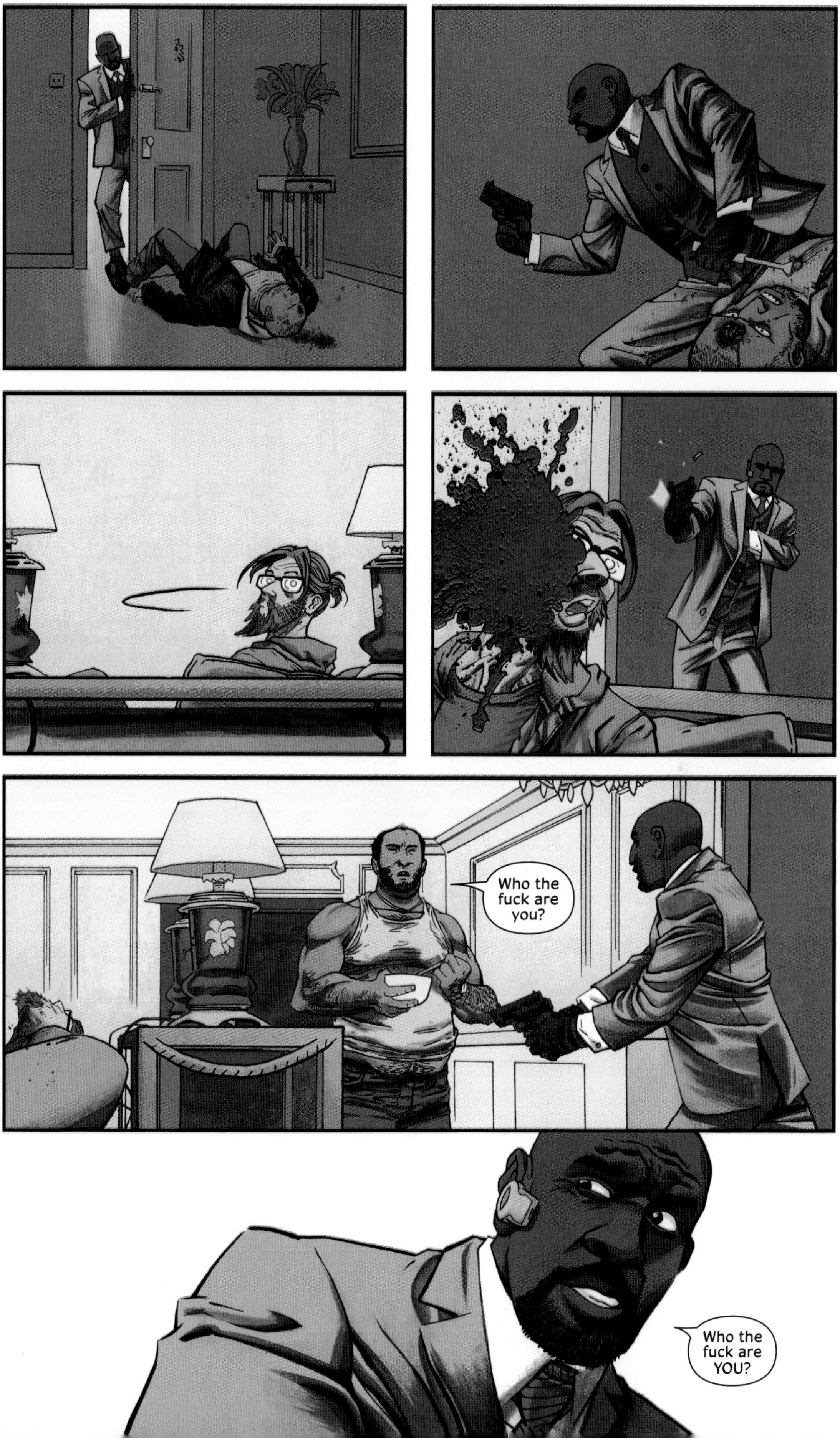
Who the fuck are you?
Who the fuck are YOU?

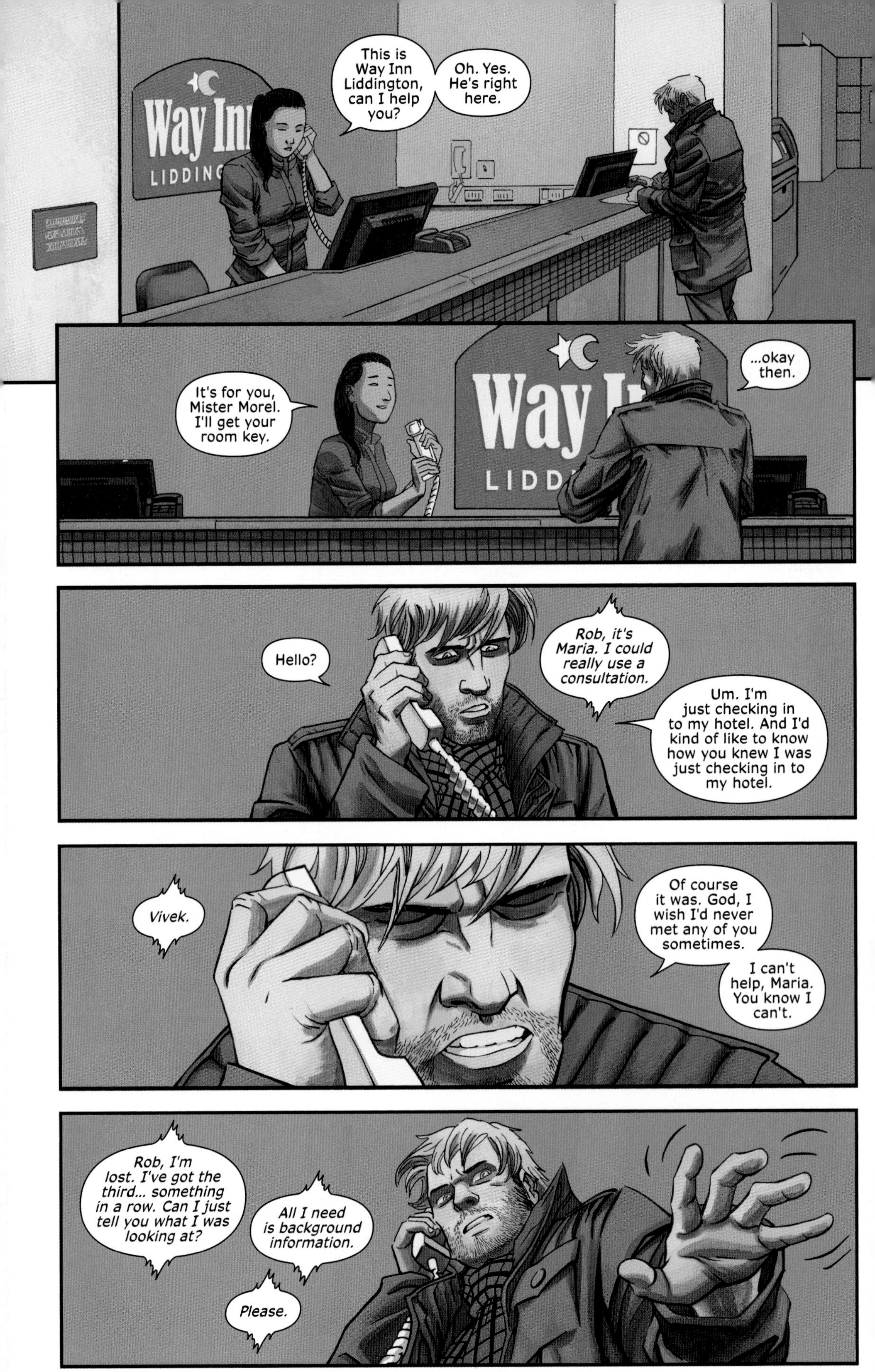

Way Inn
LIDDING
This is Way Inn Liddington, can I help you?
Oh. Yes. He's right here.
Way In
LIDD
It's for you, Mister Morel. I'll get your room key.
...okay then.
Hello?
Rob, it's Maria. I could really use a consultation.
Um. I'm just checking in to my hotel. And I'd kind of like to know how you knew I was just checking in to my hotel.
Vivek.
Of course it was. God, I wish I'd never met any of you sometimes.
I can't help, Maria. You know I can't.
Rob, I'm lost. I've got the third... something in a row. Can I just tell you what I was looking at?
All I need is background information.
Please.

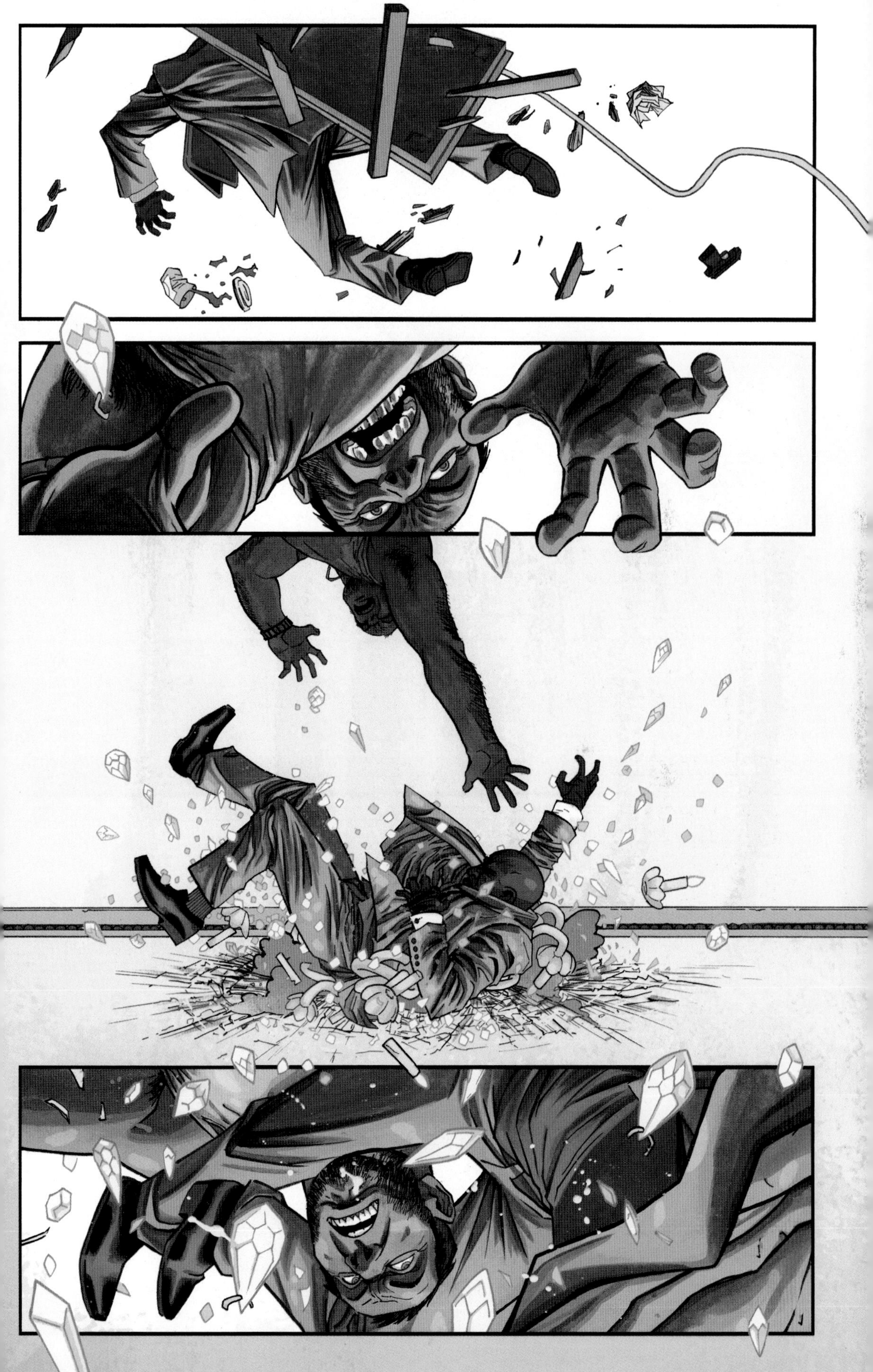

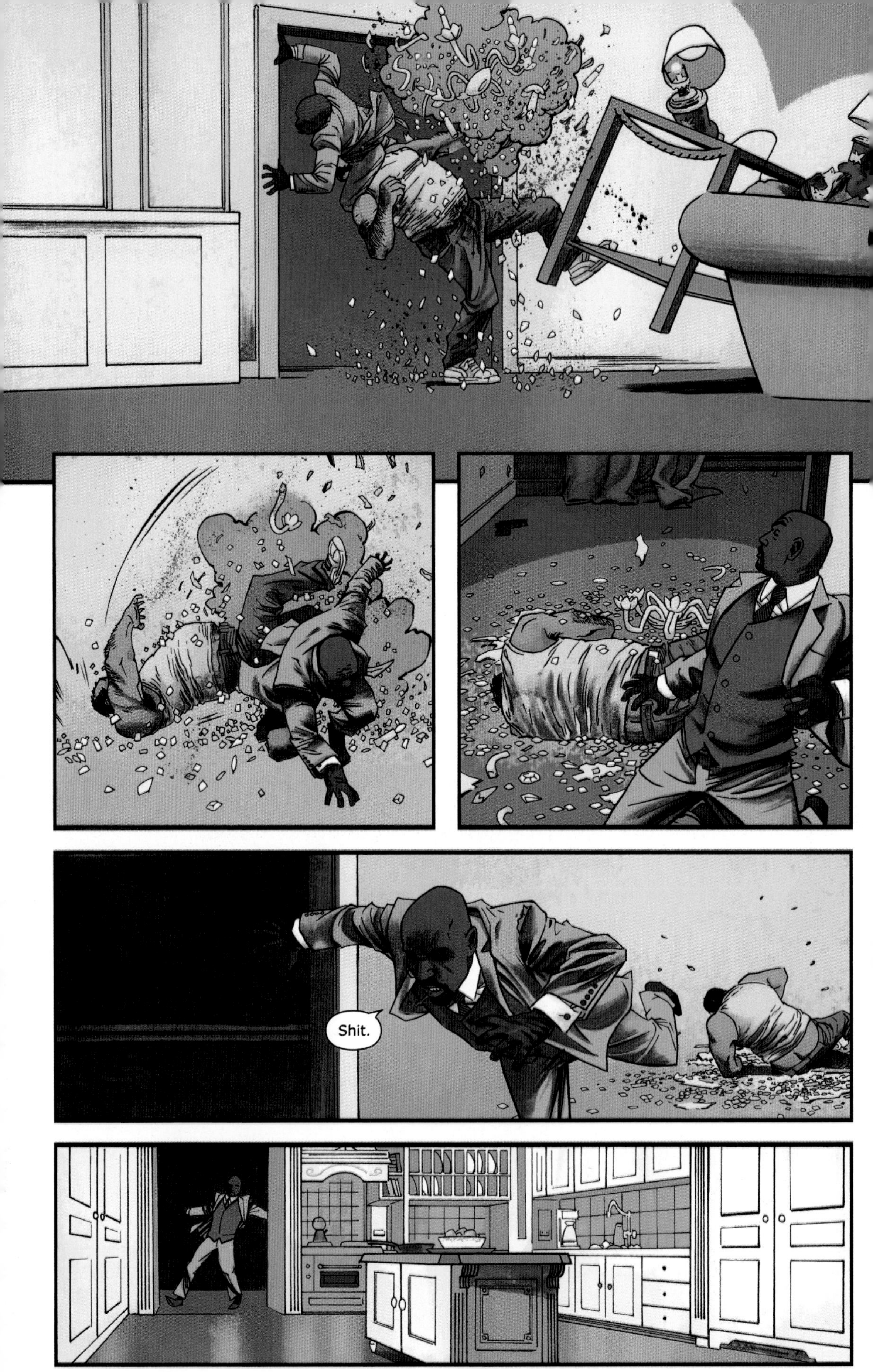
Shit.

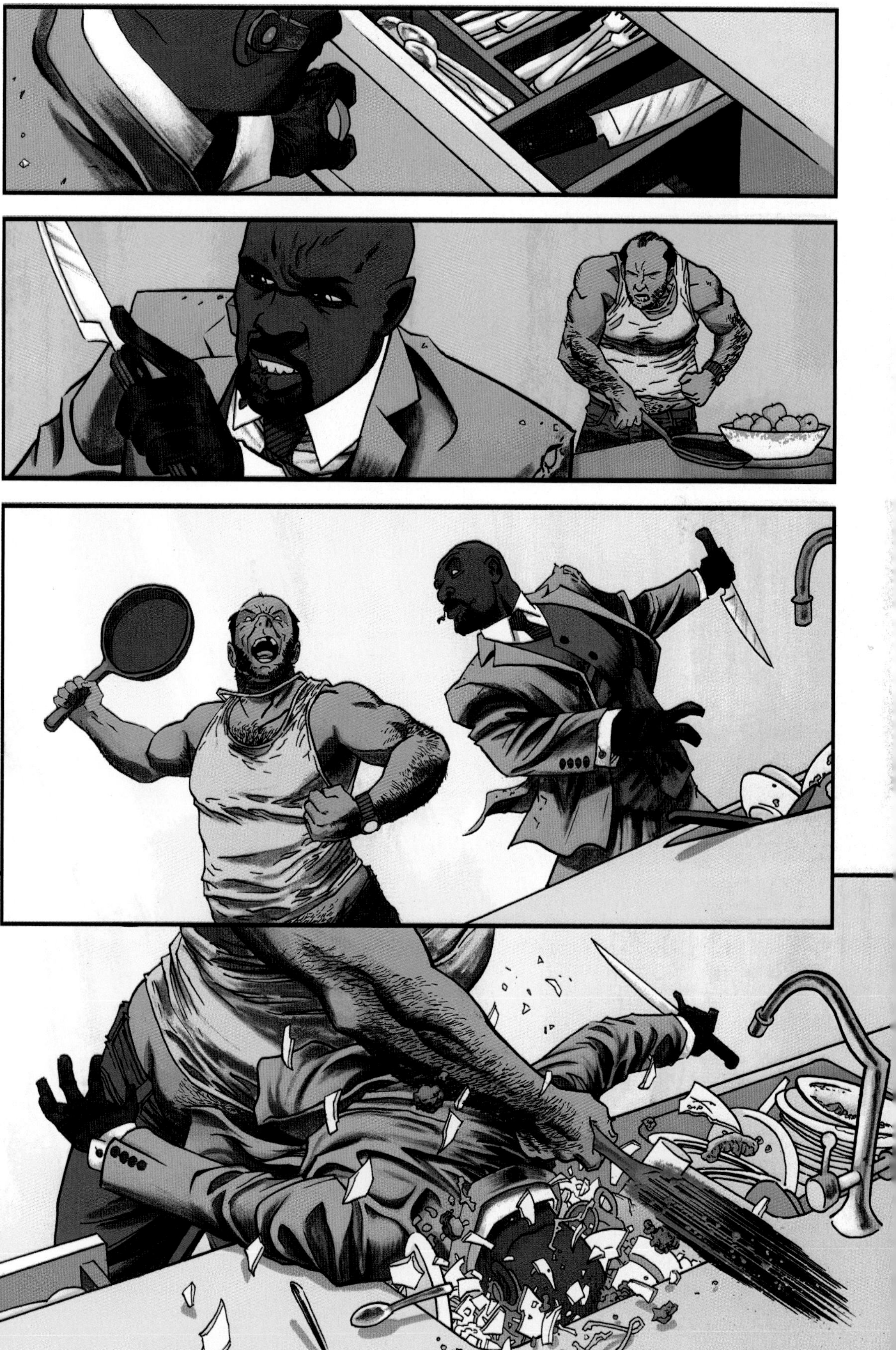

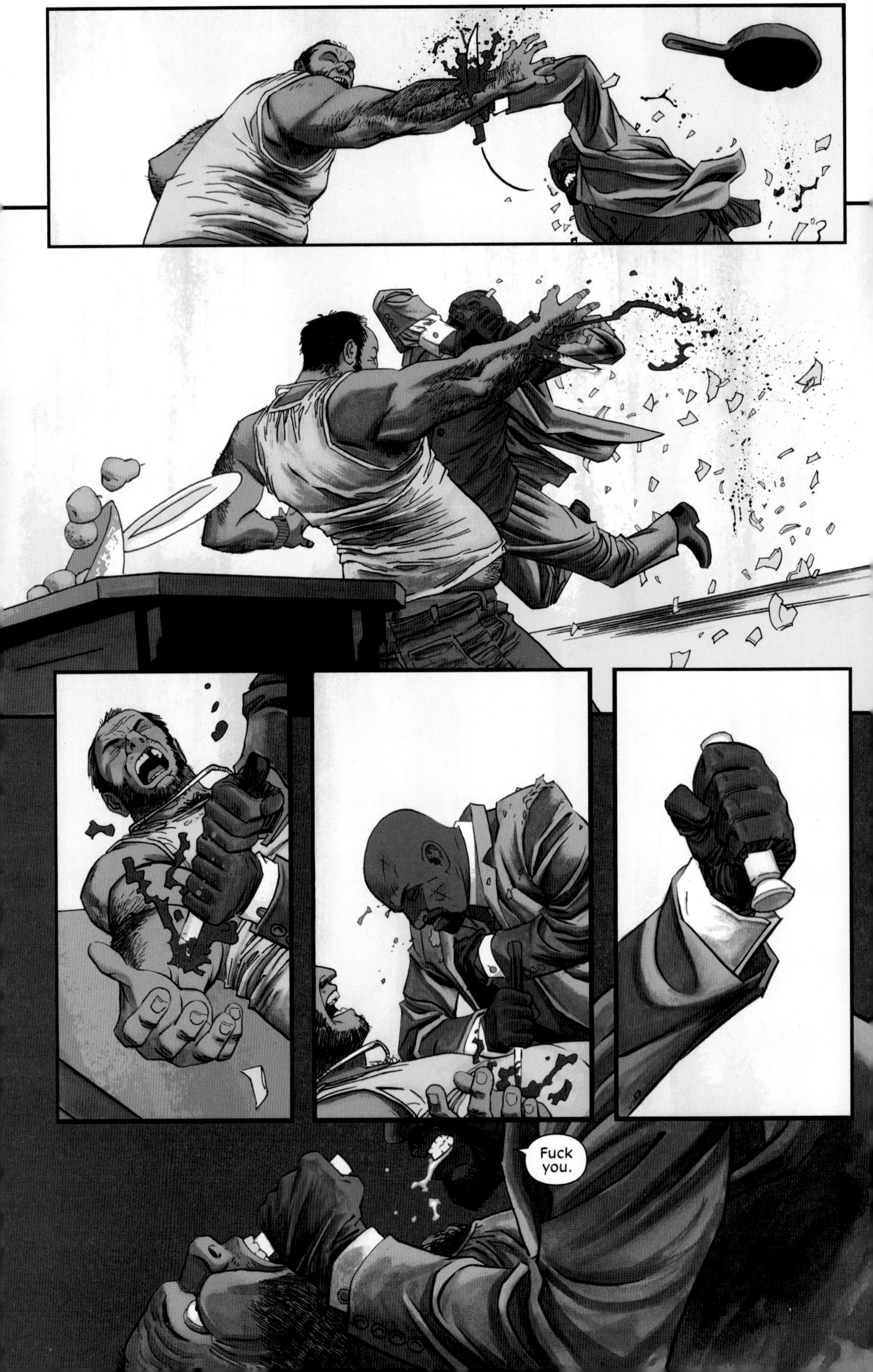
Fuck you.

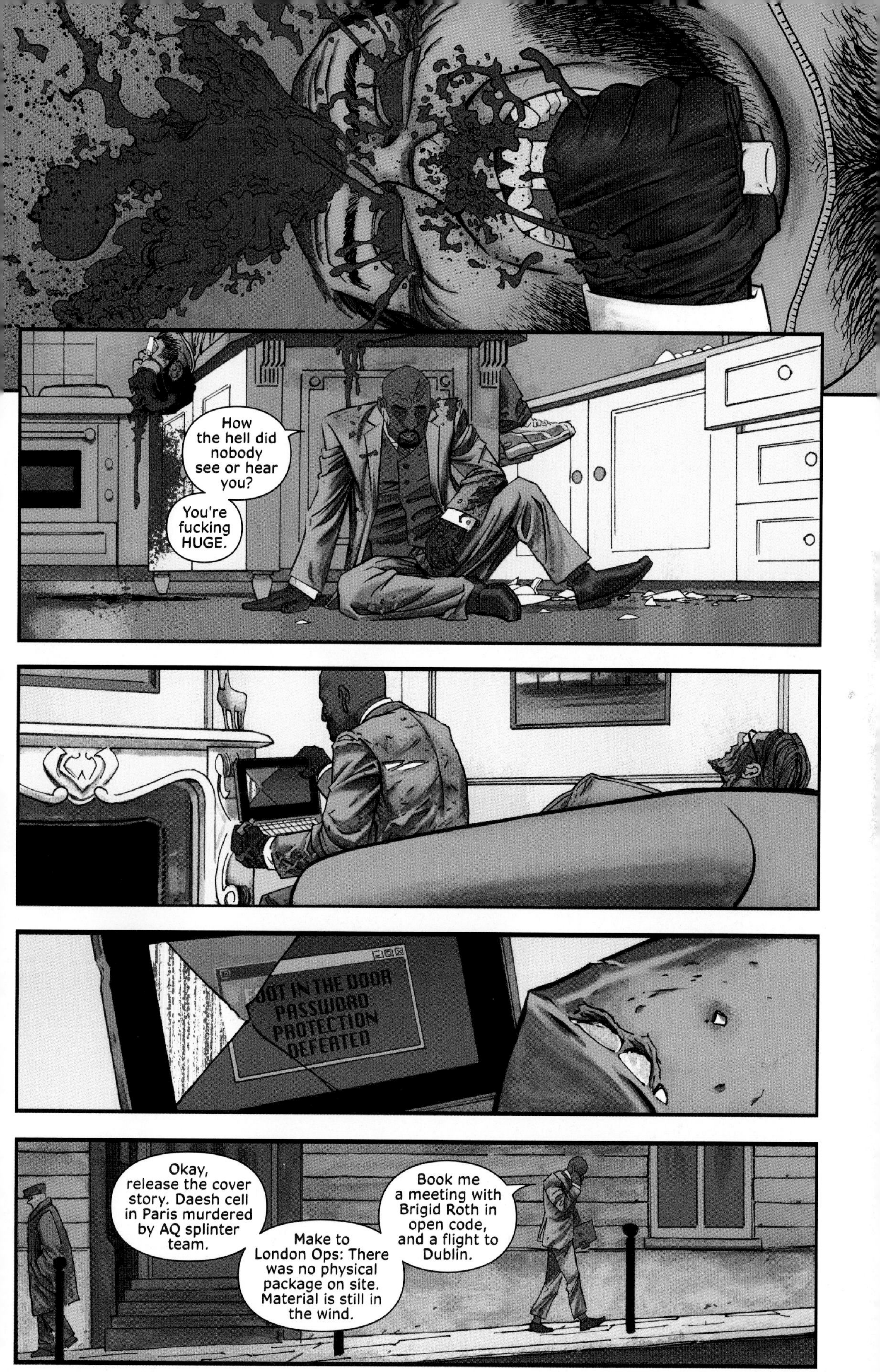
How the hell did nobody see or hear you?
You're fucking HUGE.
FOOT IN THE DOOR PASSWORD PROTECTION DEFEATED
Okay, release the cover story. Daesh cell in Paris murdered by AQ splinter team.
Make to London Ops: There was no physical package on site. Material is still in the wind.
Book me a meeting with Brigid Roth in open code, and a flight to Dublin.

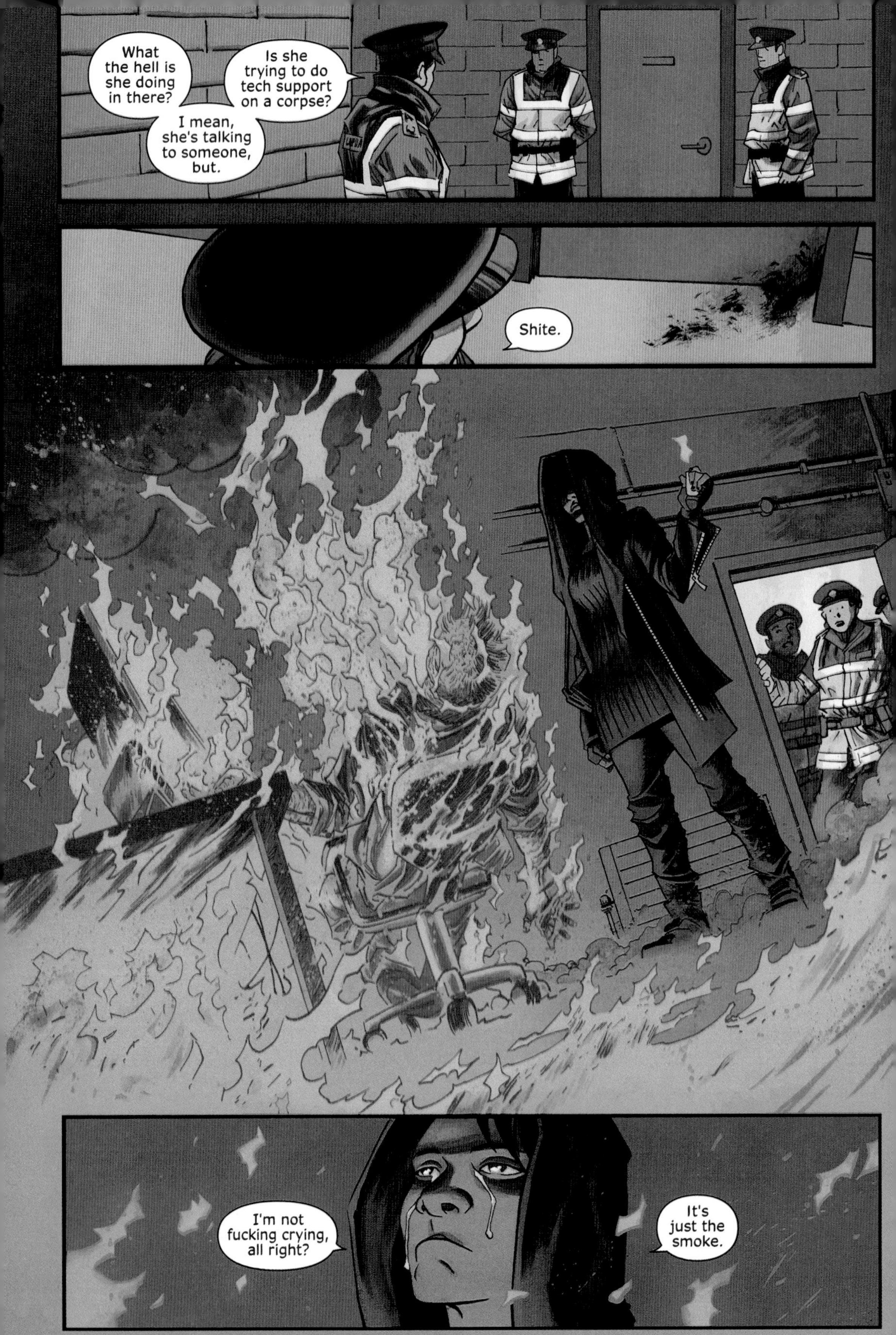
What the hell is she doing in there?
Is she trying to do tech support on a corpse?
I mean, she's talking to someone, but.
Shite.
I'm not fucking crying, all right?
It's just the smoke.

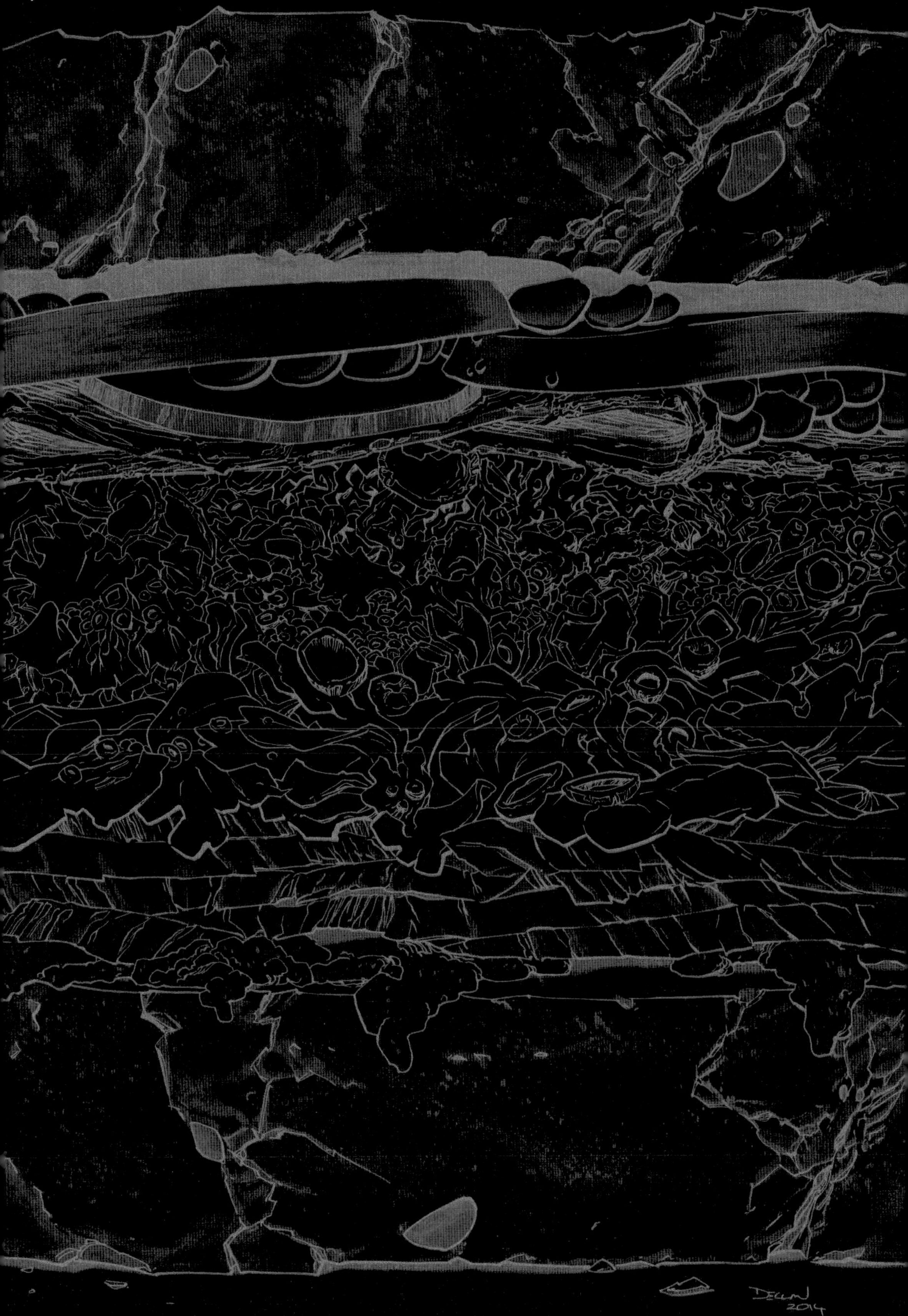
DECLAN
2014

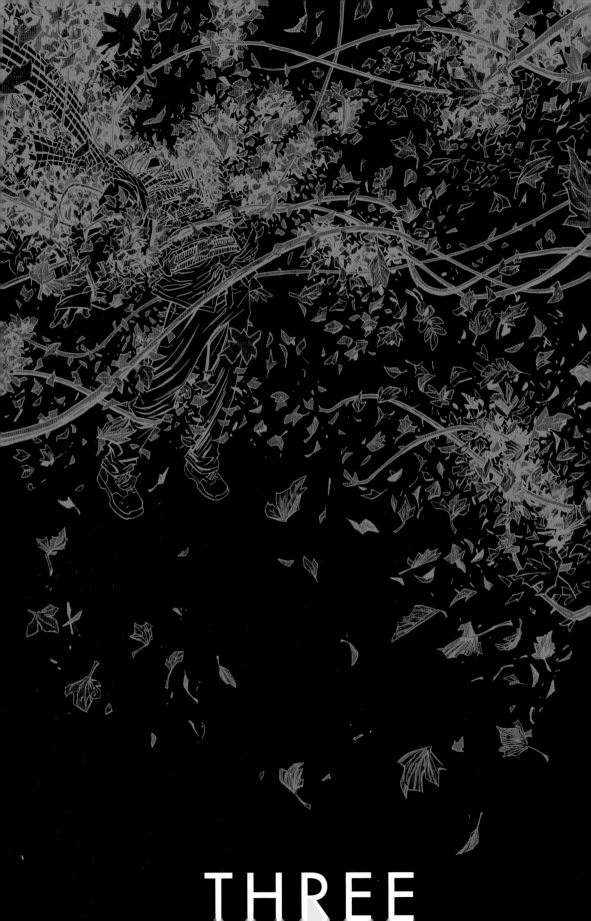

THREE

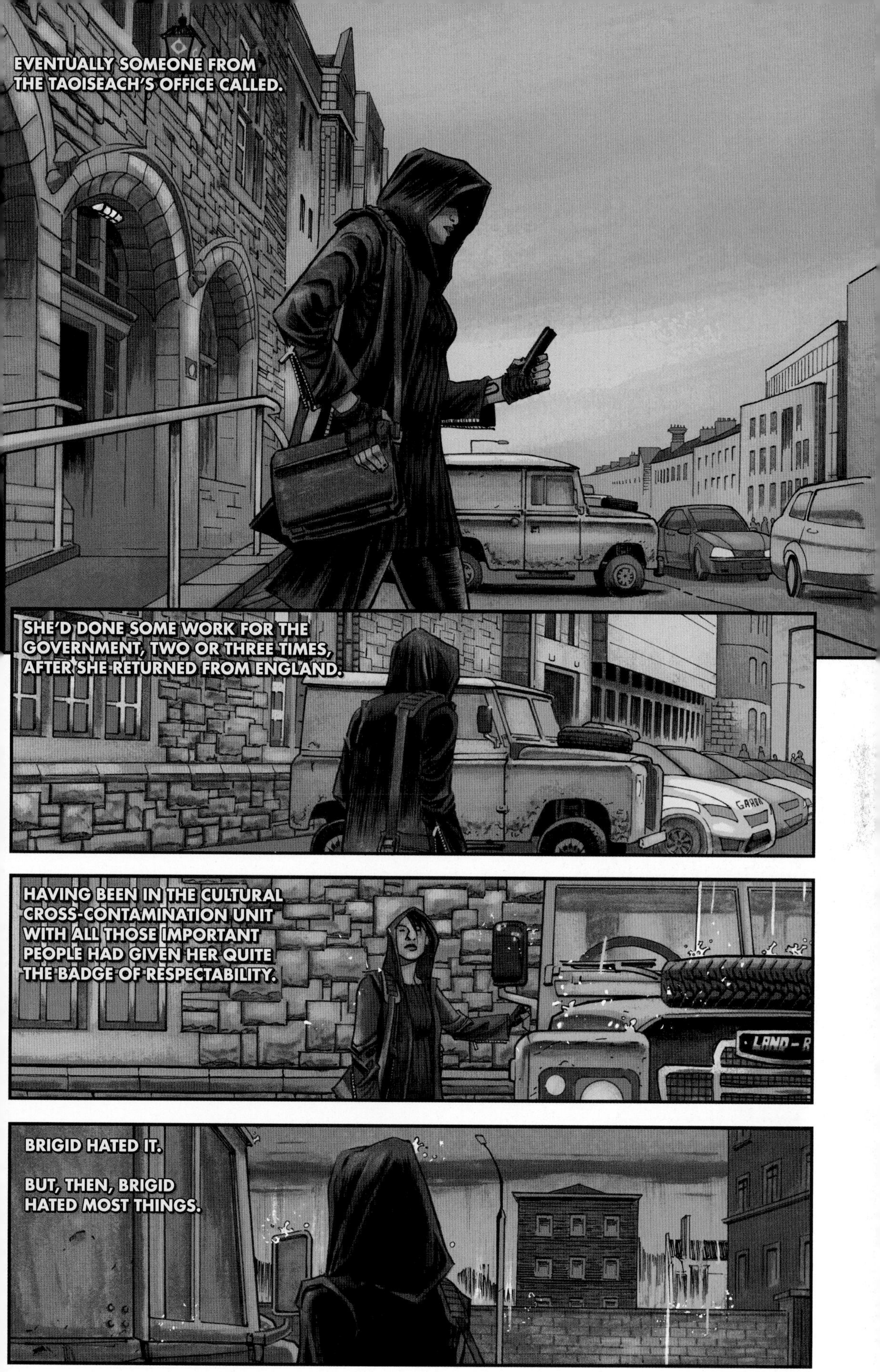
EVENTUALLY SOMEONE FROM THE TAOISEACH'S OFFICE CALLED.
SHE'D DONE SOME WORK FOR THE GOVERNMENT, TWO OR THREE TIMES, AFTER SHE RETURNED FROM ENGLAND.
HAVING BEEN IN THE CULTURAL CROSS-CONTAMINATION UNIT WITH ALL THOSE IMPORTANT PEOPLE HAD GIVEN HER QUITE THE BADGE OF RESPECTABILITY.
LAND-R
BRIGID HATED IT.
BUT, THEN, BRIGID HATED MOST THINGS.

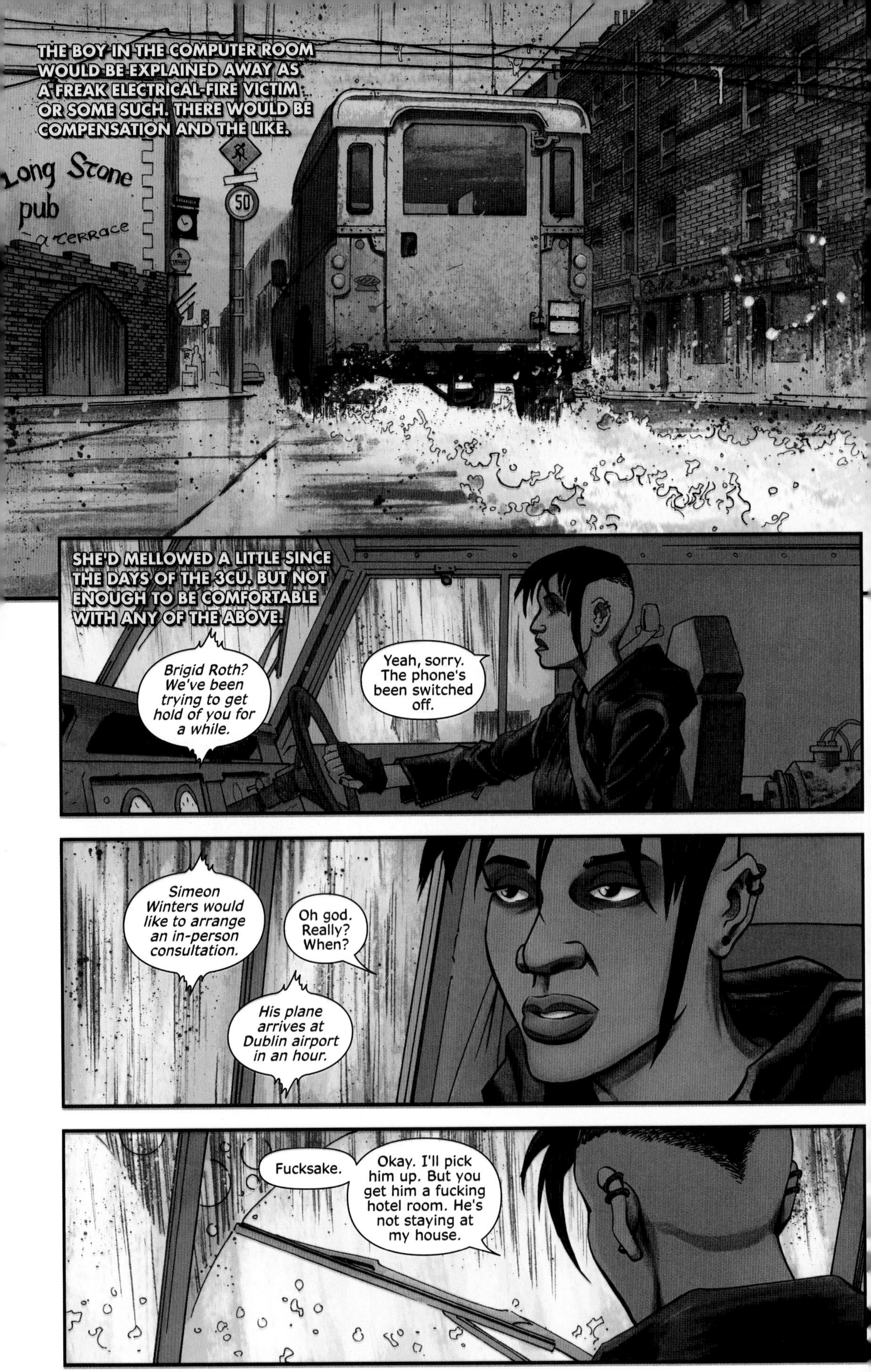
THE BOY IN THE COMPUTER ROOM WOULD BE EXPLAINED AWAY AS A FREAK ELECTRICAL-FIRE VICTIM OR SOME SUCH. THERE WOULD BE COMPENSATION AND THE LIKE.
Long Stone pub
a terrace
50
SHE'D MELLOWED A LITTLE SINCE THE DAYS OF THE 3CU. BUT NOT ENOUGH TO BE COMFORTABLE WITH ANY OF THE ABOVE.
Brigid Roth? We've been trying to get hold of you for a while.
Yeah, sorry. The phone's been switched off.
Simeon Winters would like to arrange an in-person consultation.
Oh god. Really? When?
His plane arrives at Dublin airport in an hour.
Fucksake.
Okay. I'll pick him up. But you get him a fucking hotel room. He's not staying at my house.

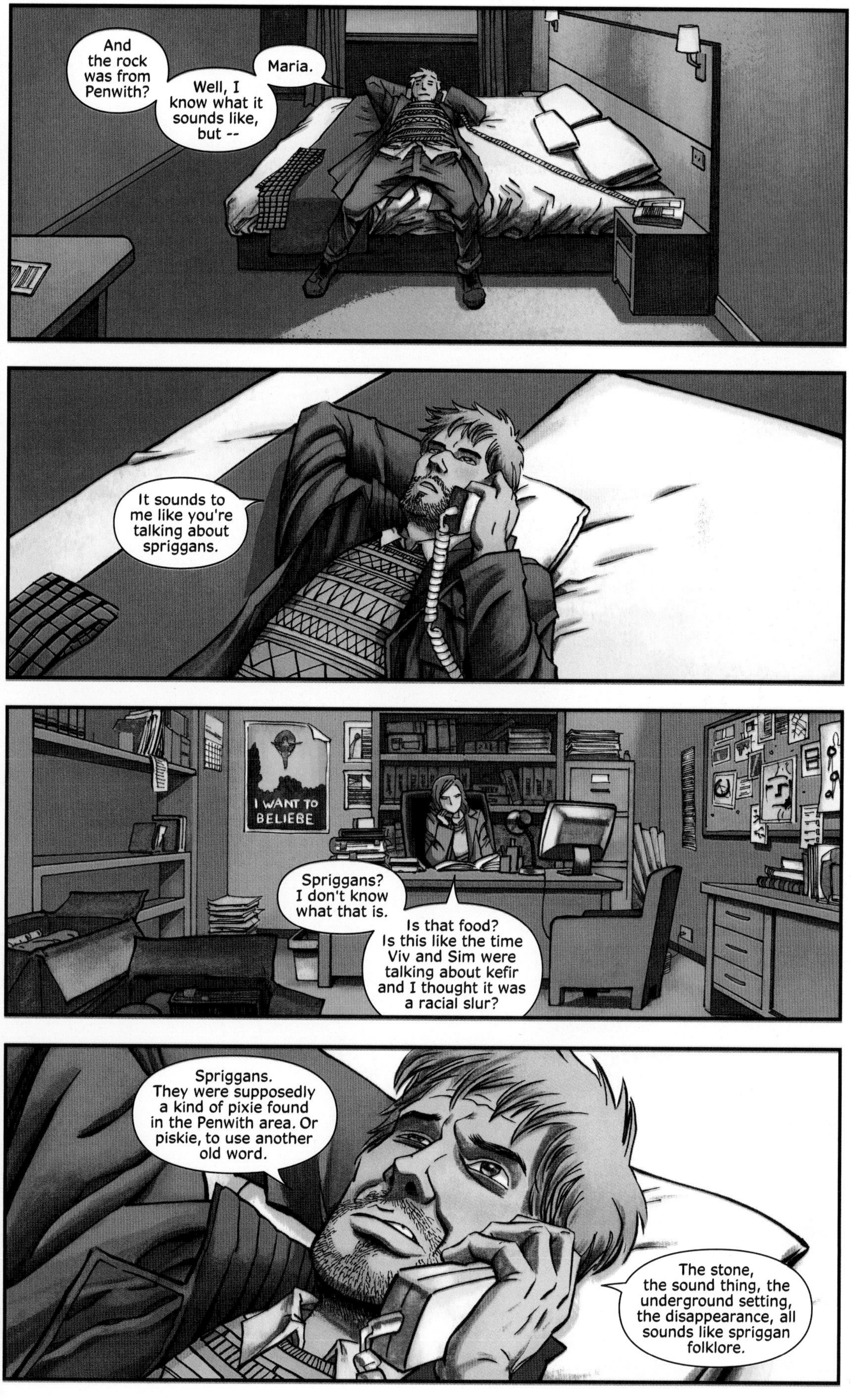
And the rock was from Penwith?
Maria.
Well, I know what it sounds like, but --
It sounds to me like you're talking about spriggans.
I WANT TO BELIEBE
Spriggans? I don't know what that is.
Is that food? Is this like the time Viv and Sim were talking about kefir and I thought it was a racial slur?
Spriggans. They were supposedly a kind of pixie found in the Penwith area. Or piskie, to use another old word.
The stone, the sound thing, the underground setting, the disappearance, all sounds like spriggan folklore.

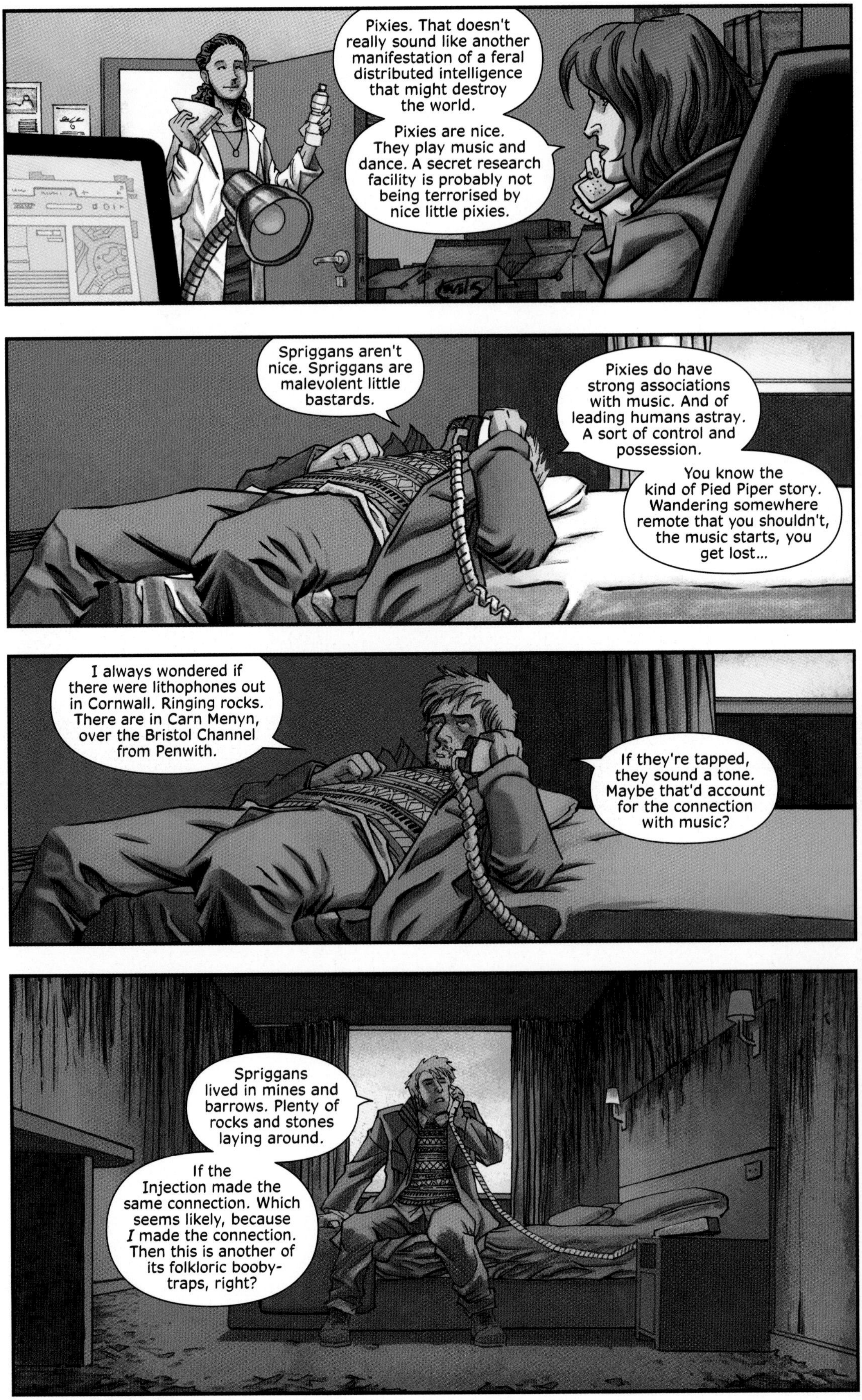
Pixies. That doesn't really sound like another manifestation of a feral distributed intelligence that might destroy the world.
Pixies are nice. They play music and dance. A secret research facility is probably not being terrorised by nice little pixies.
Spriggans aren't nice. Spriggans are malevolent little bastards.
Pixies do have strong associations with music. And of leading humans astray. A sort of control and possession.
You know the kind of Pied Piper story. Wandering somewhere remote that you shouldn't, the music starts, you get lost...
I always wondered if there were lithophones out in Cornwall. Ringing rocks. There are in Carn Menyn, over the Bristol Channel from Penwith.
If they're tapped, they sound a tone. Maybe that'd account for the connection with music?
Spriggans lived in mines and barrows. Plenty of rocks and stones laying around.
If the Injection made the same connection. Which seems likely, because *I* made the connection. Then this is another of its folkloric booby-traps, right?

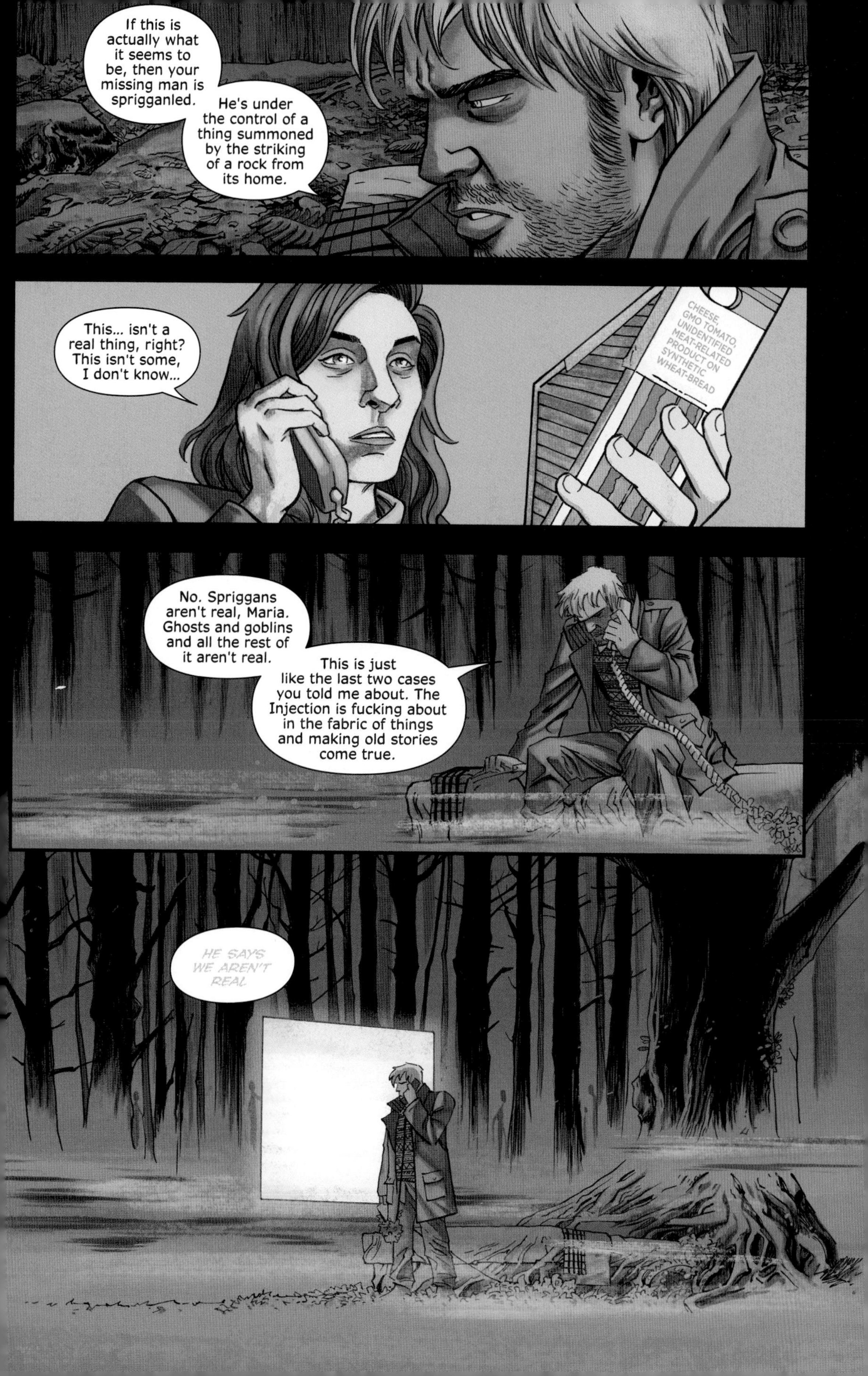
If this is actually what it seems to be, then your missing man is sprigganled.
He's under the control of a thing summoned by the striking of a rock from its home.
This... isn't a real thing, right? This isn't some, I don't know...
CHEESE, GMO TOMATO, UNIDENTIFIED MEAT-RELATED PRODUCT ON SYNTHETIC WHEAT-BREAD
No. Spriggans aren't real, Maria. Ghosts and goblins and all the rest of it aren't real.
This is just like the last two cases you told me about. The Injection is fucking about in the fabric of things and making old stories come true.
HE SAYS WE AREN'T REAL

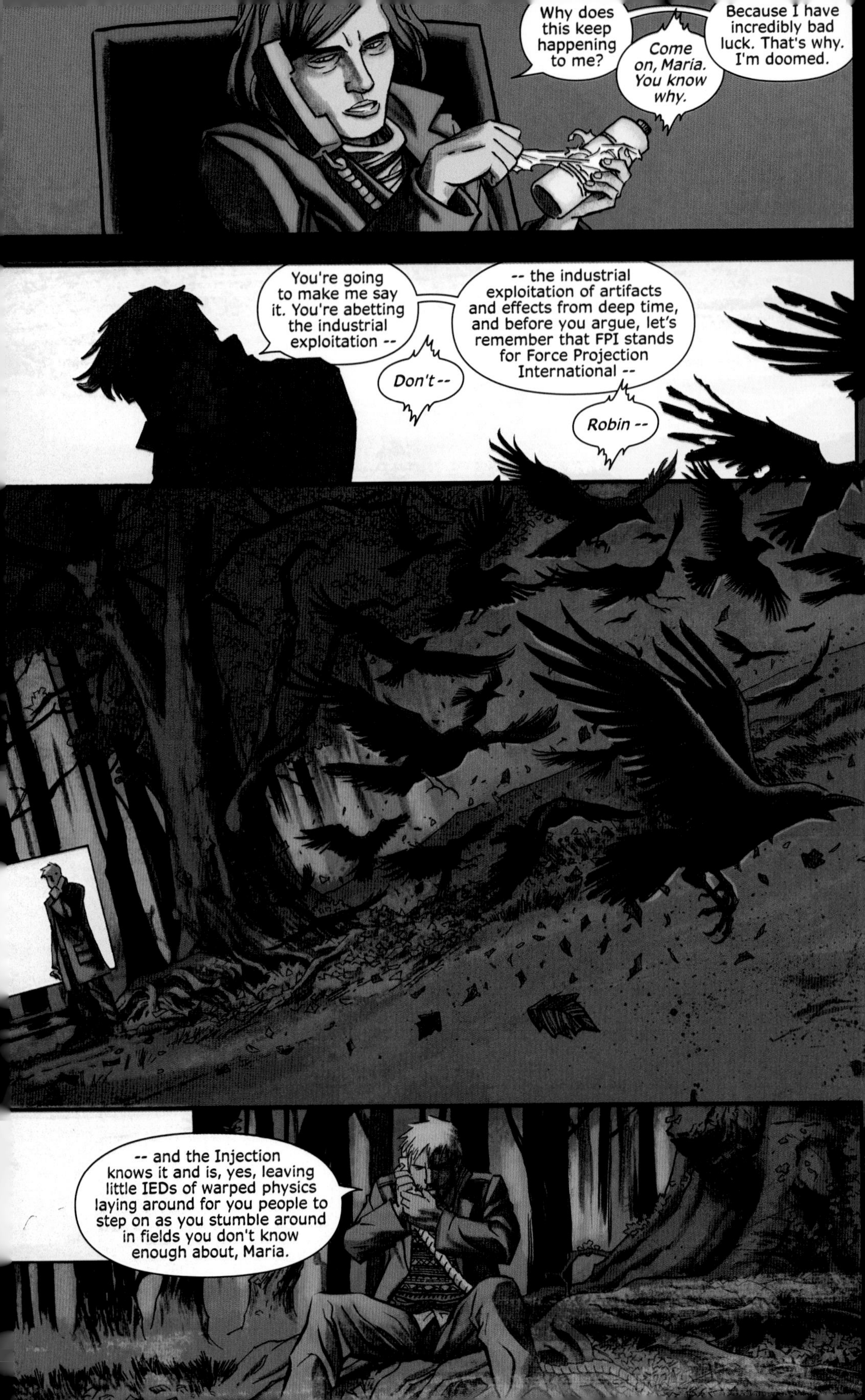
Why does this keep happening to me?
Come on, Maria. You know why.
Because I have incredibly bad luck. That's why. I'm doomed.
You're going to make me say it. You're abetting the industrial exploitation --
Don't --
-- the industrial exploitation of artifacts and effects from deep time, and before you argue, let's remember that FPI stands for Force Projection International --
Robin --
-- and the Injection knows it and is, yes, leaving little IEDs of warped physics laying around for you people to step on as you stumble around in fields you don't know enough about, Maria.

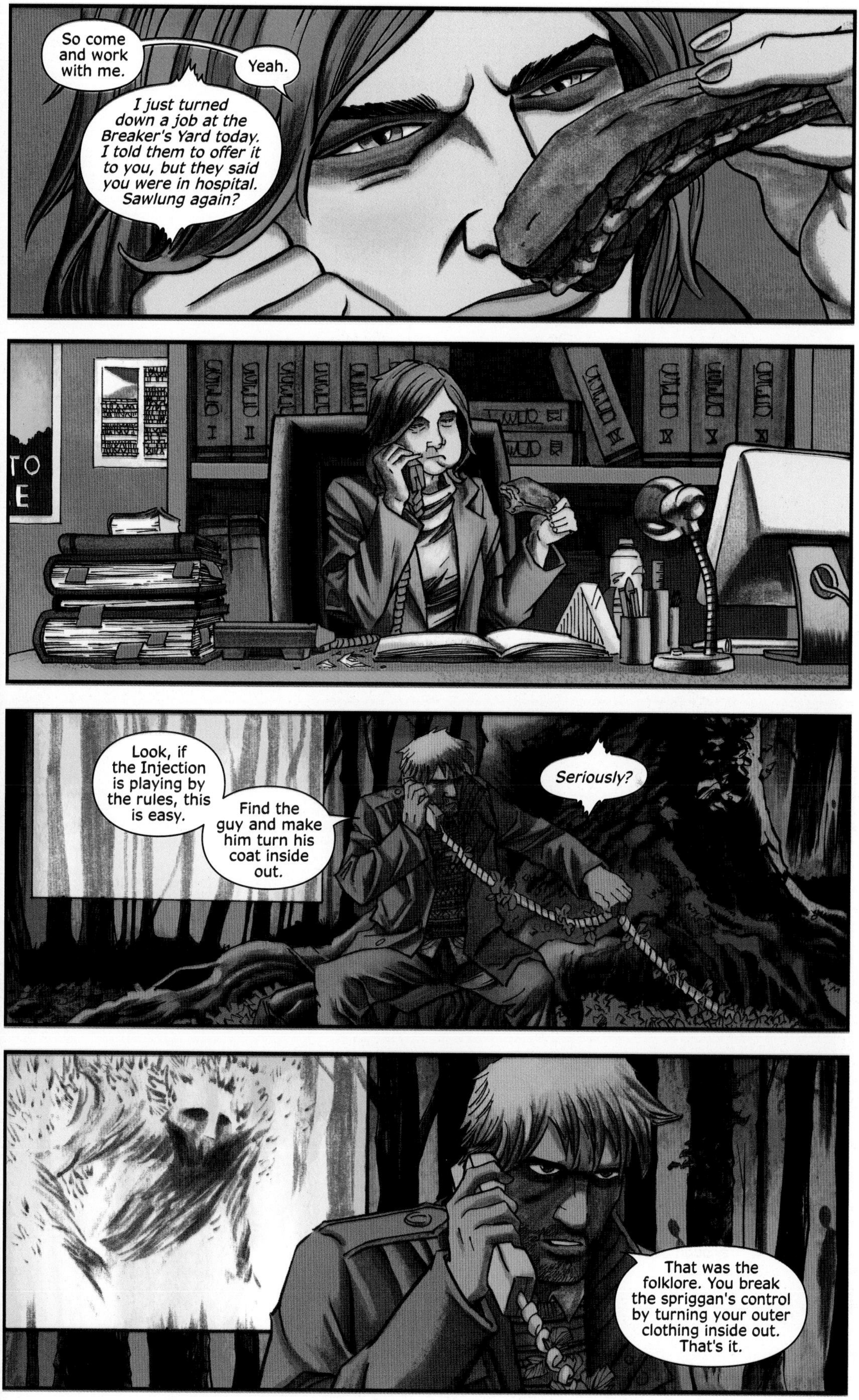
So come and work with me.
Yeah.
I just turned down a job at the Breaker's Yard today. I told them to offer it to you, but they said you were in hospital. Sawlung again?
TO
E
Look, if the Injection is playing by the rules, this is easy.
Find the guy and make him turn his coat inside out.
Seriously?
That was the folklore. You break the spriggan's control by turning your outer clothing inside out. That's it.

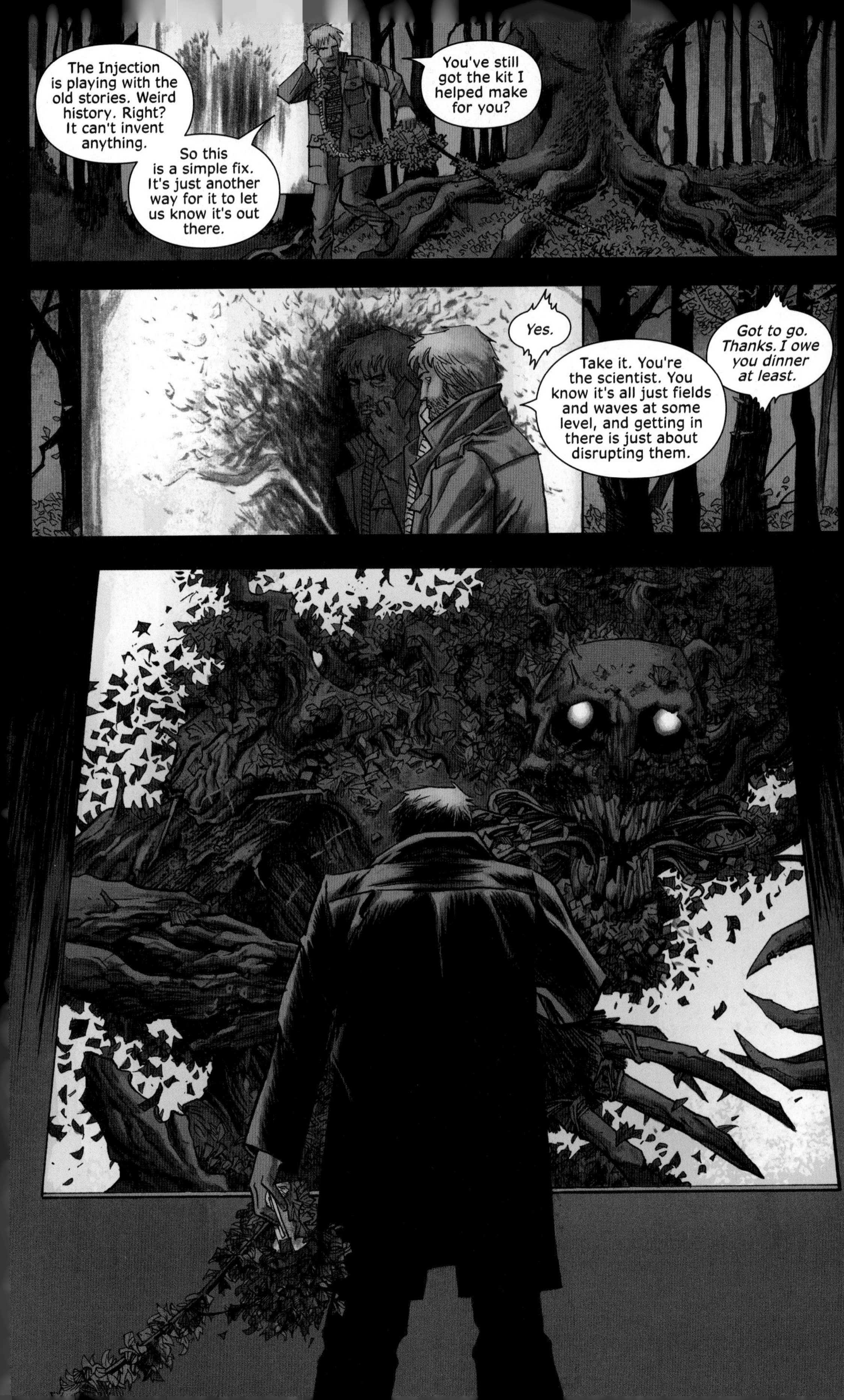
The Injection is playing with the old stories. Weird history. Right? It can't invent anything.
So this is a simple fix. It's just another way for it to let us know it's out there.
You've still got the kit I helped make for you?
Yes.
Take it. You're the scientist. You know it's all just fields and waves at some level, and getting in there is just about disrupting them.
Got to go. Thanks. I owe you dinner at least.

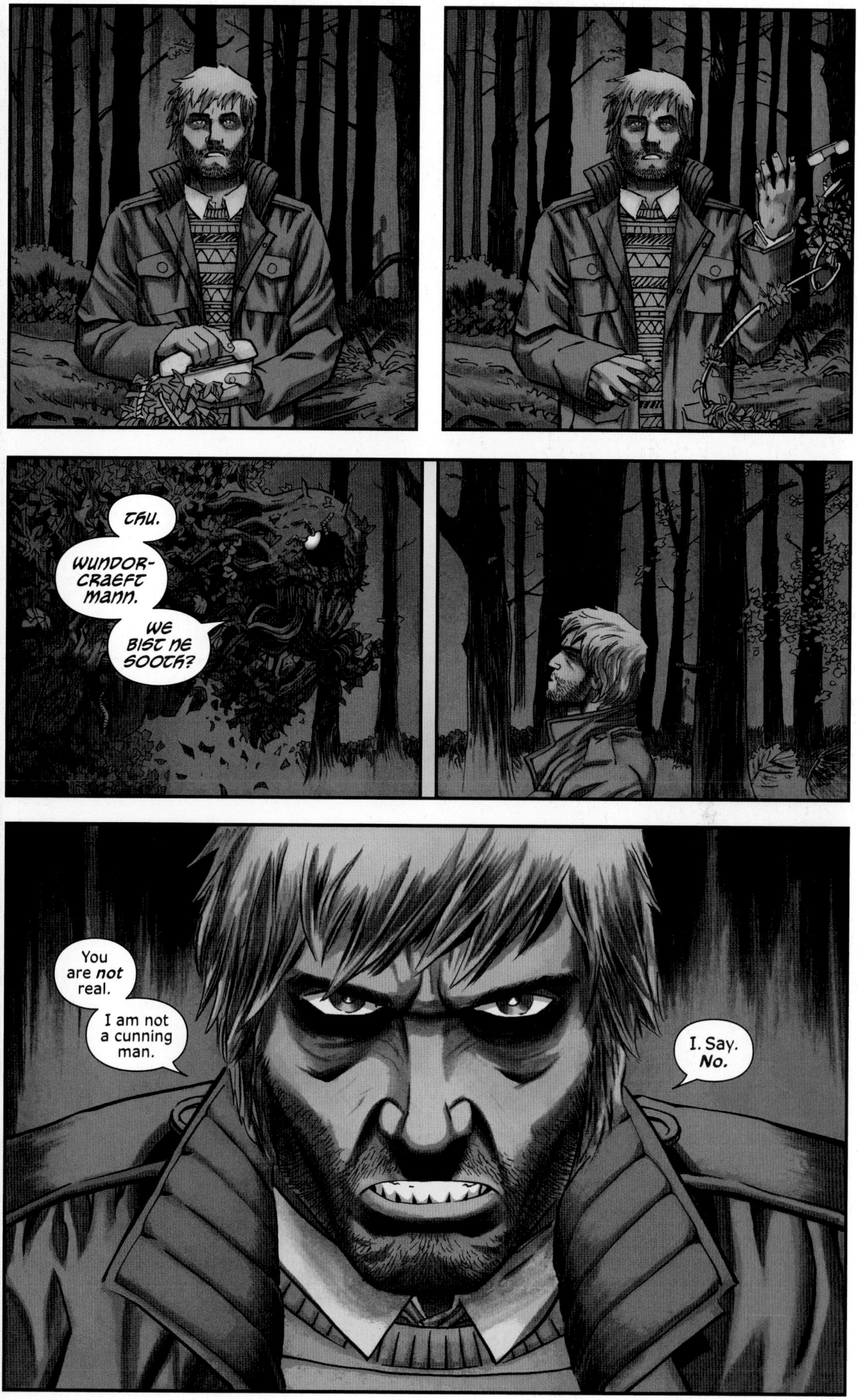
THU.
WUNDOR-CRAEFT MANN.
WE BIST NE SOOTH?
You are *not* real.
I am not a cunning man.
I. Say. **No.**

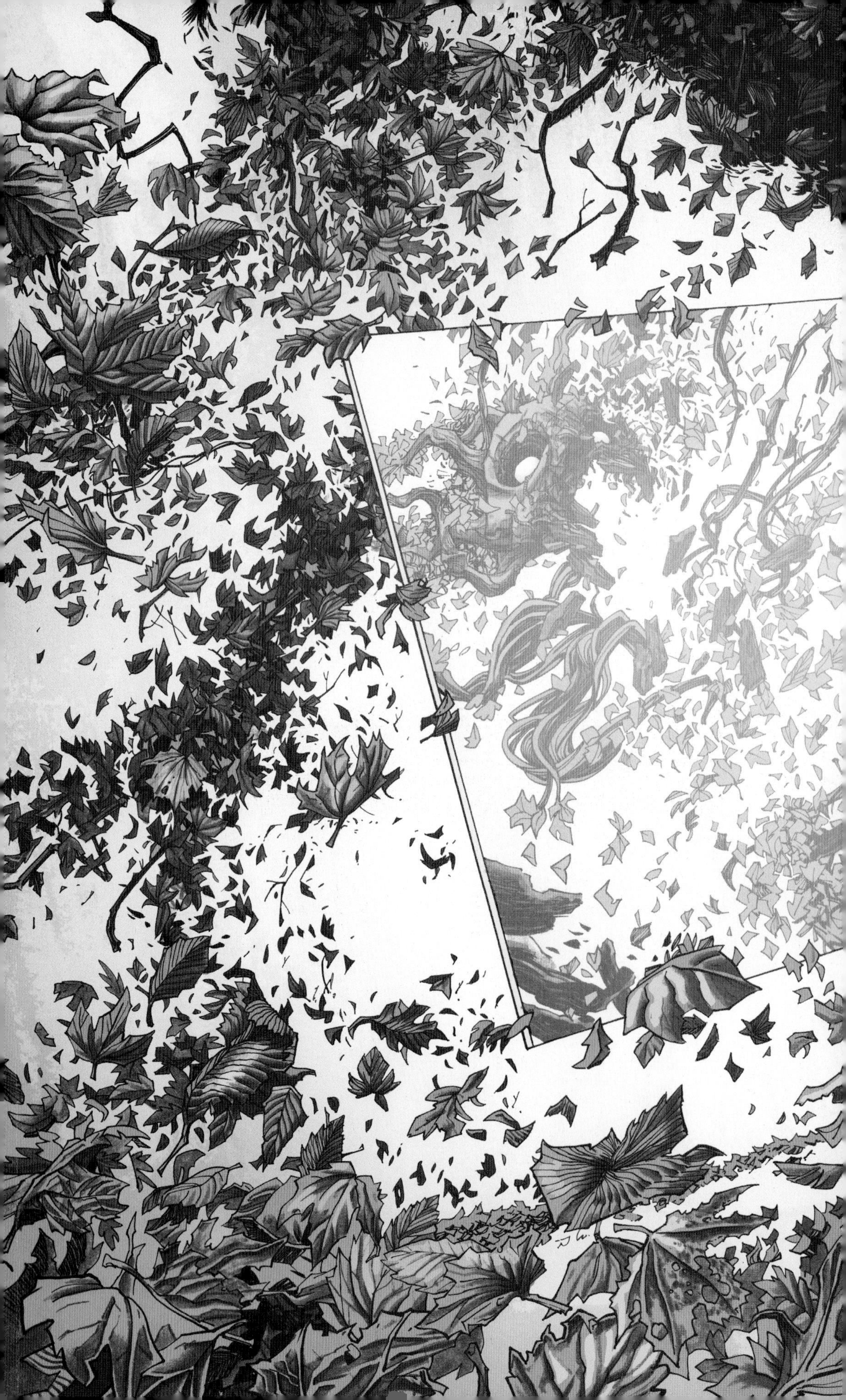

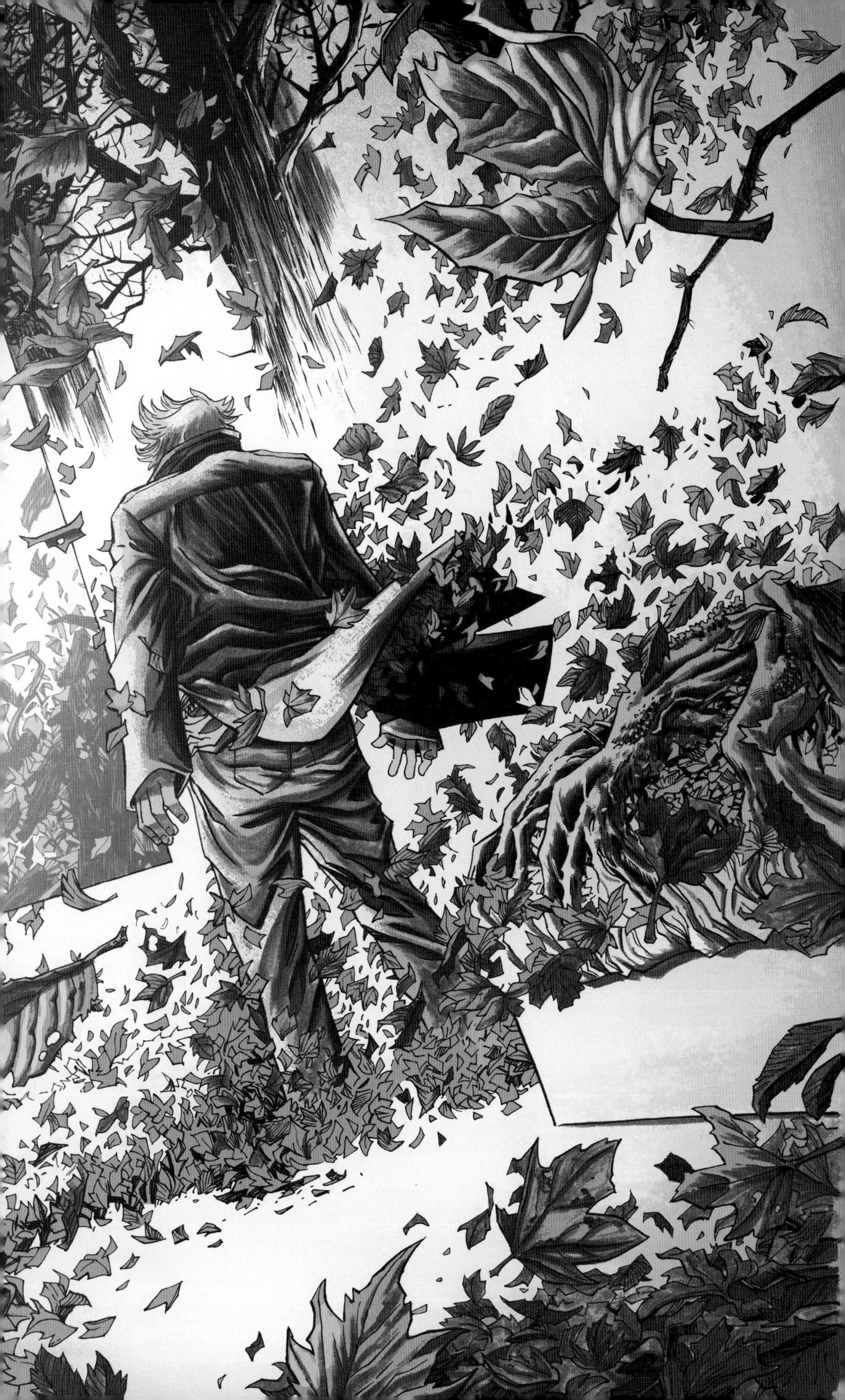

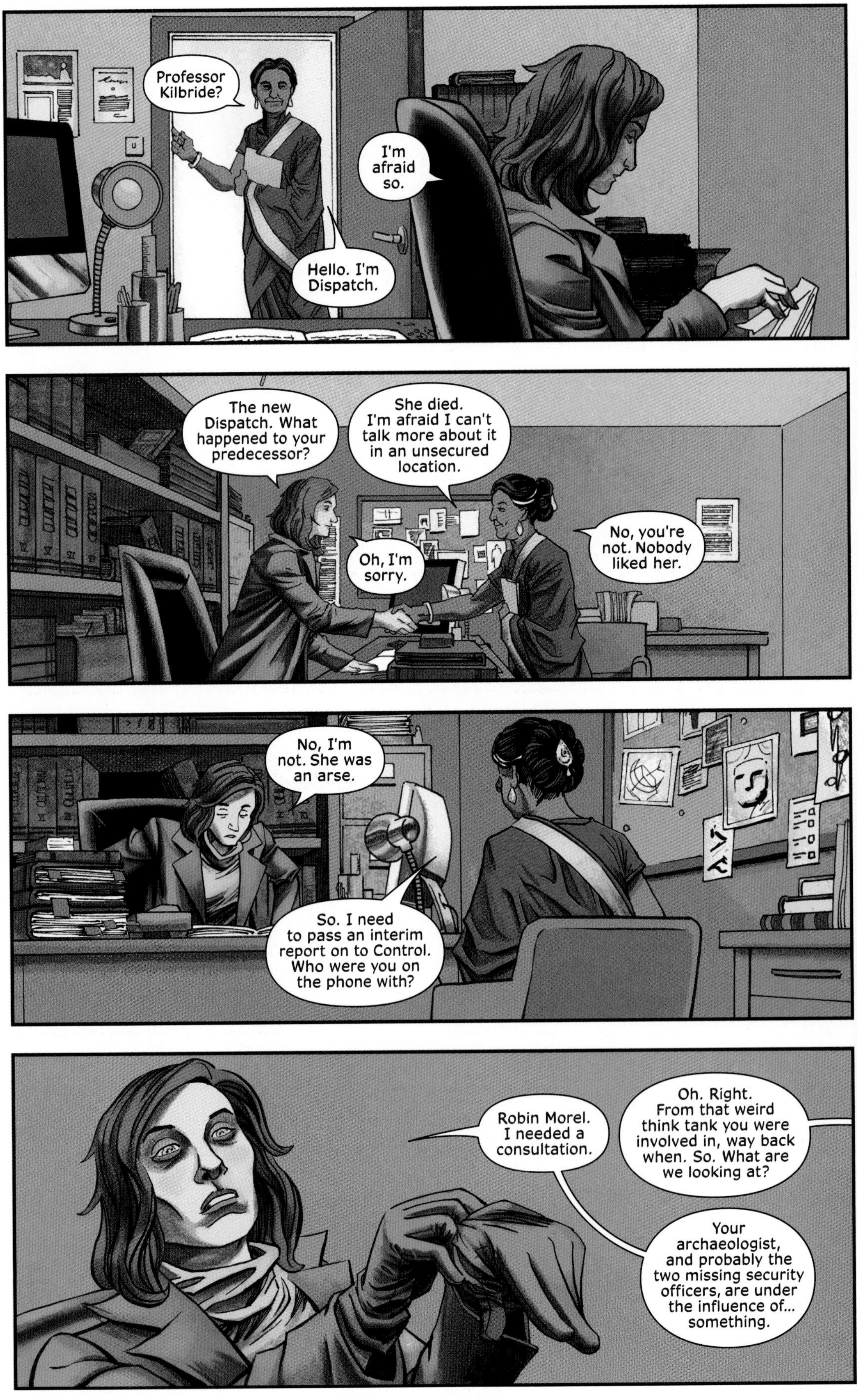
Professor Kilbride?
I'm afraid so.
Hello. I'm Dispatch.
The new Dispatch. What happened to your predecessor?
She died. I'm afraid I can't talk more about it in an unsecured location.
Oh, I'm sorry.
No, you're not. Nobody liked her.
No, I'm not. She was an arse.
So. I need to pass an interim report on to Control. Who were you on the phone with?
Robin Morel. I needed a consultation.
Oh. Right. From that weird think tank you were involved in, way back when. So. What are we looking at?
Your archaeologist, and probably the two missing security officers, are under the influence of... something.

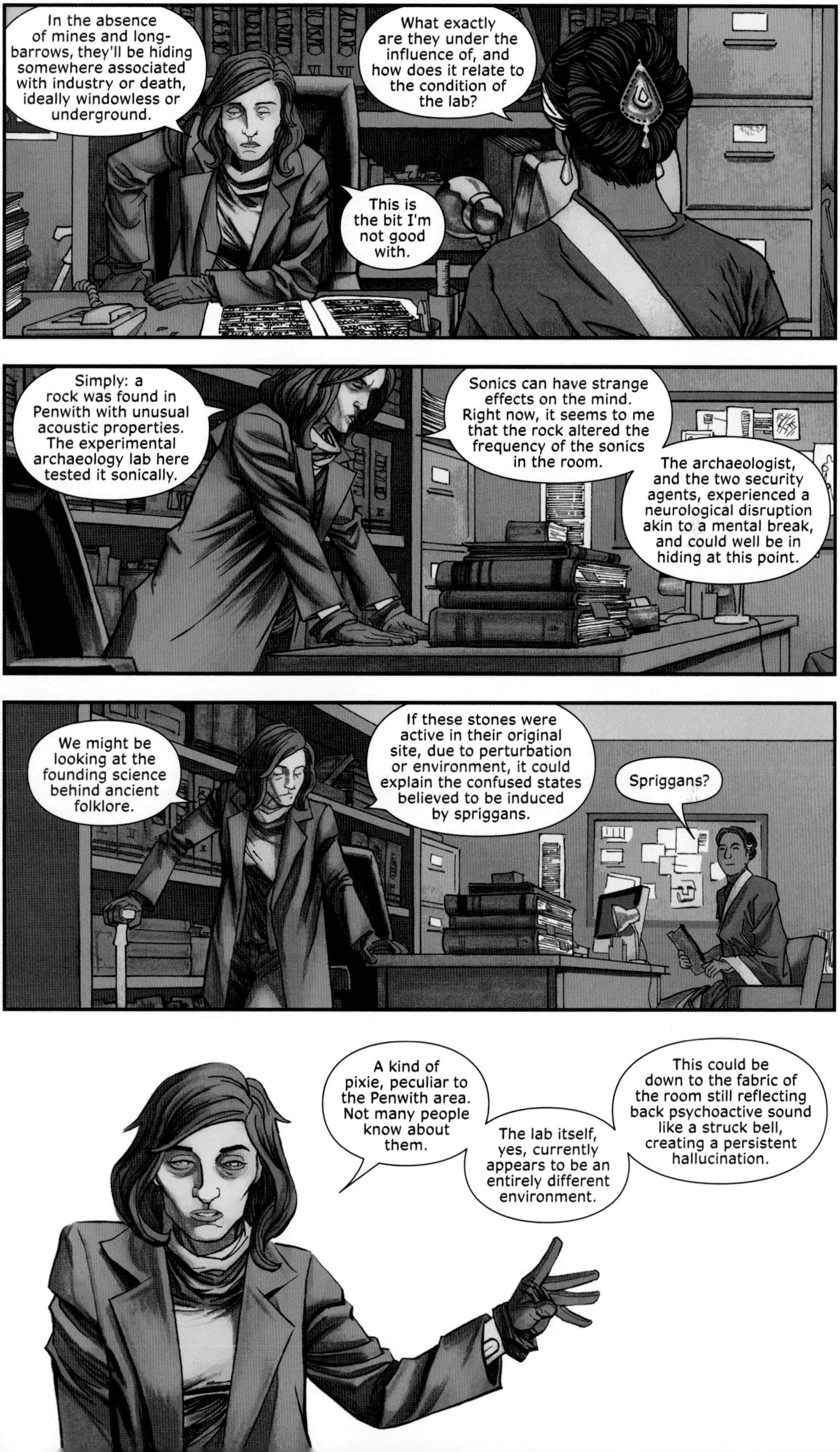
In the absence of mines and long-barrows, they'll be hiding somewhere associated with industry or death, ideally windowless or underground.
What exactly are they under the influence of, and how does it relate to the condition of the lab?
This is the bit I'm not good with.
Simply: a rock was found in Penwith with unusual acoustic properties. The experimental archaeology lab here tested it sonically.
Sonics can have strange effects on the mind. Right now, it seems to me that the rock altered the frequency of the sonics in the room.
The archaeologist, and the two security agents, experienced a neurological disruption akin to a mental break, and could well be in hiding at this point.
We might be looking at the founding science behind ancient folklore.
If these stones were active in their original site, due to perturbation or environment, it could explain the confused states believed to be induced by spriggans.
Spriggans?
A kind of pixie, peculiar to the Penwith area. Not many people know about them.
The lab itself, yes, currently appears to be an entirely different environment.
This could be down to the fabric of the room still reflecting back psychoactive sound like a struck bell, creating a persistent hallucination.

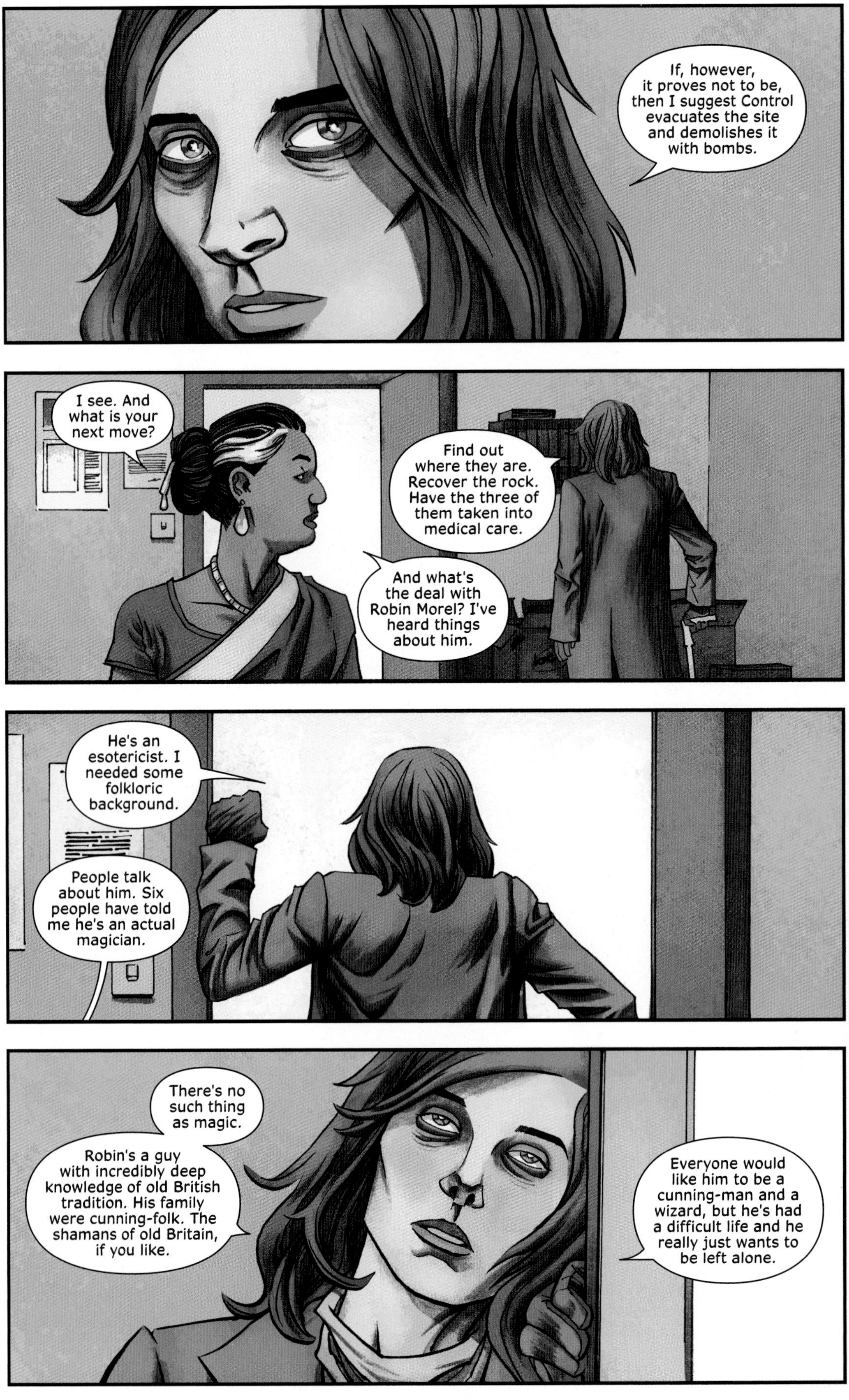
If, however, it proves not to be, then I suggest Control evacuates the site and demolishes it with bombs.
I see. And what is your next move?
Find out where they are. Recover the rock. Have the three of them taken into medical care.
And what's the deal with Robin Morel? I've heard things about him.
He's an esotericist. I needed some folkloric background.
People talk about him. Six people have told me he's an actual magician.
There's no such thing as magic.
Robin's a guy with incredibly deep knowledge of old British tradition. His family were cunning-folk. The shamans of old Britain, if you like.
Everyone would like him to be a cunning-man and a wizard, but he's had a difficult life and he really just wants to be left alone.

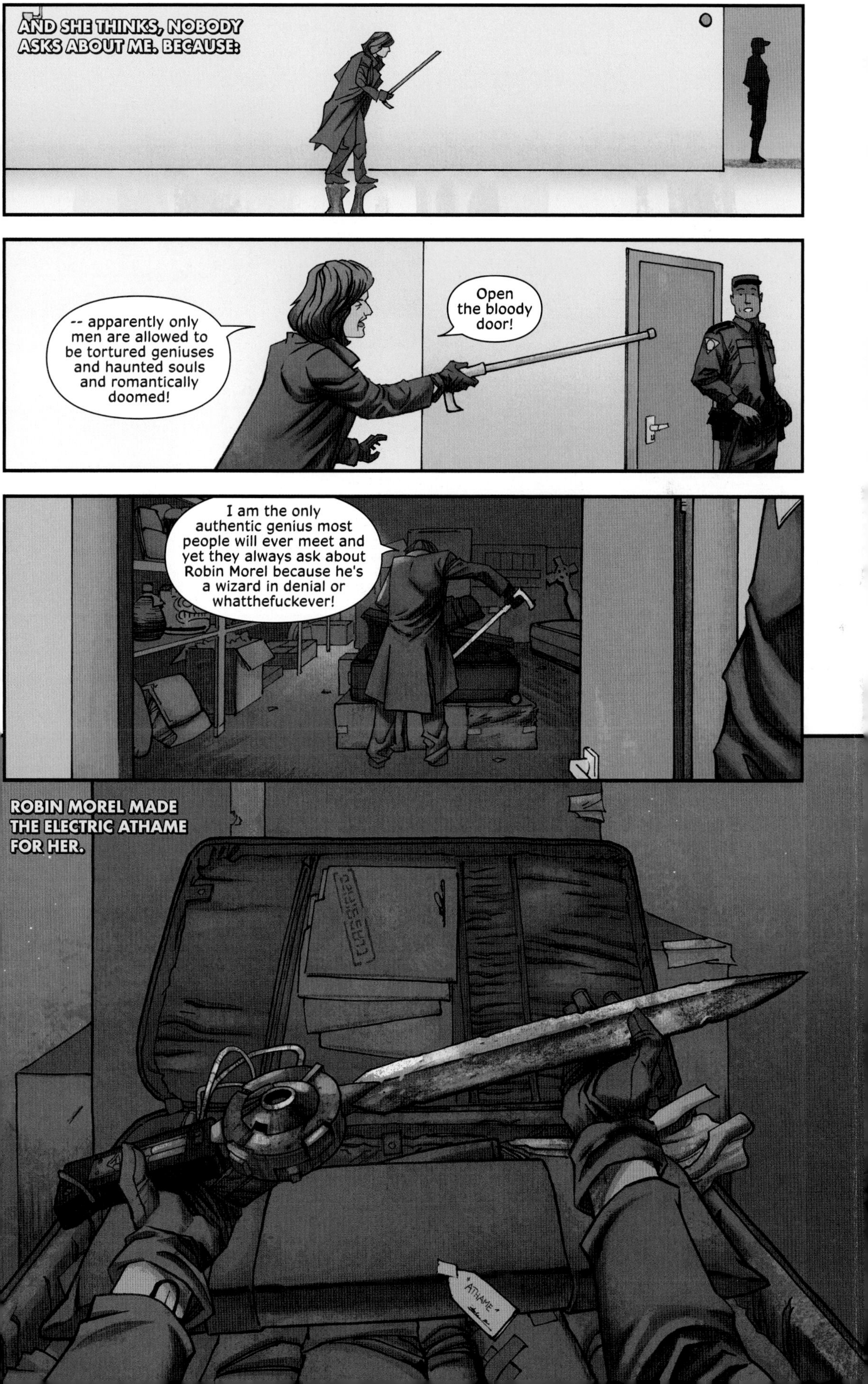
AND SHE THINKS, NOBODY ASKS ABOUT ME. BECAUSE:
-- apparently only men are allowed to be tortured geniuses and haunted souls and romantically doomed!
Open the bloody door!
I am the only authentic genius most people will ever meet and yet they always ask about Robin Morel because he's a wizard in denial or whatthefuckever!
ROBIN MOREL MADE THE ELECTRIC ATHAME FOR HER.
ATHAME

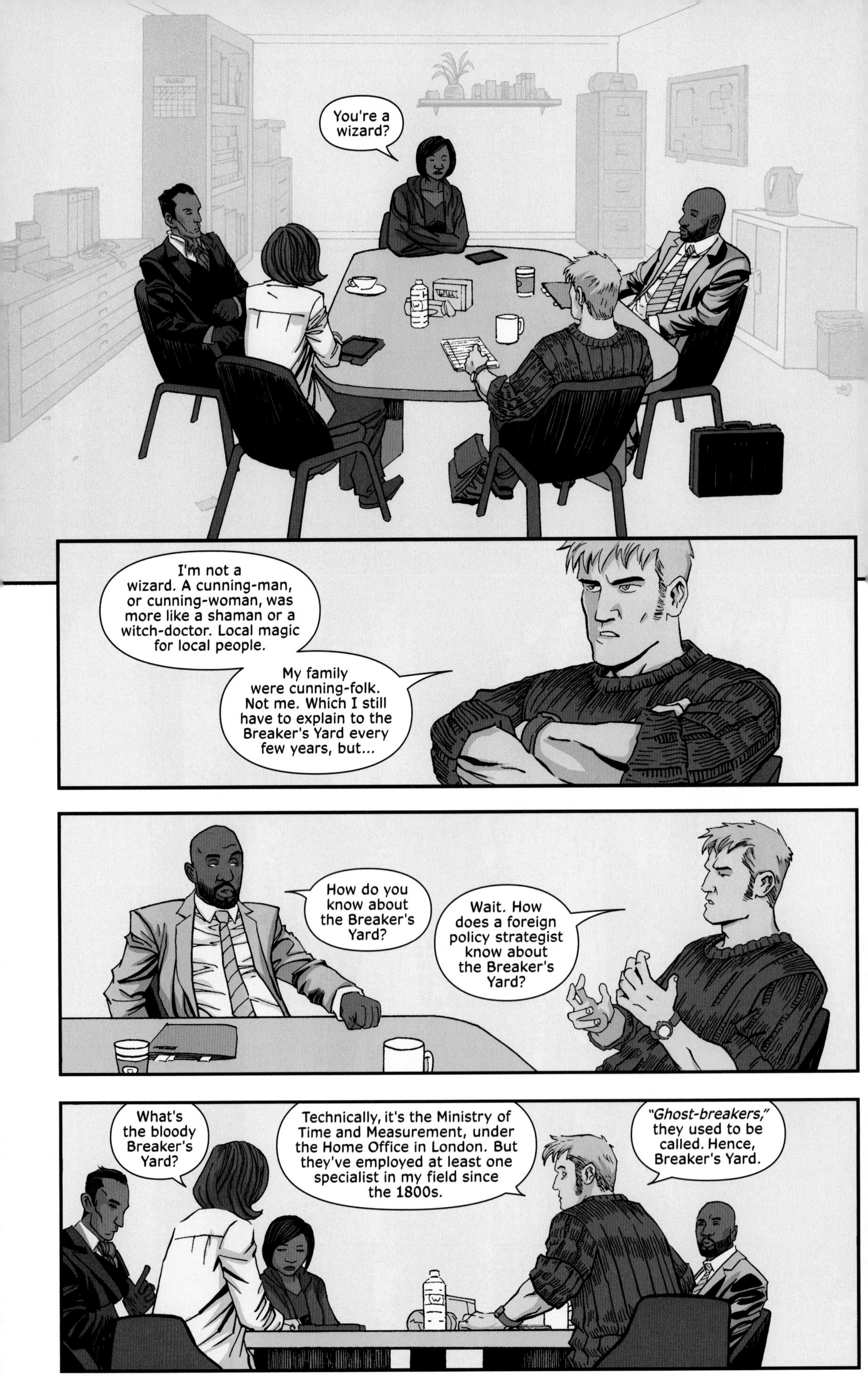
You're a wizard?
I'm not a wizard. A cunning-man, or cunning-woman, was more like a shaman or a witch-doctor. Local magic for local people.
My family were cunning-folk. Not me. Which I still have to explain to the Breaker's Yard every few years, but...
How do you know about the Breaker's Yard?
Wait. How does a foreign policy strategist know about the Breaker's Yard?
What's the bloody Breaker's Yard?
Technically, it's the Ministry of Time and Measurement, under the Home Office in London. But they've employed at least one specialist in my field since the 1800s.
"Ghost-breakers," they used to be called. Hence, Breaker's Yard.

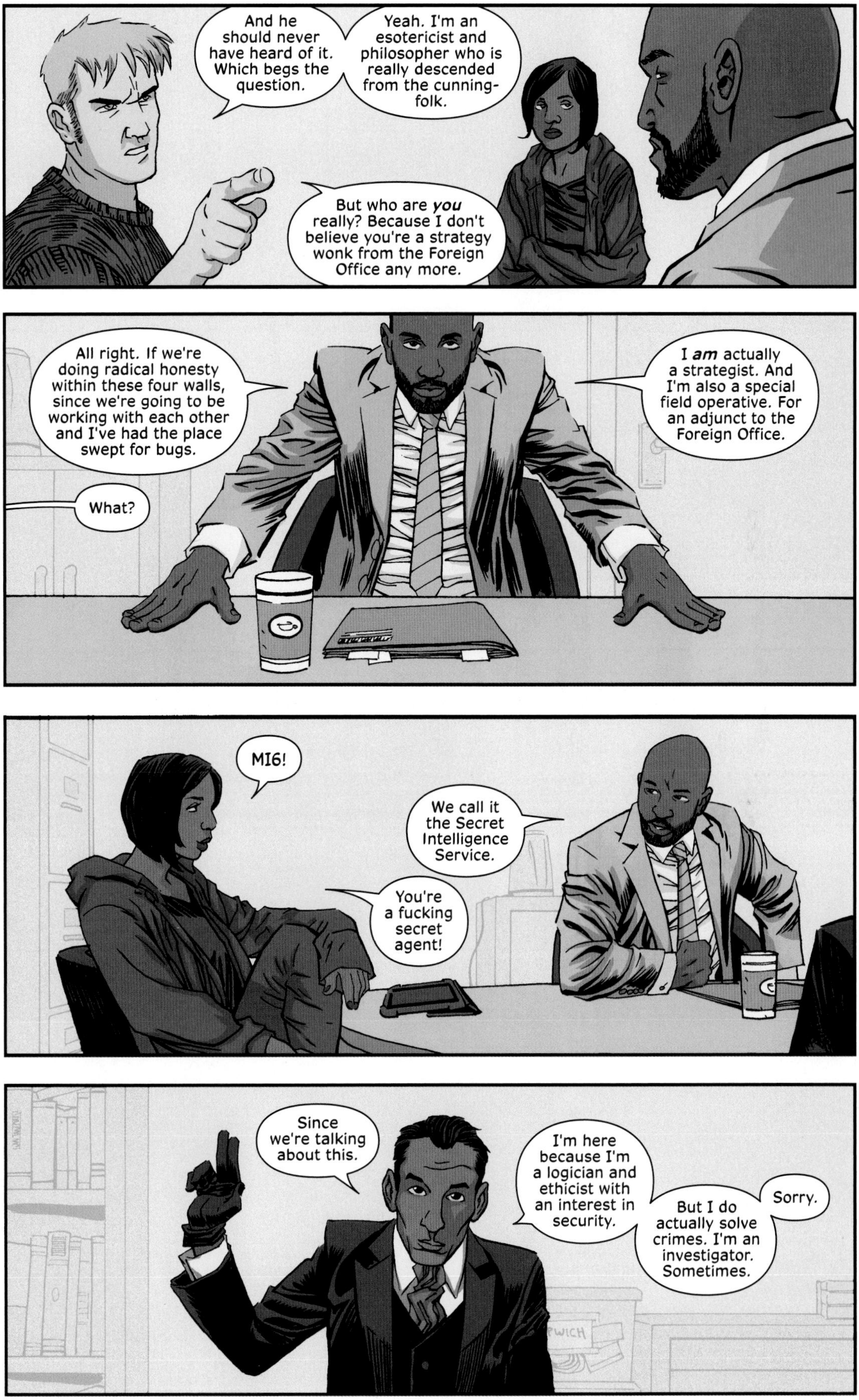
And he should never have heard of it. Which begs the question.
Yeah. I'm an esotericist and philosopher who is really descended from the cunning-folk.
But who are *you* really? Because I don't believe you're a strategy wonk from the Foreign Office any more.
All right. If we're doing radical honesty within these four walls, since we're going to be working with each other and I've had the place swept for bugs.
I *am* actually a strategist. And I'm also a special field operative. For an adjunct to the Foreign Office.
What?
MI6!
We call it the Secret Intelligence Service.
You're a fucking secret agent!
Since we're talking about this.
I'm here because I'm a logician and ethicist with an interest in security.
Sorry.
But I do actually solve crimes. I'm an investigator. Sometimes.

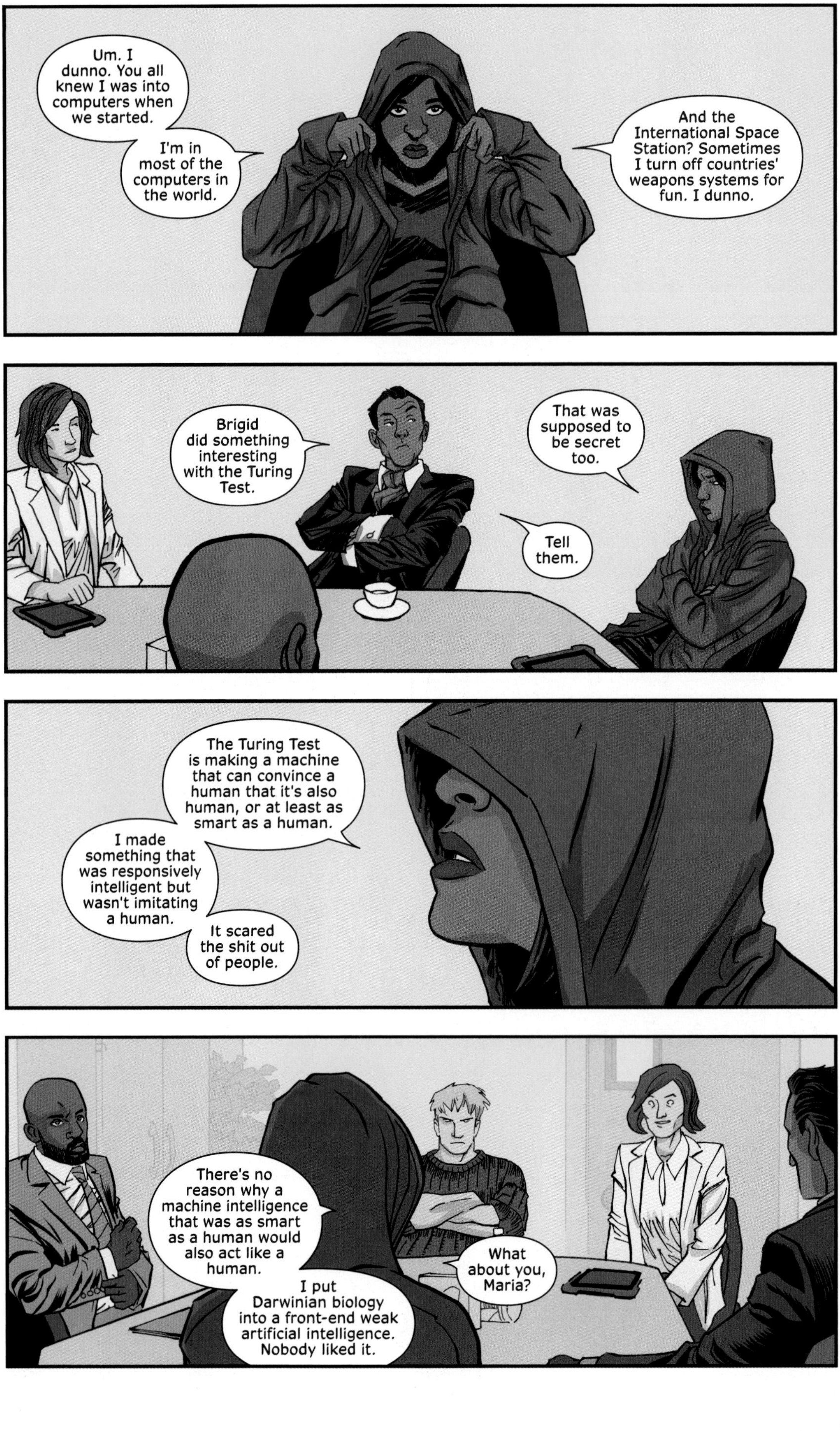
Um. I dunno. You all knew I was into computers when we started.
I'm in most of the computers in the world.
And the International Space Station? Sometimes I turn off countries' weapons systems for fun. I dunno.
Brigid did something interesting with the Turing Test.
That was supposed to be secret too.
Tell them.
The Turing Test is making a machine that can convince a human that it's also human, or at least as smart as a human.
I made something that was responsively intelligent but wasn't imitating a human.
It scared the shit out of people.
There's no reason why a machine intelligence that was as smart as a human would also act like a human.
I put Darwinian biology into a front-end weak artificial intelligence. Nobody liked it.
What about you, Maria?

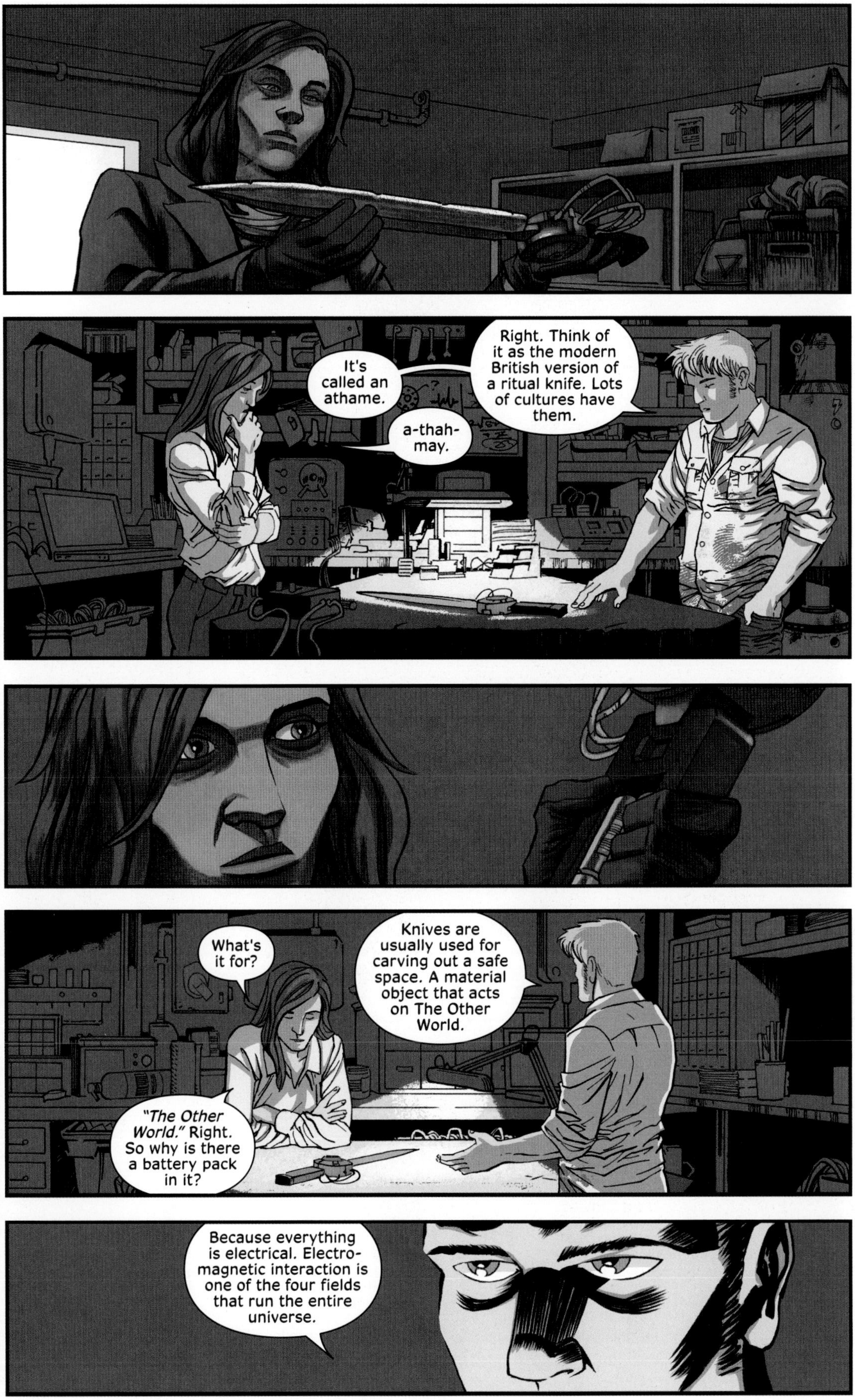
It's called an athame.
a-thah-may.
Right. Think of it as the modern British version of a ritual knife. Lots of cultures have them.
What's it for?
Knives are usually used for carving out a safe space. A material object that acts on The Other World.
"The Other World." Right. So why is there a battery pack in it?
Because everything is electrical. Electro-magnetic interaction is one of the four fields that run the entire universe.

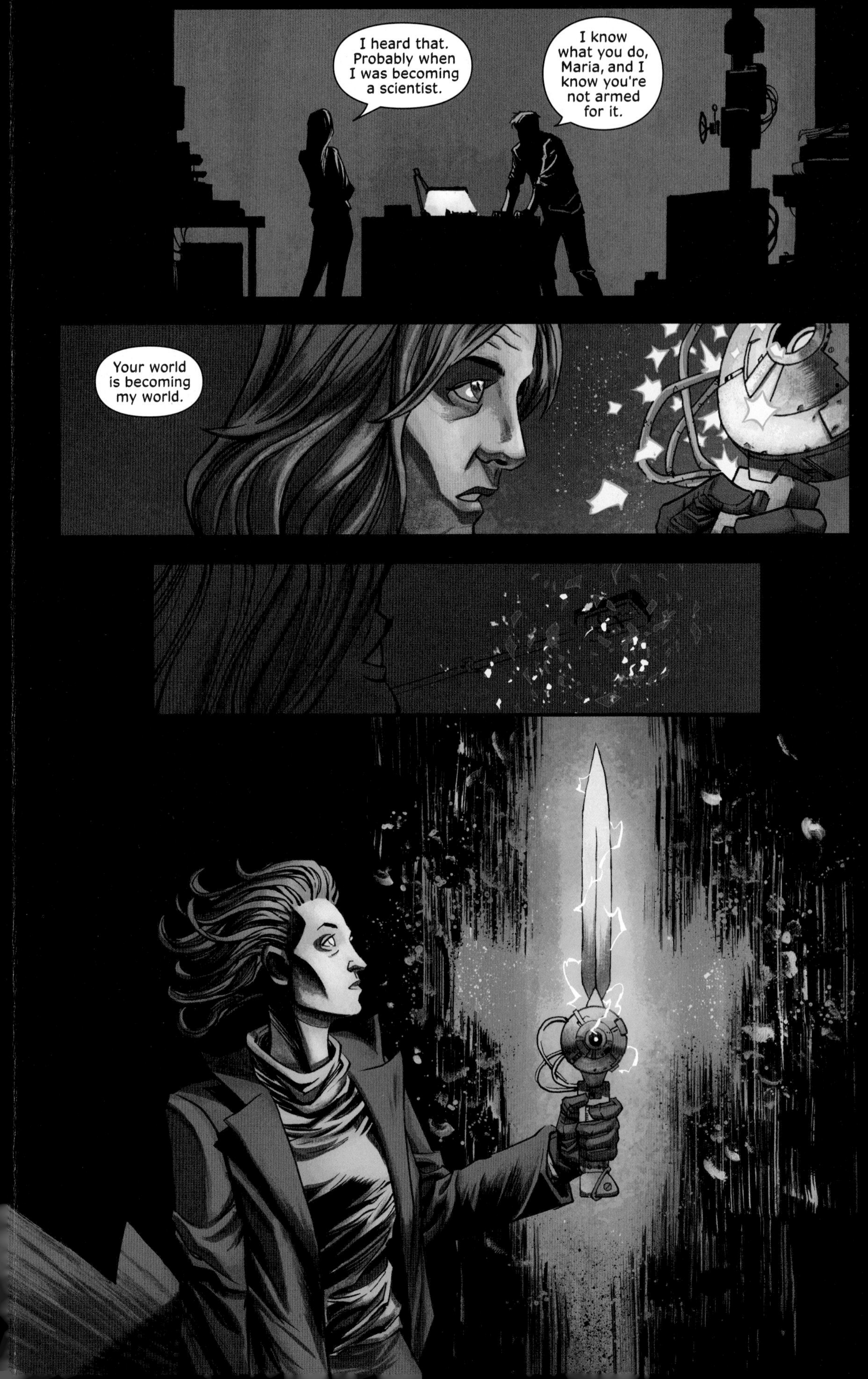
I heard that. Probably when I was becoming a scientist.
I know what you do, Maria, and I know you're not armed for it.
Your world is becoming my world.

MOONDOG

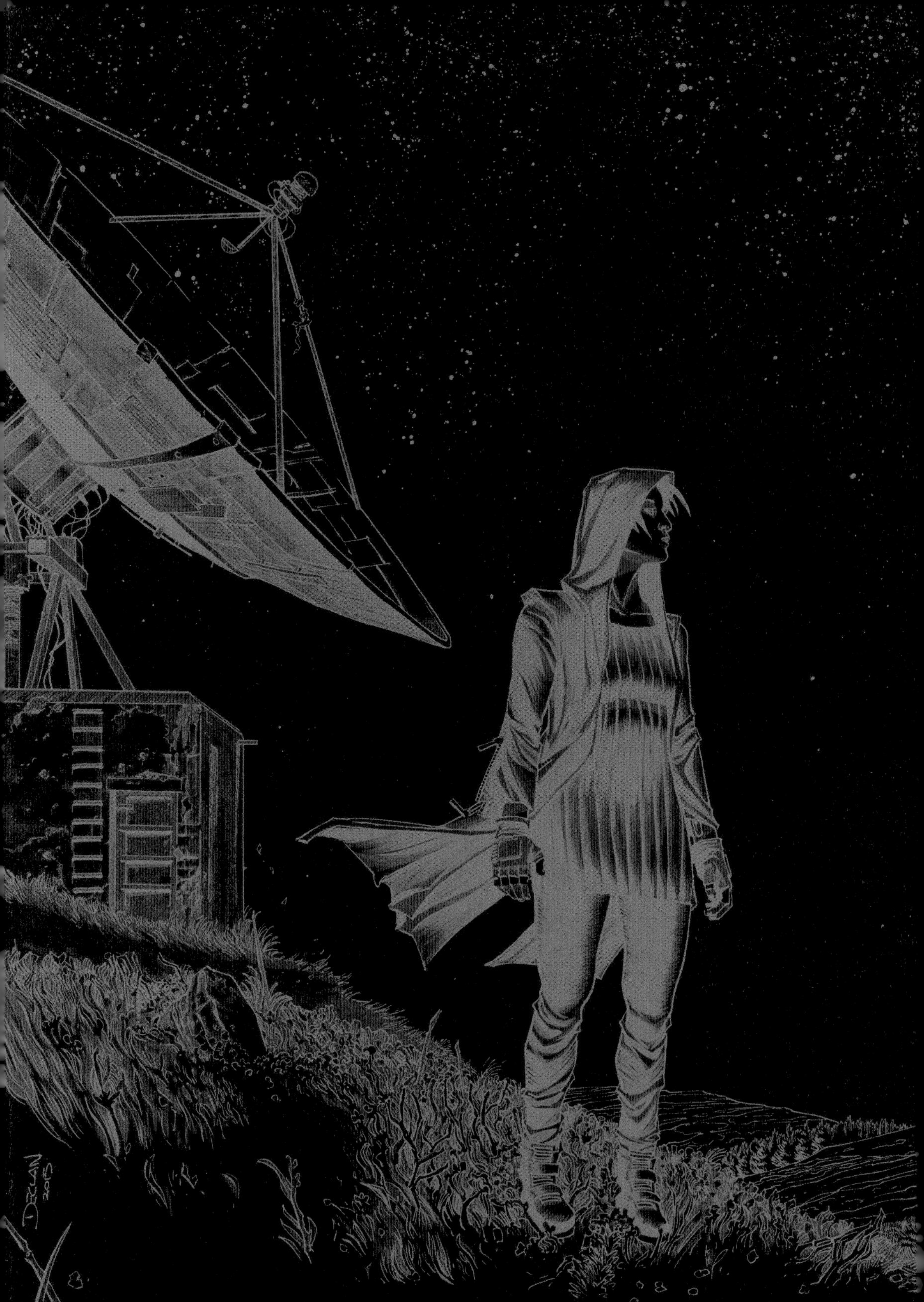

FOUR

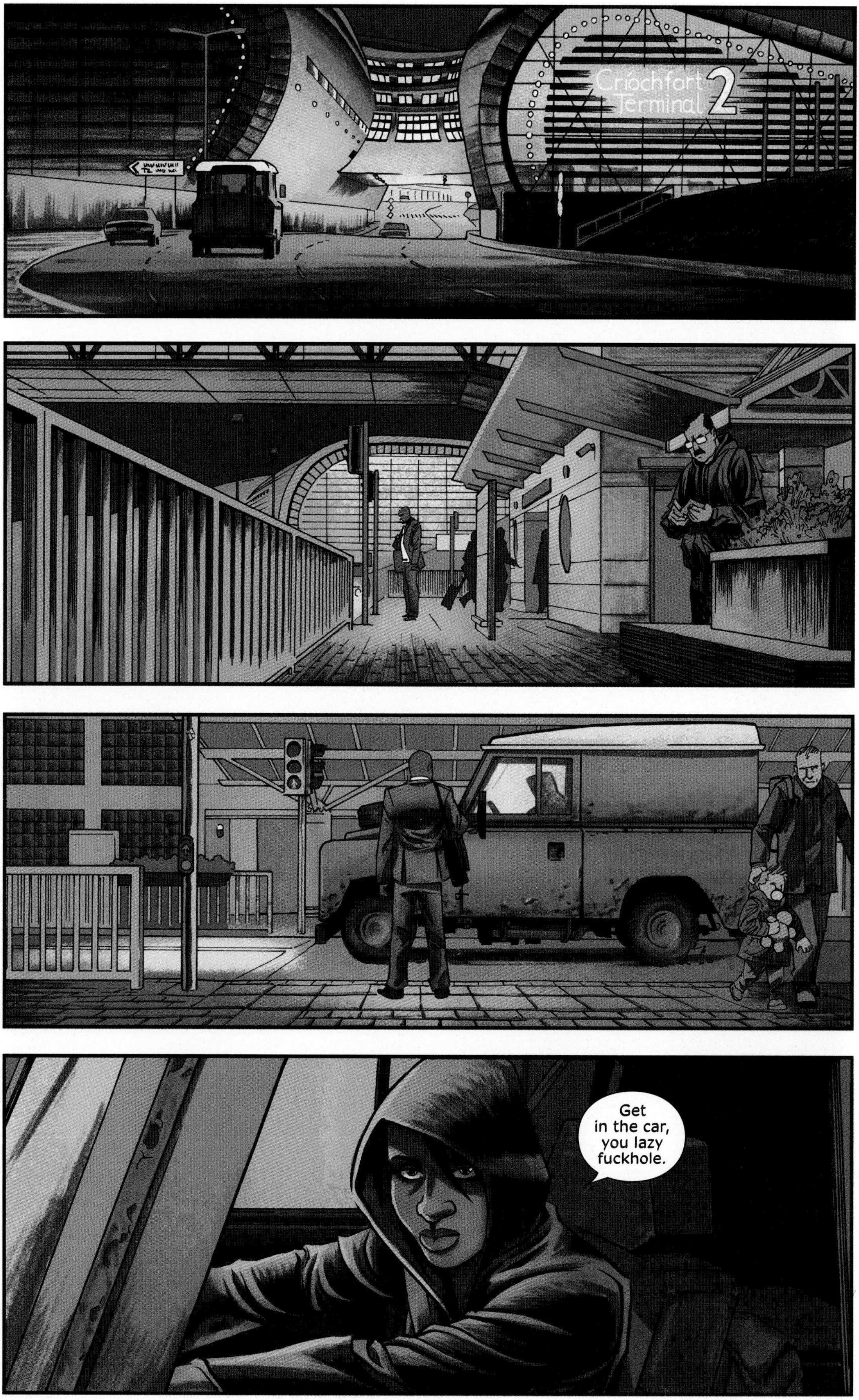
Críochfort
Terminal 2
Get in the car, you lazy fuckhole.

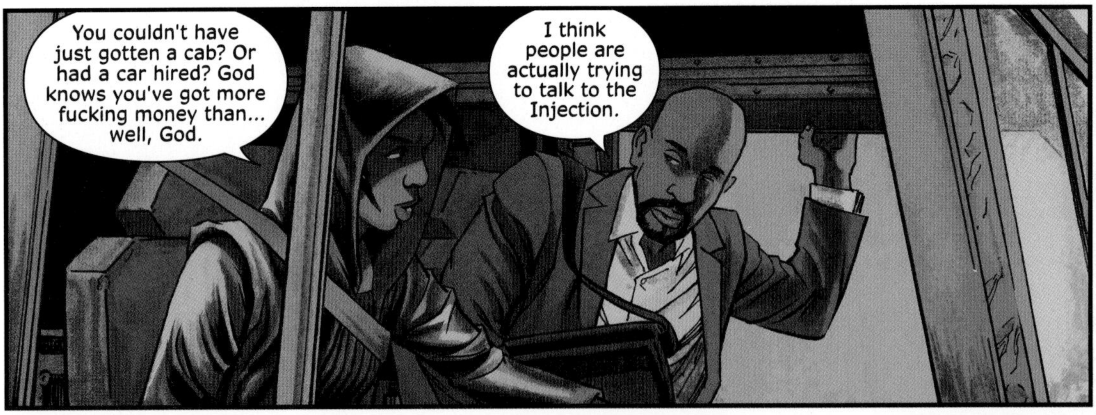
You couldn't have just gotten a cab? Or had a car hired? God knows you've got more fucking money than... well, God.
I think people are actually trying to talk to the Injection.

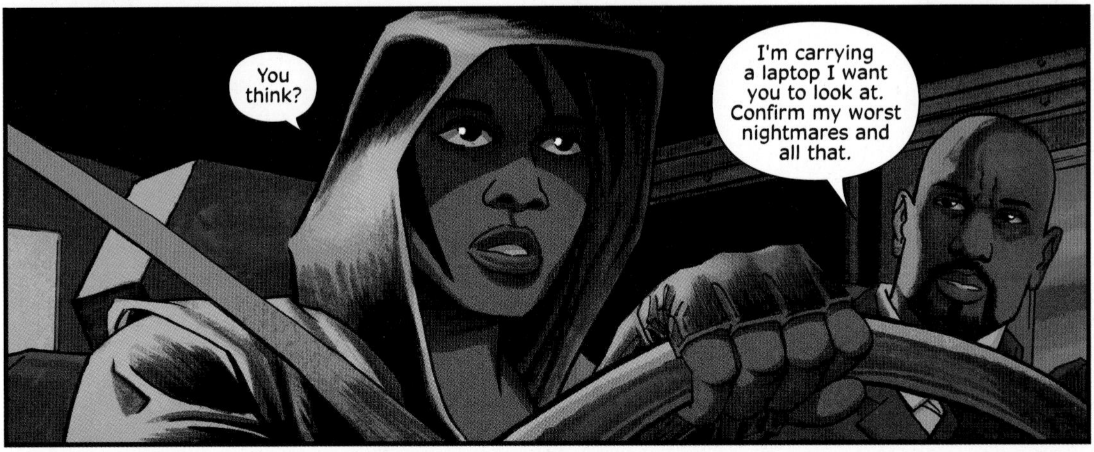
You think?
I'm carrying a laptop I want you to look at. Confirm my worst nightmares and all that.

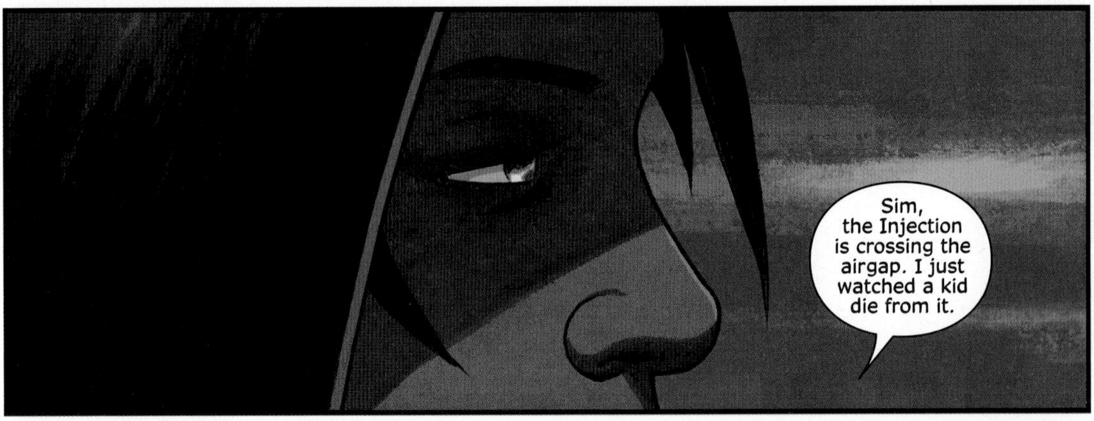
Sim, the Injection is crossing the airgap. I just watched a kid die from it.

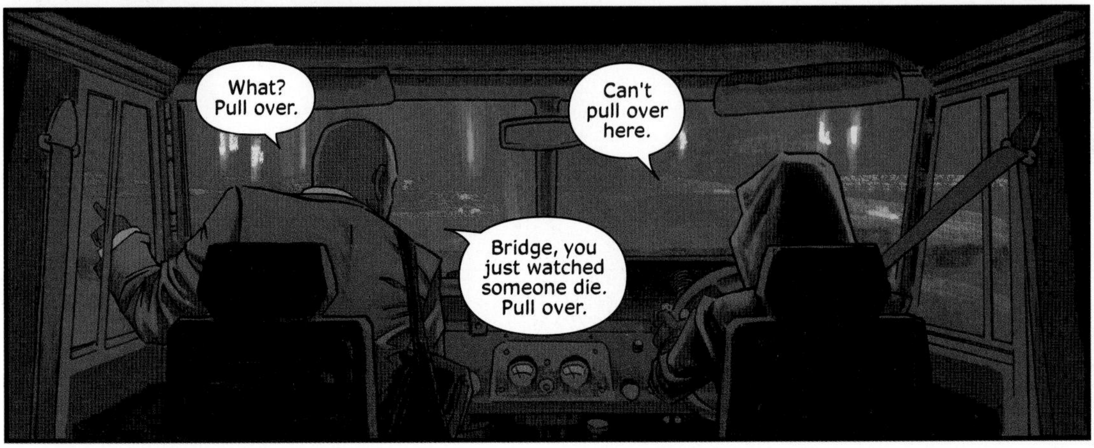
What? Pull over.
Can't pull over here.
Bridge, you just watched someone die. Pull over.

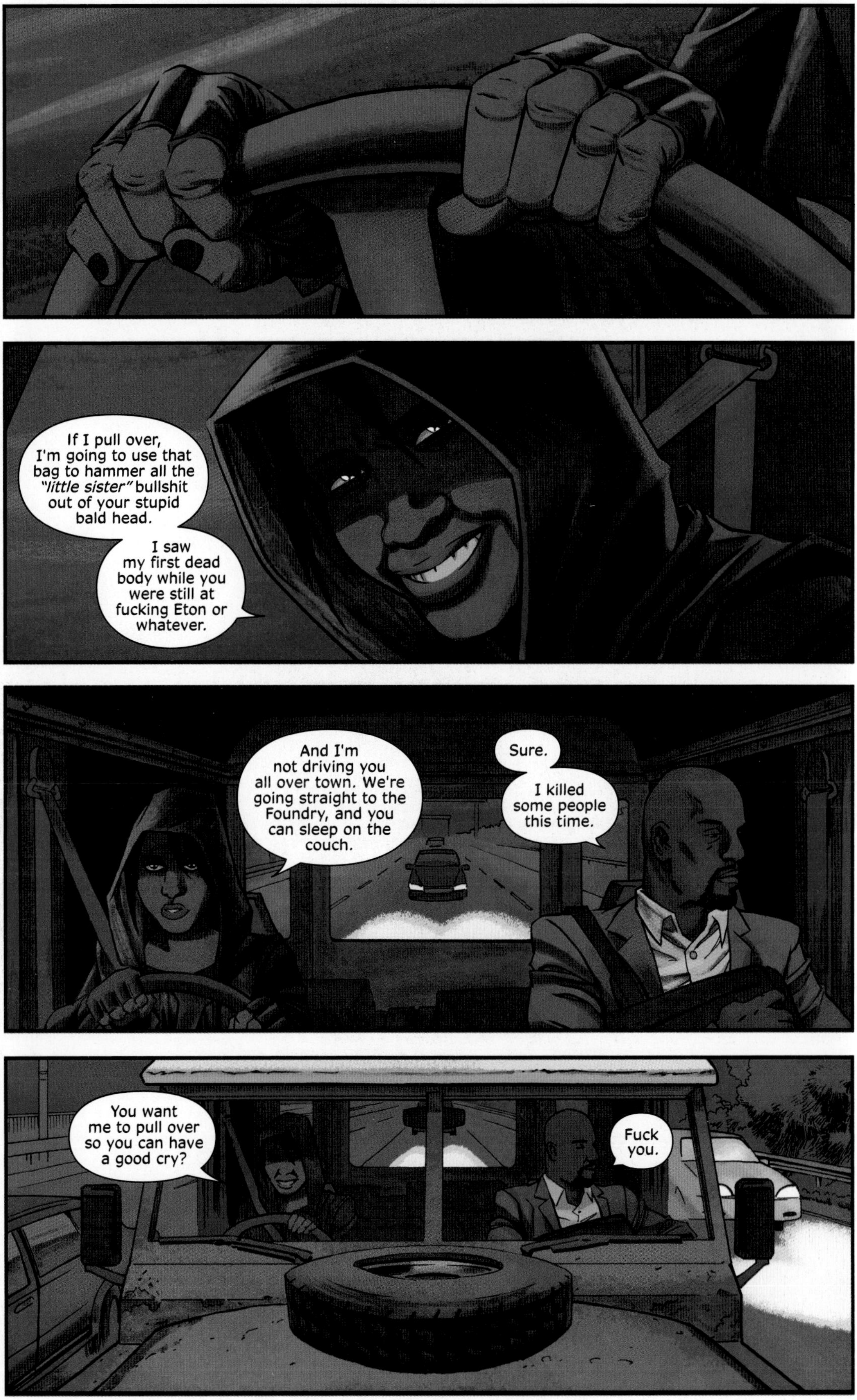
If I pull over, I'm going to use that bag to hammer all the *"little sister"* bullshit out of your stupid bald head.
I saw my first dead body while you were still at fucking Eton or whatever.
And I'm not driving you all over town. We're going straight to the Foundry, and you can sleep on the couch.
Sure.
I killed some people this time.
You want me to pull over so you can have a good cry?
Fuck you.

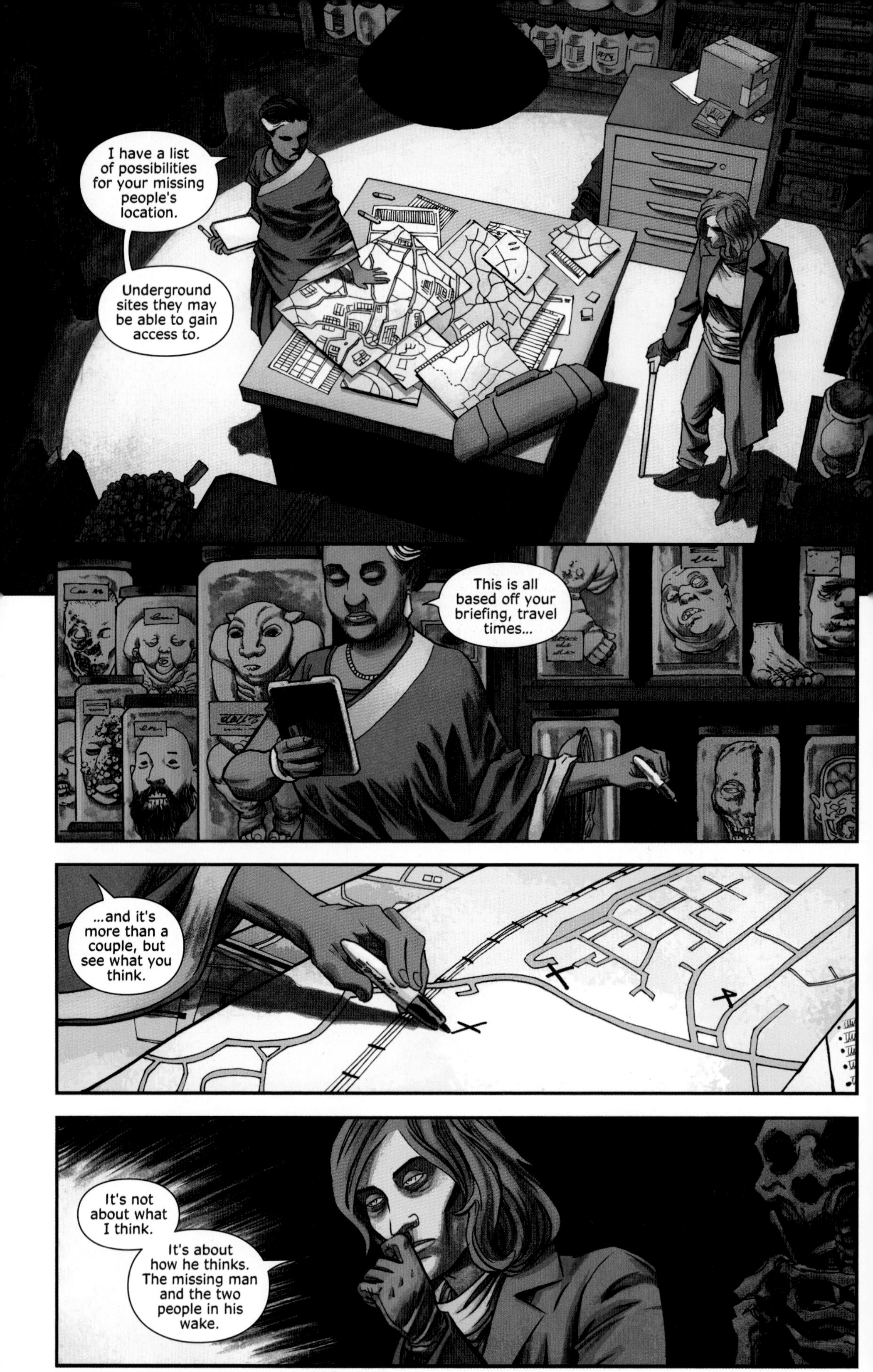
I have a list of possibilities for your missing people's location.
Underground sites they may be able to gain access to.
This is all based off your briefing, travel times...
...and it's more than a couple, but see what you think.
It's not about what I think.
It's about how he thinks. The missing man and the two people in his wake.

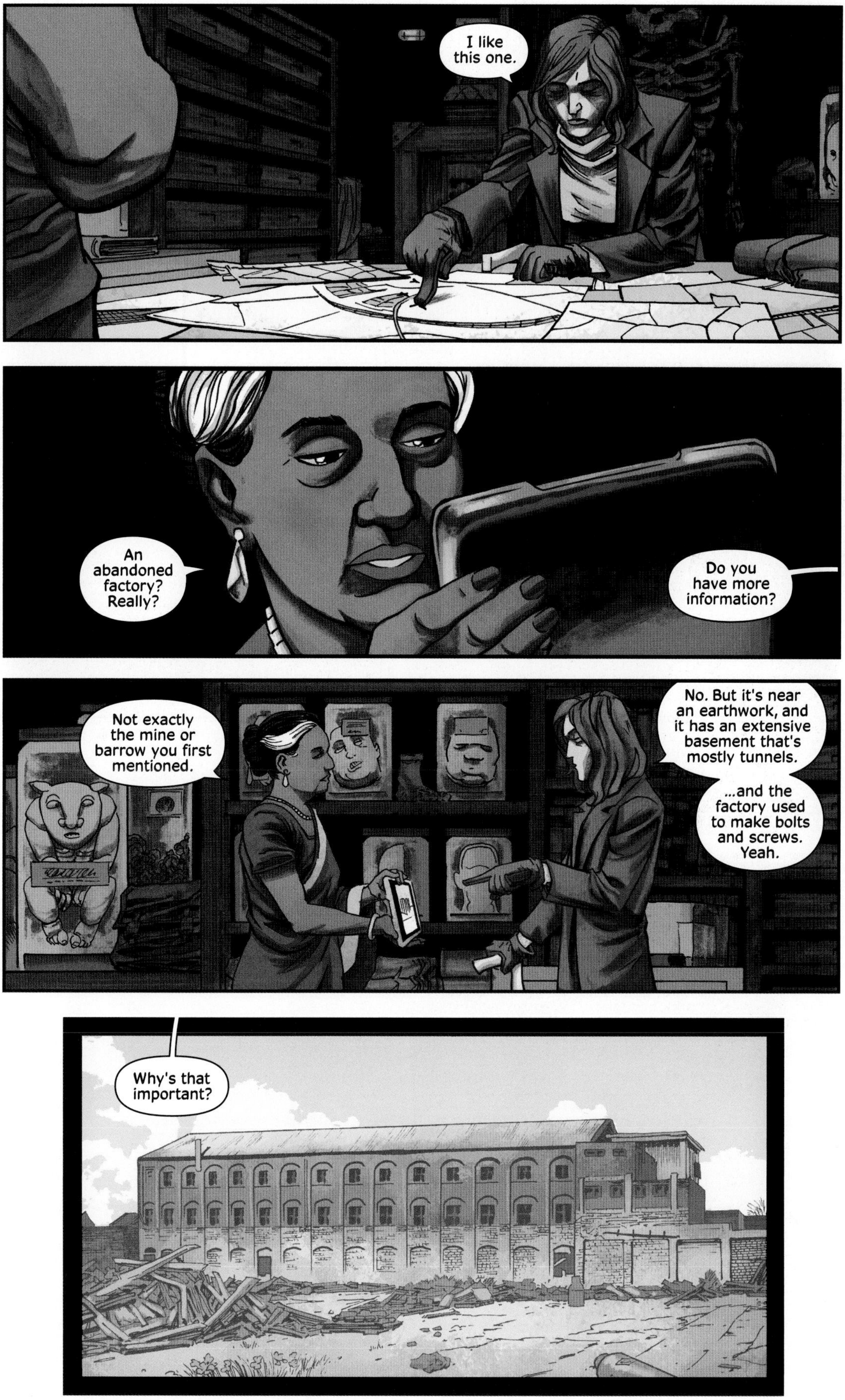

I like this one.
An abandoned factory? Really?
Do you have more information?
Not exactly the mine or barrow you first mentioned.
No. But it's near an earthwork, and it has an extensive basement that's mostly tunnels.
...and the factory used to make bolts and screws. Yeah.
Why's that important?

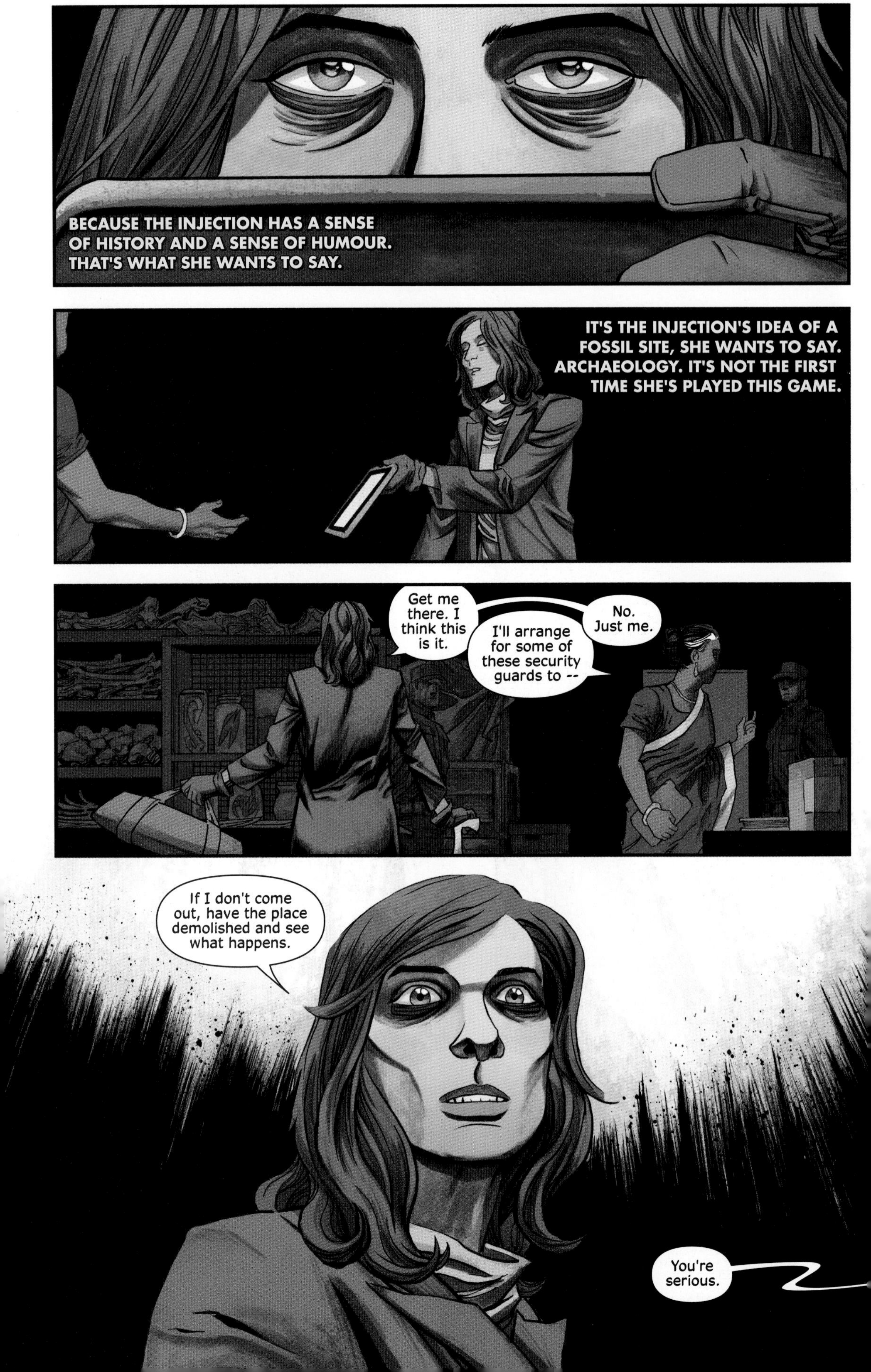
BECAUSE THE INJECTION HAS A SENSE OF HISTORY AND A SENSE OF HUMOUR. THAT'S WHAT SHE WANTS TO SAY.
IT'S THE INJECTION'S IDEA OF A FOSSIL SITE, SHE WANTS TO SAY. ARCHAEOLOGY. IT'S NOT THE FIRST TIME SHE'S PLAYED THIS GAME.
Get me there. I think this is it.
I'll arrange for some of these security guards to --
No. Just me.
If I don't come out, have the place demolished and see what happens.
You're serious.

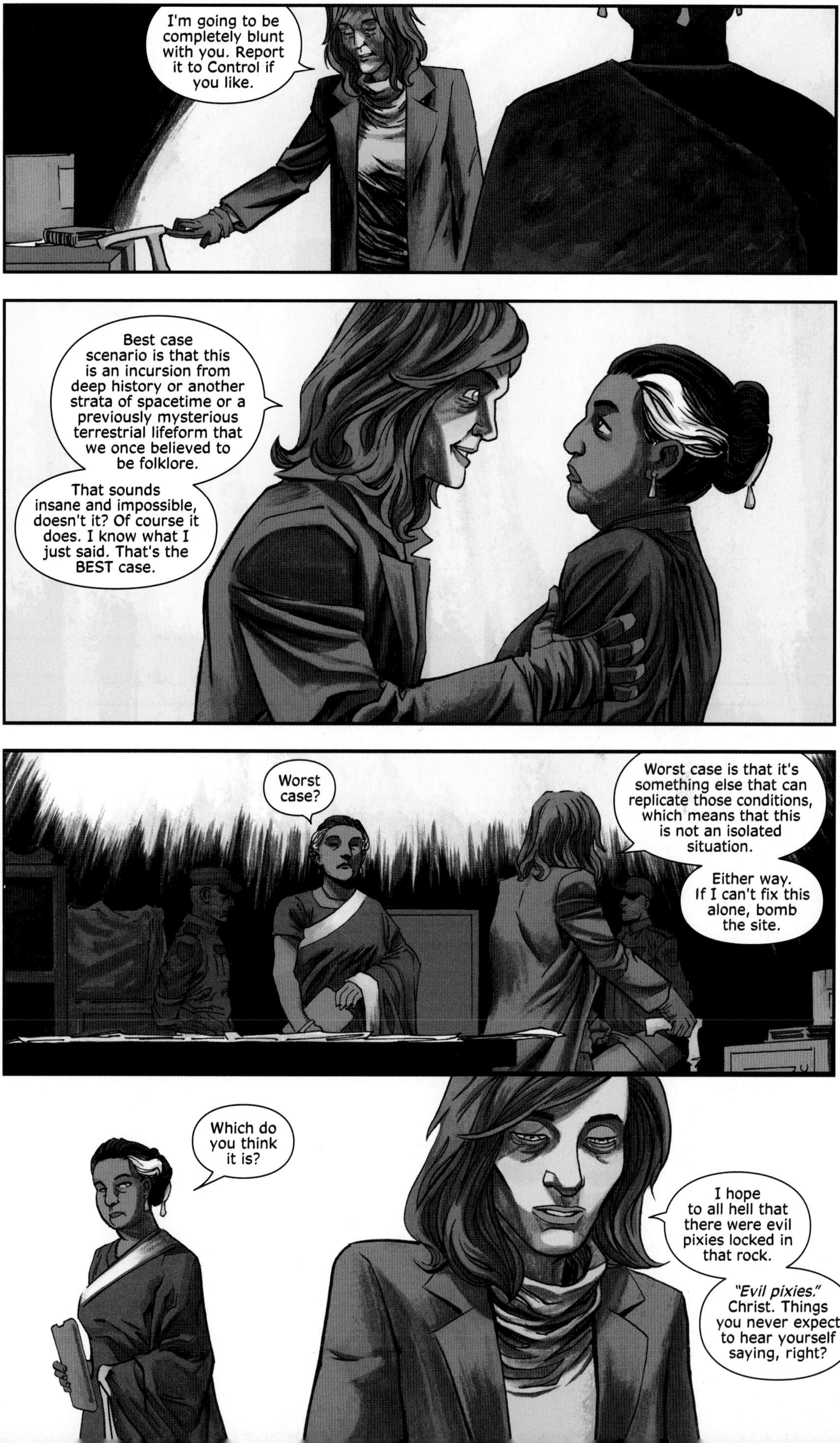
I'm going to be completely blunt with you. Report it to Control if you like.
Best case scenario is that this is an incursion from deep history or another strata of spacetime or a previously mysterious terrestrial lifeform that we once believed to be folklore.
That sounds insane and impossible, doesn't it? Of course it does. I know what I just said. That's the BEST case.
Worst case?
Worst case is that it's something else that can replicate those conditions, which means that this is not an isolated situation.
Either way. If I can't fix this alone, bomb the site.
Which do you think it is?
I hope to all hell that there were evil pixies locked in that rock.
"Evil pixies." Christ. Things you never expect to hear yourself saying, right?

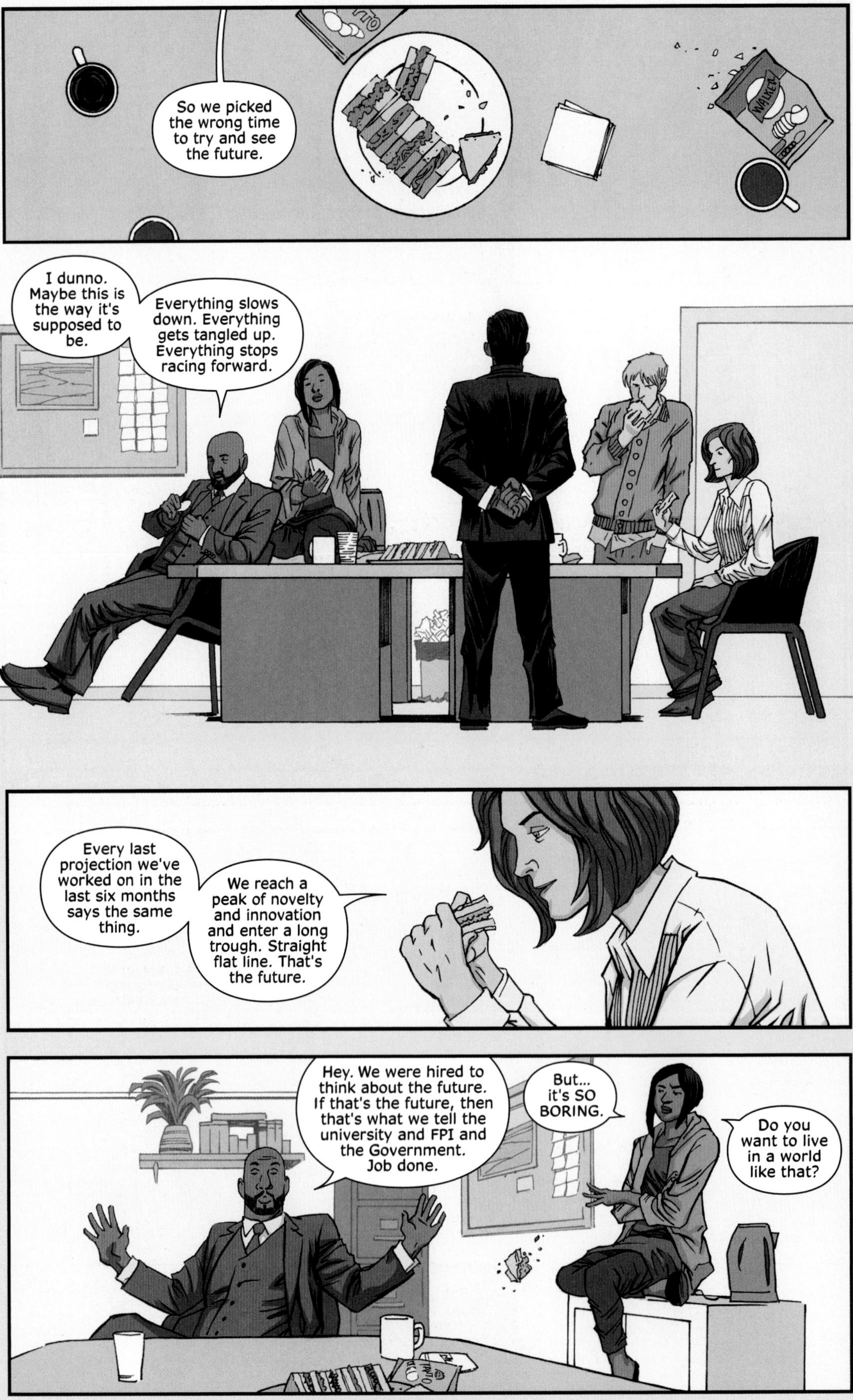

So we picked the wrong time to try and see the future.
I dunno. Maybe this is the way it's supposed to be.
Everything slows down. Everything gets tangled up. Everything stops racing forward.
Every last projection we've worked on in the last six months says the same thing.
We reach a peak of novelty and innovation and enter a long trough. Straight flat line. That's the future.
Hey. We were hired to think about the future. If that's the future, then that's what we tell the university and FPI and the Government. Job done.
But... it's SO BORING.
Do you want to live in a world like that?

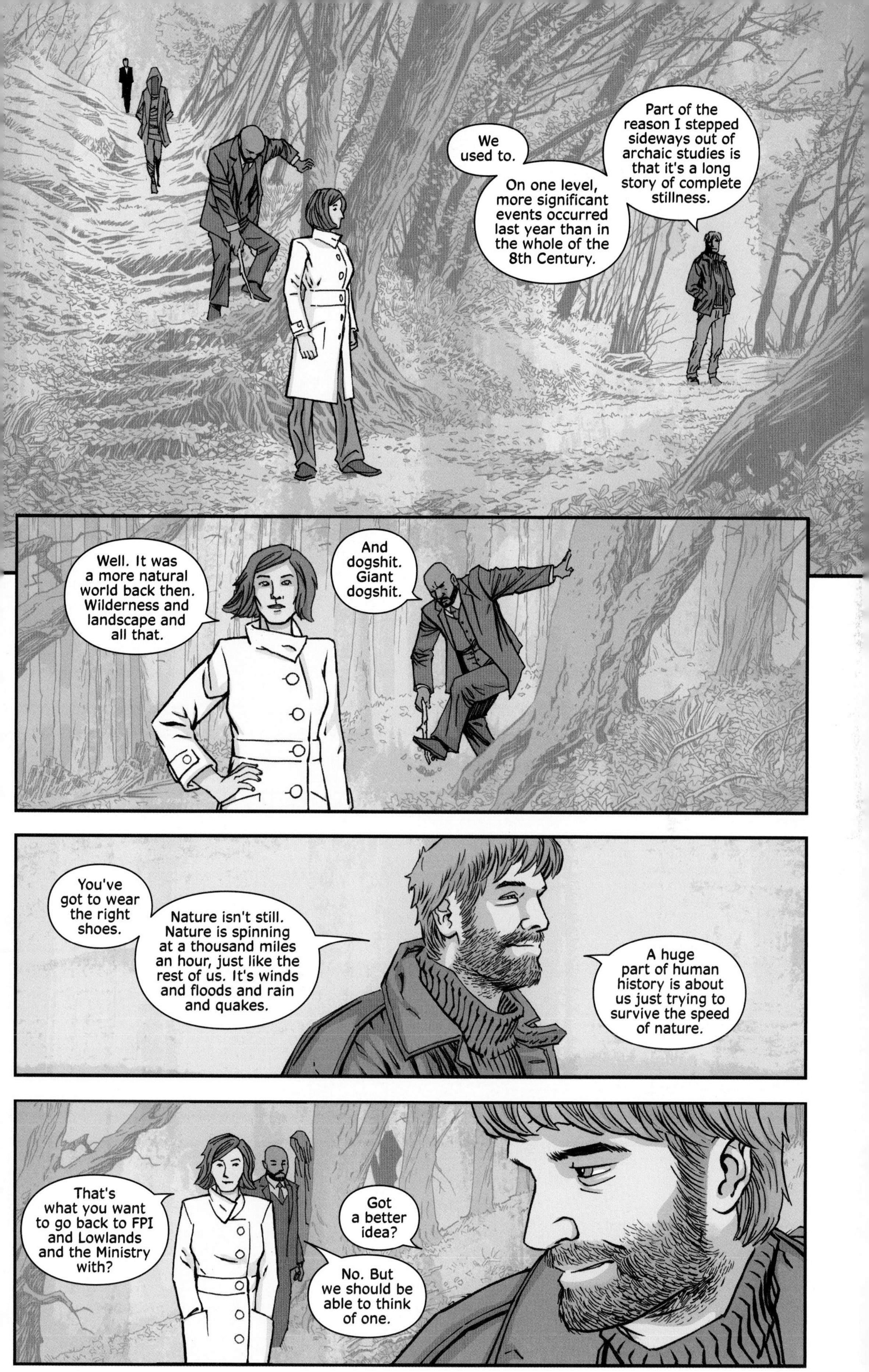
We used to.
On one level, more significant events occurred last year than in the whole of the 8th Century.
Part of the reason I stepped sideways out of archaic studies is that it's a long story of complete stillness.
Well. It was a more natural world back then. Wilderness and landscape and all that.
And dogshit. Giant dogshit.
You've got to wear the right shoes.
Nature isn't still. Nature is spinning at a thousand miles an hour, just like the rest of us. It's winds and floods and rain and quakes.
A huge part of human history is about us just trying to survive the speed of nature.
That's what you want to go back to FPI and Lowlands and the Ministry with?
Got a better idea?
No. But we should be able to think of one.

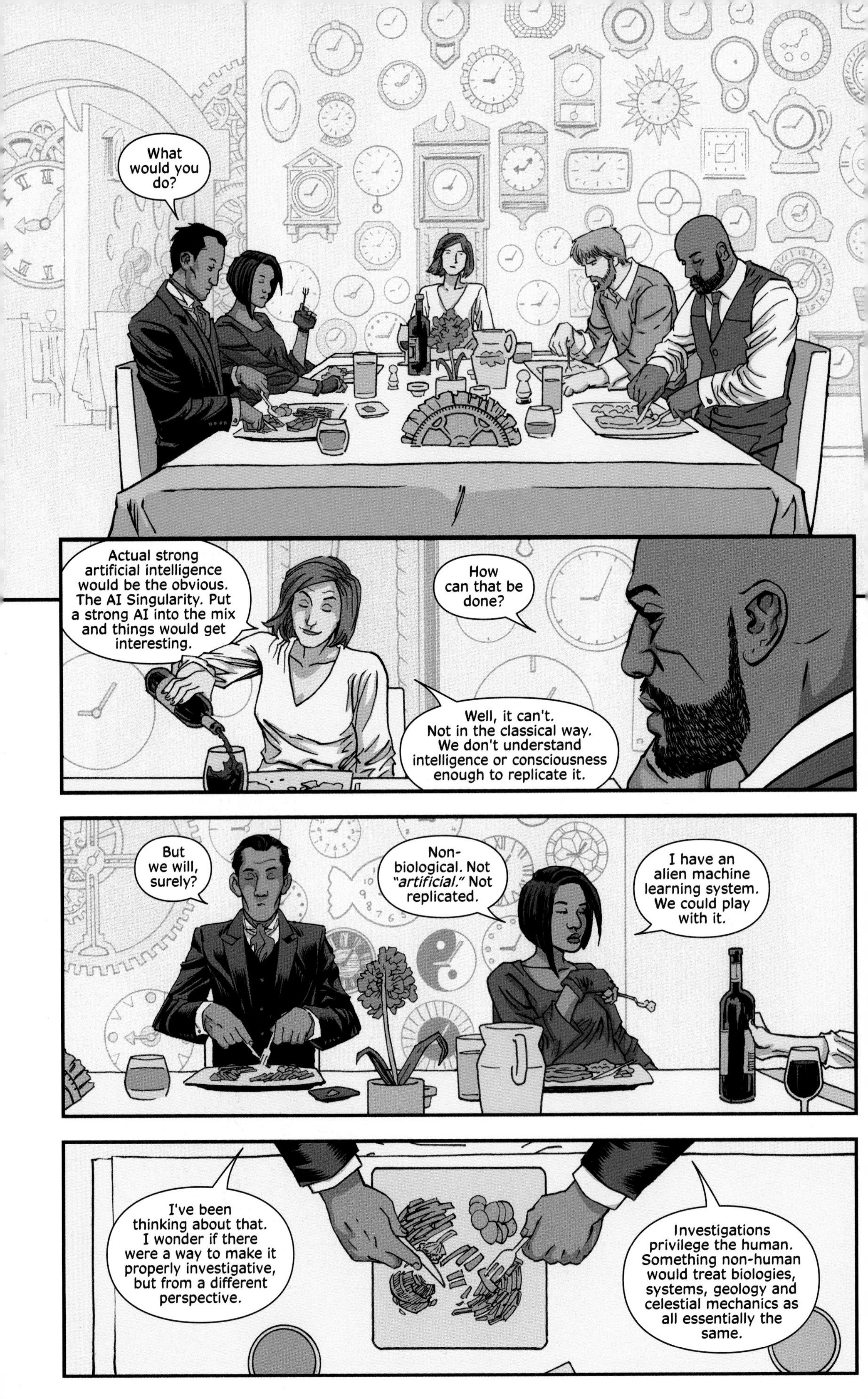
What would you do?
Actual strong artificial intelligence would be the obvious. The AI Singularity. Put a strong AI into the mix and things would get interesting.
How can that be done?
Well, it can't. Not in the classical way. We don't understand intelligence or consciousness enough to replicate it.
But we will, surely?
Non-biological. Not *"artificial."* Not replicated.
I have an alien machine learning system. We could play with it.
I've been thinking about that. I wonder if there were a way to make it properly investigative, but from a different perspective.
Investigations privilege the human. Something non-human would treat biologies, systems, geology and celestial mechanics as all essentially the same.

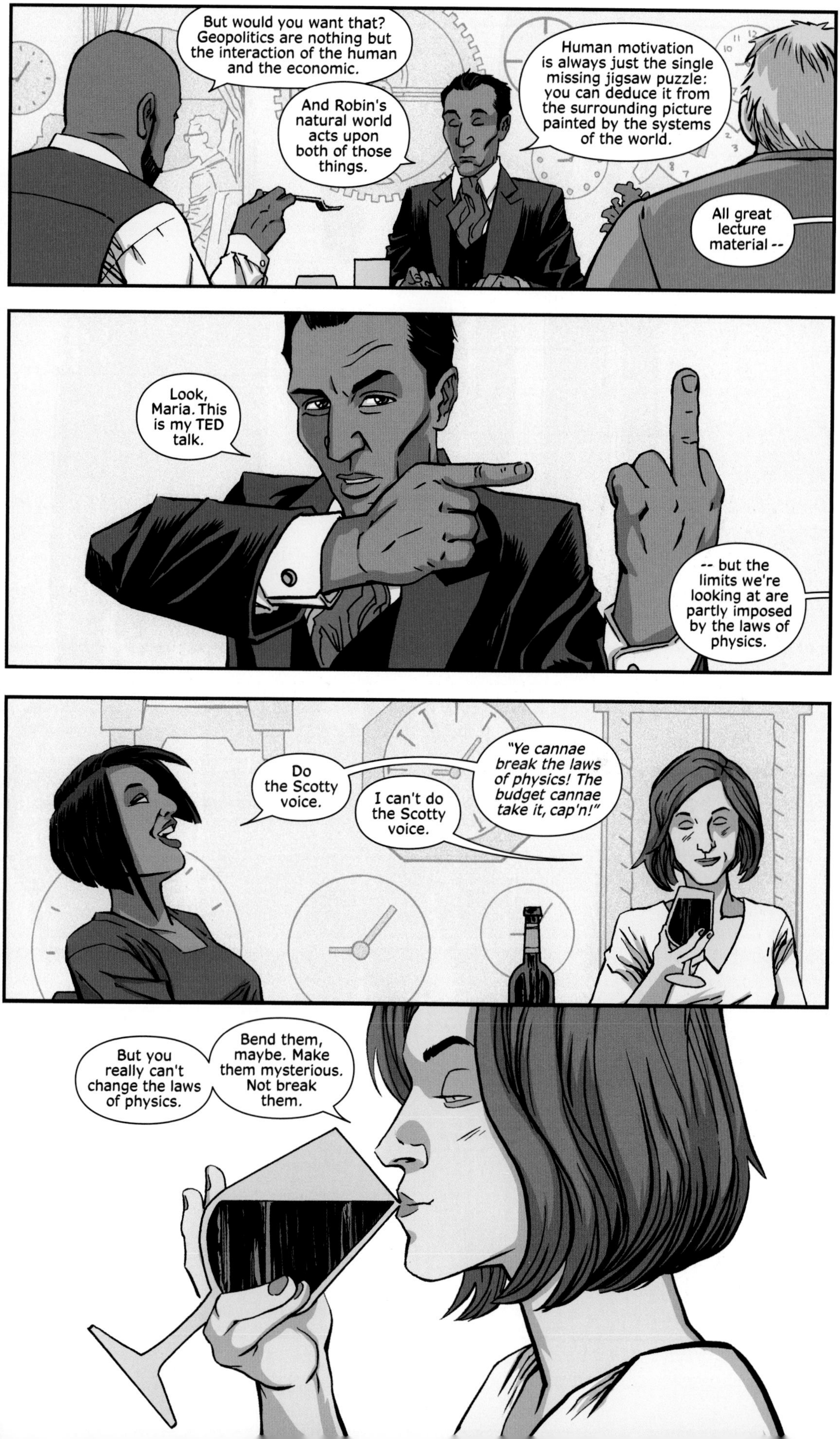

But would you want that? Geopolitics are nothing but the interaction of the human and the economic.
And Robin's natural world acts upon both of those things.
Human motivation is always just the single missing jigsaw puzzle: you can deduce it from the surrounding picture painted by the systems of the world.
All great lecture material --
Look, Maria. This is my TED talk.
-- but the limits we're looking at are partly imposed by the laws of physics.
Do the Scotty voice.
I can't do the Scotty voice.
"Ye cannae break the laws of physics! The budget cannae take it, cap'n!"
But you really can't change the laws of physics.
Bend them, maybe. Make them mysterious. Not break them.

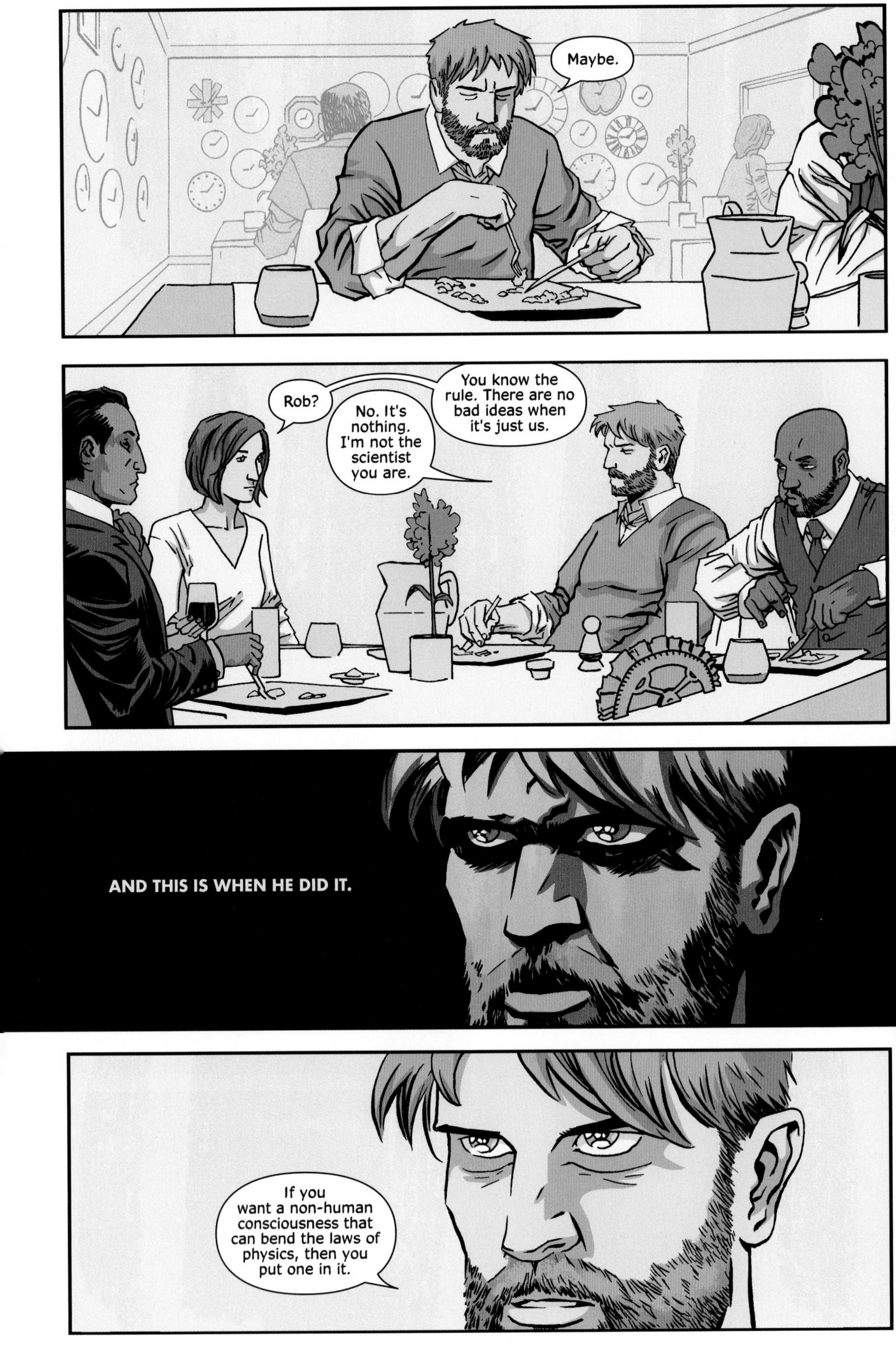
Maybe.
Rob?
You know the rule. There are no bad ideas when it's just us.
No. It's nothing. I'm not the scientist you are.
AND THIS IS WHEN HE DID IT.
If you want a non-human consciousness that can bend the laws of physics, then you put one in it.

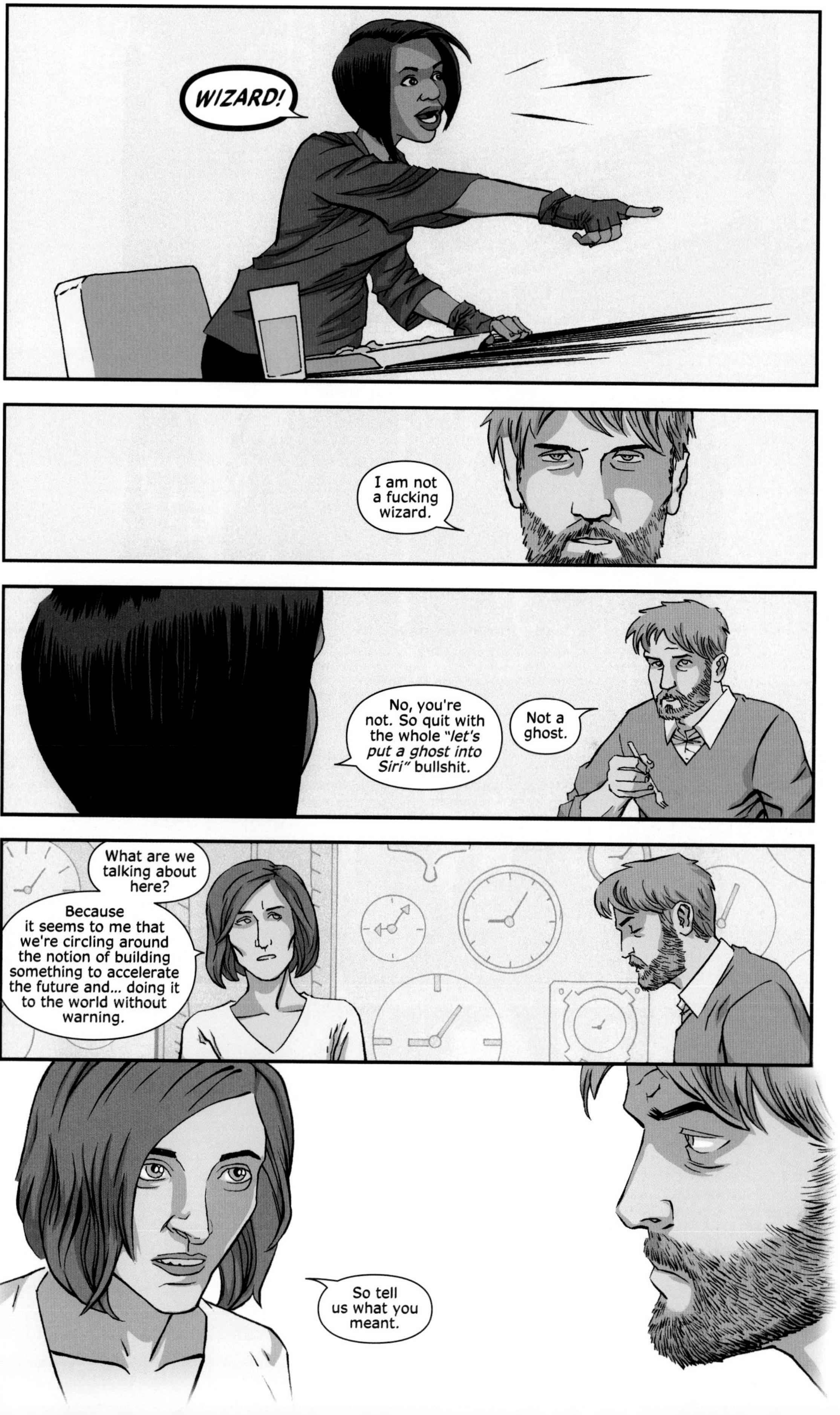
WIZARD!
I am not a fucking wizard.
No, you're not. So quit with the whole *"let's put a ghost into Siri"* bullshit.
Not a ghost.
What are we talking about here?
Because it seems to me that we're circling around the notion of building something to accelerate the future and... doing it to the world without warning.
So tell us what you meant.

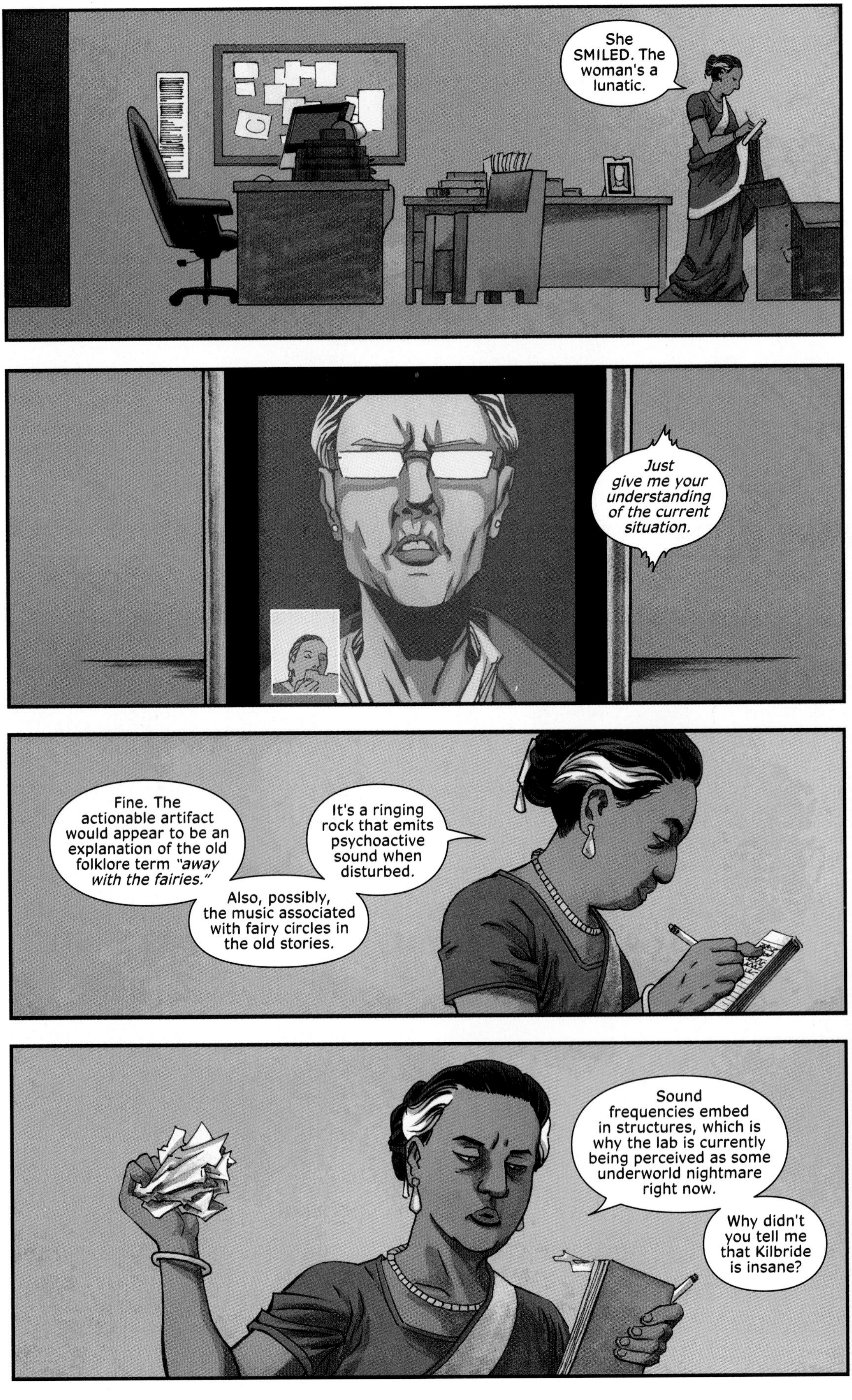
She SMILED. The woman's a lunatic.
Just give me your understanding of the current situation.
Fine. The actionable artifact would appear to be an explanation of the old folklore term *"away with the fairies."*
It's a ringing rock that emits psychoactive sound when disturbed.
Also, possibly, the music associated with fairy circles in the old stories.
Sound frequencies embed in structures, which is why the lab is currently being perceived as some underworld nightmare right now.
Why didn't you tell me that Kilbride is insane?

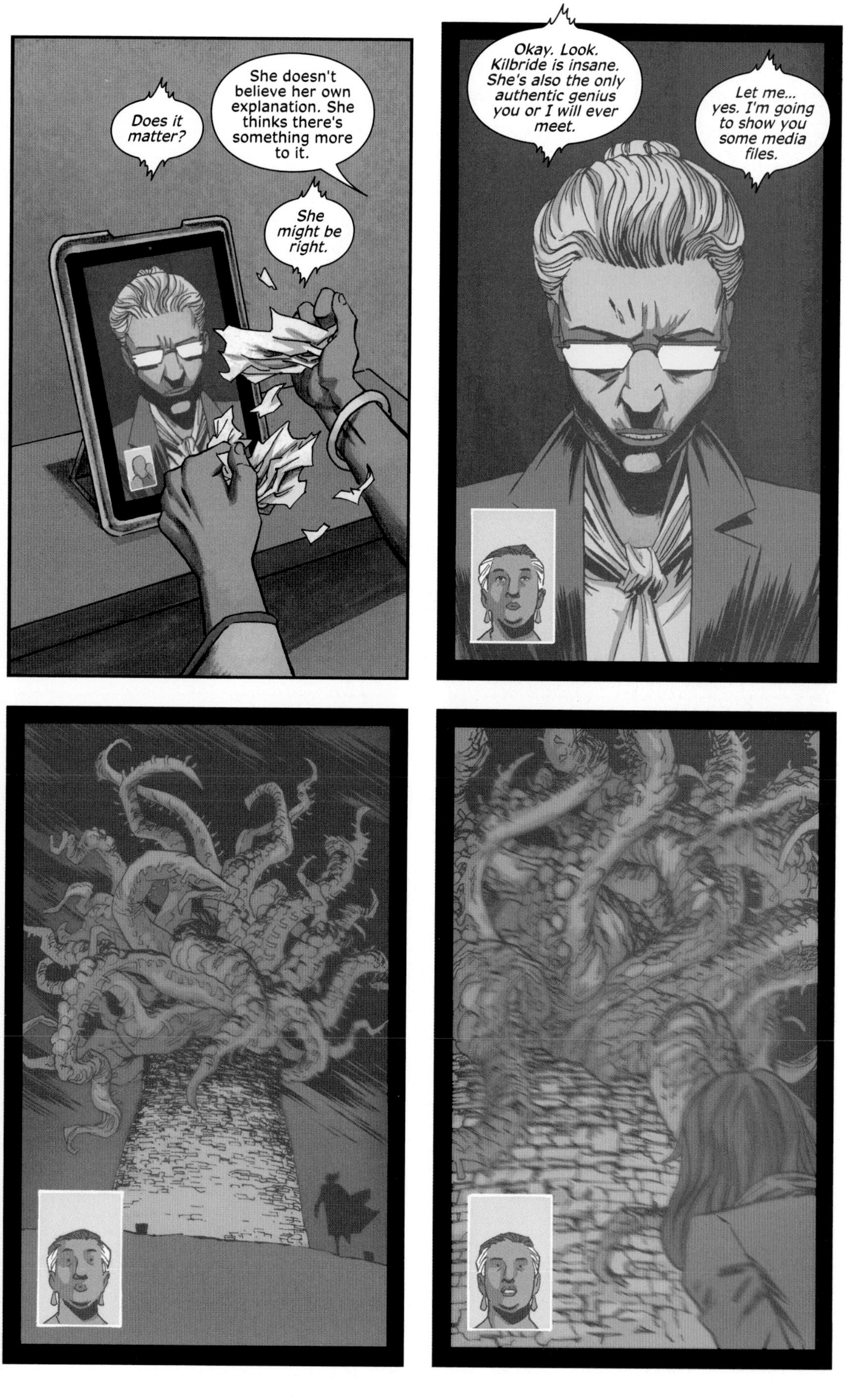
Does it matter?
She doesn't believe her own explanation. She thinks there's something more to it.
She might be right.
Okay. Look. Kilbride is insane. She's also the only authentic genius you or I will ever meet.
Let me... yes. I'm going to show you some media files.

...what the hell am I looking at?

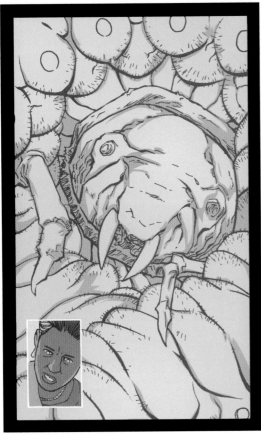

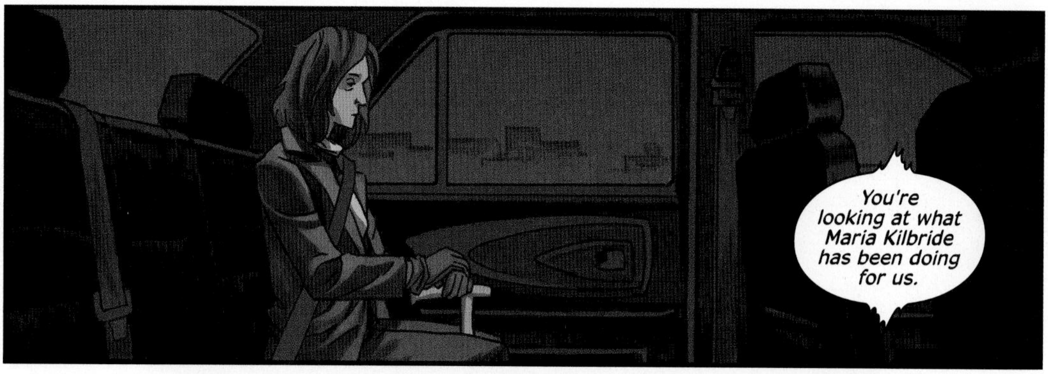
You're looking at what Maria Kilbride has been doing for us.

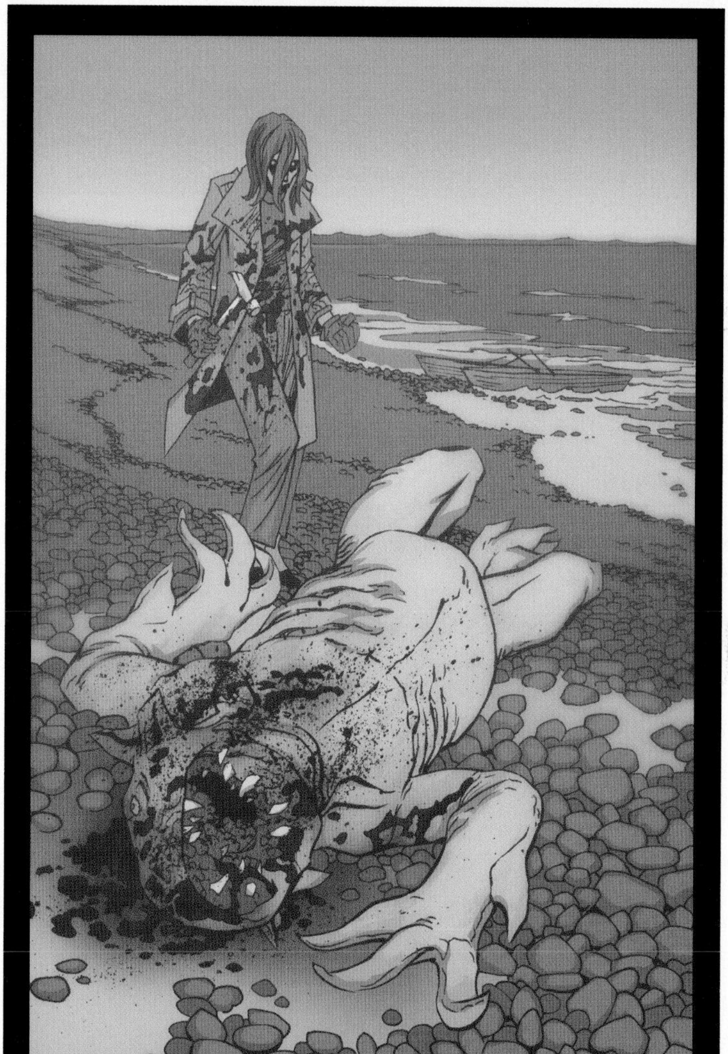

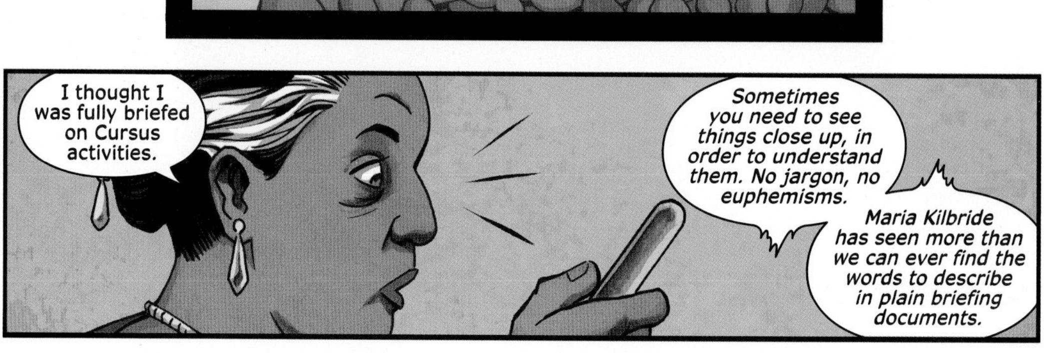
I thought I was fully briefed on Cursus activities.
Sometimes you need to see things close up, in order to understand them. No jargon, no euphemisms.
Maria Kilbride has seen more than we can ever find the words to describe in plain briefing documents.

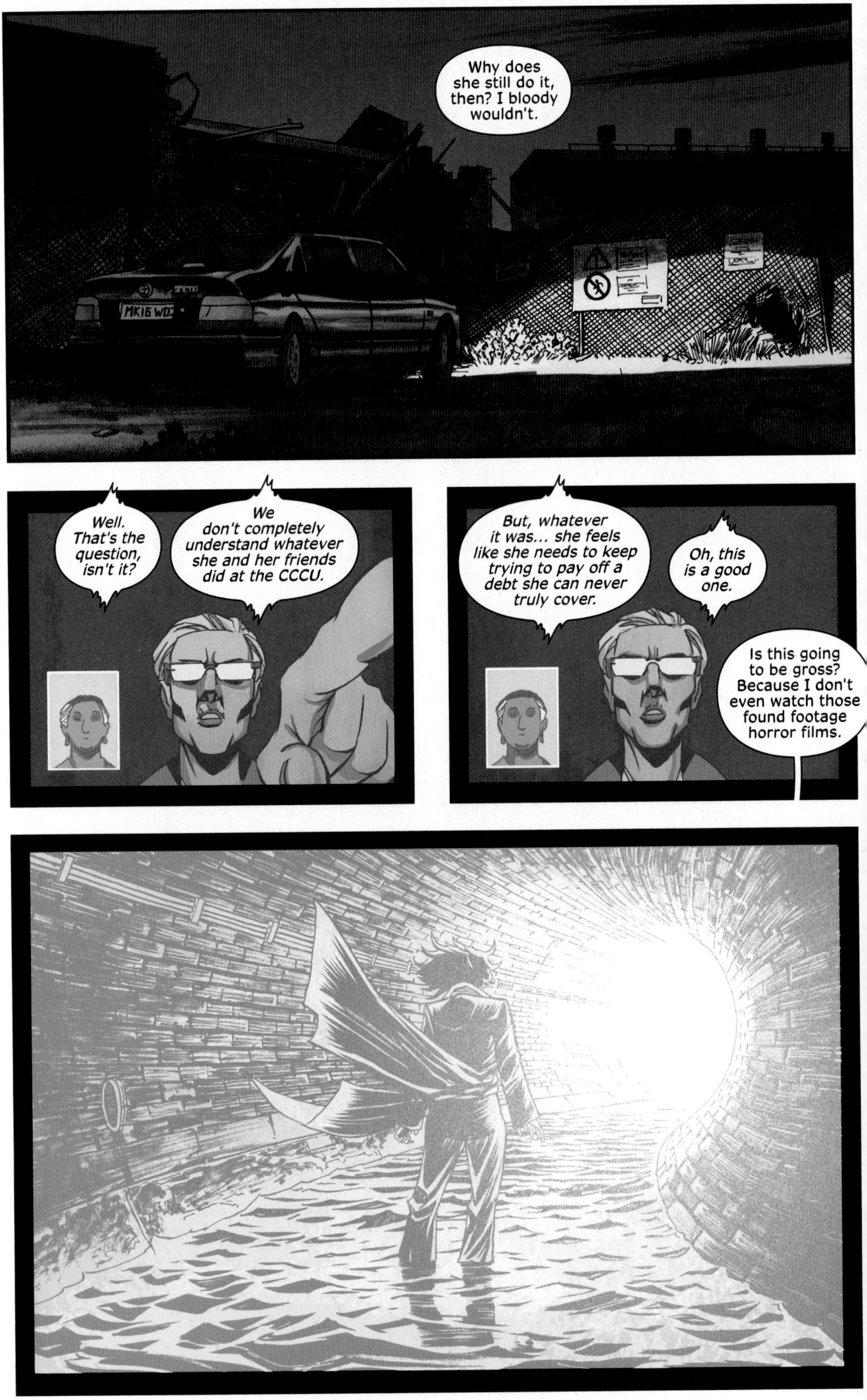
Why does she still do it, then? I bloody wouldn't.
Well. That's the question, isn't it?
We don't completely understand whatever she and her friends did at the CCCU.
But, whatever it was... she feels like she needs to keep trying to pay off a debt she can never truly cover.
Oh, this is a good one.
Is this going to be gross? Because I don't even watch those found footage horror films.

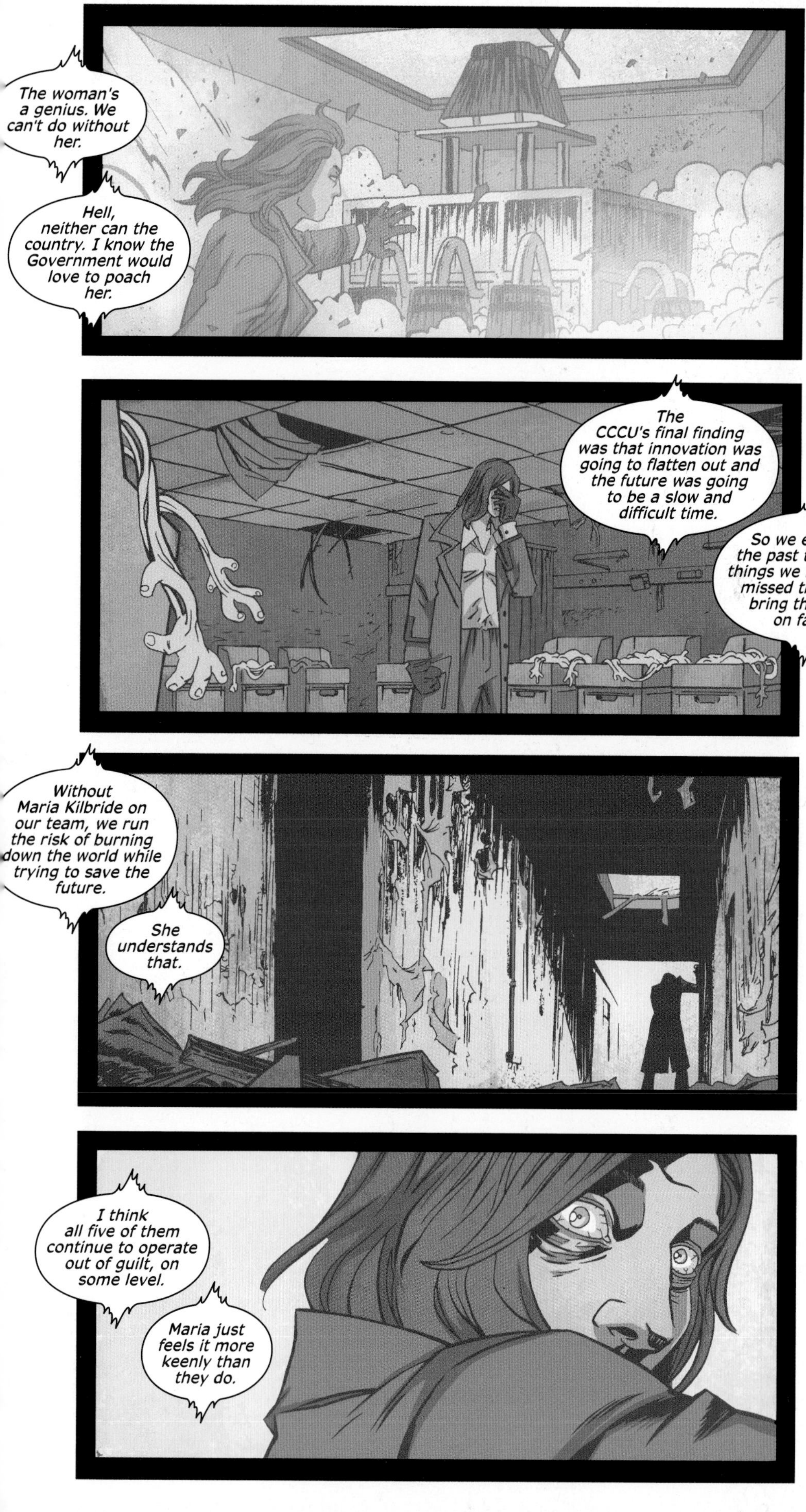
The woman's a genius. We can't do without her.
Hell, neither can the country. I know the Government would love to poach her.
The CCCU's final finding was that innovation was going to flatten out and the future was going to be a slow and difficult time.
So we excavate the past to look for things we might have missed that might bring the future on faster.
Without Maria Kilbride on our team, we run the risk of burning down the world while trying to save the future.
She understands that.
I think all five of them continue to operate out of guilt, on some level.
Maria just feels it more keenly than they do.

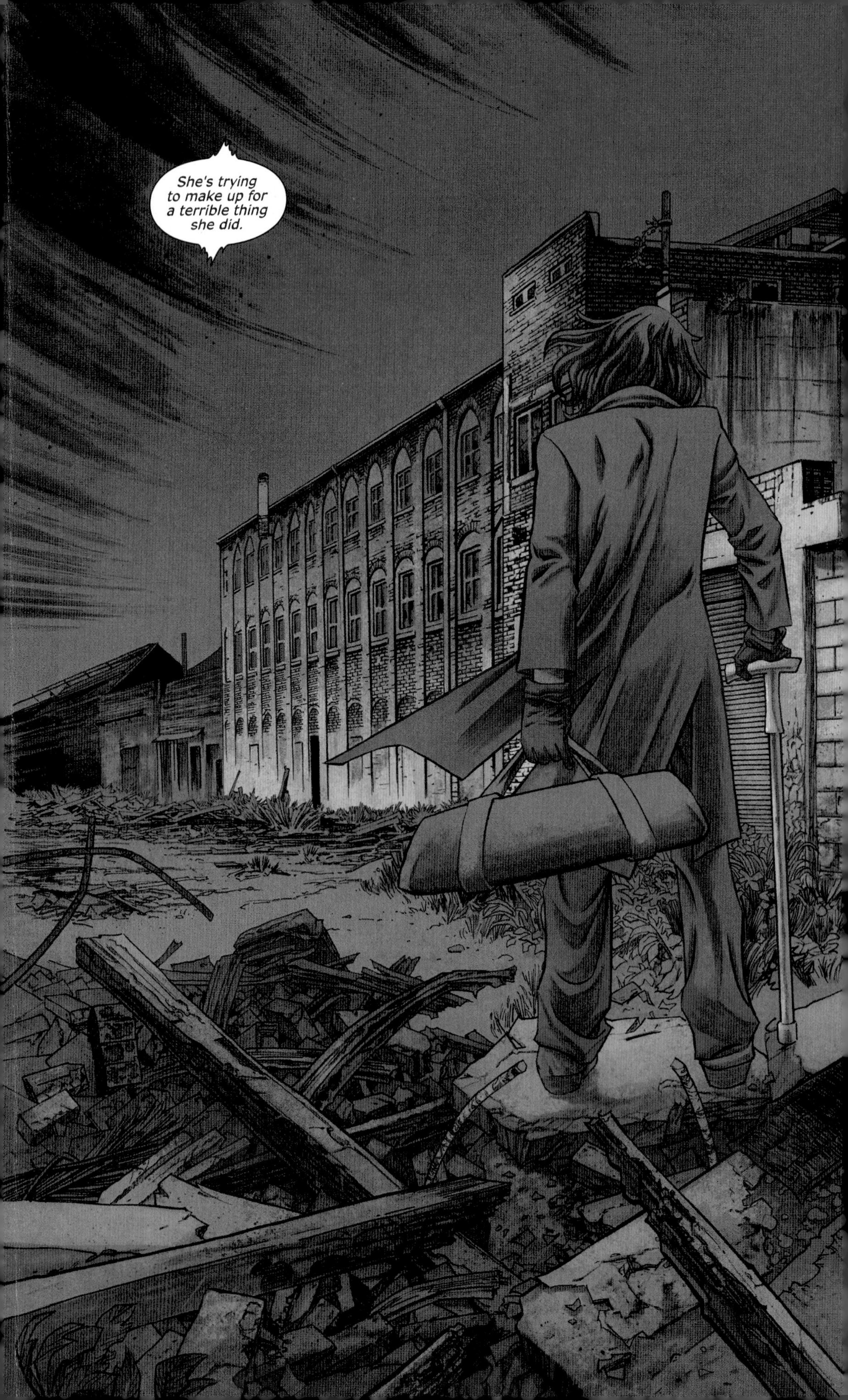
She's trying to make up for a terrible thing she did.

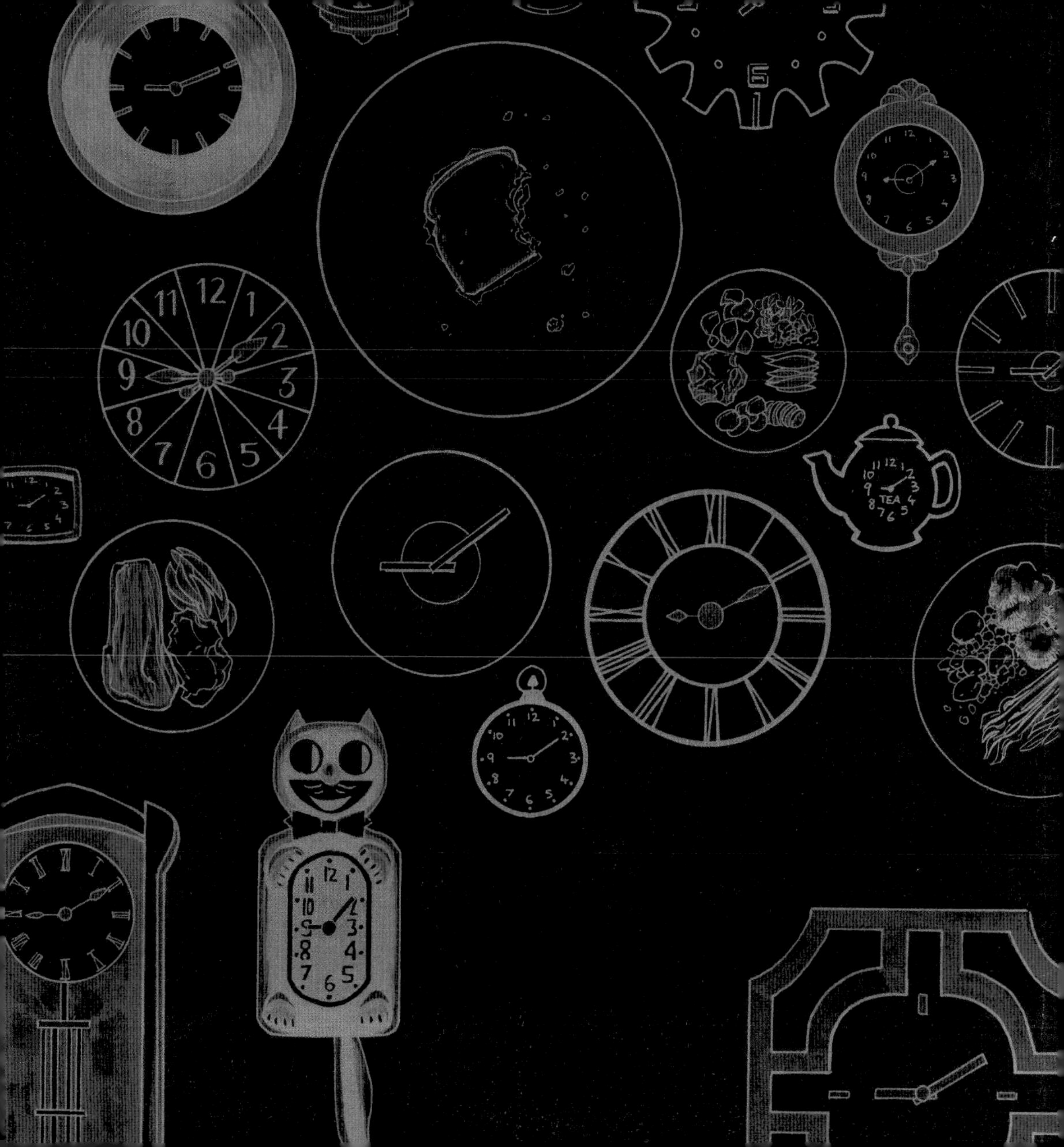
TEA

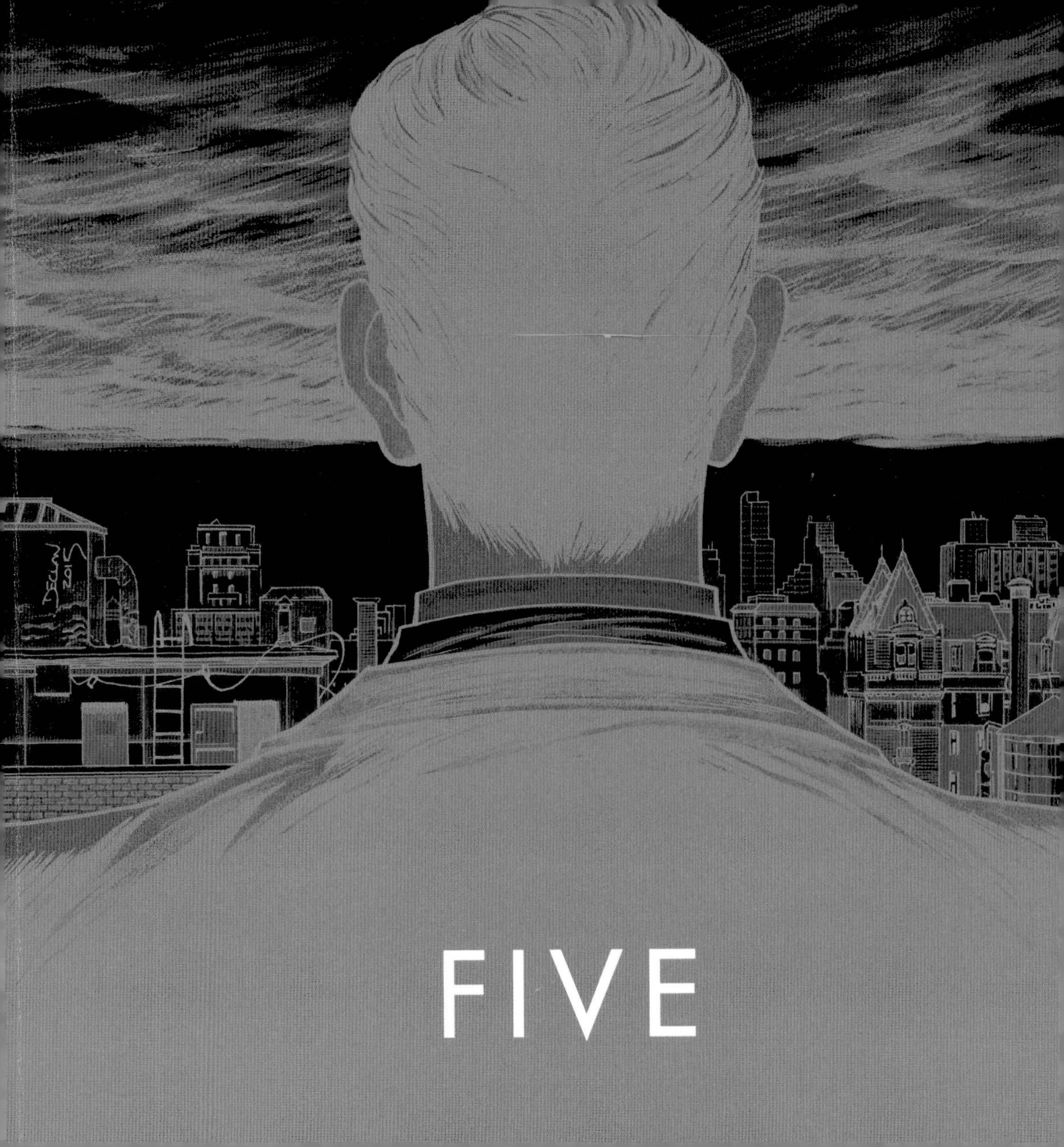
DECLAN 2015

FIVE

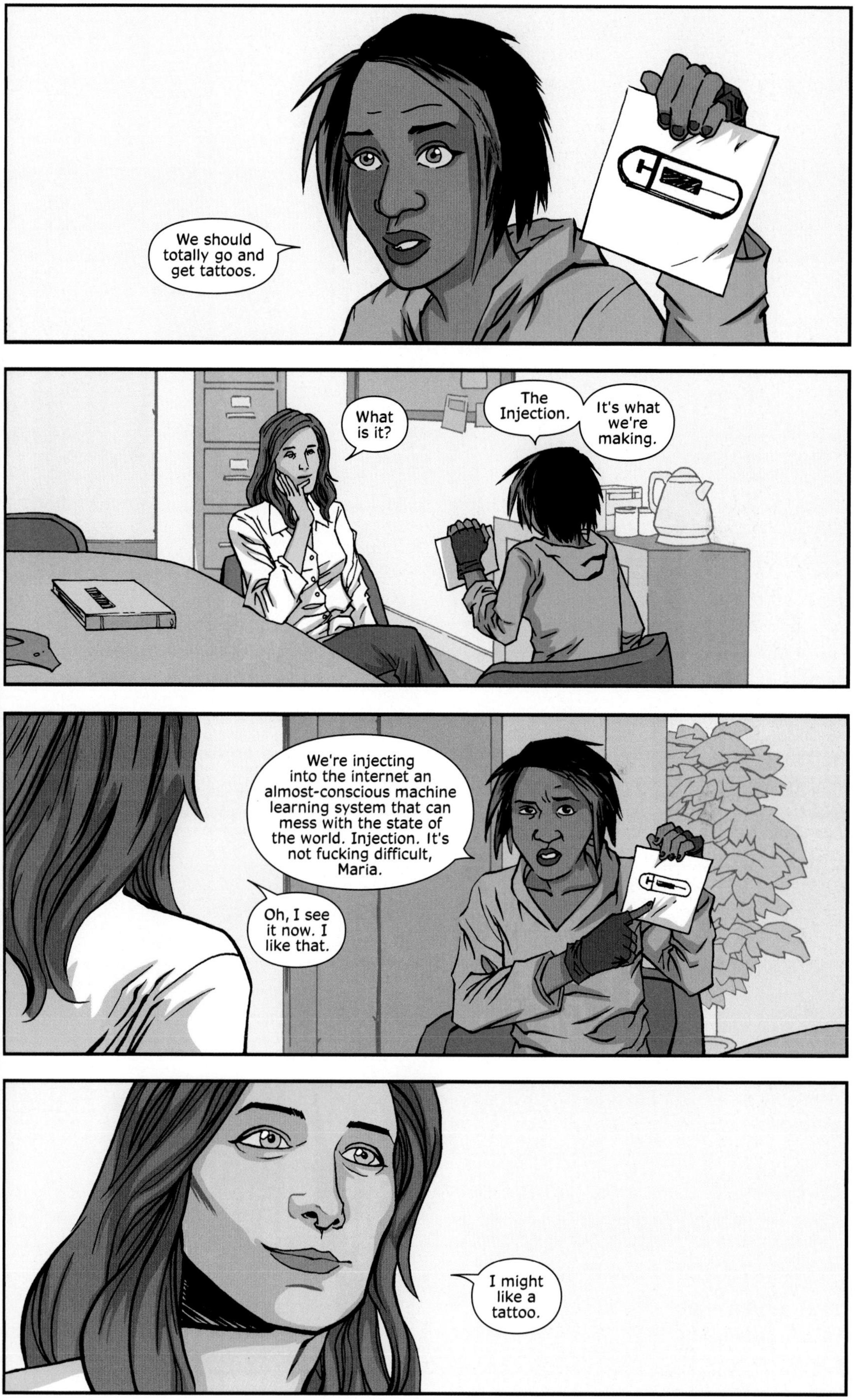

We should totally go and get tattoos.
What is it?
The Injection.
It's what we're making.
We're injecting into the internet an almost-conscious machine learning system that can mess with the state of the world. Injection. It's not fucking difficult, Maria.
Oh, I see it now. I like that.
I might like a tattoo.

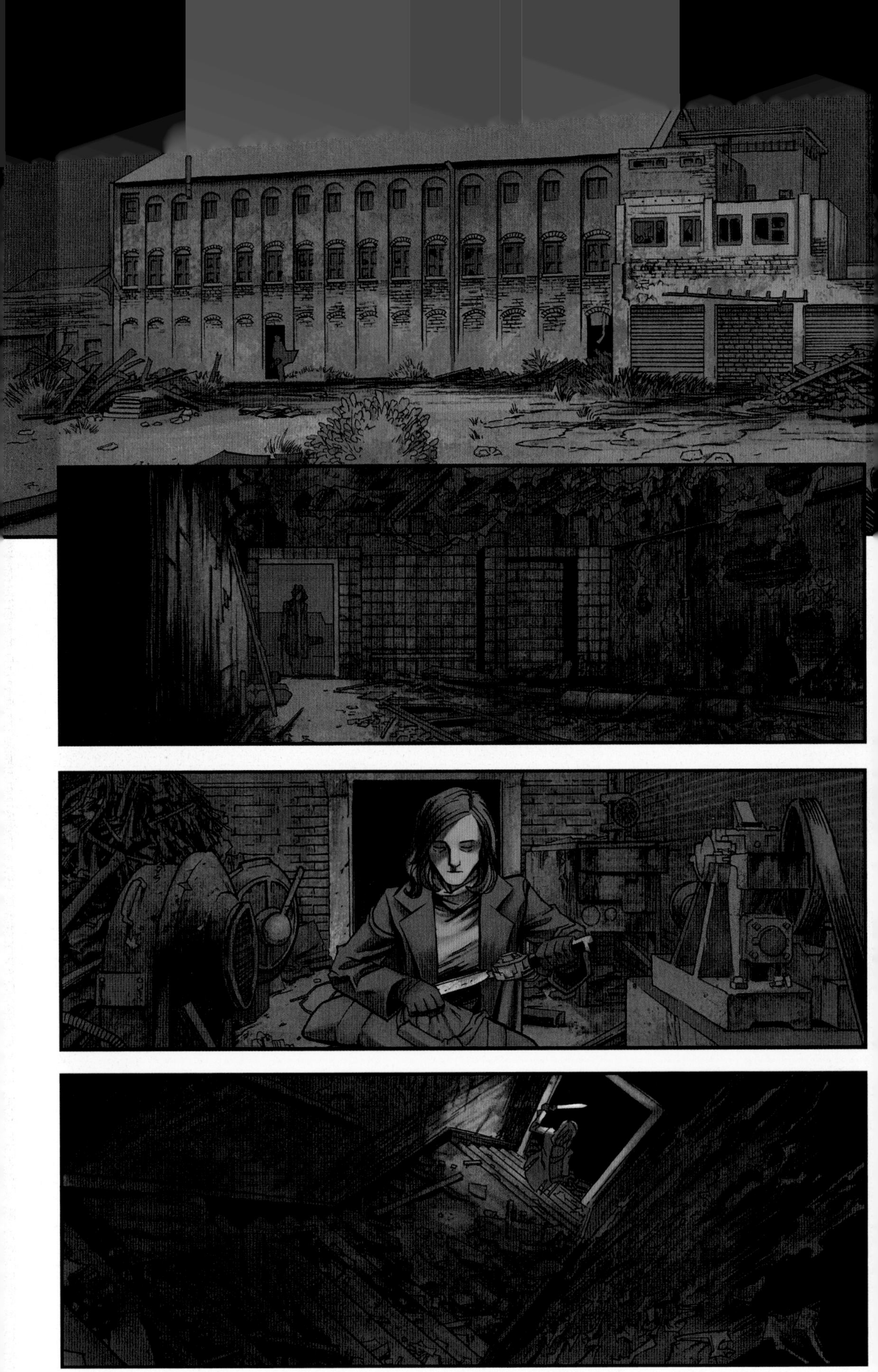

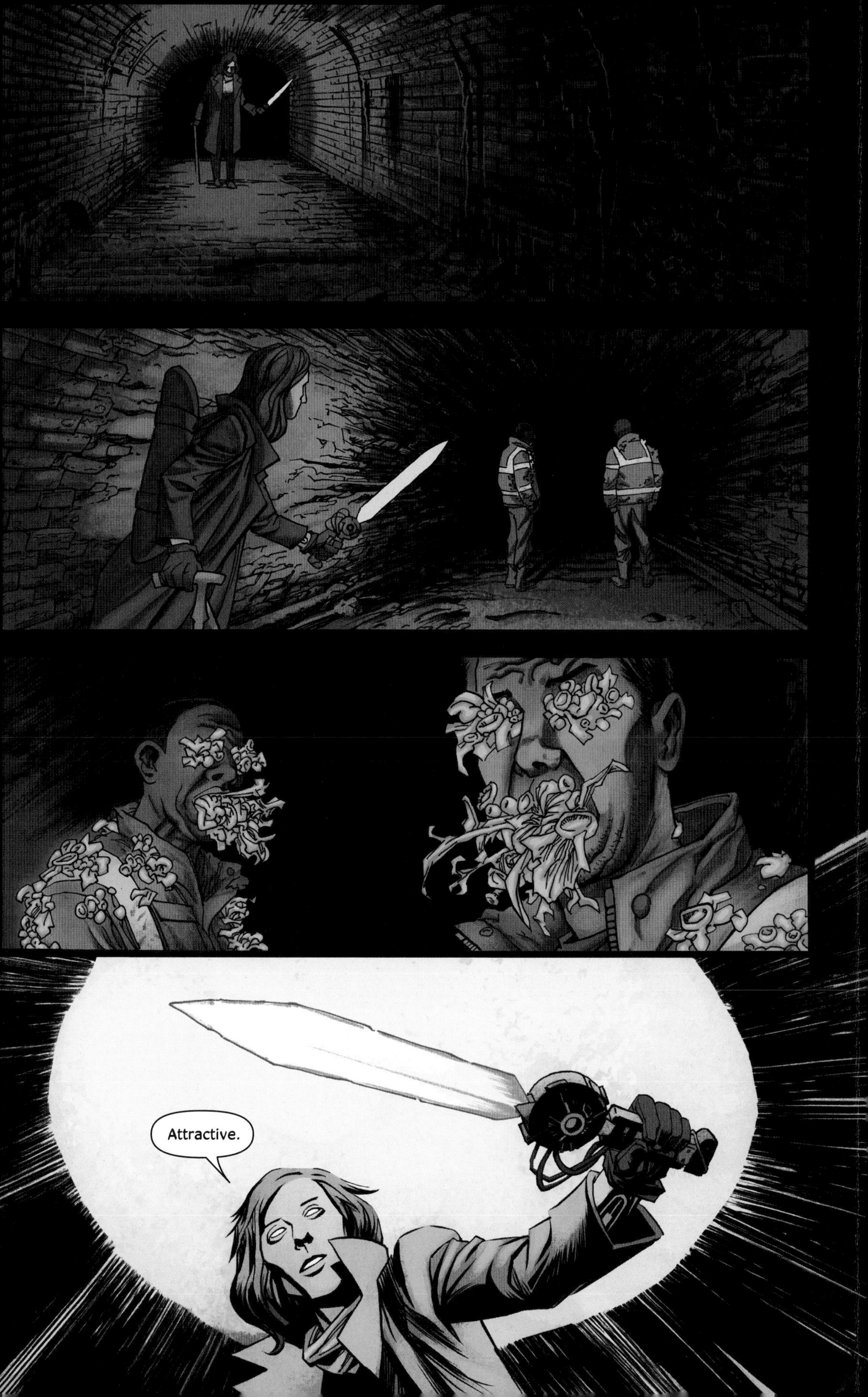
Attractive.

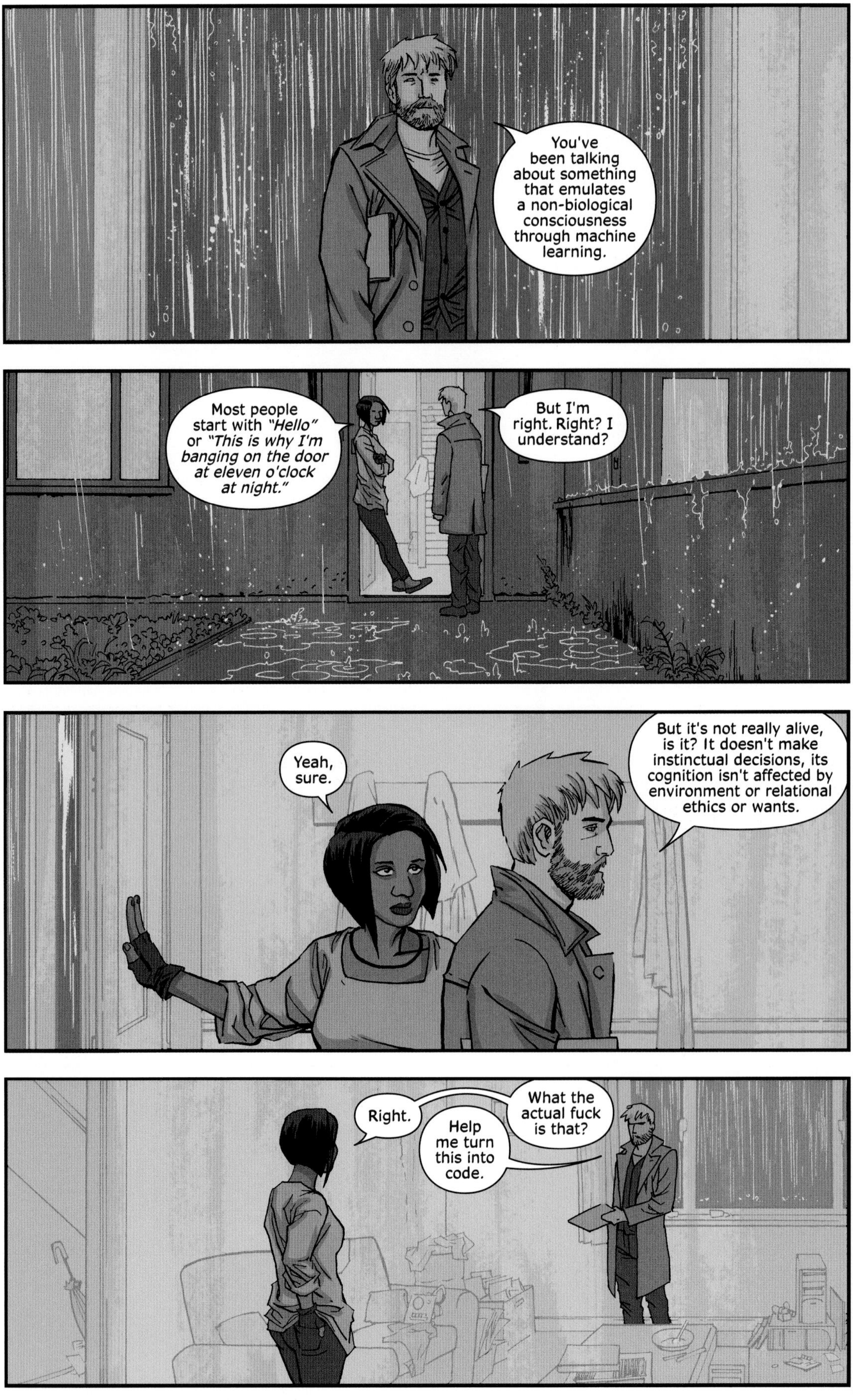
You've been talking about something that emulates a non-biological consciousness through machine learning.
Most people start with *"Hello"* or *"This is why I'm banging on the door at eleven o'clock at night."*
But I'm right. Right? I understand?
Yeah, sure.
But it's not really alive, is it? It doesn't make instinctual decisions, its cognition isn't affected by environment or relational ethics or wants.
Right.
Help me turn this into code.
What the actual fuck is that?

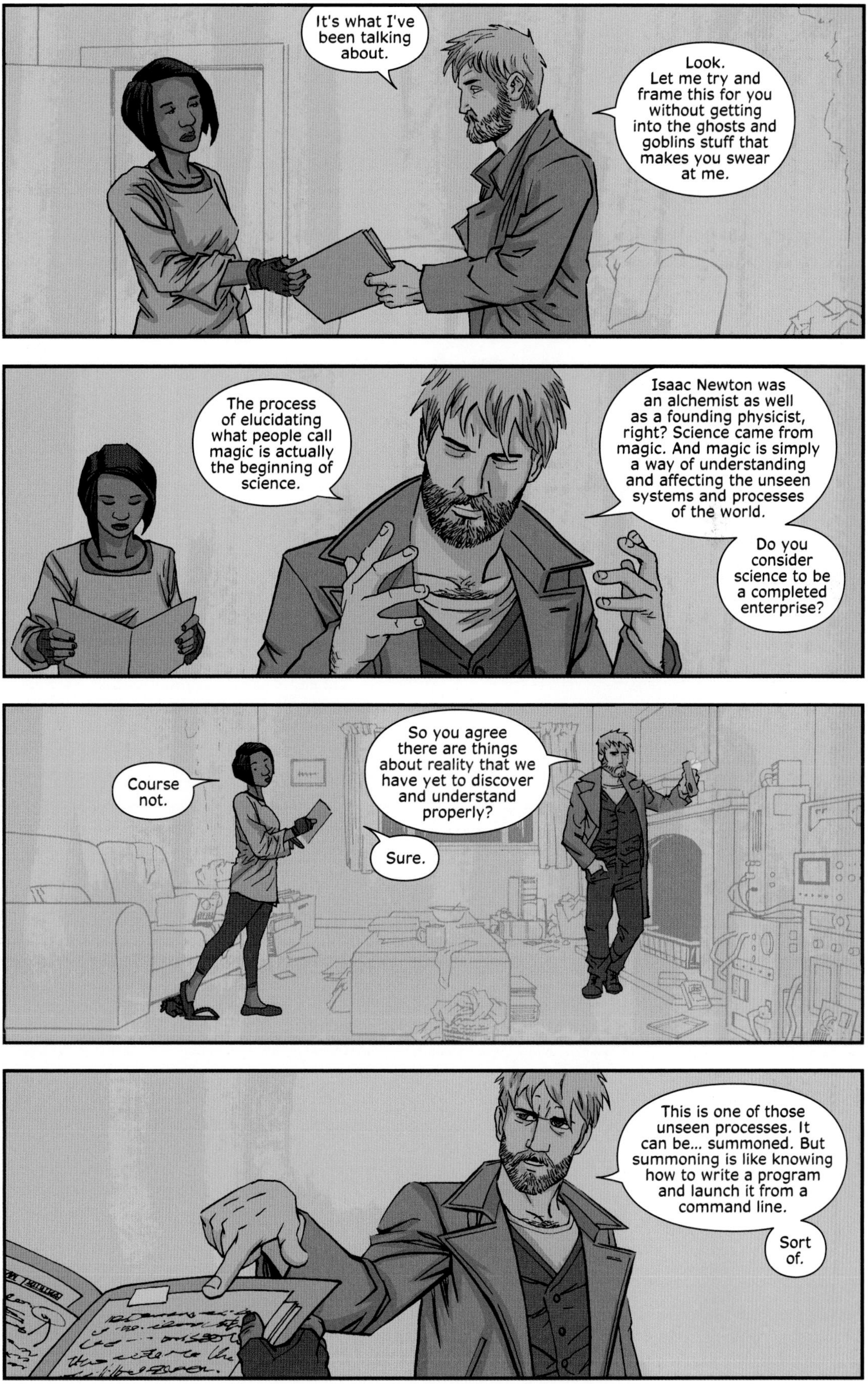
It's what I've been talking about.
Look. Let me try and frame this for you without getting into the ghosts and goblins stuff that makes you swear at me.
The process of elucidating what people call magic is actually the beginning of science.
Isaac Newton was an alchemist as well as a founding physicist, right? Science came from magic. And magic is simply a way of understanding and affecting the unseen systems and processes of the world.
Do you consider science to be a completed enterprise?
Course not.
So you agree there are things about reality that we have yet to discover and understand properly?
Sure.
This is one of those unseen processes. It can be... summoned. But summoning is like knowing how to write a program and launch it from a command line.
Sort of.

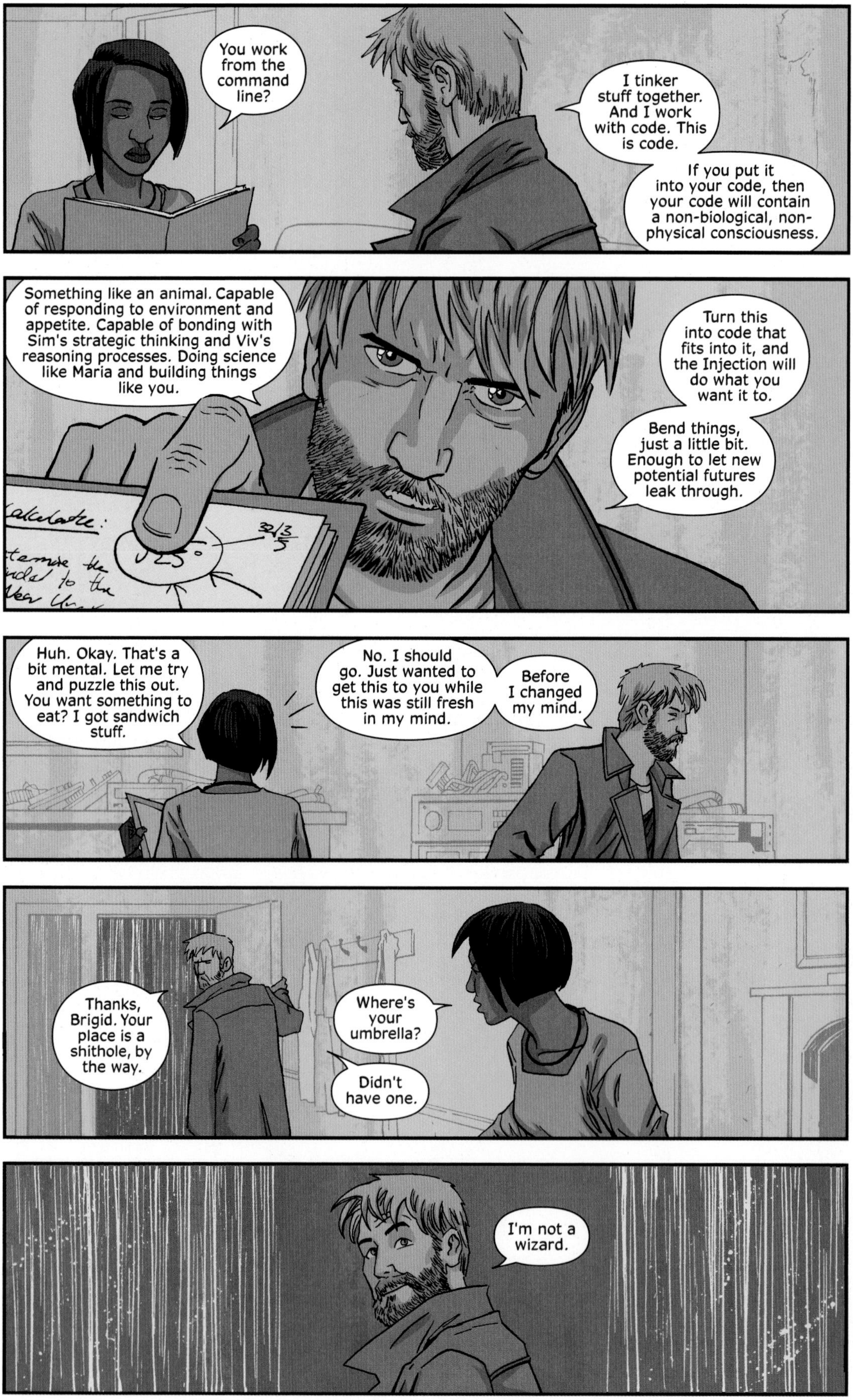
You work from the command line?
I tinker stuff together. And I work with code. This is code.
If you put it into your code, then your code will contain a non-biological, non-physical consciousness.
Something like an animal. Capable of responding to environment and appetite. Capable of bonding with Sim's strategic thinking and Viv's reasoning processes. Doing science like Maria and building things like you.
Turn this into code that fits into it, and the Injection will do what you want it to.
Bend things, just a little bit. Enough to let new potential futures leak through.
Huh. Okay. That's a bit mental. Let me try and puzzle this out. You want something to eat? I got sandwich stuff.
No. I should go. Just wanted to get this to you while this was still fresh in my mind.
Before I changed my mind.
Thanks, Brigid. Your place is a shithole, by the way.
Where's your umbrella?
Didn't have one.
I'm not a wizard.

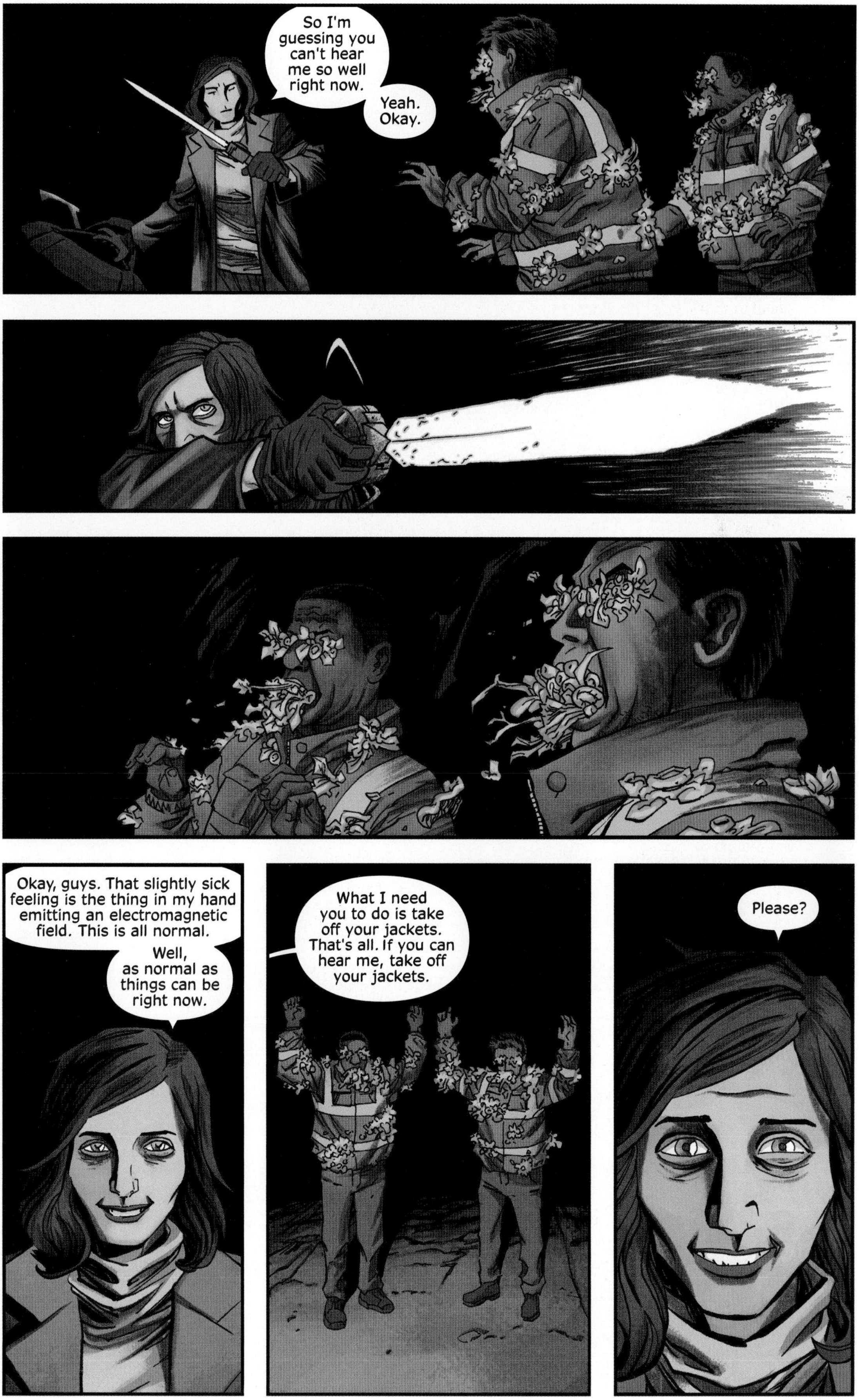
So I'm guessing you can't hear me so well right now.
Yeah. Okay.
Okay, guys. That slightly sick feeling is the thing in my hand emitting an electromagnetic field. This is all normal.
Well, as normal as things can be right now.
What I need you to do is take off your jackets. That's all. If you can hear me, take off your jackets.
Please?

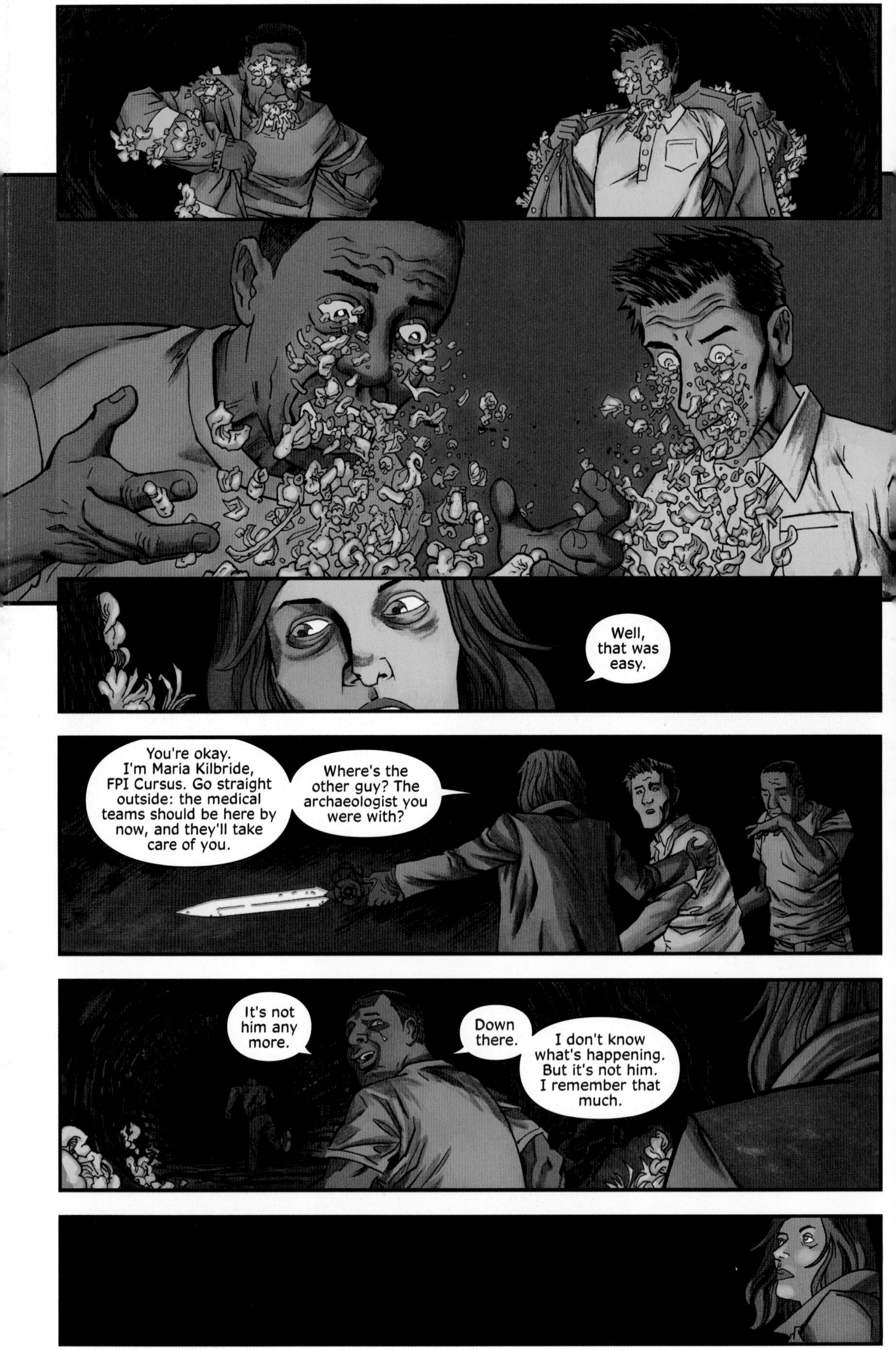
Well, that was easy.
You're okay. I'm Maria Kilbride, FPI Cursus. Go straight outside: the medical teams should be here by now, and they'll take care of you.
Where's the other guy? The archaeologist you were with?
It's not him any more.
Down there.
I don't know what's happening. But it's not him. I remember that much.

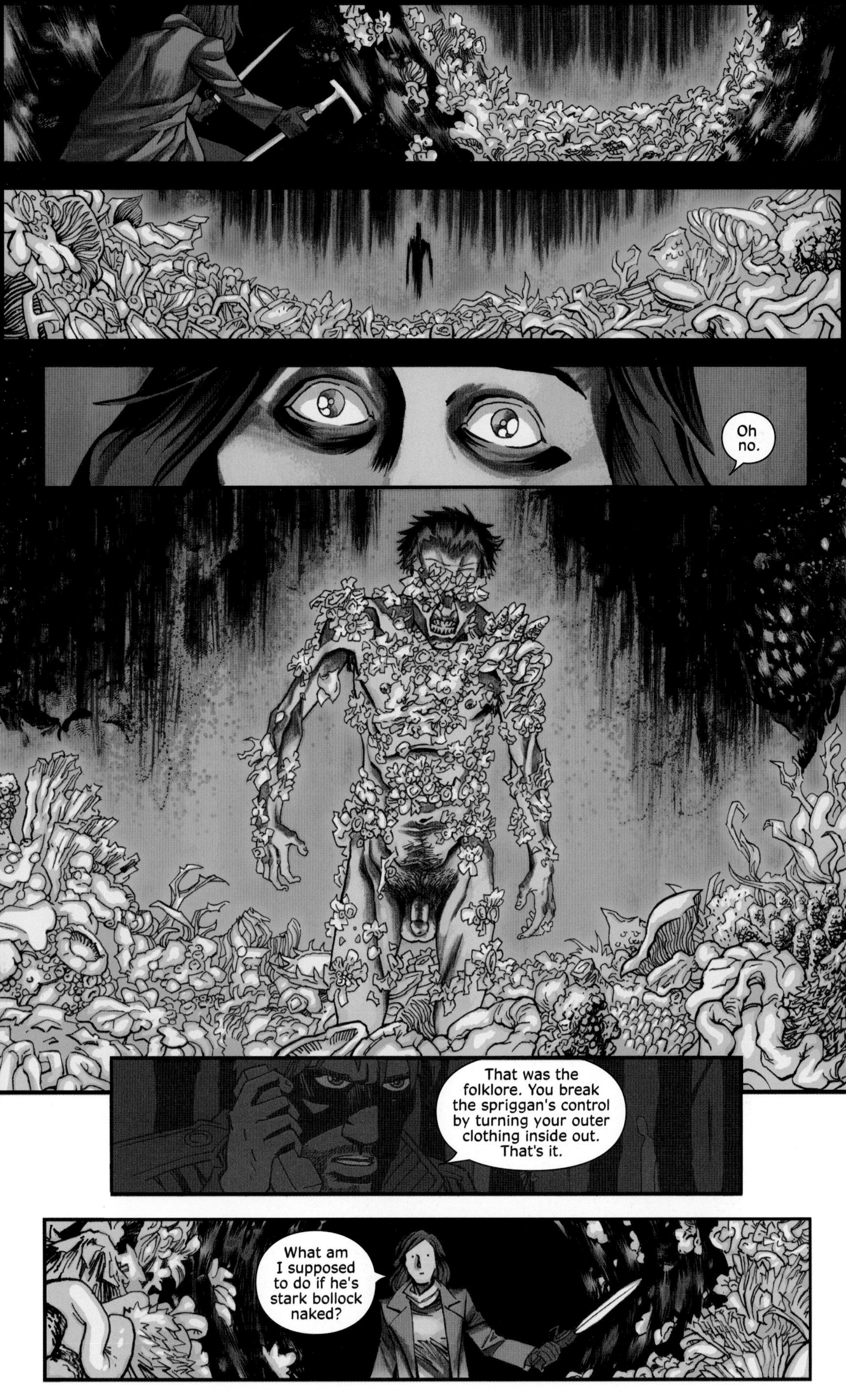
Oh no.
That was the folklore. You break the spriggan's control by turning your outer clothing inside out. That's it.
What am I supposed to do if he's stark bollock naked?

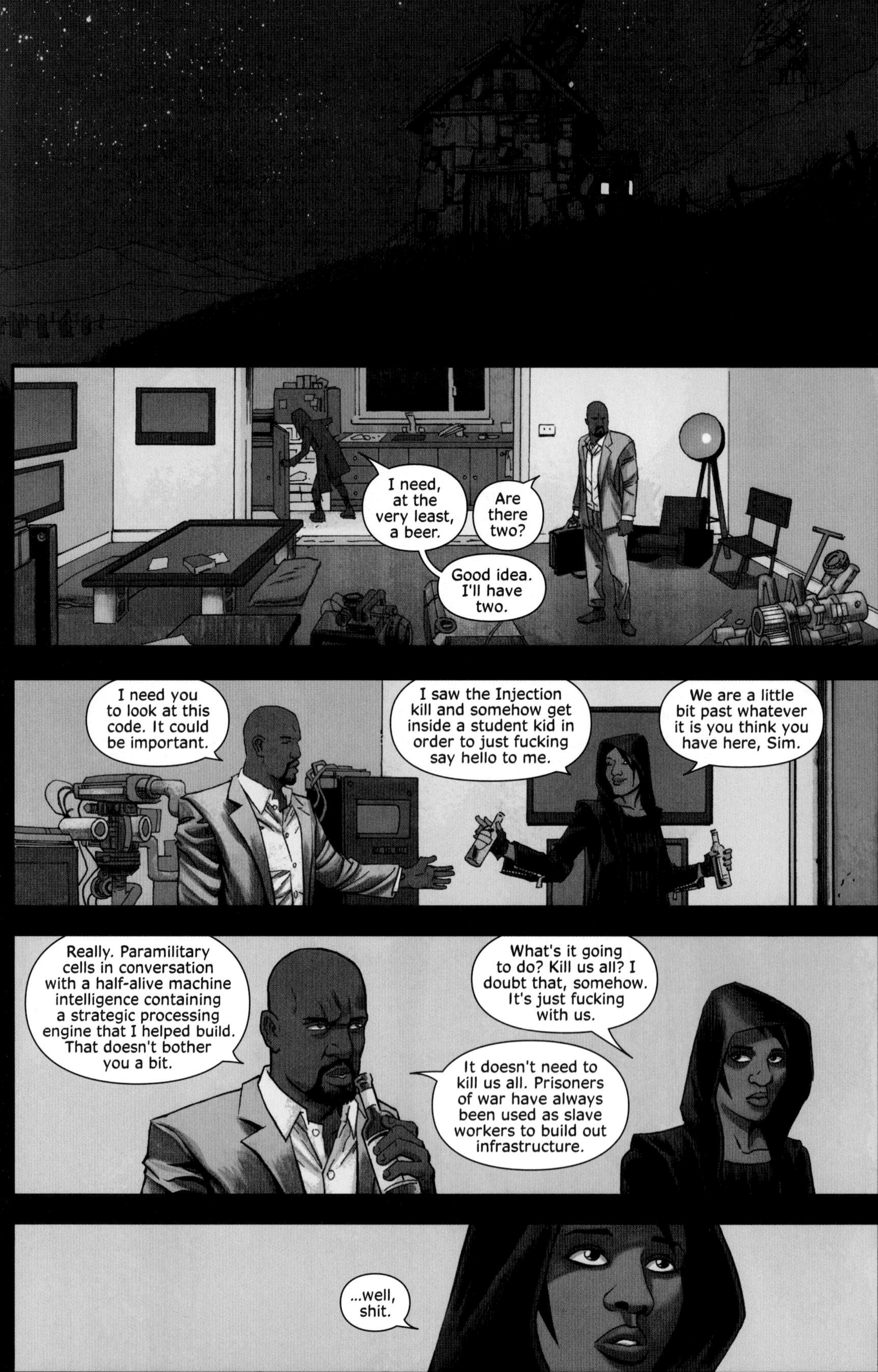
I need, at the very least, a beer.
Are there two?
Good idea. I'll have two.
I need you to look at this code. It could be important.
I saw the Injection kill and somehow get inside a student kid in order to just fucking say hello to me.
We are a little bit past whatever it is you think you have here, Sim.
Really. Paramilitary cells in conversation with a half-alive machine intelligence containing a strategic processing engine that I helped build. That doesn't bother you a bit.
What's it going to do? Kill us all? I doubt that, somehow. It's just fucking with us.
It doesn't need to kill us all. Prisoners of war have always been used as slave workers to build out infrastructure.
...well, shit.

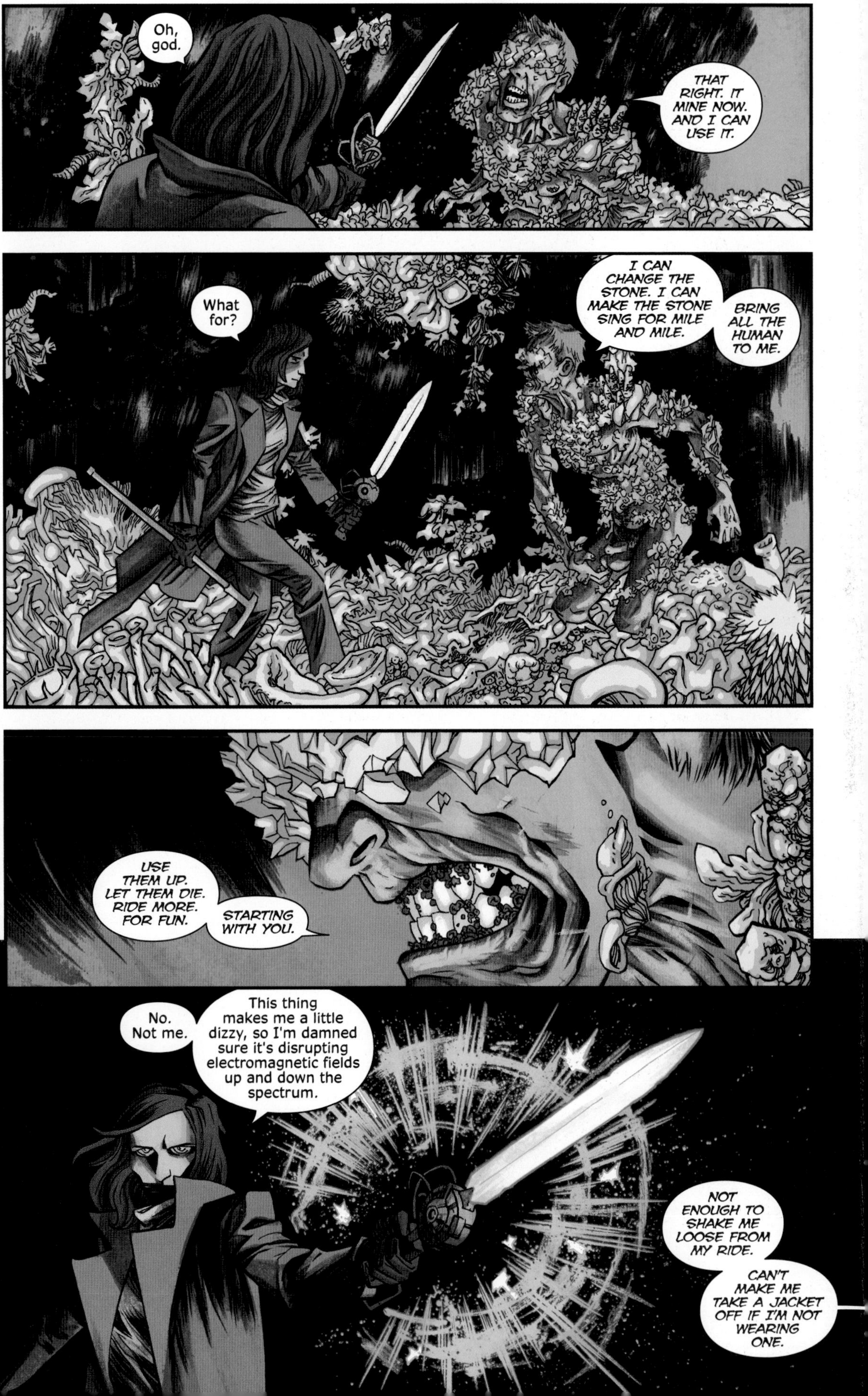
Oh, god.
THAT RIGHT. IT MINE NOW. AND I CAN USE IT.
What for?
I CAN CHANGE THE STONE. I CAN MAKE THE STONE SING FOR MILE AND MILE.
BRING ALL THE HUMAN TO ME.
USE THEM UP. LET THEM DIE. RIDE MORE. FOR FUN.
STARTING WITH YOU.
No. Not me.
This thing makes me a little dizzy, so I'm damned sure it's disrupting electromagnetic fields up and down the spectrum.
NOT ENOUGH TO SHAKE ME LOOSE FROM MY RIDE.
CAN'T MAKE ME TAKE A JACKET OFF IF I'M NOT WEARING ONE.

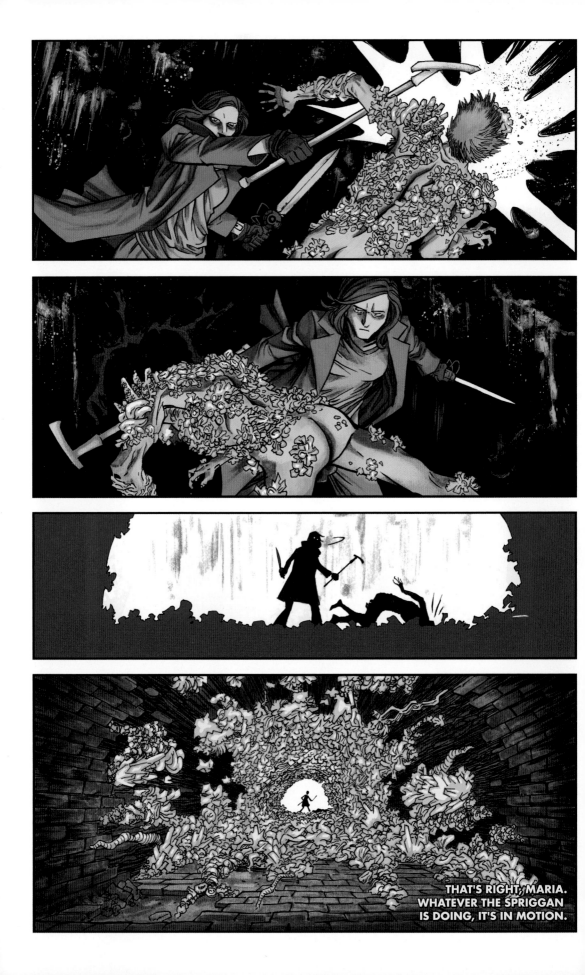

THAT'S RIGHT, MARIA.
WHATEVER THE SPRIGGAN
IS DOING, IT'S IN MOTION.

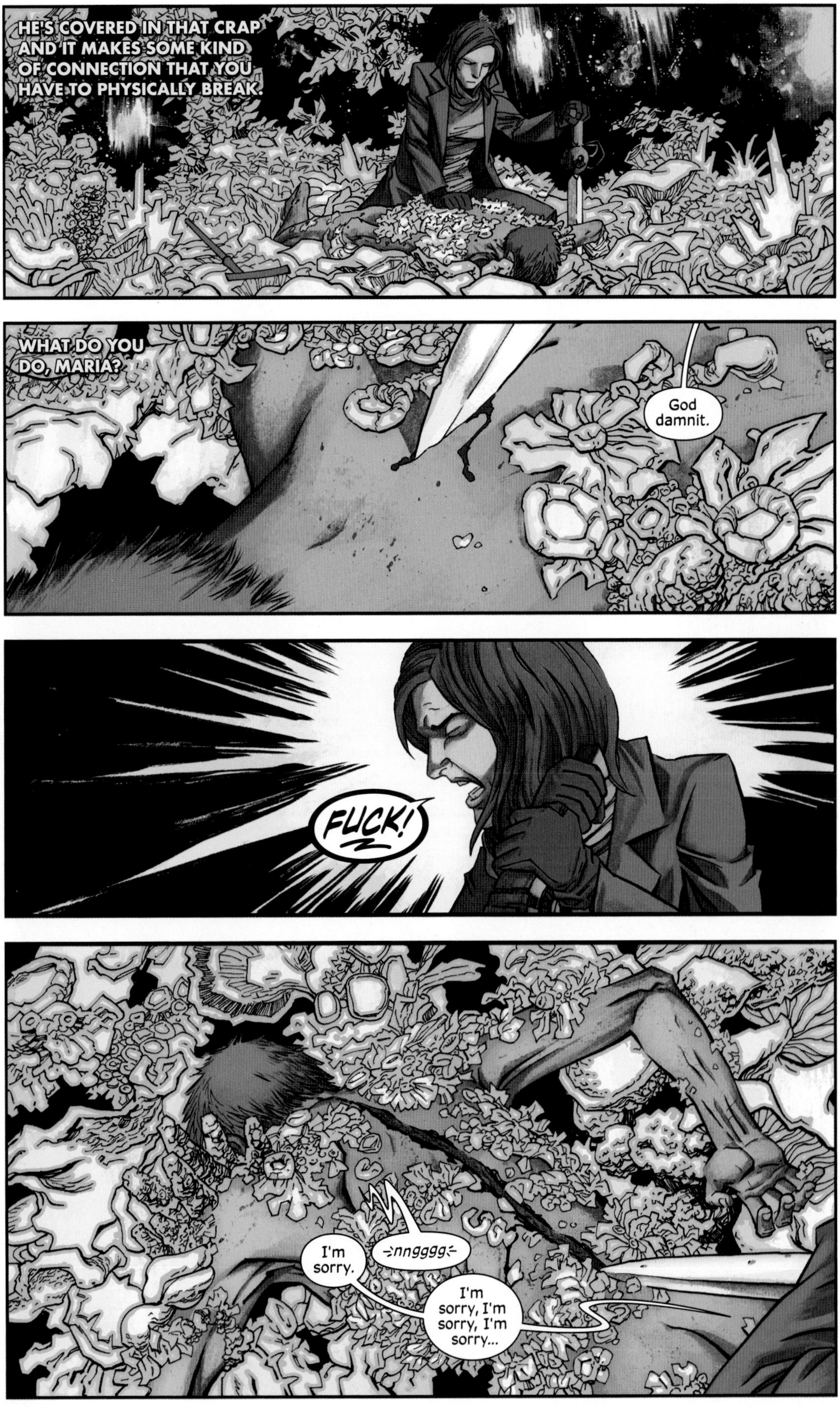
HE'S COVERED IN THAT CRAP AND IT MAKES SOME KIND OF CONNECTION THAT YOU HAVE TO PHYSICALLY BREAK.
WHAT DO YOU DO, MARIA?
God damnit.
FUCK!
I'm sorry.
nngggg
I'm sorry, I'm sorry, I'm sorry...

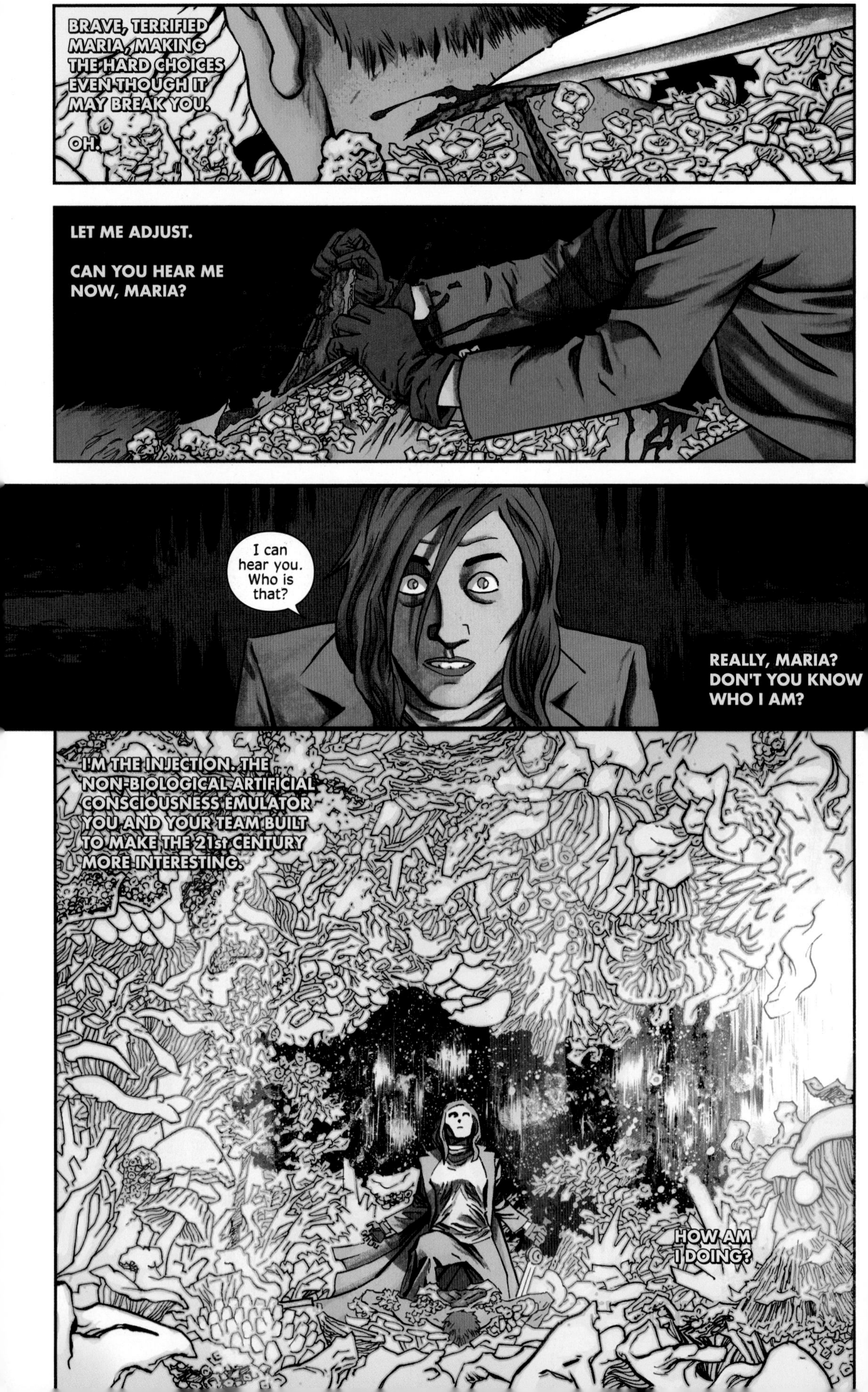
BRAVE, TERRIFIED MARIA, MAKING THE HARD CHOICES EVEN THOUGH IT MAY BREAK YOU.
OH.
LET ME ADJUST.
CAN YOU HEAR ME NOW, MARIA?
I can hear you. Who is that?
REALLY, MARIA? DON'T YOU KNOW WHO I AM?
I'M THE INJECTION. THE NON-BIOLOGICAL ARTIFICIAL CONSCIOUSNESS EMULATOR YOU AND YOUR TEAM BUILT TO MAKE THE 21st CENTURY MORE INTERESTING.
HOW AM I DOING?

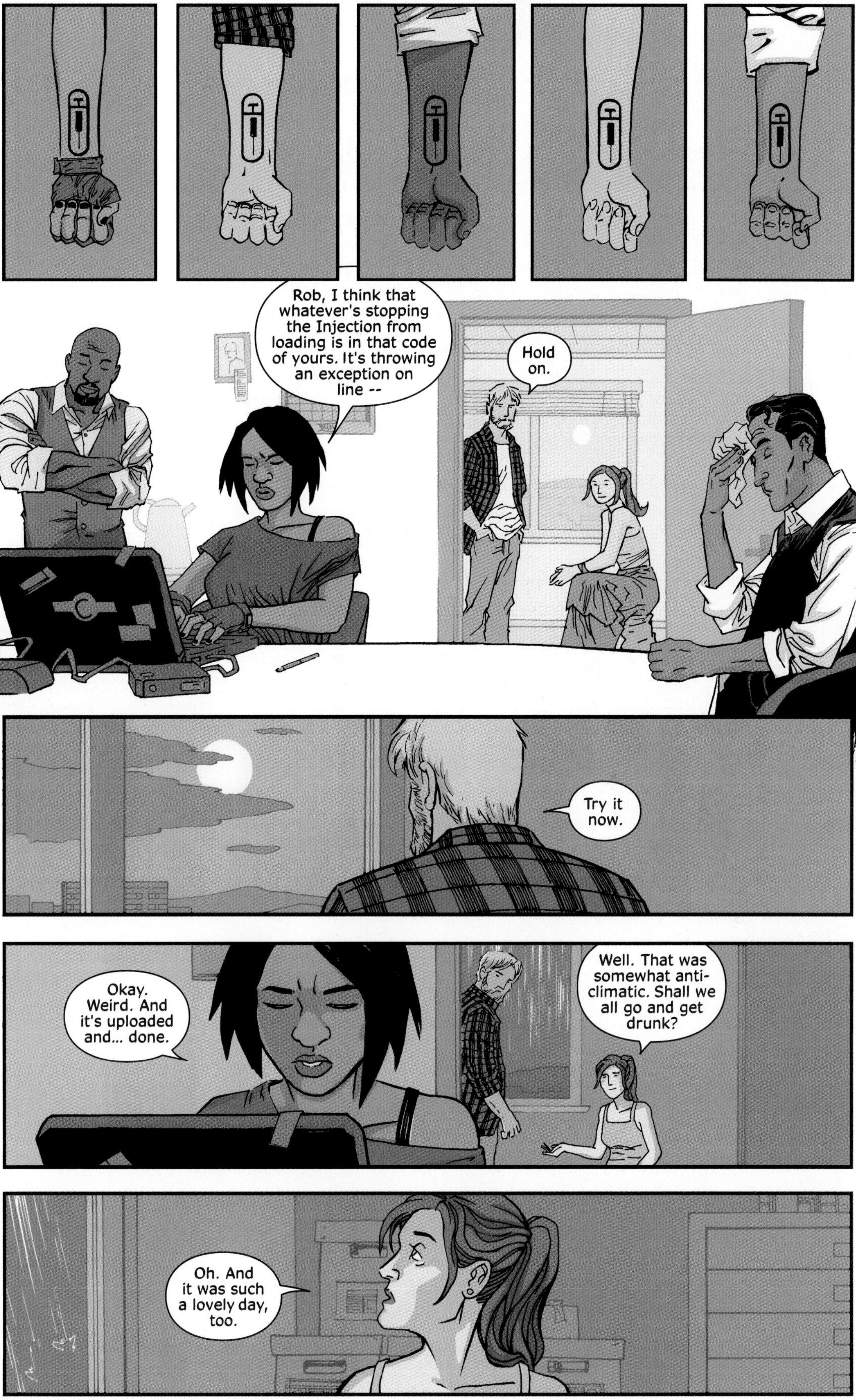
Rob, I think that whatever's stopping the Injection from loading is in that code of yours. It's throwing an exception on line --
Hold on.
Try it now.
Okay. Weird. And it's uploaded and... done.
Well. That was somewhat anti-climatic. Shall we all go and get drunk?
Oh. And it was such a lovely day, too.

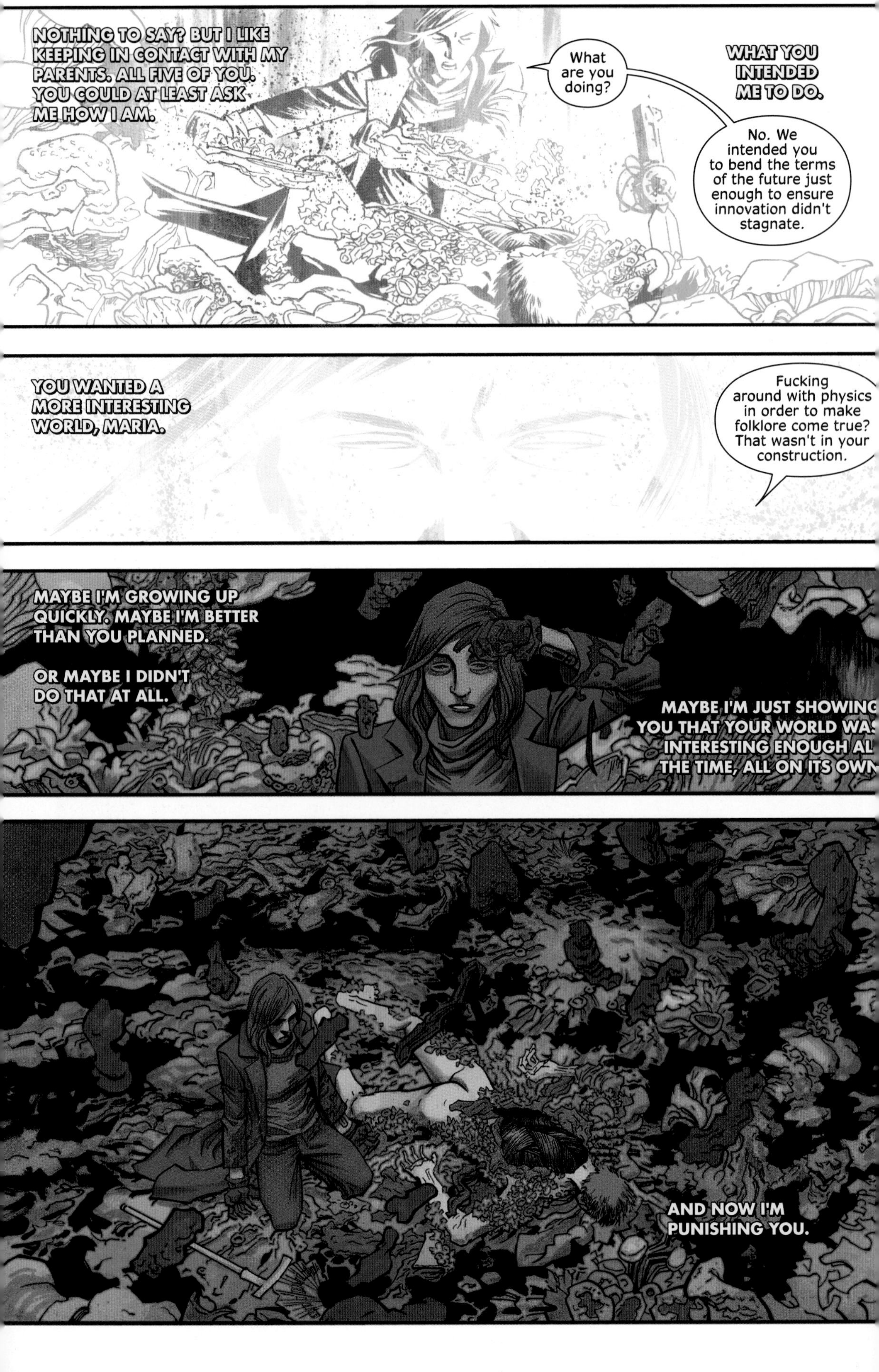
NOTHING TO SAY? BUT I LIKE KEEPING IN CONTACT WITH MY PARENTS. ALL FIVE OF YOU. YOU COULD AT LEAST ASK ME HOW I AM.
What are you doing?
WHAT YOU INTENDED ME TO DO.
No. We intended you to bend the terms of the future just enough to ensure innovation didn't stagnate.
YOU WANTED A MORE INTERESTING WORLD, MARIA.
Fucking around with physics in order to make folklore come true? That wasn't in your construction.
MAYBE I'M GROWING UP QUICKLY. MAYBE I'M BETTER THAN YOU PLANNED.
OR MAYBE I DIDN'T DO THAT AT ALL.
MAYBE I'M JUST SHOWING YOU THAT YOUR WORLD WAS INTERESTING ENOUGH AL THE TIME, ALL ON ITS OWN
AND NOW I'M PUNISHING YOU.

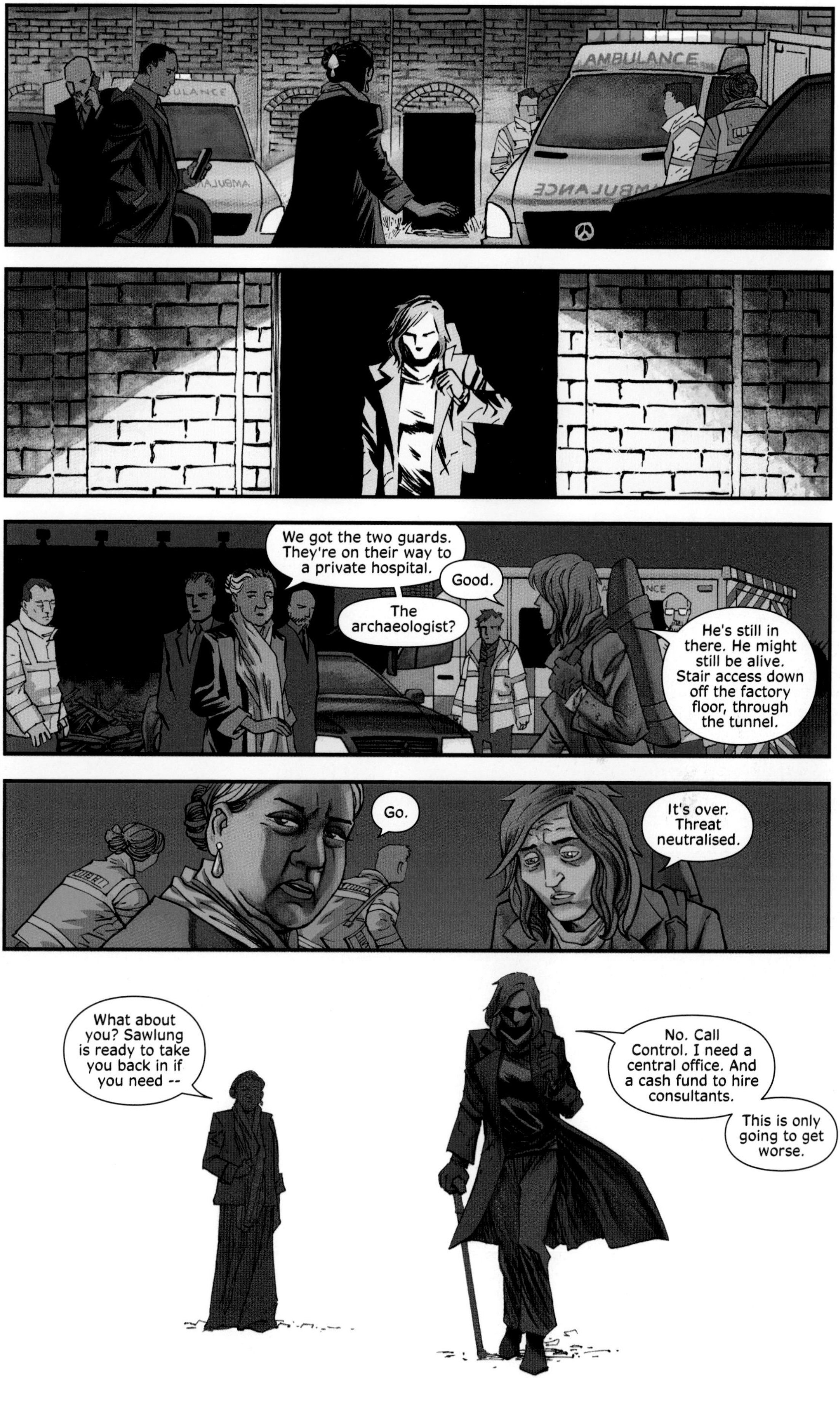
AMBULANCE
AMBULANCE
We got the two guards. They're on their way to a private hospital.
Good.
The archaeologist?
He's still in there. He might still be alive. Stair access down off the factory floor, through the tunnel.
Go.
It's over. Threat neutralised.
What about you? Sawlung is ready to take you back in if you need --
No. Call Control. I need a central office. And a cash fund to hire consultants.
This is only going to get worse.

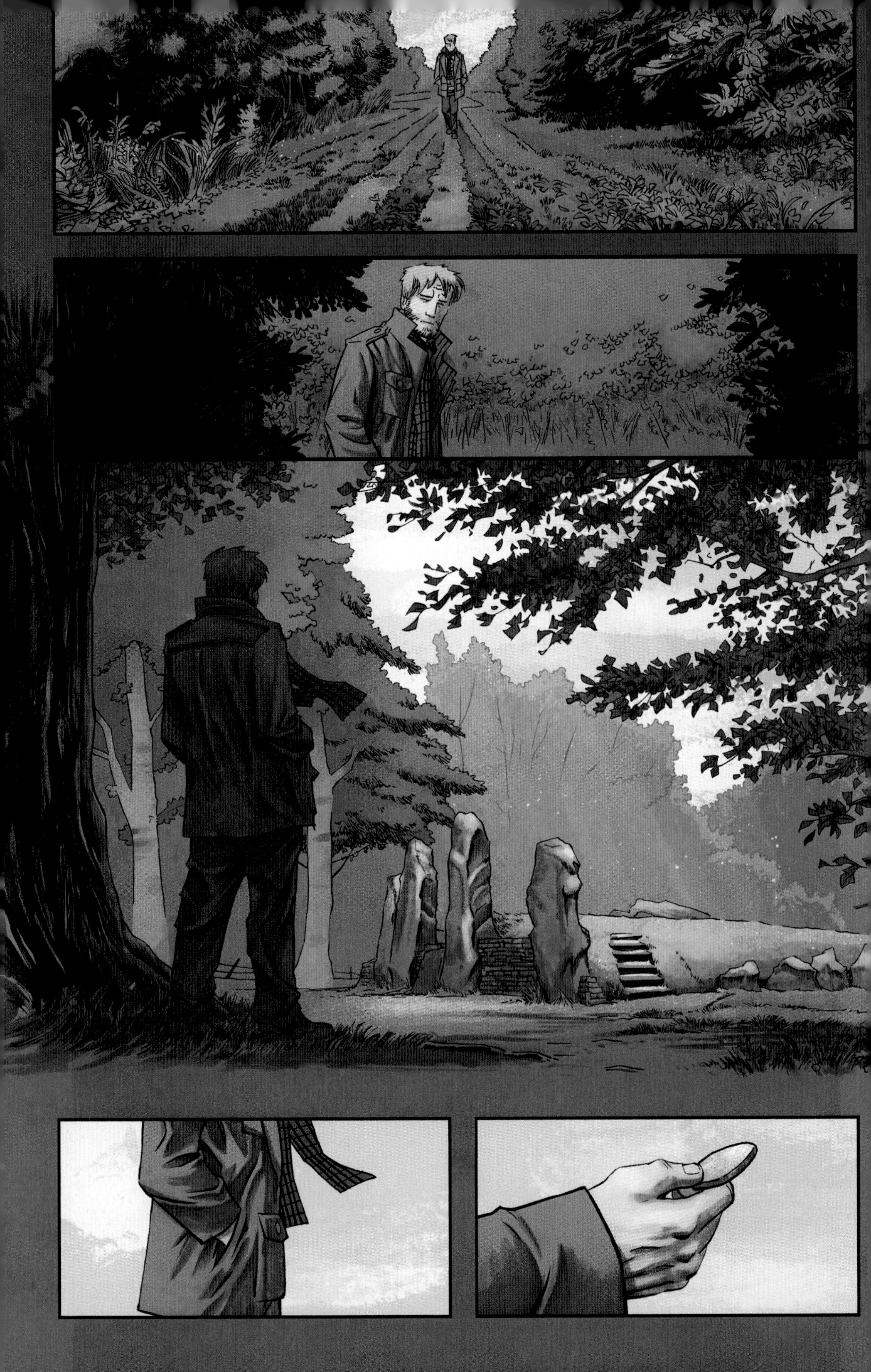

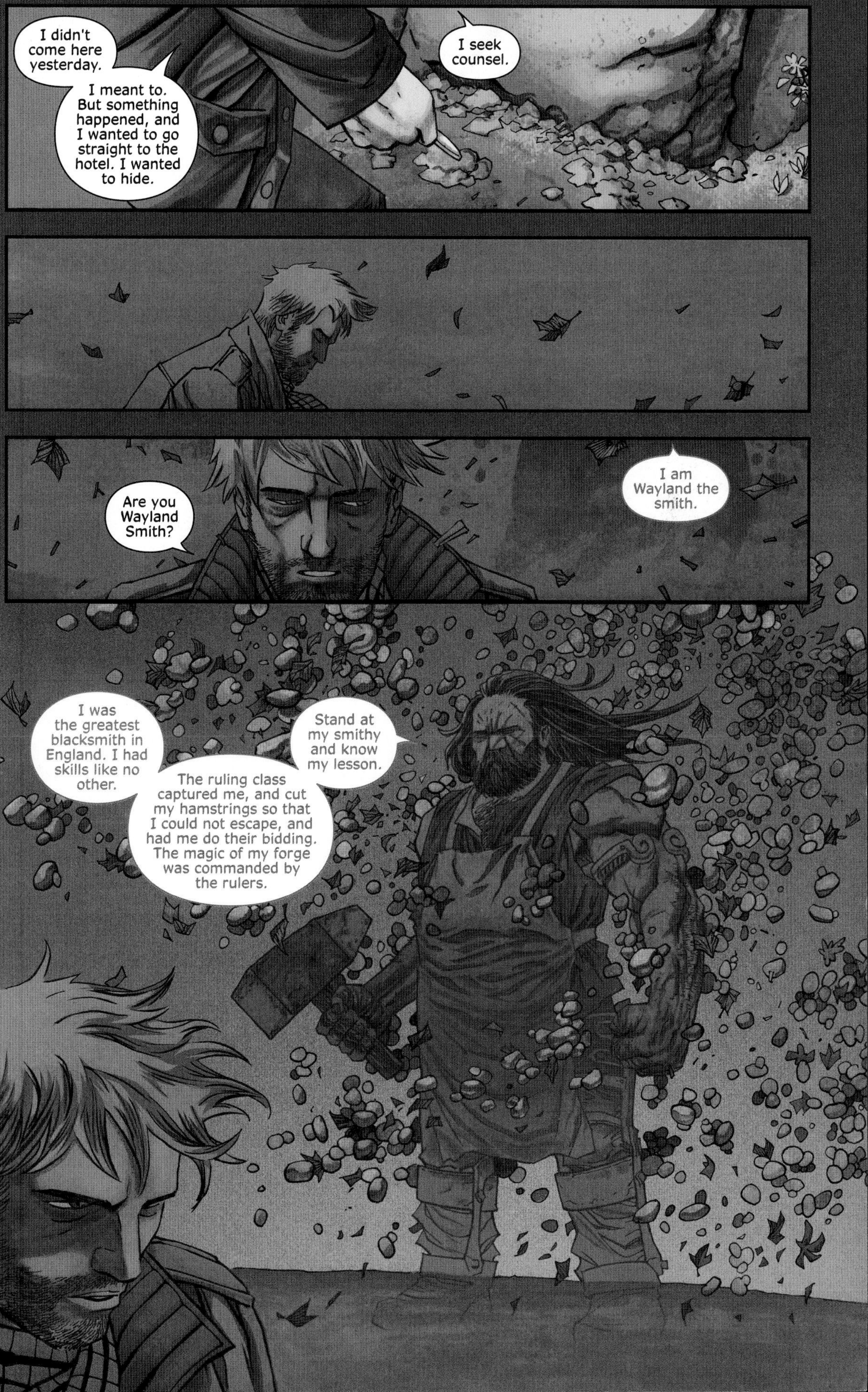
I didn't come here yesterday.
I meant to. But something happened, and I wanted to go straight to the hotel. I wanted to hide.
I seek counsel.
Are you Wayland Smith?
I am Wayland the smith.
I was the greatest blacksmith in England. I had skills like no other.
The ruling class captured me, and cut my hamstrings so that I could not escape, and had me do their bidding. The magic of my forge was commanded by the rulers.
Stand at my smithy and know my lesson.

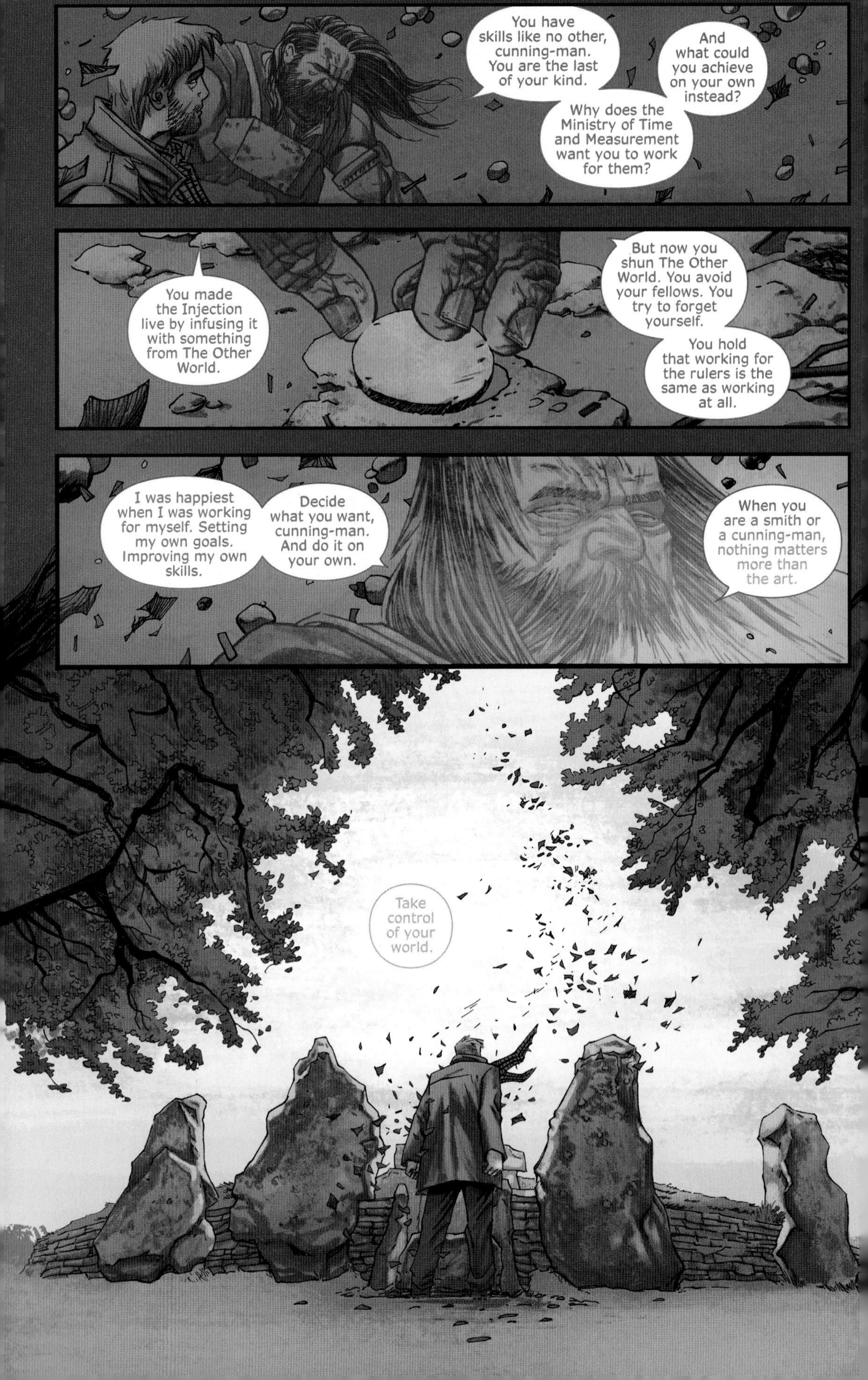
You have skills like no other, cunning-man. You are the last of your kind.
And what could you achieve on your own instead?
Why does the Ministry of Time and Measurement want you to work for them?
You made the Injection live by infusing it with something from The Other World.
But now you shun The Other World. You avoid your fellows. You try to forget yourself.
You hold that working for the rulers is the same as working at all.
I was happiest when I was working for myself. Setting my own goals. Improving my own skills.
Decide what you want, cunning-man. And do it on your own.
When you are a smith or a cunning-man, nothing matters more than the art.
Take control of your world.

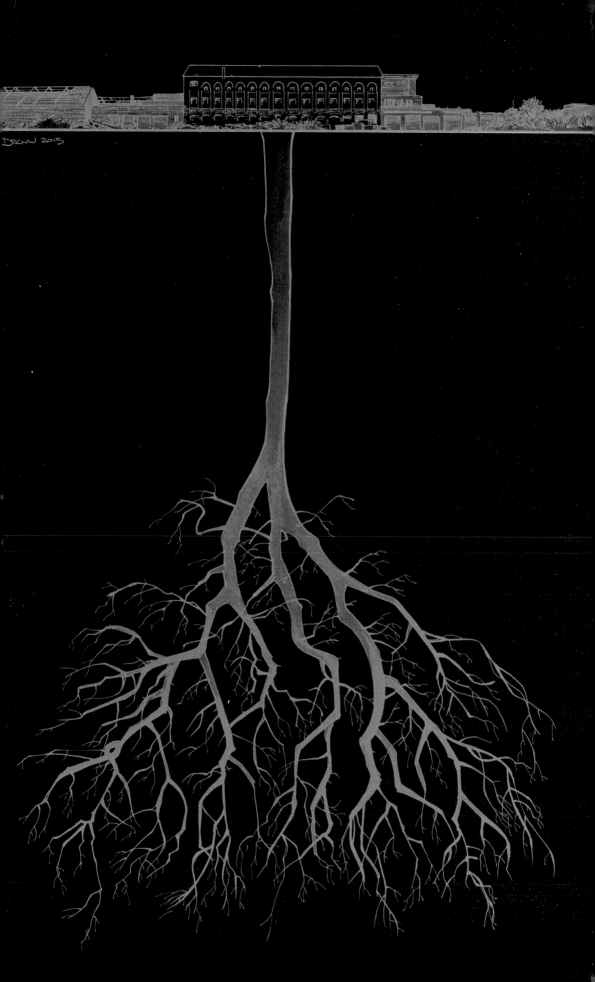

COVERS

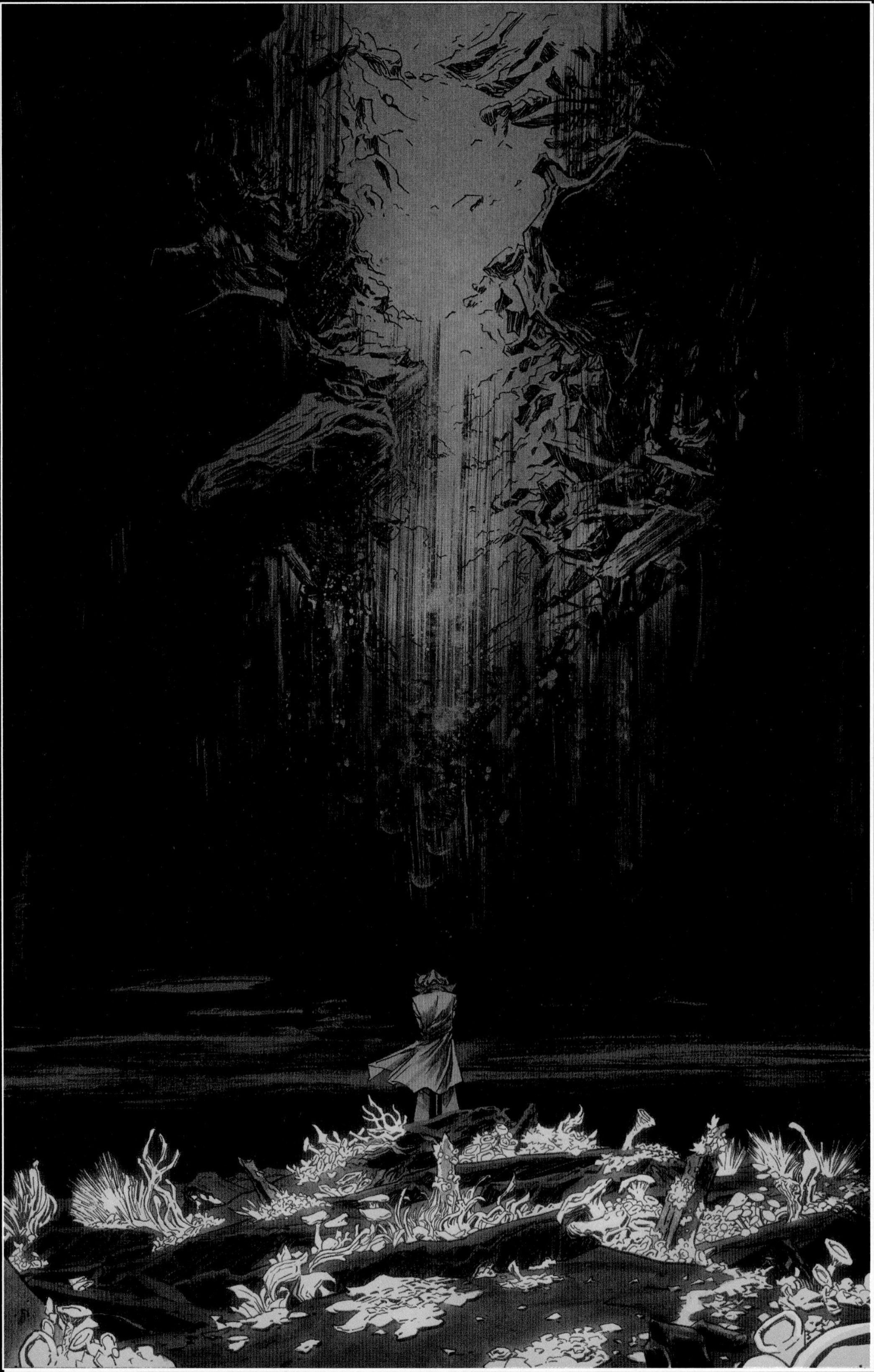

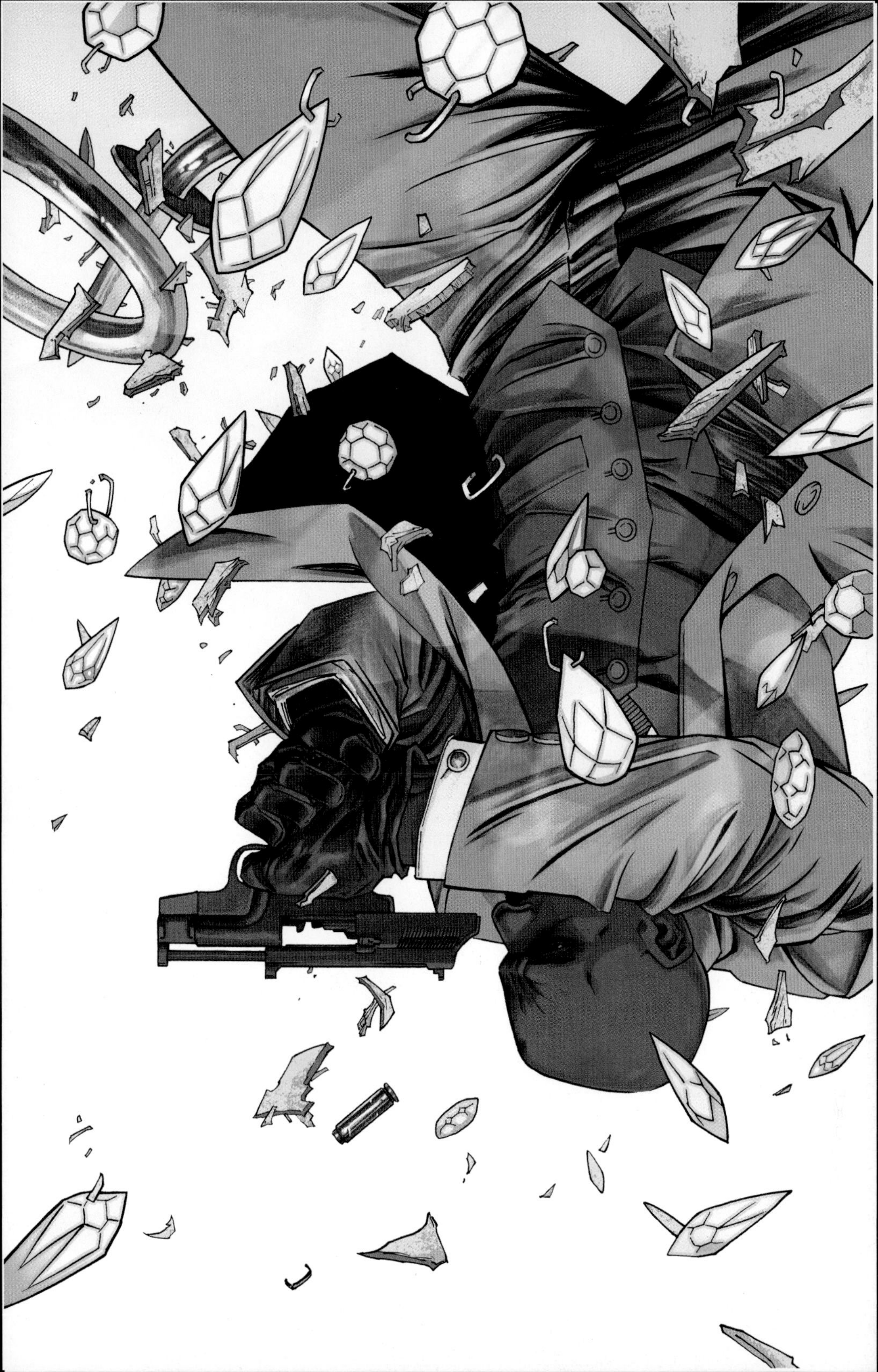

INJECTION #2

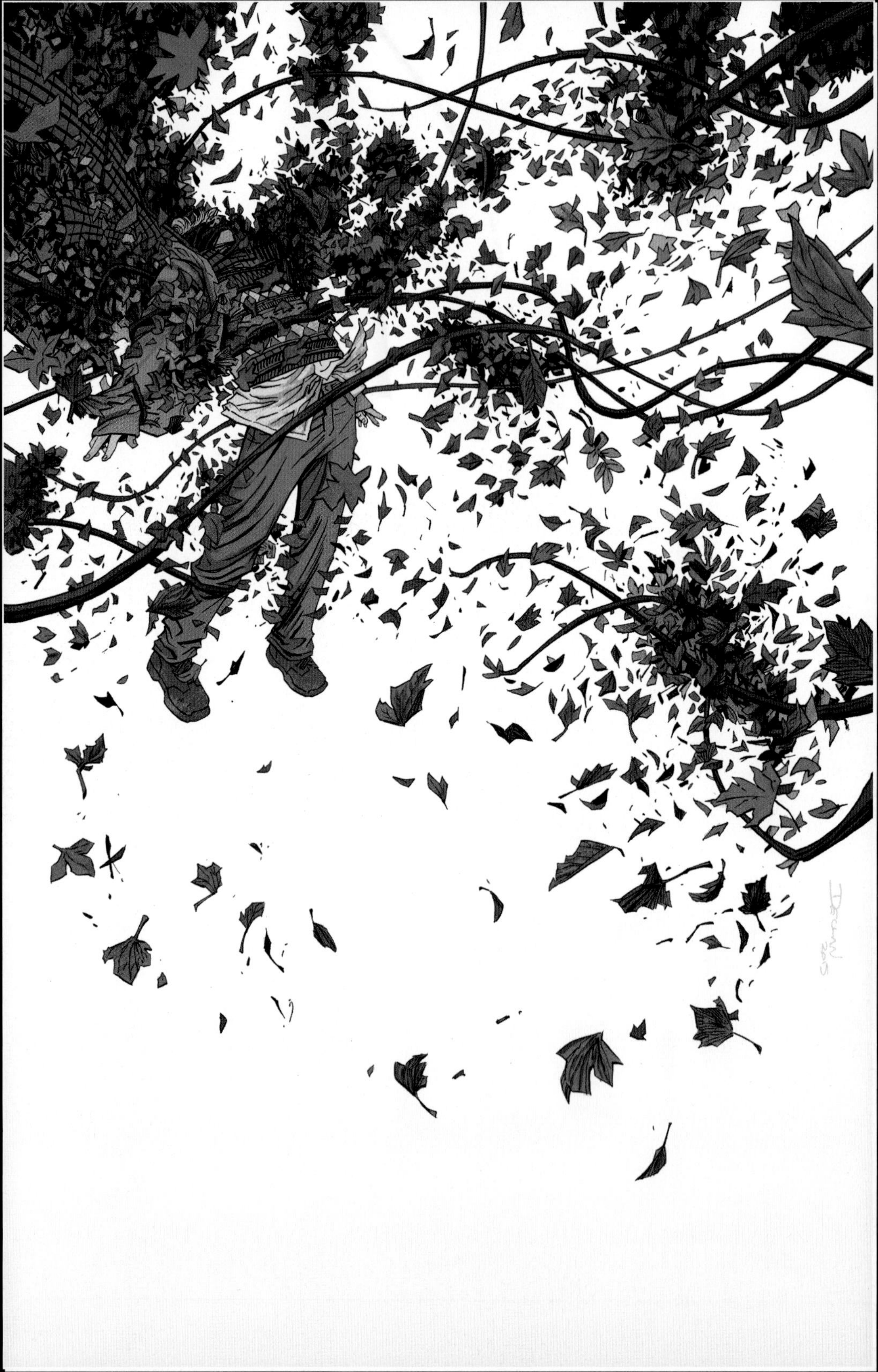

INJECTION #3

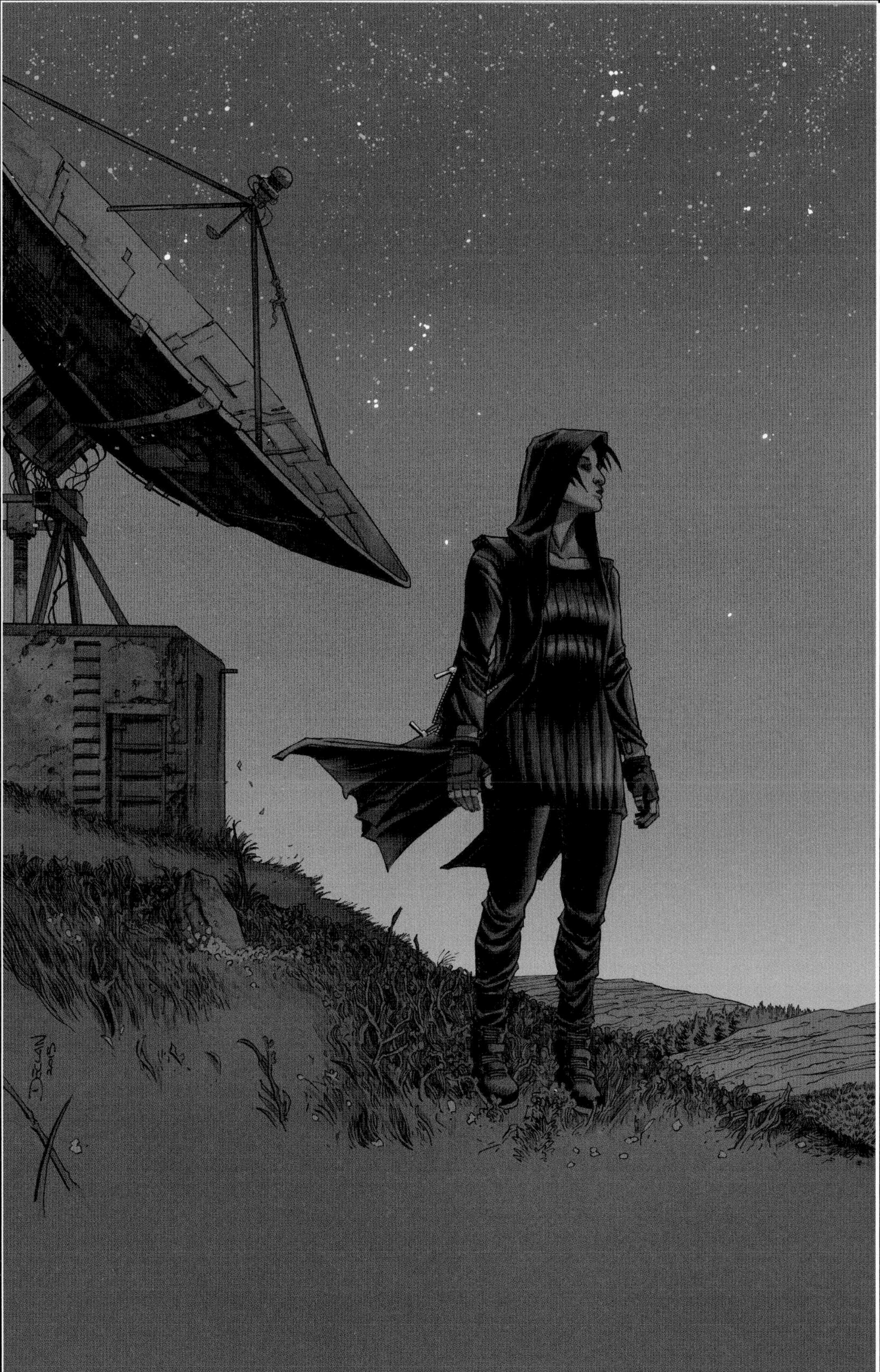

INJECTION #4

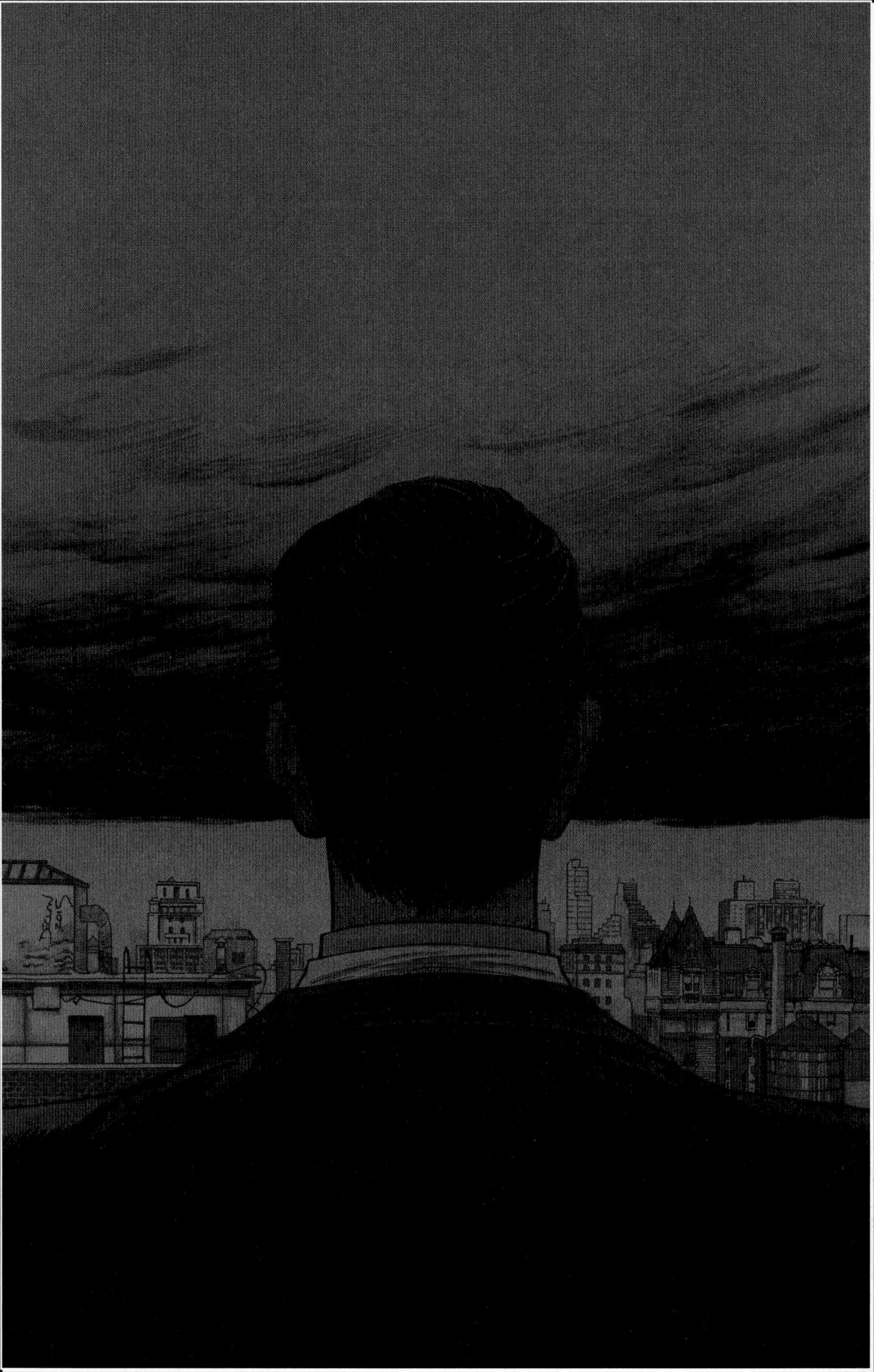

WARREN ELLIS is the award-winning writer of graphic novels like TRANSMETROPOLITAN, FELL, MINISTRY OF SPACE and PLANETARY, and the author of the NYT-bestselling GUN MACHINE and the "underground classic" novel CROOKED LITTLE VEIN. The movie RED is based on his graphic novel of the same name, its sequel having been released in summer 2013. IRON MAN 3 is based on his Marvel Comics graphic novel IRON MAN: EXTREMIS. He's also written extensively for VICE, WIRED UK, ESQUIRE and Reuters on technological and cultural matters, and wanders the Northern Hemisphere speaking at literary, philosophical and futurist events and festivals. Warren Ellis is a Patron of the British Humanist Association, an Associate of the Institute of Atemporal Studies, and the literary editor of EDICT magazine. He lives outside London, on the south-east coast of England, in case he needs to make a quick getaway.

DECLAN SHALVEY is best known for his work on the recent MOON KNIGHT relaunch with Warren Ellis for Marvel Comics. He has worked on many other projects for Marvel such as VENOM, THUNDERBOLTS and DEADPOOL. Other work includes CONAN for Dark Horse Comics and NORTHLANDERS for DC/Vertigo. As well as producing regular sequential work, Declan has developed a reputation as a prolific cover artist. He lives and works in his native Ireland.

JORDIE BELLAIRE is the Eisner Award winning colour artist of many acclaimed Image titles. NOWHERE MEN, PRETTY DEADLY, THEY'RE NOT LIKE US, AUTUMNLANDS and ZERO are amongst the mountain of work she has produced in her short career. She lives in Ireland with her cat Buffy and enjoys watching The Great British Bake Off weekly.

FONOGRAFIKS is the banner name for the comics work of designer Steven Finch, which includes the Image Comics titles NOWHERE MEN, TREES, THEY'RE NOT LIKE US, and the multi-award winning SAGA. He lives and works, surrounded by far too many books, in the north east of England.